My Weekly

'Original, poignant and heart-warming'
Sadie Pearse

Virginia Macgregor is the author of *What Milo Saw*, *The Return of Norah Wells*, *Before I Was Yours*, *You Found Me* and the young adult novel *Wishbones*. Her fifth novel for adults, *The Children's Secret*, will be out in the UK in November 2019. Her work has been translated into over a dozen languages. After graduating from Oxford University, she worked as a teacher of English and Housemistress in three major British boarding schools. She holds an MA in Creative Writing and now writes full time. Virginia is married to Hugh, who is Director of Theatre at St. Paul's School in Concord, New Hampshire. They moved to New Hampshire from the UK in July 2016 and live at St. Paul's with their two daughters, Tennessee Skye and Somerset Wilder and by the time this novel is published, they will have a new little boy too.

As Far as the Stars

Virginia Macgregor

ONE PLACE. MANY STORIES

HQ
An imprint of HarperCollins*Publishers* Ltd
1 London Bridge Street
London SE1 9GF

This edition 2019

1
First published in Great Britain by
HQ, an imprint of HarperCollins*Publishers* Ltd 2019

ISBN: 978-0-00-821732-7

MIX
Paper from
responsible sources
FSC™ C007454
FSC
www.fsc.org

This book is produced from independently certified FSC™ paper to ensure responsible forest management.

For more information visit: www.harpercollins.co.uk/green

Printed and bound in Great Britain by
CPI Group (UK) Ltd, Croydon, CR0 4YY

To my beloved husband, Hugh, who never stops believing in what I do.

Silently, one by one, in the infinite meadows of heaven,

Blossomed the lovely stars, the forget-me-nots of the angels.

Henry Wadsworth Longfellow
Evangeline: A Tale of Acadie

DAY 1
SATURDAY 19TH AUGUST, 2017

Prologue

On the I-81, heading for Nashville, a yellow Buick comes to an abrupt halt.

A girl swerves onto the hard shoulder and hits the brakes.

Then she checks the message on her phone again.

Damn it!

She thumps the steering wheel.

She checks the clock on the dashboard, takes a breath and then puts the car back into gear.

She takes the next exit, gets back onto the I-81 and heads back to DC, praying that her brother's plane will be on time.

A continent away, a pilot looks at the paper model sitting on the dashboard in his cockpit: a warbler, a tiny bird that can fly for three days across the Atlantic without landing.

He never takes it for granted: how miraculous this is, to be up here, hundreds of miles from the earth. And at night, to see the stars, up close.

He thinks of his son, who made the paper bird. In a few hours, they'll be together and then a holiday, just the two of them. He's going to try harder this time.

Beyond the paper bird, through the thick glass windows, the sky is that endless kind of blue. His eyes aren't big enough to take it all in.

It's morning. The day is starting.

It's going to be a beautiful day, the pilot thinks. *A beautiful flight. Not a whisper of wind. A smooth parabola through the sky from one continent to the other.*

He's done this route hundreds of times. Sometimes, he jokes that he could do it in his sleep.

He cranes his neck and looks down. They're passing the west coast of Ireland. In a few more minutes they'll leave behind the land and then, for thousands of miles, it'll be just him and his passengers and crew, flying between sea and sky.

There are times when he's so happy up here that he wishes he could fly for ever. That there was no land to go back to.

The plane is flying steady now. He switches the controls to autopilot; there's no more need for his intervention, not for a good while.

He sits back and looks back out at the sky.

Across the Atlantic, at Dulles International Airport in DC, a seventeen-year-old boy waits by the arrivals gate. He sits on the floor, his back pressed into the wall.

It'll be hours before his father's plane lands, but he doesn't mind waiting. Airports are like home for him. He's good at blocking out the noise and the people. All those comings and goings.

He pulls a scrap of paper out of his backpack and starts folding.

A few miles off the coast of western Ireland, where the sea is so deep it's black, a fisherman stands in his boat, pulling in a net. He's been out since before light.

He hears the drone of the engine before he sees the plane. He lives under the flight path, so over the years he's become used to the sound, to how the rhythm of the planes weave between the currents of the sea.

But still, it takes him by surprise: to see them up there, those big metal birds, carrying all those people through the sky.

The sea he understands: a wooden raft floating on the waves is as ancient as the world. But the planes, they never seem quite right.

He holds up his hand and waves. He knows that it's too far for the pilot to see him, but still, he likes to do it.

The sun's so strong – the sky so blue – he has to close his eyes.

Behind his eyelids, there's darkness and then stars. And when he blinks them away and tries to adjust again to the brightness, he thinks the plane will be gone – far off on its journey through the sky. A few moments peace until the next one.

But the plane hasn't gone: it's still there.

He's familiar with this trick of time and distance, how it seems as though the planes are not moving at all, when really, they're tearing through the sky faster than anything on land or sea.

He keeps staring at the plane, a straight, white arrow piercing the blue sky.

But then the plane seems to change direction. Its angle shifts. Its wings tilt to one side.

Maybe it's steading itself, he thinks, having reached altitude. But usually the planes climb higher, especially the big airliners.

He blinks again.

Strangely, now, it looks like the plane is slowing down.

The fisherman rubs his eyes. *I'm getting old,* he tells himself. *And I'm tired. I was up early; I've been staring at the sea for too long.*

He thinks of going home. Of taking off his wet clothes. Of washing the salt from his skin and then climbing into bed for a few hours' rest.

His eyes adjust.

He can see clearly now.

And then something makes him stand up in his boat and tilt his head up to the sky and wave frantically, even though he knows that no one can see him.

He's not just tired. And his eyes are fine.

Something's wrong.

The plane is no longer ascending. And it's not adjusting its position. Its tail is too high in relation to its body; its nose is dipping. And though the force of the engines keep propelling the plane forward, there's a strange stalling sound, a grinding through the air that echoes across the sea.

He watches and watches as the plane tilts and dips and slows.

And starts to fall.

Chapter One

12.25 EST
Dulles International Airport, Washington DC

Even before I step into the arrivals lounge I see the chaos.

People push in and out of the sliding doors, their cells clamped to their ears.

Cars crowd the pick-up zone.

Everyone's walking too fast.

I knew it would be busy: it's the end of the summer and people are flying in for the solar eclipse. But this is insane.

As we get closer to the airport building, Leda lets out a long whine like someone's stepped on her tail. Ever since we turned off the highway, she hasn't let up: barking and yelping and doing that high-pitched whimpering thing.

Leda's my brother's dog. A small, scrappy, caramel-coloured mongrel with shiny black eyes and stiff, worn fur. She looks more like an old-fashioned teddy bear than a dog.

She's cowering in the footwell like something's spooked her.

And I can't shake the feeling either: something's wrong.

But I push the feeling down to the pit of my stomach. I can't go there, not now. I have to focus.

Leda whines again.

'Pipe down,' I call back to her. 'You'll see him in a second.'

Leda's been missing Blake all summer. I told Blake he should take her with him to London but he said Leda would be better off with me. Which is probably true. Just because Blake loves her, it doesn't mean he remembers to feed her or walk her or let her out to pee.

I park the car a bit too close to the main walkway but it's so busy it's the only space I can find. And who's going to moan about stumbling over a 1973 mustard yellow Buick convertible, right? I should charge a viewing fee.

Leda jumps up and down on the back seat, her ears flapping.

'Okay, okay.'

I lift her out and then throw my telescope over my shoulder – it's the only thing I'd mind being stolen from the car. In fact, I'd be *delighted* if someone stole the two dresses spread out across the back bench. One's for the rehearsal dinner (yellow), one's for the wedding (sky blue): both sewn by Mom. They're the kind of dresses I wouldn't be caught dead in, not in real life, but my big sister, Jude, is getting married, and that's a big deal, so I gave in.

For the past year and a half, everything's been about my sister, Jude's, wedding. At least all this will be over soon and we'll be able to go back to our normal lives.

As I walk to the terminal entrance I get out my cell and text Blake:

Hurry. You can smoke in the car.

I hate it when Blake smokes when he's driving, but if we wait for him to have a smoke outside he'll end up talking to someone and then he'll want to take down their cell number (Blake's got more friends than any sane person can remember), and then he'll notice the colour of the sky or a sad-looking piece of trash on the sidewalk and feel inspired to write down some lyrics. And then he'll find a reason to have a second cigarette and he'll suggest we take a detour somewhere, for the hell of it, and before we know it, we'll have missed the whole wedding.

And, besides Jude and Stephen, the bride and groom, if there's one person this wedding can't go ahead without, it's Blake. He's singing the song. *The* song.

When I step into the arrivals lounge, things look even worse.

The people clutching the flowers and *Welcome Home* banners don't look like they're meant to look: bouncy with excitement about seeing whoever it is they came to collect. They look stressed out.

A red-faced man has one of the airport staff by his shirt collar and is yelling into his face.

The *something's wrong* feeling pushes back up my oesophagus and I get that biley taste at the back of my throat.

It has nothing to do with you, I tell myself. *Just focus on finding Blake.*

I breathe slowly in and out until I feel better.

I check my phone again and read Blake's last message:

ETA: 10.15am.

Followed by another message a few minutes later:

See you at Dulles.

Dulles! As in Dulles International Airport in Washington DC.

DC is where we live. And Dulles is the airport Blake's flown in and out of a million times. I've lost track of the number of Heathrow-Dulles flights I've booked for him. I joke that I'm the one who always brings Blake home, to our small apartment in Washington, to our family. *You're my guiding star, Air,* he jokes. Only it's not a joke: if it weren't for me, God knows where Blake would end up.

Which might be the reason he got confused – maybe he thought he was just flying into Dulles, coming home, as usual, and that I'd pick him up and that we'd drive to the wedding together.

But that wasn't the plan. And I'd told him the plan a million times:

Mum, Dad and Jude were driving down to Nashville a week ahead to make preparations for the wedding.

I'd follow a few days later.

And I'd pick him up at Nashville airport and bring him to the hotel.

Book a flight to Nashville, I'd told him, over and over, knowing it would take a while to sink in.

Nashville is where the wedding is taking place. It's the city where Dad grew up and took us for every holiday when we were kids. And it's the city Blake loves more than anywhere in the world.

It made sense for him to fly straight into Nashville: it allowed him to squeeze in a few extra gigs in London before the wedding. He'd already complained about having to cut his UK tour short.

I look at my phone again. I still can't believe that he flew into Dulles. Seriously? The airports are 700 miles apart, in totally different states – in different time zones for Christ's sake. It's not like they're easy to mix-up.

Though I shouldn't be surprised. Blake is mess-up central.

Two days ago, I got this random voicemail from him. It wasn't even from his phone – which is why I didn't pick up. He explained that he'd lost his cell and that he was borrowing a phone. There was so much noise in the background that he was shouting. He was probably at a gig.

Then he landed the bombshell:

Can you book the return flight for me? Run out of cash. Thanks sis, got to go. Love you.

Casual. Totally casual.

Blake only ever books one-way tickets. His plans are constantly changing, so it doesn't make sense to book more than a few days ahead. And he's always short of cash. So I guess I shouldn't have been surprised. Only, this *was* different: it was forty-eight hours before our sister's wedding.

And I'd reminded him – like a thousand times – that he had to book a return flight well in advance.

But had he listened to any of my very clear instructions about the wedding? About where it was taking place and when and at what time and which airport he had to fly into?

No. Obviously, no.

And, two nights ago, when he left that message, saying that he hadn't booked his flight yet – like it was nothing – did I bail him out, *again*?

Yes. Obviously, yes.

So, even though it was three in the morning and I was so tired I could barely keep my eyes open, I got out the debit card Mom and Dad set up for me, and booked the flight from Heathrow to Nashville, as planned.

Jude, Blake and I all have a card with separate accounts set up in our names. It's Mom and Dad's way of teaching us to be responsible with money. Only Blake keeps maxing his out and then I have to bail him out with my card. The thing is, Mom gets alerts when any of us spend more than $50 so I texted her, explaining that Blake had forgotten to book a return ticket and that he didn't have any money but that she didn't need to worry, I was on it. Everything was going to be fine. Blake messing up is a scenario she's familiar with. She answered with: *OK. Just get him here.*

Mom never blames Blake for anything. She never even blames him for maxing out his debit card. She's got this massive blind spot where he's concerned. Being pissed off at how Mom is totally soft when it comes to Blake is one of the few things Jude and I bond over.

Then I sent a text message to the phone he'd called from with the flight details for the totally overpriced last-minute ticket. That I'd meet him at Nashville airport and take him to the hotel.

I sent him a few other texts too, not caring what stranger would read them first, telling him how pissed I was that he'd woken me up and how expensive the flight was and that he'd better be on time.

He never answered any of my texts.

I don't really believe in praying: I don't think anyone out there is listening. Except, perhaps, some life form on a planet we haven't discovered yet. But not a God-like figure. Not someone who directs our lives. That night, though, I found myself begging that if there was some force out there who decided whether things work out or get fucked up, that Blake would get my messages. That whoever he'd borrowed a phone from would pass them on. That he wasn't some random guy off the street that Blake would never see again.

I guess I begged – or prayed, or whatever – because I knew that this time Blake had to get his shit together. That he had to make it back for the wedding.

The next time I heard from him was the text he sent me when I was halfway to Nashville saying that he was landing in Dulles. The text was from a different number, probably another phone he borrowed.

You mean Nashville!

I'd texted back.

No. Dulles. See you soon, sis.

And then nothing.

Had he not received any of my messages when I booked his flight? Did he end up booking a flight on his own? He was always borrowing money off people; maybe he'd found a way to pay the airfare. And then he'd got it wrong: he thought we were meant to meet up in Dulles and drive down to Nashville together. But that had never been the plan. I'd explained it to him.

But then Blake's not good at listening. Not when it comes to practical, everyday stuff.

So, this was another typical Blake fuck-up. Only worse: a fuck-up on top of a fuck-up.

I clench my hands, digging my fingernails into my palms.

Focus, I think. *Just focus on finding Blake.*

I'm really late. Two hours late. So, I guess all these stressed-out looking people, they've been here for a while already.

There's a toddler screaming. But besides him and the red-faced yelling guy, everything's a weird kind of quiet, people walking around with wide, glazed eyes like they've lost something.

I've been to this airport more times than I can remember – I'm Blake's personal taxi service – and it's never felt like this. And when I see how lost those people look, I feel bad – like I should be asking them if I can help or something – but I don't have time to be helpful in other people's lives right now: I've got to find Blake, get him into the car and start driving.

That's if he's even here. Knowing Blake, he's probably got on a plane to Hawaii or Iceland or bloody Timbuktu.

I check my phone again.

No. Dulles. See you soon, sis.

Though, in the grand-Blake scheme of things, his message doesn't really mean much. I've lost count of the number of times he's told me where he's planning to go, only to find out that he's ended up somewhere else altogether.

Maybe his brain went into autopilot; maybe he thought he was coming home to DC, like he usually does. Or maybe his brain was tired or hungover or in its general state of Blake-like distraction and he texted *Dulles* because that was what he was used to texting.

Maybe, at this exact moment, he's standing at the arrivals gate of Nashville International Airport – like he was meant to all along.

God, I shouldn't have turned the car round. I should have gone to Nashville as planned, assumed that he was on the plane I'd booked for him, ignored his random text.

If you made me drive all the way to Dulles for nothing, I'm not doing anything for you ever again, I say to him in my head. *And this time, I mean it.*

Dulles. Nashville. Dulles. Nashville. The words crash around in my brain.

Where the hell are you, Blake?

He should have some kind of electronic tag.

I take a breath.

I've got to concentrate on one thing at a time. Assume he's here. Then work out from there. A clear, logical method.

I search the area around the arrivals gate. Blake's hard to miss. He's really tall and skinny and has this crazy black hair that stands up a mile with all the gel he puts in it – it's longer than mine. It's a bit of a family joke – how Blake's hair is longer than mine, and how many products he has in the bathroom, and how long he takes grooming himself.

When we tease him, he says it's part of his brand.

Blake's been honing his brand since he was five years old when this music teacher at school told him he had a talent – and that he was cute, which, she explained, was a winning combination.

When I can't find him, I scan the arrivals screen for his flight. Within a few seconds, I've found it:

10.15 UKFlyer0217 From London Heathrow:
DELAYED.

Chapter Two

12.40 EST

I look back at the screen to make sure I've got it right.

But the word's still there:

DELAYED.

It doesn't make any sense. Blake texted me before he got on the plane. If it had been delayed, he'd have known – and they wouldn't have let passengers get onto the plane, not that early.

Though sometimes they get everyone on and then pull everyone off again. If there's a technical error or something. That could have happened.

But who cares what happened? If we're late for any of the wedding stuff, Mom's going to kill me.

I go up to a guy wearing what I recognise as a UKFlyer uniform:

'Excuse me—'

He spins round. His eyes are wide and kind of jumpy. UKFlyer officials have this way of looking totally calm. Like, even if the airport was on fire, every hair would stay in place. Mom says it's a British thing. But this guy doesn't look calm, not at all. Which is weird. Like it's weird that everyone around me is acting so stressed out. It's not like they've all got weddings to go to – or Moms like mine. Planes get delayed all the time.

'The plane – the one that's been delayed,' I say to the UKFlyer guy. 'I was meant to pick someone up.' I pause. 'Or I *think* I was. It's complicated. Could you check the passenger list for me?'

He stares at me and blinks like I'm not speaking English.

I rephrase, trying to calm myself down enough to get the words out in the right order:

'I need to check whether my brother was meant to be on the plane that's been delayed.'

'I'm afraid we can't release that information.'

'I'm his sister.'

'We still can't release that information. Not at this point.'

'What point?'

He looks at me like I'm about two years old – or totally crazy – or both. I mean, shouldn't I know if the person I've come to collect was on the plane? And if I don't, isn't that weird?

Yeah, it's weird. But then he doesn't know Blake. Infuriatingly unpredictable Blake.

'I'm sorry I can't help,' the guy says, his eyes still darting around. 'I've got to go.'

My heart starts doing this weird arrhythmic pounding thing.

This can't be happening.

If I screw up even the tiniest part of this wedding, Mom will never forgive me. She's planned every last detail. It's been her life for like a year.

On the surface, my allocated job for the wedding is simple: Blake. Get Blake to Nashville. *In good time.* Get him to the family breakfast and then the rehearsal dinner and then, crucially, the wedding, wearing a morning suit: top hat, coat and waistcoat, like Jude wanted – and ready to sing.

After Jude and Stephen have said their vows, during the eclipse, Blake is going to perform the song he's written for their big day. The song that Jude – and Mom – and every guest at Mom's perfectly choreographed wedding, would remember for the rest of their lives. I reckon most of Jude's friends accepted the invitation just so they could drool over Blake Shaw's big blue eyes and gravelly voice. Not that I'd tell her that.

The only one who's heard the song is me; I practised it with him over a million times before he left for London. And I made him promise to keep practising while he was away – *This time, the charming-Blake-improv, won't cut it,* I told him.

It's my job to give Blake a hard time – to balance out the rest of the world that thinks the sun shines out of his butt.

My body tenses up. If he messes up the song, I'm going to kill him, like *properly* kill him.

I take a breath.

Yeah, *on the surface,* getting Blake to the wedding was meant to be simple. But Blake's never simple. Which is why I was given the job. Managing Blake is *always* my job. Besides working my butt off to get a higher Grade Point Average than the boys in my Advanced Physics class and looking at the night sky through a telescope, sorting out my big brother's life is my primary occupation. When one of his songs hits the charts and he makes millions, I'm *so* taking a cut.

Leda won't stop fidgeting so I put her down and rub my eyes. The world blurs. I blink and look over at the people who are here to welcome the passengers off the Heathrow flight. And that's when I see him.

Scruffy, tangled blond hair falls over his forehead. His hair's longer than mine. Way longer. Though I guess that isn't hard. A year ago, I chopped all my hair off: went for a pixie. Blake loved it. Mom freaked. Jude looked kind of pleased, like now I definitely wouldn't be competition in her daily one-woman beauty parade. At first, Dad didn't say anything, he only kind of smiled with that twinkle he gets in his eye when he knows I've done something that's kind of out there. Later, when Mom was out of earshot, he told me he thought it looked modern, which I guess was a compliment.

Anyway, this guy's hair is long and tangled and looks like it's been hacked at by a pair of kid's safety scissors. It brushes the top of his round tortoiseshell glasses, which make his eyes look huge. They're light grey, like when the sun's fighting to get through the clouds.

He's skinny and pale in that fade into the background kind of way.

In other words, he's the kind of guy, that, unlike Blake, people walk right past.

But that's what makes me notice him – the fact that he's sitting on the floor, really still, out of everyone's way.

When you're part of my family, the quiet-keep-it-to-themselves types seem to belong to a different species. Even Dad, who's this bookish Classics professor, can be kind of loud and overexcited when he talks about his favourite (not very famous) Greek goddess, Pepromene.

Anyway, the quiet guy's head is bent over a piece of paper that he's folding over and over. He's totally lost in what he's doing – it's like all this craziness isn't even touching him.

For a second, looking at him and how calm he is, my heart stops hammering and I think that things might turn out okay. That they've made a mistake. That – with the proviso that Blake *did* get onto the flight to Dulles – any second now, he's going to walk towards me, his guitar case slung over his shoulder, waving and looking guilty for having messed up his flight – but smiling too. Because that's also part of his brand: the massive smile that makes his cheeks dimple; the smile that takes over his entire face; the smile that makes whoever's looking at him think it's just for them.

Someone shoves past me and I'm snapped back into the present.

Leda jumps up and down like a mad thing.

And then an announcement blares out through the terminal speakers:

Attention please ladies and gentlemen, this is a call for all those meeting passengers on Flight UKFlyer0217 from Heathrow. Please come to the information desk.

Chapter Three

13.31 EST

We're in a room now, behind the security gates. It's all taking too much time. And it's making me nervous. Why couldn't they simply tell us what they had to tell us over the speakers or put a note on the arrivals screen? Why herd us all together like this for a plane that's been delayed?

I shouldn't be here. I should get back into the car and drive to Nashville.

Just tell me where you are, Blake! I say through gritted teeth.

I look up at a digital clock on the wall. The wedding starts in less than forty-eight hours. By 9 a.m. tomorrow we're meant to be having this family breakfast, some special family time before all the mad preparations for the wedding day start. It'll be the last time it's just the five of us. Mom's booked a table at Louis's, a diner-cum-bar on Music Row, near Grandpa's flat. It's open twenty-four hours a day, acknowledging that most musicians, like Blake, don't really follow the same waking and sleeping cycles that the rest of us do. There's a small stage where people can get up and play or sing. Blake loves it. Grandpa would take him there when he was little. He's always going on about how, when he hits it big one day, he'll buy it up from the owner who's like a hundred years old. So breakfast at Louis's was meant to be a big deal for Blake too. And if he'd arrived at DC at the time he was supposed to, and we drove through the night, stopping a few times to stay sane, we might have made it. Just. Now, it would take a miracle.

And then the rehearsal dinner tomorrow night. We absolutely have to make it in time for that.

My head hurts at the thought of all the wedding stuff I'm going to have to get through in the next two days and how, right now, I'm hundreds of miles away from where I should be – with no sign of Blake.

I just wish someone would tell us whether the plane has been delayed by an hour or ten or if it has been cancelled altogether. To sort out this mess, I needed facts I could work with.

I look back at the clock. 13.33.

Right now, Blake and I should be in the hotel in Nashville, going through the song, steaming the creases out of our wedding clothes, keeping Mom from having a nervous breakdown, and trying really hard to bite our tongues about the fact that our sister, who graduated from Julliard and had this amazing glittering career ahead of her as a concert pianist, ditched it all to get married and have babies.

The security checks took for ever. Even though none of us are flying, the airport staff still had to scan our bags and our bodies – and everyone was carrying all the wrong stuff, like liquids and nail scissors and lighter fluid – because it's not like we were prepared for any of this.

My telescope beeped like a hundred times when it went through the X-ray machine, and even when I took it out and explained what it was (and reminded them that there was an eclipse happening tomorrow so carrying a telescope around was totally normal – that, in fact, *not* carrying a telescope around when there's an eclipse is what should concern them), they still looked at me suspiciously.

And then I had a row with them about Leda coming through with me – especially as she wouldn't stop jumping long enough for them to scan her properly. In the end, I said she was a service dog and that I'd start fitting if she didn't come with me, so they let her through. It's a trick Blake uses all the time.

Then they took ages writing down everyone's names and numbers.

Which, I wanted to tell them, was double standards; taking *my* information and not giving me the information *I* wanted. Like whether Blake was on the plane.

And now we're waiting for someone to tell us something – *anything* – about what's going on.

I've got this massive headache from all the waiting and the stressing about Blake not being on time and the fact that this room doesn't have any windows. It should be illegal: rooms where you can't see the sky.

I'll be there, no matter what, Blake said to me like a zillion times.

And I know he will. He gets how important this is. And he's never broken a promise to me – not once. Sometimes his promises take a while to materialise; sometimes, his promises have to go through an obstacle course of fuck-ups like this one – but Blake always comes through for me in the end.

Which makes me think that I'm wasting time hanging around with all these people rather than finding out where he really is. If Blake was on the plane and it was delayed, he will have found another way to get to the wedding.

So, I check my phone again. Still nothing.

There aren't enough chairs so I'm sitting on the floor with Leda on my lap. She's finally gone to sleep, knackered from all that whining and jumping.

The guy I saw at the arrivals gate is sitting on the floor again, leaning against this massive backpack he's been lugging around. And he's folding another bit of paper, some old flyer he's picked up. I think he's recreating the Washington Monument, though the model he's making is so tiny it's hard to tell.

I remember how, when we moved from London to DC, and Dad took us round all the tourist stuff, the first thought I had when I saw the monument was that it looked like a rocket about to shoot off into the sky. But then my brain has a habit of shaping everything it sees into some kind of space-related universe.

I look back at paper-folding guy. It's cool, how he's made this really accurate model out of a bit of scrap paper. And I'm about to go over and tell him that when he sighs, stands up, scrunches the model up into a ball and throws it in a trash can.

Blake does that too – when he's frustrated with how a song's going. You can tell whether his composing is going well or badly by how many bits of balled up notation paper there are on his bedroom floor.

Except the model the guy made was good – like *amazingly* good. I think about going to rescue it from the trash, but then people around me start shifting and shushing and I get distracted.

I look up in time to see a short, bald official in a UKFlyer uniform climbing onto a chair. He tries to get our attention, but everyone speaks over him, shouting out questions.

So, I stick two fingers in my mouth and whistle.

A few people give me a dirty look, like what I did was inappropriate. But it works: the room goes still.

The paper-folding guy looks up at me, his eyes big and grey behind his glasses, and smiles.

Everyone else turns to face the UKFlyer representative.

'I'm sorry that we haven't been able to give you more information about the flight—'

'Oh, for Christ's sake!' It's the man I saw earlier, the one with the red face.

'If you bear with me—'

But he's lost us. We all know that he hasn't got any more of a clue about what's going on than we do.

Which totally pisses me off. I need to know what's happening so that I can work out, for sure, whether Blake's going to make it to the wedding or not. Unless Blake shows up right now, we're already too late to make it to the family breakfast, news which will cause a minor earth tremor when it reaches Mom.

My heart sinks. It's the middle of the summer vacation and everyone's coming over to see the solar eclipse: it would take a miracle for him to find a seat on another plane. And if Blake doesn't get onto another flight – and soon; if he ends up stuck in Heathrow, he'll miss the rehearsal dinner too. God, he might not even make it to the wedding on time.

And it's not as if we can delay the wedding – like we usually delay things for Blake being late. Because the whole point of the wedding is that it's meant to happen *during* the eclipse. And the eclipse isn't going to hang around for anyone – not even my brother. On Monday 21st of August 2017, between 13.25 and 14.26 (there's a time-zone change between the states of Virginia and Tennessee), the moon's shadow will rush across Nashville at 1,800 mph, and Jude will marry her high school sweetheart, Stephen. And they'll live happily ever after.

Or that was what was meant to happen. Before this – whatever it is – got in the way.

I look at my phone. Mom's left another message.

Did you pick up Blake's suit?

I text back quickly:

Yes.

Then I put my phone away.

You want to know the *really* ironic thing? It was my idea. Having the wedding during the eclipse. It was genius. A kill-two-birds-with-one-stone kind of genius. Four birds, actually.

Bird One: the solar eclipse is a big deal for me. Skies and planets and stars – basically, everything that's not on earth – is what I spend all my time thinking about. This is the first total solar eclipse to sweep across the entire USA in ninety-nine years and Nashville is the largest city in the path of the totality. Having a special family event connected to it felt cool.

Bird Two: Mom wanted a wedding that trumped all her friends' daughters' weddings – and none of those got married or are planning to get married during the eclipse. The idea totally got me into Mom's good books.

Bird Three: Nashville's kind of a home away from home for us. When we were little we'd visit all the time, squeezing into Grandpa's tiny flat on Music Row. Grandpa was Blake's hero. He played the electric guitar and they'd jam together for hours. Gran passed away before we had the chance to meet her so we were Grandpa's only family. Blake was the one who made sure that Grandpa never felt alone. Anyway, all our happiest family memories are from that time. When Grandpa passed away, Dad decided to keep the flat, for all of us but for Blake mainly, who totally loves Nashville. One day Blake wants to live there – there and London, his two favourite cities in the world.

Anyway, that's kind of Bird Four: holding the wedding in Music City was a way to guarantee that Blake would show up and that he'd buy into the whole wedding thing. Blake loves Nashville. He sees himself as the blended reincarnation of Johnny Cash and Jimi Hendrix – with a bit of Dolly Parton thrown in for good measure: Blake's got this kind of hip androgynous thing going, which is also part of his brand. When people ask him if he's gay or bi or something, he says: *You fall in love with a person, not a gender.* Which gives him this sexy, mysterious vibe that make girls – and guys – even more into him.

Anyway, when I suggested the eclipse, just for a moment, Mom and Dad looked at me like I was the special one. Like they do with Blake because he's this really talented musician with good looks and has this totally magnetic personality. Like they look at Jude because she's pretty and because she's marrying a guy who's going to law school, like Mom did, and is going to give them a million grandchildren.

So, I'd done well.

Only I didn't factor in the fact that Blake might not show.

I start to feel dizzy, like the ground is falling away from under me.

The UKFlyer guy looks out across the room, like he's hoping that someone's going to save him so that he can get down and not have to do this anymore.

A woman with a baby asleep in a sling walks up to the counter where the guy's standing and looks up at him, her eyes bloodshot.

'Please tell us what's going on.' She says it in this really quiet voice, but we all hear her.

The guy stares down at her kid, like he's never seen a baby before. His eyebrows scrunch together and his shoulders slump.

'Please,' she says again.

And then it's like something clicks. He rolls back his shoulders, tilts up his head, opens his mouth and says it, the thing that no one in this room is ready to hear:

'It's missing.' He clears his throat. 'The plane's missing.'

Chapter Four

15.23 EST

It's been two hours since the UKFlyer official told us that the plane is missing. The plane with 267 crew and passengers on it. And Blake. Possibly. Or possibly not. I'm not sure what's worse: knowing for sure that the person you're waiting for is on a plane that's vanished into thin air or not knowing whether the person you're waiting for even got on the plane. I guess I do know. I guess that being on a missing plane is worse. But still, you get my point: this whole situation sucks.

I text Blake for like the millionth time – on both the numbers, the one from the other night when he asked me to book the flight and the other one where he told me that he was heading to Dulles. And I get that it's stupid because he's probably nowhere near either of those phones right now, but I don't know what else to do.

Where are you?

I wait a beat.
Still no answer.
So, I text his actual cell in the hope that he found it:

Hi Blake, please tell me where you are – got to get to the wedding.

I shove my phone into the back pocket of my shorts and look around at the people who've been waiting with me for more news. They've gone quiet, like they're scared to say anything out loud.

How can a plane just disappear? It's not like Mom's car keys or Dad's hairline. We're talking about thousands of tons of aluminium with hundreds of people on it. And it's not like it's an obscure route – planes from Heathrow land in DC all the time: it's a clean, well-worn journey over the Atlantic. And they'd have been in contact with air traffic control the whole way, wouldn't they?

Ground crew from the airline hand out water bottles and meal vouchers, like we're the victims of some kind of natural disaster. Then they let us go back to the arrivals lounge where the cafes and restaurants are.

Whenever someone from UKFlyer talks to us, they say the same thing:

We're on the case.

We'll keep you updated on any developments.

Try not to worry.

So, we wait.

And wait.

And wait some more.

Which is driving me totally crazy. Because waiting is the one thing I can't afford to do right now.

Blake's going to be fine. He's *always* fine. Being fine is in his DNA. Born under a lucky star and all that.

What's *not* going to be fine is him ruining our sister's wedding.

The arrivals terminal has got even busier. A few people managed to get chairs. Most of us are standing or sitting on the floor.

I notice the toddler who was screaming earlier, sprawled on his dad's lap, asleep.

And I notice the quiet, tangle-haired guy. He's making another paper model from a sheet of newspaper, some kind of small bird, its wings spread wide. It's totally amazing how quickly he makes those models. And how they go from being this big piece of paper to a tiny representation of something, like he's creating a miniature world.

He brings the newspaper bird over to the woman with the baby, who's been crying for what feels like the last hour. She's taken him out of his sling and is bouncing him on her knee to calm him down. It takes her a few seconds to notice the guy standing there, with his paper bird.

He holds it out to her. She looks up at him.

'For your baby,' I hear him say.

The mom takes the bird from him, places it in her open palm and stares at it, as though she's waiting for it to flap its wings and take off. When the baby notices the bird, he stops crying and starts swiping at it with his chubby fingers.

'Thank you,' the mom says.

The guy gives her this nod, accompanied by a little bow, and then goes back to sitting on the floor and takes another piece of scrap paper out of his backpack.

And then a new wave of people pours through the arrivals gate.

That's the worst thing about all this: the fact that other planes are landing all the time. Planes full of people – including planes from Heathrow.

I keep scanning the passengers coming through, hoping to see Blake's crazy black hair sticking up over everyone's heads. I'm totally ready to storm up to him and make a scene, to lay into him for, well, being Blake: late, disorganised, unaware of anything else that's going on in the world besides himself – and infuriatingly loveable with it so that just as I'm yelling at him I'll want to hug him too. Because I've missed him this summer. I miss him whenever he's away.

I get my phone out to text him again but then realise how stupid it is when I don't even know what number to call, so I put it away.

Blake probably lost his cell on purpose. He gave up his smart phone a few years ago, claiming that it interfered with his creativity. The one he's got now only texts and calls and rarely has much connectivity. Mom makes him have it for safety reasons – and so we can stay in touch with each other as a family. But if he had a choice, he'd toss it in the trash.

We get weird looks from the people who come to collect the passengers from the other planes: they're wondering why we're all hanging out here in the arrivals lounge. But then they find whoever it is they came for and walk off and we get left behind again.

I sit with my back against the wall.

My phone buzzes. I grab it out of my pocket thinking that, at last, Blake's getting in touch.

But it's a message from Mom.

41

Has Blake landed? Tried to call him, no answer.

I get that stomach-acid taste at the back of my throat again.

I texted her when I left DC – the first time. Before I got halfway to Nashville and had to turn around again because my brother messed up his travel plans. Which I haven't told her about. What Mom *thinks* is happening is that I'm standing in Nashville International Airport waiting to pick Blake up and that we're going to drive to the hotel together and that we'll be showing up anytime now.

Not yet

I text back.

What's going on?

She texts back, almost as soon as I've sent my message.

Plane's late

I write back.

And then my phone starts ringing. It's Mom. Obviously. She wants more information.

I don't answer.

Because I'm a coward.

Because I can't face having to explain it all to her: Blake getting on the wrong plane and me having to drive all the way back to DC and that there's a chance we might not make it for the family breakfast. That if I

42

don't get some answer soon, we might not make it for the wedding itself.

All the saliva in my mouth dries up. I can't let myself go there. He's going to make it. He has to.

Can't talk

I text back.

She'll think I'm driving. That will buy me some time. She sends another message:

Remember we're having breakfast at Louis's.
Okay.

I text back.

I'm really feeling sick now.

I should tell her what's going on but she'll implode. And then she'll tell Jude and Jude will fall apart. And Dad will have to deal with it and Dad's a crisis-avoider so he'll panic and then go into hiding somewhere, which will make Mom even more mad.

Telling them that it's even worse than me and Blake being late for the wedding stuff – that his plane's gone off radar, that no one knows where he is – isn't even an option.

I screw my eyes shut to block out the world.

This is the last time I'm covering for you, Blake, I say to myself. *The last damn time.*

I was nine the first time Blake disappeared. The first time I had to lie for him.

He snuck into my room in the middle of the night, his guitar case and a holdall slung over his shoulder.

43

'Tell them to let me sleep in.'

I was still asleep myself – it was three in the morning – so I wasn't registering what he was telling me.

'What?' I asked.

'Tomorrow morning. Tell them not to disturb me. Tell them I'm sleeping.'

I sat up and rubbed my eyes.

'Mom and Dad?' I asked.

He nodded.

'Where are you going?'

'Not sure yet.'

Blake's words didn't make sense. At age nine this was how the world worked: when you left one place you did so with the express intention of going to another specific location.

So I changed my line of questioning.

'*Why* are you going?'

'To play.' He tapped his guitar case.

'Why can't you play here?'

'I need inspiration.'

Blake was always going off to find inspiration. He was always going off period.

I have a restless soul, Air, he'd say, sounding like he was thirty rather than thirteen.

That didn't make sense to me either, not then.

'Why can't you find inspiration here?' I asked.

He raised his big black eyebrows. 'Really?'

'Yeah, really.'

'I need some space, Air.'

He'd said it before. That the music – and the lyrics – wouldn't come here, at home. I thought that it was a mean thing to say. Like being with us was stopping him from doing what he loved most.

'When are you coming back?' I asked.

He shrugged.

'You can't sleep in for ever.'

He grinned in that goofy way he had that made me feel warm and happy and like everything was good with the world.

'For ever? It won't be for ever, Air.'

'So why are you taking a holdall?'

'In case.'

'In case what?'

'In case I need some of my stuff.'

I sat up taller. 'People don't need their stuff if they're coming back quickly.'

'Just cover for me, Air – will you do that?'

'What if Mom goes into your room and finds out that you're not there?'

He tilted his head to one side. The gel in his hair had worn off, so long dark strands fell into his eyes.

'You're the smart one in the family, Air, you'll find a way to cover for me.'

Then he kissed the top of my head and walked off to my window – the one that had access to the street below.

'You *are* coming back, aren't you?' I asked.

I was worried that one day Blake would go so far that he'd get lost – or decide that coming back was too much hassle. He loved Mom and Dad and Jude and me but that didn't mean he was going to live with us for ever. And he didn't like DC. Blake was always going on about how he couldn't wait to be eighteen, how then he could do anything he wanted.

When his body was halfway out of the window, he turned around and smiled:

'For you little sis?' He smiled. 'I'll always come back.'

He blew me a kiss then pulled his guitar case and holdall through the window.

'And even if I don't –' he went on.

I leapt out of bed, ran up to the window and leant out. 'Even if you *don't*? What's that's supposed to mean?'

He put his fingers under my chin and tilted my face up to the sky.

'They're always there, right?'

It was a clear night so although the light pollution in DC was bad, the sky still looked amazing: like someone had pierced a thousand holes in the black canopy of the sky letting the light that lived behind it shine through.

'Yeah, they're always there.'

'Well, so am I – like your stars.'

'*My* stars?'

He nodded.

Blake knew how much I loved them, even then.

When I was nine years old, I'd thought that was a wonderful thing to say: that he'd always be with me, because the stars were always with us too. But when I got older and understood about how old the stars were and the whole light years–distance thing – and the fact that it's basically impossible to measure the distance between us and the stars – I realised that what he told me that night wasn't anywhere close to wonderful. He was basically telling me that even if I could still see him, he might be millions of light years away.

Nothing's been confirmed yet.

Any moment now I might get a text from Blake saying that he got a flight to Nashville after all. Which means that he'll make it for the family breakfast – that it'll just be me who misses it. Which won't be a big deal.

Or that he was late for the flight and got onto one that's arriving later. Which, depending on his arrival time, will at least give us enough time to get to Nashville for the rehearsal dinner.

Whatever happens, we'd be there for the wedding. And, in the end, that's all that matters.

Or that bald UKFlyer guy who's in charge of keeping us up to date will tell us that the plane's back on radar, that air traffic control got it wrong, and that the UKFlyer0217 has landed. That the passengers are coming through passport control and that, in a few minutes, they'll be with us.

'Can I borrow your phone?'

Leda's head shoots up from my lap. She thumps her tail against my thigh so hard that I put my hand on it to press it down.

I look up too. He's standing there, the pale, tangle-haired, paper-folding guy. And he's staring at me, his eyes wide behind his tortoiseshell glasses.

'My mobile's out of charge,' he explains.

Yeah, he definitely sounds English, like Mom and our relatives back in the UK. Mom's got a bit of a Scottish lilt because that's where she lived until she was ten and all her family come from there, but mostly she sounds English.

The guy adjusts his glasses and keeps staring at me.

'Sure.' I hand him my cell, relieved that I don't have to keep looking at Mom's messages popping up.

When he starts swiping at the screen, I notice that his fingers are shaking.

I've been so swept up with thinking about my family and the wedding and what's going to happen in the next forty-eight hours if Blake doesn't show up, that I kind of forgot that all these people around me are also waiting for news about those they came to collect. Blake could be anywhere right now, but they *know* that their loved ones are on the plane. And maybe they don't have families like ours – or moms like our mom – to hold them all together.

While he's using my phone, I look past him at a TV screen on the far side of the room. And then I notice some of the people who've been waiting with us, getting to their feet and turning to look at it too.

Which makes the guy look up from my cell and turn to the TV screen as well.

It's the ABC news feed that's been on this whole time with weather reports and the latest from the Yankees–Red Sox game and details about tomorrow's eclipse.

Except none of those things are on the screen.

Instead, there's a grainy picture. It keeps wobbling out of focus: a large piece of metal, floating on the sea.

Chapter Five

15.37 EST

It's when I see that bit of grainy footage on ABC News that I know for sure.

Blake wasn't on that plane.

He can't have been.

He didn't know what he was texting: he's probably in Nashville, wondering where the hell I am. I shouldn't have turned around so fast. I should have kept going to Nashville, stuck to our plans.

And if he's not in Nashville, then he's probably somewhere else altogether. Like still in London, playing in a hip bar somewhere.

'I've got to get out of here,' I say, taking my phone back.

I swing my telescope onto my back, grab Leda and head towards the terminal doors. She makes her body go limp so I have drag her along the floor.

'Get up,' I say to her, yanking harder.

As I walk, I send Mom a text.

Blake messed up. We're not going to make it for the family breakfast. Please don't worry, Mom, we'll be there soon.

I put my phone in the pocket of my shorts and try not to think about the bomb I've just landed on Mom.

I yank Leda again but she won't move. Her head is twisted back towards the group of people we've been waiting with, the ones who came to meet the UKFlyer0217. That's when I notice the guy again and suddenly, I feel bad for walking away like that and even though I totally don't have the time for this, I walk back to him.

Leda follows, suddenly cooperative.

'I'm sorry,' I say to him. My eyes well up. 'For whoever...' I look back at the screen. The bit of metal floating on the sea. Then I look at my watch. 'But I've got to go.'

I don't know what's going on. With the plane. With where Blake is. But I've made a decision: I've got to get to the wedding. Whatever it takes. I have to be there for Mom and Dad and Jude. If Blake doesn't show, I'll find an excuse for him.

Jude needs this: her perfect wedding, getting married to Stephen.

Mom needs it.

We all do.

And if Blake doesn't show up on time, *I'll* sing the damn song.

I can't play the guitar and my voice is totally average and I get shit scared of standing in front of even one person and performing. But I've been practising it with Blake ever since Jude announced she was engaged, so I know the words. Yeah, I'll sing it. And it won't be great. And Jude will be sulky as hell about it. But hopefully all the other wedding stuff will distract her and everything will sort of be okay.

And when Blake does turn up – like he always does – he's going to owe me, big time. More than he's ever owed me.

For a beat, the guy keeps staring at me, and then he says:

'Don't you think you should stay?' He shifts nervously from foot to foot. 'I mean, there could be more information. We've been told to wait.' He blushes like saying even these few words to me is painful. 'It's better to stay together at times like this,' he adds.

'At times like this?'

'Yeah.'

He makes it sound like this is the kind of situation that people find themselves in more than once in their lives. And like he's some kind of expert.

'I'll keep checking my phone,' I say – because I can't tell him the truth: that I don't need to stay because that bit of metal floating in the sea has nothing to do with my brother.

I feel bad for leaving him. He looks like he could do with having someone stay with him, but I've got to get on the road.

Chapter Six

15.48 EST

Except, when I get to the car, it's not there.

Blake's car.

The mustard yellow 1973 Buick convertible that he loves like it's a living thing.

The car which has my rehearsal dinner dress in it, and my bridesmaid's dress and Blake's suit and Leda's food.

The car Dad was going to drive Jude and Stephen to the airport in after the wedding, to catch the flight to Florence for their honeymoon.

The car that was my one chance of getting to the wedding on time.

Leda barks at the empty space where I parked it, like she's seeing a ghost.

My head spins.

I look around and then spot a parking notice taped to a post next to where I left the Buick.

I peel it off but I already know what's happened.

Shit. Shit. Shit.

It's been impounded. *Obviously*, it's been impounded – it's what happens when you leave a car illegally parked in the pick-up zone for close to three hours. I've given Blake this lecture before. Blake who parks anywhere, anyhow, thinking he'll get away with it because he's Blake Shaw and that somehow makes him untouchable.

I put Leda down. She pees against the post where the parking notice was taped and then starts whimpering.

I feel like screaming. At the sky and the sun and all the planes flying overhead. At whoever it is who decided to land me in this shit storm of a situation.

I think of Blake's car on the back of some horrible truck being carted to an impounding lot miles and miles from here.

I think about how much money it will cost to get it back – money I don't have.

And I think about how long all this is going to take.

But instead of screaming, I take my telescope off my back and sit down on the sidewalk. I slump my shoulders and all the oxygen goes out of my body.

Leda lies down beside me and rests her head on my lap.

I stroke the spot she likes to have rubbed behind her ears: a soft, silky bit, the colour of gold, amongst all the rough, straggly fur.

'What are we going to do?' I ask her.

She looks up at me with her dark, glassy eyes like she's asking me the exact same question.

I wrap my arms around her and close my eyes.

Chapter Seven

16.14 EST

I don't know how long I sit there on the sidewalk, staring at the tarmac, willing my brain to work out some kind of plan to make all of this okay. But by the time I look up again, the sun's so low, it blinds me.

Which is why I don't notice him, not at first.

I put my hand over my brow to block out the sun, which lights up his hair – the tangled strands look like comets.

The sun reflects off his glasses too, so hard that I can't see his eyes.

Leda gets up and runs around him, which makes him look nervous so I pat the space beside me to get her to sit down again.

For a second, I let myself believe that the fact that he's standing there – the fact that he's coming out of the airport – means that they've released new information. That the plane made it after all.

'Is there any news?' I ask.

He shakes his head. 'I needed to get out of there for a bit.'

My heart slumps.

'I thought you were leaving?' he says.

'So did I.'

'You changed your mind?'

I shake my head, too tired to explain. And too pissed about the car.

He sits down beside me but keeps a space between us like he's scared to get too close. But then he holds out his hand, which feels weirdly formal, but I take it anyway. His skin's cool. It feels nice.

'I'm Christopher,' he says. 'As in Columbus. I can't believe that I just said that.'

'*As in Columbus*?' I laugh and, for a second, it feels like a bit of my body comes back to life.

'My dad has a thing about explorers.'

With his tangled blond hair and his pale skin and his rosy cheeks, he looks more like Christopher Robin out of *Winnie The Pooh* than the rugged coloniser of the New World.

'Parents dump you with a whole load of shit when they give you a name, hey?'

He blushes. Maybe I offended him. Maybe he likes being associated with Christopher Columbus.

'I'm Air. As in, Ariadne.'

It's Blake who nicknamed me Air – as soon as I was born. Because he thought it was a totally cool name. As opposed to the totally nerdy name Dad picked out for me. For my baptism, when I was seven, Blake even wrote a song for me, using all these clever metaphors about breath and air and being in the world.

He looks up at me. 'Ariadne. The goddess of mazes and labyrinths.'

'You know?'

Nobody knows. Nobody except my geeky parents who fell in love over Greek myths at Oxford. My geeky parents who were totally pissed at Blake for changing my name basically as soon as they'd given it to me.

'Home-schooled,' he says.

'Sorry?'

'I was home-schooled until I was sixteen. Dad made me study all the old stuff. Latin, Greek, the myths. He got tutors for me. And when he had the time, he took me to museums. Anyway, that's how I know.'

'You were home-schooled in England?'

'Not really *in* England. Not really at home, either.'

'You weren't home-schooled at home? How does that work?'

He blushes again, which makes his pale grey eyes stand out even more.

'My dad travels so much that it was either take me with him or put me in a boarding school. I'm in a boarding school now, but I was home-schooled until last year.' He pauses. 'Well, *away*-schooled – I had some tutoring whenever we were in London but most of the time Dad taught me when we were travelling.' The corners of his mouth go up. 'Dad and the internet.'

'Why boarding school now?'

'So I can get my A-levels and go to university. Dad said it would be easier having the structure of a school to help me through that rather than figuring it out on our own.'

He hasn't mentioned his mom, which probably means she's not around in some way and I don't want to upset him by asking.

'I'm from England too,' I say. 'Was. Lived there until I was four. Which is why Americans think I'm English and English people think I'm American.'

'I like it – your accent.'

'It makes me sound like I don't belong anywhere.'

'Is that a bad thing?' He gives me a small, sideways smile.

I hadn't ever thought of it being a good thing. But perhaps he's right. Perhaps it's kind of cool not being locked into one particular place. 'I guess not.'

'So how come you lived in England?' he asks.

'Mom's English – well Scottish-English. Dad went to do a semester at Oxford, which is where they met.'

'Where they fell in love over Greek myths?' he says.

'Yeah. Mom was meant to be doing international law but she kept taking all these other classes too. Anyway, Dad ended up loving Oxford so much he stayed for years. They got married. Had kids.'

'And then you moved to the US?'

'Mom got a gig at the White House. As an international human rights lawyer.'

'Wow.'

'Yeah. She's a high achiever.'

'And your dad?'

'Classics professor at Georgetown. He still misses Oxford but he'd go anywhere for Mom.'

He looks at me, curious, like my friends sometimes do when I talk about Mom and Dad and how close they are.

He leans back and closes his eyes. Behind his glasses, he's got these crazily long, light eyelashes. 'It's warm out here,' he says.

'Yeah.'

A beautiful warm afternoon.

I think about Mom, Jude and Dad working really hard to get things ready for the wedding. And how Mom must be coping with the news that we're not going to make the breakfast. I picture them sitting there tomorrow morning, staring at two empty chairs and how Mom will be totally freaking out and how Dad will be trying to calm her down and how Jude will be thinking that it's typical that we're both off somewhere else without her. She feels left out when it comes to the three of us. All those birth order theories don't apply to us. Blake's the middle child but he gets all the attention. Jude's the eldest but that doesn't make her feel special – she's the one who feels like she's being overlooked. As for me, I'm the opposite of the spoilt and indulged youngest child – I'm the one whose job it is to sort out my brother and sister's problems and fights.

My eyeballs sting like I'm going to cry, because I know that it's totally not fair. There are times when Jude's sulkiness about not getting enough attention has annoyed the hell out of me but if there's one time that Jude shouldn't feel left out, it's at her wedding.

I sniff back the tears.

Leda nestles in closer to Christopher. He sits up and pats her head gently.

'She yours?' he asks.

'My brother's. I'm babysitting.'

He puts out his hand and Leda puts her head into it like she's looking for a treat.

'I love dogs – all animals really,' Christopher says.

He keeps stroking her. Leda's tilting her head back so far now it's like she's in some kind of trance. He's totally good with her.

'Do you have any pets?'

Christopher shakes his head. 'I was never allowed. Too much moving around.'

He keeps stroking her and I can tell, from how his shoulders drop and his body sinks into itself, that Leda's making him feel more relaxed too.

'So, what happened?' Christopher asks. 'I thought you needed to be somewhere.'

'I did.' I look back at the space where I parked the Buick. 'They took my brother's car.'

'Your brother?' He frowns and knits his eyebrows together: they're blond and tangled, like his hair. 'The one who owns the dog?'

'The very same.'

'He's the one you came to pick up?'

'Yeah. Sort of. It's a long story. I think I got it wrong. Or he got it wrong. Anyway, he's not here.'

'Right.'

I hand him the parking notice. 'They took the car.'

'From the car park?'

I shake my head. 'From here.'

'Here?'

I nod.

'Right *here*?'

'I was in a hurry – we were already late.' My throat goes thick. 'I know it was a stupid thing to do but I texted Blake to come straight out; I thought it would only take a few minutes before we'd be back in the car.' Tears prick the back of my eyes; I blink hard to make them go away. 'I didn't know all this would happen.'

'Are you okay?' asks Christopher.

And then it all comes out.

'My sister's getting married on Monday, during the eclipse, on this amazing rooftop terrace in a hotel in Nashville. And I should be there already but I thought

Blake got on the wrong plane so I came back to collect him and now he's not here and he's not answering my texts and I don't know how to tell my family – and now I don't have a car anymore.' I gulp. 'I don't know what to do.' My words tumble over each other so quick I'm pretty sure I don't make any sense. 'So no, nothing's even close to okay.'

I shut my eyes to push the tears back in.

'Can I help?' Two perfect pink circles form at the top of his cheeks.

It's a weird thing to ask. But it's kind of nice too – to have someone helping me out for a change.

'Help?' I ask.

'To get your car back,' he says.

He makes it sound so simple. And it makes me feel better – that there's one thing I might be able to sort out in this whole tangled mess I'm in.

'I'm fine,' I say.

'I'd like to help.'

'You would?'

He gives a quick nod. 'Take my mind off things for a bit – you know?'

It hits me again. That someone he knows – someone he cares about – is on the plane that's gone missing.

His brow is scrunched up and he's squinting into the sun and I get it, that he needs this.

'Yeah, I know,' I say.

He studies the parking notice and then says, 'Have you called the number yet?'

I shake my head.

'The tow truck might not have got very far. We could explain.'

'Explain?'

60

'What's going on,' he says. 'That these are special circumstances.'

Our eyes catch his and, for a beat, we don't say anything.

'You think that would work?'

In my experience, traffic enforcement doesn't do special circumstances, especially for people our age.

'We could try,' he says.

Leda gives out a small bark and thumps her tail against the sidewalk, like she's agreeing with him.

I bite the side of my thumbnail and notice that my sky-blue nail varnish is chipped. I went to have a manicure before I left DC – on instruction from Mom. To match the bridesmaid's dress I'm meant to wear tomorrow.

Then I get out my phone and dial the number.

Chapter Eight

16.45 EST

I watch Christopher grab a sheet from an old in-flight magazine from his backpack and start folding. I don't even know what he's making but I can tell that he's enjoying it, the feel of the skin of the paper as he rubs it between his fingers. He looks relaxed like he did when he was stroking Leda.

I snatch glances at him through the corner of my eye, hoping that he doesn't realise that I'm staring. It takes my mind off things, looking at this weird English guy who's got nothing to do with my life or what's going on in Nashville or with Blake. How he's sitting here, folding that bit of paper, as though it's another ordinary day.

It's weird that he's this calm, because as bad as I've got it with Blake and the wedding and everything, Christopher has it way worse. Someone he knows was on the plane that's crashed. God, I haven't even asked him who he came to meet or why he was here. I've been so busy thinking about myself. And he's the one who must be going through hell. And yet he's sitting here, like he's got some special information that no one else does. As if that floating piece of metal doesn't mean the same to him as it does to the rest of us:

that the crash was bad. Really bad. As in, it's unlikely anyone survived.

Leda puts her muzzle on Christopher's lap and keeps slobbering on him, but he doesn't seem to mind.

'I didn't ask you…' I stutter.

'Sorry?'

'I never asked you, who you came to meet.' My voice breaks a bit. 'I mean, who you were collecting at the airport.'

'Oh.' He goes quiet for a bit. 'Dad. I came to collect my dad.'

'I'm sorry.'

He doesn't answer. I guess it's all too much to take in right now. That's probably why he came out here, so he could get away from thinking about his dad being on that plane.

'So, what brought you to DC?' I ask.

'I came to do research for a school project. *The future of American politics*.' He puts quote marks round his words with his fingers. 'Dad's been working for the last week and he knew he was flying into DC so he thought it would make sense for me to come earlier – to do some work – and for him to join me afterwards.'

'You came all the way to DC for a school project?'

'Dad gets cheap flights. And he said it would make my project stand out – to do on-the-ground research.'

'Wow, that's commitment.'

'Dad believes in doing things properly.'

'Sounds like my mom.'

He makes another fold in his paper.

'You really study American politics in the UK?'

He nods. 'Dad made me take politics as an A-level. He wants me to understand.'

'Understand what?'

He looks up at me and smiles. 'Everything, basically. But the state of the world as it is now, I guess. And America's kind of central to understanding that.'

'Central to understanding how we're fucking up the world, you mean?'

He laughs and his face relaxes for the first time.

'Maybe,' he says. 'I guess we're all a bit responsible for that.'

I think about the blazing rows Mom and Dad have about politics over dinner and how the one thing they agree on is that our current president is single-handedly tearing down every good thing about our country. As far as I'm concerned, the mess the world's in is another reason for going into space.

'You enjoy that? Studying American politics?' I ask.

He looks back into his hands. 'Not really.' Then he looks up again quickly. 'I mean, no offence—'

I smile. 'None taken.'

'It's not really my thing.'

'But you're doing it anyway?'

He looks back down. 'Dad's made a load of sacrifices – for my education. It's the least I can do.'

'Studying something you don't enjoy seems like quite a big price to pay if you ask me.'

He stops folding and stares into his hands.

'I mean, you should still get to study what you want to study,' I add. 'You only live once and all that.'

I think about how supportive Mom and Dad have been about my whole wanting to be an astronaut thing and how, even though they're worried, they're kind of supportive of Blake and his music, and how they're letting Jude do her own thing too, even though they're sad that she gave up her piano. I guess we're lucky. Not all kids get parents like that.

'It's not so bad,' Christopher says. 'Dad gets me to see cool places. And once I'd done all the school stuff – tours of the White House, the museums – I got to go to the National Gallery of Art. I loved walking around the Sculpture Garden. Some of those artists are amazing.'

'I go there too – all the time! To the gallery – and the Sculpture Garden. It's one of my favourite places in DC.'

'Really?'

I nod. 'Who knows, we might have crossed paths.'

The corners of his mouth turn up.

I wonder whether I'd have noticed Christopher walking past me or sitting on the edge of the fountain in the Sculpture Garden. I mean, if we hadn't been thrown together like this at the airport.

'So, you've been walking around DC on your own for a whole week? Isn't that kind of lonely?'

He starts folding again, making sharp, tight corners, pressing down with the side of the thumbnail to make the edges smooth.

'I don't mind,' he says after a while. 'I've got used to it. Dad works a lot and it's kind of fun, getting to know a new city on your own.'

I like to be on my own too, when I'm discovering something for the first time: like identifying a star through my telescope, or researching a planet.

'I suppose I get that,' I say. 'It makes you focus more – when you're on your own, I mean.'

65

He nods.

'What's the boarding school like?' I ask. 'It must have been a bit of a shock, after home-schooling or away-schooling or whatever it is you did.'

'It's okay. Mostly. A bit male.'

'A bit male?'

'All boys.'

'Wow.'

'Which is why I'm nervous.'

'About what?'

He gulps. I watch his Adam's apple slide up and down his throat.

'Talking to you,' he says.

'Well, you're doing a better job than most of the guys at my high school.'

The tops of his cheeks go an even deeper red.

'There's a lot of rugby too. I'm not so good at that.'

I look at his long, white fingers folding those bits of paper. No, I can't imagine he'd like to be in the middle of a rugby scrum.

He goes back to folding the paper over and over into all these tiny, intricate folds. Then he puts it down beside him on the pavement, half-made so I can't quite work out what it is – whether it's another bird, because there's a kind of wing, or whether it's the sail of a ship.

He looks over at the doors to the airport terminal and then glances at his watch.

'You worried about the plane?' I say and then I regret it. Of course he's worried about the plane. The reason he's out here, sitting with a random girl with a dog on a sidewalk, is because he's trying not to think about it.

He shrugs.

66

'Dad's planes aren't usually late.'

It's a weird thing to say; as if anyone had the power to decide if their plane is going to be late.

'There's probably been a mix up,' he adds.

I think of that floating bit of metal again and how it didn't look like a mix up to me.

I swallow to ease the dryness in my throat and then get up and start pacing again, craning my neck in the hope that I'll see Blake's yellow Buick rounding the corner.

Christopher goes back to folding his piece of paper.

Then I sit down again – a bit closer to him than I intended. Our legs touch. I don't know whether I should move to give him more space or whether moving will seem rude like I don't want to sit close to him.

I check my phone. Just more *Where are you?* And *Call me?* messages from Mom. Nothing from Blake. I sigh and start biting the side of my nail. I'm jittery but at the same time my body and my brain feel frozen, like I couldn't get up off this pavement, not in a million years.

I look back down the road. At least when the Buick shows up I can *do* something. Get behind the steering wheel, start driving, clock up the miles to Nashville so that I have a chance of getting to the wedding on time.

I look back over at Christopher.

'Thanks,' I say.

'For what?'

'For hanging out with me.'

'It's better than being in there,' he says, looking back at the airport terminal. 'Much better.'

A taxi pulls up a few yards away from us.

Leda barks.

Three people step out.

A woman in a trouser suit, red hair tumbling down her shoulders; as she stumbles out onto the pavement, she gets out a compact mirror and starts applying lipstick.

Behind her, a guy with one of those fuzzy microphones on the end of a stick.

Behind him, a guy with a camera balancing on his shoulder.

I get up and put my hands on my hips. 'What the hell?'

Leda barks louder.

The woman spots us, puts away her lipstick and her mirror and walks up to us, her heels clacking on the sidewalk.

She stops in front of us, pauses, like she's settling into a role, brushes a strand of hair over her shoulder and then says:

'Did you two come to meet the plane?'

'No,' I say, quickly, before Christopher has the time to say anything.

If having a mom for a lawyer has taught me anything, it's that you don't talk to journalists. Especially to journalists who look like her.

The microphone guy and the camera guy come and stand beside her. They're pointing their respective pieces of equipment at us.

The woman – the reporter – turns to Christopher. 'You?'

Christopher looks at me. I shake my head.

The woman's waiting for him answer.

'No,' Christopher says.

She looks at us suspiciously. 'You two kids don't want to be on TV?'

Leda's barking is really loud now, so loud that the woman takes a step back.

'No, we don't want to be on TV.' I yank Christopher away from the reporter.

The woman steps closer. 'What's that?' She looks down at Christopher's hands – at the paper model he's holding.

I look down too.

My insides flip.

He made a plane. A paper plane.

Slowly, he scrunches it up into a ball.

'It's nothing,' he says.

The woman shrugs. 'Come on,' she tells her guys with the microphone and the camera and then walks off.

I watch her stride through the sliding doors into the terminal building and get a sick feeling at the back of my throat. She's going to interrogate all those poor people inside. She's going to make them feel even worse about what's happening. At least she's left Christopher alone.

When she's gone, I sit back down.

Christopher sits down too. He lets out a long sigh like he's letting out a whole lot of air that's been building up inside him.

'Dad would hate that,' he says.

'Hate what?'

'All the fuss. The reporters. They say they want to help but they don't. They make everything worse.'

'They don't *help*?' I ask.

He shakes his head. 'When he's not doing his regular job, Dad does charity work: he goes to disaster relief zones, after earthquakes and fires and stuff. He can get there quicker than most people. He goes to deliver supplies. And he says that the reporters focus on the wrong stuff and make people more scared. And when people are scared, bad things happen. Keeping people calm, making people feel safe – that's what matters.'

It's weird. Sometimes, when Christopher talks about his dad, I get the feeling that he doesn't really like him, that they're not close, but then he says something like that and it's like his dad's his hero.

'I'm sorry—' he stutters. 'They get to me, that's all.'

'It's okay, I understand,' I say. 'That's why I told her to get lost.'

He nods. 'Thanks.'

Leda flops between us.

We sit there, listening to the planes taking off and landing. So many planes. So many people.

Then, all of a sudden, Christopher looks up at me.

'About your brother – I think it's going to be okay. UK Flyer has one of the best safety records.'

'Blake's not on the plane.'

Because he's not. He's not where he's meant to be. He's probably miles from the wedding. But there's no reason he'd be on the plane that's crashed. That's not an option.

Christopher doesn't answer.

Leda shuffles in closer between us.

And for a long while, neither of us say anything.

We just keep waiting.

Chapter Nine

17.32 EST

It takes us over an hour to get the car back. Christopher was right, it hadn't reached the impound lot yet. When I got through to the state police, I told them that my brother was on the plane that's gone missing, the one that's on the news. I felt bad for lying but telling them the truth – that I don't know where Blake is and that I'd just parked illegally because I was in a rush – wouldn't have got my Buick back. Anyway, it worked.

I hope the reporter didn't get any of me on film. Mom always has the news on, especially news from DC, in case she needs to rush back to the White House to give some kind of legal advice. She'll get so mad if sees me standing at Dulles right now. And if she catches wind of the fact that I've been caught up in this whole plane crash thing, she'll totally flip.

After that reporter left, I went back into the airport terminal to get some food and water for Leda. The TV screen was still showing the same picture of that bit of metal floating on the sea. It turns out that the stretch of ocean is off the coast of Ireland, which they're saying was at the beginning of the plane's route. But all kinds of crap gets washed up into the ocean, right? That's what I want to tell Christopher, who's been really quiet since the reporter left us.

When the tow-truck guy finishes giving us a lecture on not parking illegally, he gets out one of those wireless credit card terminals and holds it out to me.

And I freeze.

I've spent all my cash on gas, having my nails done, and getting the sun filter for my telescope. And using the emergency credit card is out: first, because I already pulled out a large sum paying for Blake's flight and second, because Mom will get an email alert. And she's smart: she'll notice that the transaction was made to some parking fine business in DC.

'We take credit or debit,' the guy says.

'You're kidding, right?'

I'm hoping that if I act surprised enough, he might change his mind. It's a trick Blake taught me.

Except the guy looks at me like I'm an idiot. I should have learnt this lesson already: Blake's tricks minus his charm don't work.

'No, I'm not kidding,' he says, his voice deadpan.

'You're seriously making me pay a fine?'

'Yeah. It's policy,' the guy says.

I consider pointing out that it's not policy to drive a car back to its owner once it's been towed. And that policies don't really count when it comes to our particular situation. But he's been pretty accommodating up to now and I don't want him to take the car away again.

'I can't afford that,' I say, staring at the $200 displayed on his terminal.

The parking control officer rolls his eyes.

'I could lend you some money,' Christopher says.

My first instinct is to say no.

Mom and Dad have raised us never to borrow money from anyone. Well, they've raised me and Jude not to borrow money from anyone. Blake does his own thing. Plus, I feel bad – I don't even know Christopher. And I don't know when I'll be able to pay him back or how.

But I can't stop thinking about how, if I leave now, I can still make it to the rehearsal dinner.

'Thanks,' I say.

When the guy drives back off, I put Leda in the back and get into the driver's seat.

Then I sit there, the door open, staring at the silver guitar pendant hanging from the rear-view mirror; I gave it to Blake for his eighteenth birthday, three years ago. I can't believe he's actually twenty-one. You're meant to be a proper grown-up by then, aren't you? But Blake has this Peter Pan thing going on. He'll never really be old.

In the rear-view mirror, I see my two dresses and Blake's suit and hat box, laid out on the back.

And then I look at the rest of the car, like it's the first time I see it. The scuffed leather bench seats in the front and back. The beige top, folded down. It's awesome. Old and kind of rusty and it rattles whenever you go over sixty mph. But it's totally awesome. Like Blake.

A hard lump forms at the back of my throat.

I close the car door, put my left hand on the steering wheel and I'm about to switch on the ignition when I notice something else: the photograph taped to the dashboard. I'm ten years old, standing on this tall rock above a swimming hole. Blake's holding my hand. We're about to jump.

Jude must have taken the picture. It was the first time Blake took us there – Blue Springs in the Cherokee National Forest, Tennessee.

I switch on the ignition.

And then I realise that he's still standing there.

'Do you have someone?' I ask.

He looks at me, his grey eyes wide. 'Someone?'

'Someone you can call – or go to?'

He looks back at the arrivals lounge and then back at me like he's struggling to make up his mind about something.

'Where were you meant to go?' I prompt. 'After you picked up your dad—' Then I stall.

I grip the steering wheel harder. 'Well, where were you and your dad meant to stay? When he got here, I mean?'

Please may he have someone. A friend. A relative. A contact from his dad. He can't stay here alone.

'Oregon,' he says. 'A connecting flight. To see the eclipse.'

'Wow, Oregon,' I say. 'That's cool.' Because Oregon's where I would have chosen to be – if it weren't for the wedding. I mean, Nashville's a cool place to see the totality, but Oregon is where it all starts.

I wonder whether, in a different lifetime, without the wedding and without the plane going missing, Christopher and I might have met out there, at the beginning of the eclipse. And then I think about how we might have crossed walking around the Sculpture Garden in DC. Blake wrote this song, ages ago, about how when you're meant to be meet someone, you get loads of chances – you brush past them over and over until BAM! you finally notice each other. I'd always thought that was a bit slushy and romantic – and too superstitious for my scientific world view. But maybe there's something in it.

'So, you have someone you know in Oregon?' I ask. And then I feel stupid. They're going on a holiday, why would they know anyone there? And even if they did know someone there, it's miles away – it's not like a friend in Oregon is going to help Christopher with what he's going through here in DC.

'No, we were going to stay in a hotel.' His eyes go far away, like he's trying to picture being there. 'And Dad booked us a place on a sailing boat,' Christopher says. 'He wanted to see the eclipse from the water.'

A silence hangs between us: the silence of what was meant to happen if his life hadn't just been turned upside down.

'What about your mom?' I ask.

He stares at me and blinks.

'Was she meant to come with you – to see the eclipse?' I ask.

And I know it's overstepping. And that he would have mentioned his mom already if she were in his life. But I can't drive away thinking that he's going to be here on his own. There has to be someone he can call.

He shakes his head.

'Is she back in England?'

He shakes his head again. 'Atlanta.'

'Your mom lives in *Atlanta*?'

He nods.

75

'I've got a parent from each side of the pond – like you. Only the other way around. Mum's American, Dad's English.'

That was in Blake's song too: how when you meet someone you were meant to meet you find out all this crazy stuff you have in common that can't be explained away.

'They're not together,' he says.

'They're divorced?'

'They never got married.'

'Oh.'

'They separated shortly after Mum had me.'

'Do you go to Atlanta to visit her?' I ask.

He shakes his head.

I know I'm in a minority: the kid of parents who are still together – more than that, who love each other. And that even though Mom's totally crazy in the way she organises every second of our lives; and even though Dad's too much of a wuss to ever stand up to her and say *No, life's already hard enough without another one of your mad projects*; and even though Jude annoys the hell out of me with her throwing away her life to be a 1950s housewife, and Blake drives me crazy in the way he thinks the whole world revolves around him – I love them more than anything. All four of them. And I know that that makes me one of the lucky ones. I've got a family. A proper family. The most incredible family in the world.

'Have you called her?' I ask. 'Your mom? To tell her what's going on.' My breath is tight in my throat. 'With the plane.'

He shakes his head. 'I didn't know what to say.' He pauses. 'It's like too much time has passed – too much has happened. We can't just pick up where we left off.'

I look at him and think about how he helped me get the car back, and the thought of him going back into that airport terminal on his own makes my heart sink.

'Perhaps it would help if you saw her face to face.'

His head snaps up.

'I could take you part of the way to Atlanta,' I suggest. 'I'm heading in that direction. Sort of.'

Leda jumps up and starts thumping her tail on the tarmac, like she's totally up for taking Christopher with us.

He bites the side of his lip and looks back at the door to the arrivals lounge.

'As soon as there's any news, it will be all over the TV and the internet,' I say. 'It's not like you'll find out more by staying here. And you'll go crazy waiting. Come with me – you can charge your phone in my car and I'll drive you to Knoxville. There'll be a bus to Atlanta from there.'

He doesn't say anything.

'I could do with the company,' I say.

Leda starts licking Christopher's arm.

'And it looks like she wants you to come too.'

Then, very slowly, he nods. 'If you're sure.'

'I'm sure.'

I shove the dresses and the suit to one side on the back seat to make room for his backpack and lift the binder from my summer internship at the Air & Space Museum off the passenger seat.

Leda jumps into the back.

And then Christopher gets in beside me.

Chapter Ten

20.45 EST
1-66

It takes us ages to get out of DC because of the traffic. When we finally do, I relax for a bit and look up at the sky. It's dark. And now that we've left the city, it's clearer; there are billions of stars. The moon. A pale, round disc in the sky. Tomorrow night, it won't be there at all, not the night before the eclipse. Well, it will be there – it's always there, like the stars – we just won't see it.

I wonder what it would be like to see the eclipse from the moon; to watch a long, dark shadow slicing the earth while the rest of the world stays bright. Now that would be even more amazing than being in Oregon.

One day I'll live somewhere where it's so clear it'll be like living in the sky itself. When Mom was a kid she spent her summer holidays way up in the north of Scotland, and she says that there are islands there where you can see more stars than you ever thought existed.

The warm, night air brushes against my arms and my face, cool against my eyes.

It feels good to let my body go numb, not to have to think.

The only sound comes from the engine, a low hum, the tyres clicking over ridges in the road and Leda, who keeps letting out her random yelps in her sleep.

I still don't know where Blake is, and the news of what happened to the plane and Christopher's dad is hanging over us like this horrible black cloud. But it feels good to have left the airport behind and to just be driving.

I look over at Christopher. After he plugged his cell into the lighter socket, he sat back and stared out of the windscreen. And he hasn't stopped staring. Like he's hoping that the night sky will give him an answer.

As the wind rushes past us, the smell of his skin and his clothes drifts over to me: pines needles and rain-wet earth, like he lives deep in a forest somewhere.

Besides Dad and Blake and a couple of boys in my Physics class at school, I don't really hang around guys much. Which means that, if he were here now, Blake would totally be giving me a hard time about this.

And then it comes back to me: the reason I'm in this weird situation – driving my brother's Buick through the night with a strange guy from England – is because Blake's missing.

Christopher hasn't said anything since we left Dulles, which is kind of a relief; my brain's been on overdrive ever since I got to the airport and I don't have the energy to talk or process any more information.

So, I keep my eyes on the road, let the warm air wash over me and push the CD player into its slot.

The sound system's the only concession Blake made to updating the car. He wants the Buick to be true to its 1970s spirit. Yeah, the car has a spirit. For Blake, everything's got a spirit.

The CD spins and then music starts coming out, and it takes a second to sink in. The singer's voice.

Suddenly, I can't breathe.

My hands go numb on the steering wheel and the car starts swerving to the middle of the road.

'Hey! Watch out!' a voice yells beside me.

I hear Leda barking from the back seat – loud, strong barks, way louder than her usual whining.

Then I hear her scramble down into the footwell, like she does when she's scared.

The next thing I see are headlights, huge, beaming in through the windscreen: a truck is coming towards us, head on.

My heart's hammering.

A hand reaches past me and pulls the steering wheel hard until the car swerves to the side of the road.

Then I lose control of the wheel and I'm thrown against the door.

The tyres screech.

Leda yelps from the footwell.

The car spins and, for a second, I think this is it, this is where it ends.

And then everything stops.

We're on the hard shoulder, facing the wrong way. The side of my body feels bruised from the impact against the door. My head's spinning. Blood's pounding in my ears.

Outside my body, the only sound is the tick, ticking of the engine. And the whoosh of cars driving past us.

My throat's dry and my heart's knocking so hard I think it's going to push out of my ribs.

And I'm wondering why the airbag didn't detonate. The only way Mom agreed for Blake to drive this museum piece of a car was if he got it totally safety-checked. He said he did.

Of course, he *said* he did.

He probably decided that airbags weren't true to the car's spirit. I should have taken it to the garage myself.

I try to steady my breathing.

The weird thing is that the music's still playing. Blake's cover of Johnny Cash's 'Flesh and Blood'.

I reach out for the CD player and thump my palm against all the buttons, trying to make it stop.

'Damn it!' I yell, still thumping at the CD player.

'It's okay,' a voice says beside me. 'It's okay.'

And then I remember I'm not alone. That Christopher's sitting beside me, a guy who, a few hours ago, I didn't even know existed. A guy who, more likely than not, just saved my life.

He reaches past me, pushes on the eject button and the CD slips out.

I sit back, my whole body shaking.

Neither of us says anything.

Then, his voice low and gentle, he asks, 'What just happened?'

My eyes are closed now.

'That was him.' My words come out jagged, like my mouth has forgotten how to form words. 'That was Blake, singing.'

I open my eyes and look back at the road. Everything looks normal: cars drive past us on either side. Headlights. Tail lights. No sign of the truck that we swerved to avoid.

'I'm sorry,' I say, my voice shaking. 'It's all been too much. And then hearing Blake's voice.'

From the corner of my eye I see Christopher nod. And then he looks down at the CD player. My eyes follow his and I see Blake's handwriting scrawled in Sharpie across the top: *For Air.*

I've listened to the CD he made for me so many times it should be worn out by now.

'Your brother's a musician?'

I feel blood in my mouth; I must have bitten my cheek as we swerved away from truck.

I can't believe I haven't told him this about Blake yet. It's like you can't mention my brother's name without mentioning his music in the same breath. Blake *is* his music. And I assume that the world knows him already, which is stupid, I know. But then if you've lived with Blake, you'd understand: he was born with *Destined to be famous* stamped on his forehead.

'Yeah. He's a musician. He writes songs. Plays the guitar – has a band. He was on tour in England.' I pause. 'He's even more successful over there than he is here.' I stare out of the windscreen. 'He loves London, especially.'

I stare out of the windscreen, feeling numb. And then I cover my face with my hands and dig my fingers into my scalp. My breath is ragged, like there's not enough oxygen in the air.

'All this is so messed up,' I say.

I picture our special family breakfast at Louis's tomorrow morning without me and Blake there. How Mom will be out of her mind with worry – and totally pissed that I'm not answering my phone.

And how, if Blake doesn't show up in time for the wedding itself, I'm going to have sing instead of him. Which makes my stomach cave in on itself. He's the one everyone wants to hear.

Blake's words come back to me:

I'll be there, no matter what.

I'd guessed there would be a screw-up. There usually is with Blake. And he's made a fine art out of turning up late to things. It makes him even more noticeable – as if he needed that. But this is Jude's wedding for Christ's sake. This is different. This is the one time where he has to be on time. This is the one time where (besides the song) he doesn't get to steal the show.

I take a few breaths to calm myself down.

I'll be there, no matter what, I whisper to myself. *No matter what*. He promised.

And then I look back up at the stars.

Someone once asked me why I wanted to do it – to study the night sky, to be an astronaut. Why I was so obsessed with the world beyond the earth.

My answer was simple:

It makes me believe that anything's possible.

But it's like all that's an illusion. I feel trapped. And totally powerless. Like even if the whole universe were on my side, it wouldn't help me.

'If Blake doesn't make it to the wedding, I don't want to go either.'

Christopher waits a beat and then, in a quiet way that's louder and clearer than anyone yelling, he says:

'Whatever's going on with your brother, you'll be there. For your family.'

I stare up at him. 'I will?'

'Yes, you will,' he says firmly, like there's no alternative. He looks at me through the strands of tangled hair that fall over his forehead. 'You said that your sister's wedding was the most important day in your family's life, right?'

'Right.'

'So, you have to go.'

'But what am I meant to tell them?' I hold out my phone. 'I've got all these missed calls from Mom. She's wondering what the hell's going on.'

'Don't tell them anything. Not yet. Just focus on getting to Nashville.'

I stare at him for a second. His grey eyes are so light, they're transparent. He's doing the job I usually do: he's calming me down and telling me that it's going to be okay and getting me to focus on finding a solution. It feels nice not to be the one sorting things out for once.

I nod. 'You're right. It's going to be fine. Blake's going to show up and it'll all be fine.'

'I didn't say—'

'He'll show up,' I talk over him. 'And he'll sing his song and everyone will forget he was even late.'

I press the words into my head.

'Yeah, it's going to be fine.'

I can feel Christopher staring at me. He doesn't say anything.

84

I look at the steering wheel. Somehow, I have to find the strength to get going again – to drive those hundreds of miles to Nashville.

'You still want to be driven by someone who nearly crashed into a truck?' I ask Christopher.

He keeps looking at me. Then the corners of his mouth turn up. 'The truck was kind of in the way.'

I let out a laugh, and all the tension in my body dissipates for a moment.

'It was, wasn't it?'

'Definitely.'

'You trust me? To keep driving you?'

'Well, I don't know about that...' he says. But he's smiling. 'Yeah, I trust you.'

The thing is, I don't even know whether I trust myself anymore.

I look up again at the stars. If I'm going to be an astronaut one day – if I'm going to make it all the way up there – I'd better learn how to navigate things down here.

A low whine comes from the back of the car.

'Oh God.' I unbuckle my seatbelt and twist round to the back of the car.

Leda's cowering in the footwell, her eyes two black, glassy pools. For once, she's dead quiet. My binder and my telescope are wedged in beside her and Blake's suit has flown off its hanger and is draped over her. The hat box is in the other footwell. It's got a big dent in the side. I hope to god that the hat isn't damaged.

I rip the suit off her body, pull her out of the footwell onto my lap, wrap my arms around her neck and let out a sob. Then I hold her away from me and inspect her. There's a small cut on her ear – and on her nose too. Her whole body's shaking and I can feel her heart hammering against her ribcage. I lean in and kiss the top of her head.

'I'm sorry,' I say. 'I'm so, so sorry.'

She licks my face. Her tongue is so warm and familiar that my eyes well up and for the first time since Blake left her with me six weeks ago, I'm grateful that I've got her.

I hold her closer and look up at the sky. *Where are you, Blake?*

Christopher leans over and pets the top of Leda's head in long, gentle strokes. I can feel her relaxing against me, her heart slowing down.

For a few seconds, neither of us say anything. Then I say, 'Here.'

I place Leda on Christopher's lap.

'You look after her.'

Leda licks his hand and he leans over and kisses the top of her head, the soft patch between her ears.

'Leda likes you,' I say.

'*Leader?*'

'Yes, Leda. As in L-E-D-A. Jupiter's thirteenth moon.'

'Oh – right.'

'It was found in 1974. The moon, I mean. I can show it to you if you like.'

God, I sound like a dork.

'It's a cool name.' He pats her again, a bit more confidently this time. 'Have you had her for a long time?'

'She's Blake's. Like the car. Whenever he goes on tour, I get to babysit them. And I named her – obviously.'

'Obviously?'

'I like space.'

'As in, outerspace?'

I nod.

Leda puts a paw up against Christopher's chest and then paws at his glasses, so that he has to readjust them. Yeah, she definitely likes him.

Christopher shakes her paw like he shook my hand earlier.

'Pleased to meet you, Leda,' he says. 'Officially.'

As I lean over and give Leda a stroke, my hand brushes Christopher's bare forearm; electricity shoots through my body.

I notice Christopher's cell light up; it's been charging through the cigarette lighter. He grabs it and starts scanning through news pages. His breath goes jagged and he starts jiggling his leg.

I should ask him what's going on, but I'm not ready to take in anything else right now. I want to get back on the road and drive. Focus on getting to the wedding. And anyway, if Blake's turned up somewhere and is waiting for me to pick him up, he'll call me.

I switch on the ignition and look across the road. It's late so there aren't many cars around. I pull out onto the road, do an illegal U-turn and then press down on the accelerator.

Chapter Eleven

21.30 EST
1-81

My eyes are burning. After the adrenaline of the past few hours, it's like my body's gone into some kind of shutdown mode.

I look back at the road. A few seconds later, my eyes close. My eyelids are heavy and it takes all the energy I've got to blink them back open.

'I think I need to take a break,' I say.

Which is the last thing I want to do right now. I've got over 500 miles to cover before I get to Nashville – and, because of the eclipse, the traffic's going to be really bad as soon as people hit the road tomorrow morning.

So, I should keep going.

But if I don't take a break, I'm going to crash the car – really crash it this time. And then I'll never make it to the wedding. If that happens, Mom and Jude won't forgive me. It's one thing our unreliable brother not showing up, it's another for the always-show-up-no-matter-what-little-sister (the little sister who's meant to walk in front of Jude scattering the petals of Mom's heirloom roses) bailing.

I look over at Christopher. His eyes are closed so I guess he didn't hear me.

I lean over and shake him gently.

He rubs his eyes and yawns.

'We're stopping for a break,' I announce.

I notice a Mobil sign by the next exit and flick the indicator.

'Can you lend me a bit more money?' I ask. 'For some gas?'

I swallow hard. I hate having to ask him, but I don't have a choice. Well, I do have a choice. I could use the emergency credit card. But like I said, I'm not ready for Mom to find out where I am. Plus, she'll get the email alert and then she'll call and I'll feel like I have to pick up and I'll try to make up some excuse but she'll hear it in my voice, that something's wrong. I'm a crap liar.

'I'll pay you back.'

'Sure,' he says, getting out his wallet.

Once we're parked and I've filled up the car, I take Leda to a patch of grass for a pee and then put her back in the backseat of the car.

'We won't be long,' I say.

I noticed a sign in the window advertising coffee. It won't be Starbucks but I'll take anything to keep me awake.

I start walking away from the car and Leda yelps. And then she totally guilt-trips me: cocking her head to one side and looking at me with those big, black glassy eyes of hers.

She's still shaken up by what happened earlier, when I nearly rammed us into an oncoming truck. The blood on her ear has dried into a crusty brown. I know she's wondering where Blake is because the only reason we ever go to Dulles airport is to collect Blake. And I know that she doesn't want to be alone. But what am I meant to do? There's a big *No Dogs Allowed* sign outside the Mobil store.

She lets out a low, mournful whine.

'Okay,' I say. 'Okay.'

I look over at Christopher and get an idea.

I open the boot, pull out a fluorescent yellow sash that Mom put in there along with a whole load of other safety stuff and tie it round Leda's belly.

She starts whining again. Then she wriggles around under the sash like she's got fleas.

'It's this or you stay in the car,' I say.

Leda keeps snapping her head round and biting at the sash.

I clip on her lead and hand it to Christopher.

'She's yours,' I say. 'Look like you need her.'

'Sorry?'

'She's your service dog.'

'She is?'

'Yep.'

If you think I'm a bad liar, try watching me act. It's not pretty. I flunked every theatre class I took at school. Blake and Jude sucked up all of Mom and Dad's artsy genes.

'Okay,' Christopher says, taking the lead.

I like that about him. That he kind of goes along with things without asking too many questions. That he stays calm. And trusts me.

'You'd be good to have on a space mission,' I say.

'What?'

Did I actually say that out loud?

'Oh, nothing. Just that you're cool.'

He raises his bushy blond eyebrows. 'I'm *cool*?'

'Yeah. You are.'

I grab my telescope from the back seat, Christopher gives Leda's lead a tug, and we head into the store.

The guy behind the counter looks at Leda and you can tell he's about to say something, but then he sees Christopher and closes his mouth again. Christopher totally rocks the service dog thing. He pats Leda on the side and says, 'good dog,' and makes it seem like it's totally normal that he's bringing an animal into a no-animals-allowed place.

Blake once said that confidence was his biggest talent – that it was what made people listen to him and like him. That people are drawn to confidence because it makes them feel safe, like it's making them stronger too. Blake said that confidence was even more important than being good at singing or playing the guitar or being cute. Though he has all of those things too, of course, so I'm not sure he's really tested the theory.

I've got enough cash in my wallet to get us a couple of coffees from the dispenser. I get some chips too, from the guy at the counter. He's so busy watching the highlights of the Red Sox game that he doesn't even look away from the screen as he hands me the change.

We sit at a round, rickety metal table by the food machines, the only table in the store. I feed Leda some chips under the table. I know it's not good for her but Leda looks like she could do with some comfort food. And, more to the point, Blake's not here so he doesn't get a say.

My phone sits on the table in front of me. It keeps lighting up. More messages from Mom.

Messages from Mom asking when Blake and I are going to show up.

I type a quick message: **Blake messed up his flight. I'm waiting for him. We'll see you tomorrow. Don't stress, Mom**. I pause and then add: *Love you*.

Then I switch off the phone.

I know Mom. On the face of it, she'll seem totally calm. Make a joke of it – that it's Blake's thing – to turn up late. That we should have banked on him not making the family breakfast. That the main thing is that he's there for the wedding. That I'll get him there. Because that's what I do.

But inside, she'll be going crazy.

Because the events Mom plans never go wrong.

Mom sees every festive occasion (Halloween, Thanksgiving, Christmas, Easter, birthdays and a few other religious festivals to which we have no known affiliation) as some kind of Olympic-level competition. When we were kids, she hand-sewed every one of our Halloween costumes and baked, carved and frosted every one of our birthday cakes and, every Christmas, she scales the roof putting up Christmas lights – bolder and brighter and blinkier than any of the neighbours.

She's totally exhausting to live with. Like Martha Stewart on speed. Except that stuff isn't even her day job. She's an amazing lawyer too.

So, how does Mom do it all, I hear you ask? Simple: she never sleeps.

You've got it, Mom's both a superhero and totally annoying.

So, you can imagine that her eldest daughter's wedding was going to be a big deal. And it's an even bigger deal because Mom knows that, more likely than not, she'll only get one stab at it. Blake doesn't believe in marriage – or anything else that involves long-term commitment: he's had a steady stream of girlfriends since middle school. As for me, having a husband and kids doesn't really mix with zooming off into space.

So if Blake and I mess up Jude's wedding, she'll be upset. *Really* upset.

I wonder how Dad's handling everything right now. He's the yin to Mom's yang. The calm centre to her spinning world. He sits back and lets stuff wash over him. When Mom goes into intense mode, he slips away into his study and goes into Greek-myth world and doesn't re-emerge until things have calmed down. When Mom's doing my head in too, I sometimes join him in there. He lets me sit on the other side of his desk and read or work on my Physics homework and we pretend the rest of the world has dropped away. It makes me feel better, to sit there with Dad, even if we don't say anything.

I think about calling him and telling him everything but then I know that's not an option. Dad's like me: can't hide what he's thinking. Mom would pick up on the fact that I've been in touch right away.

When Christopher's finished his chips, he gets out his phone.

'You said there was a bus from Knoxville to Atlanta?' he says.

'Yeah, there should be.'

He looks up a few more pages.

'What time do you think we'll get there?'

'To Knoxville?' I check the clock on the far wall of the store. 'When's the earliest bus – tomorrow morning?'

'Six thirty.'

'If we drive through the night we might make it for that one.'

He nods.

And then a stillness settles between us. And I know it's because talking about the bus has brought it home that, in a few hours, we'll be saying goodbye.

He takes a paper napkin from the dispenser and folds it until it turns into a small, tight body with wings and a long, thin beak. He places it on the table and its head tilts upwards, like it's about to take flight.

It's amazing how he can make a cheap paper napkin from a gas station look this beautiful.

Sitting here, it's like we're in a bubble, our bodies pale from the fluorescent strip lights, no sound except the humming of the refrigeration units behind us.

I think about the craziness of the airport we've left behind and the investigation into what's happened to the plane and the fact that I nearly crashed the car. And I think about all the wedding preparations taking place in Nashville and how Blake and I should be there. And then I look back at Christopher, folding another napkin, a second bird to accompany the first. It reminds me of the newspaper bird he made for the mother and the child back at the airport. I wonder where they are now. I wonder who they were waiting for.

Christopher's hair falls over his glasses, and I feel like leaning forward and sweeping it away so that he can see more clearly but I don't. Because that would be weird, right? Touching a boy I hardly know? Plus, it would make him totally freak. And I realise that right now, I need him. Like

I need to go to Dad's study sometimes. Because even though he's not doing anything, he's making me feel better about this shit storm of a situation.

So, instead of touching his hair, I keep watching him. It's kind of soothing, how precise he is – and how focused. Like, while he's folding, nothing else in the world exists.

'Where did you learn to do that?' I ask.

He stops folding and looks up at me.

'Do what?'

'Those models you make.'

'*Models*?'

'Out of paper.'

'These?' He looks down at the paper birds. 'Oh, they're nothing,' he says.

'They don't look like nothing.'

He sighs, leans back in his chair and looks out through the store window. A truck is refuelling next to Blake's car.

'I used to get bored, waiting,' Christopher says.

'Waiting?'

'For Dad.' His eyes narrow in concentration and he makes another fold. 'I hung around airports a lot.'

'When you were travelling with your dad?'

'Yeah.'

'You taught yourself how to make things out of paper, then?'

'I started by making paper planes,' he says. 'I guess like any kid.'

I think back to the paper plane Christopher was making when we were waiting for the Buick to come back – and how that reporter stared at it, like it implicated Christopher in some way. The plane was amazing. A perfect replica of one of those Boeings that cross the Atlantic. But it was more than that. Its wings were alive, like those of a bird.

'I'd get scraps of paper,' he explains. 'And fold them into an arrow and shoot them around the place.' He goes quiet for a bit. 'It annoyed him.'

'Your dad?'

He nods.

'He got *annoyed* by the paper airplanes?'

'Yeah.' He goes quiet again. 'It still annoys him.'

'Sorry?'

'The paper folding. He thinks it's a waste of time. That I should be reading books or revising for my exams or planning my future. *You have to lead a Big Life, Christopher*, he's always saying.' He pauses. 'Whatever that means.'

I feel a thud in my chest. And it comes back to me, the reason we're here, in this service station that smells of oil and grease, drinking bitter coffee from a machine. And that it's way more serious than anything I'm worried about. A plane's crashed. And though he seems to be in denial about it, Christopher's dad was on that plane.

'Well I think it's cool, the things you make,' I say. 'That you're artistic.'

His eyes go wide. 'Artistic?'

'I can't even draw a stick-man.' *I can't even sing*, I think. But that, more likely than not, is what I'm going to have to do – in just over twenty-four hours. To cover Blake's ass. To make sure Jude's wedding goes to plan. 'So, I think that it's amazing – that you can make all that stuff, just out of paper. More than that – it's not even special paper like from an art shop or something. You use scraps, right? Stuff you find around the place.'

He nods.

'Well, it's awesome.' I smile. 'Eco-Art – that's trendy, right?'

'*Trendy?*'

'Yeah.'

He laughs. 'Maybe.'

'Well, I think your models are amazing.'

The tops of his cheeks blush. 'Thanks.'

A guy comes into the store. He grabs a coffee from the machine beside us and a burger from the oven. Then, he bashes into the back of my chair and my telescope falls to the floor.

'Watch out!' I say.

But the guy keeps walking, without even apologising.

Christopher leans over and picks it up.

'What's this?'

'My telescope.'

'For the eclipse?'

'Yeah – for the eclipse. But for other stuff too.'

'Other stuff?'

'I like looking at the night sky. I want to do it – professionally.'

'Professionally?'

'Yeah. Sort of.'

My cheeks get hot like they do every time I have to explain my thing about the stars and the universe and what I want to do with my life. Besides Dad, most people I tell don't get it. That what's up there is like the most important thing a human being could do. That it's the only way we're ever going to understand how we got here and why we're here now and what's going to happen next.

'I want to be an astronaut,' I say.

'Really?' He looks surprised but not a patronising only-ten-year-old-boys-want-to-be-astronauts look. It's a kind of impressed look. Really impressed. Like he understands – how wanting to go into space is the most awesome thing anyone could ever want to do.

I feel a rush of pride.

I nod. 'Yep, really.'

He looks up at me, his pale, grey eyes wide and shiny. 'That's meant to be really hard – isn't it?'

'Yeah, it's really hard. Only a tiny percentage of those trained ever go up into space. I did an internship this summer, at the Smithsonian to help my chances of getting into MIT. NASA recruits from MIT,' I explain.

'So, you're going to study engineering?'

'Yep. One more year of school—'

'One more year of school?'

'What?'

'You look – I don't know – kind of—' he stalls.

'Young?'

He nods. His face goes red.

'I skipped a grade. That's why this internship was really important. I have to prove that I'm ready.'

'Skipped a year? So you must be, what—'

'Seventeen. Just. My birthday was last week.'

Mom usually makes a fuss about birthdays but this year, mine got kind of lost in all the wedding preparations and I was busy doing my internship and Blake was in London. I didn't mind. I don't like the fuss. Dad took me out for red velvet cake at my favourite bakery in town and then we talked for hours, until it was nearly dark and the owner of the bakery had to kick us out. It was probably the best birthday I've ever had.

Christopher shakes his head. 'God, you must be really clever – skipping a grade. I can barely keep up with my own year.'

'I work hard. And starting young has advantages. If you want to be an astronaut, I mean.'

'So, when you get to MIT—'

'I'm going to do a BA in Physical Science – majoring in Astronomy. I want to understand the skies before I get into the mechanical stuff. Then I'll do a Masters in Aerospace Engineering. And after that a doctorate.'

'Wow, you've really got it all worked out.'

I nod. 'If you want to be an astronaut, you basically have to start planning from when you're born.'

'Won't it be kind of lonely – I mean, all those years of studying and then going off into space?'

'Besides my immediate family, I'm not into personal relationships, so I'll be fine. And I quite like being on my own.'

Those bushy eyebrows of his knit together. 'You're not into personal relationships?'

'Getting married and stuff,' I explain.

'Oh – right.'

'I mean, if it's a toss-up between finding the man of my dreams and having his babies or getting to land on some undiscovered planet, the choice is easy.'

'It is?'

99

'Definitely. And anyway, break-ups are distracting, right? I can't afford to be distracted, not when I'm planning a space mission.'

'Why would there be a break-up?'

'There are always break-ups. It's like a thing for astronauts: break-up statistics are high. So, it's better to be single.' I pause. 'Especially if you're a woman.'

His eyes look wider and paler than ever. Maybe I've told him too much. But then he was the one who asked all the questions.

'You'd get on with my mum.' He makes it sound like a sad thing.

'As in Atlanta Mom?' I ask. And then I feel stupid. It's not like he's got any other moms.

'Yeah, Atlanta Mum. She's a scientist. A marine biologist – sea rather than sky. But she wanted to study too – rather than having a kid, I mean. Which is why Dad looked after me.' He pauses. 'I guess that, like you, she didn't want any distractions.'

'Oh…' I don't really know what to say. I think he's just compared me to the mom who walked out on him.

'I'm sorry.' I say. 'That you didn't get to have both of your parents.'

Mom and Dad had us all pretty young. Dad was still doing his doctoral thesis at Oxford when they had Jude. Mom was finishing her legal practice course. They would never have considered giving her up though. Mom jokes about putting her down for naps in her filing cabinet at work and Dad says that she'd sit in her stroller at the back of his lectures, good as gold, and that having her around made the students like him more. I guess they worked it out. Then, one year later, they had Blake. They were so close in age people thought they were twins.

And then, four years later I came along, by which time Mom and Dad had hired an au pair from Sweden who allowed them to get on with their jobs without making us feel like we'd been abandoned. Juta drank goats milk, forced us to go on these epic hikes and cycled through Oxford, pulling us behind her in a trailer. She sang constantly – which meant that she adored Blake because he'd sing along with her. They'd do harmonies and people would stop in the street and listen.

At first we hated her but by the time she left, three years later, we thought our lives would end if she wasn't there anymore.

She's coming to the wedding too. Bringing her husband and four children.

Anyway, I wonder what I'd do. Whether I'd give a kid up if it meant being able to go into space. It doesn't feel like a fair decision. Which is why it's better not to get involved in all that to begin with. Keep things simple. And the world's overpopulated anyway.

'Sometimes it's hard,' I say. 'To make it work. But I'm sure they both still love you. Parents are parents, right, no matter how much they mess things up?'

For a while, Christopher doesn't say anything. And then, he says:

'I've never really felt like I've had parents. I mean, I haven't felt like I belonged to them – like you're meant to feel.'

'You don't feel like you belong to your parents?' That's the saddest thing I've ever heard.

'I mean – I don't feel like I come from them, like I'm one of them or that I have bits of them in me.'

I think about the bits of Mom and Dad I have in me. I thought I was more like Dad. Kind of chilled. Happy in my own company. But then, when I've got an idea for a project or when I go off on one of my rants about female astronauts, Dad looks at me and smiles and says: *You're just like your mother*. Which kind of annoys me. But when I think about what Christopher said, about not feeling part of his parents, I realise that it's not such a bad thing – having a bit of both of them in me.

He stares past me, his eyes getting that thousand-mile stare. 'I don't feel like you're meant to feel – you know, as someone's child.'

How you're *meant* to feel. Wow. I don't ever remember thinking that I was meant to feel anything with my parents. They were simply there. And so was I. And that was that. I think about what he said about how being an astronaut would be lonely – well, feeling like you don't have a family, or like you don't belong to your family, that must be way, way lonelier.

'I'm sorry,' I say.

'It's okay.' He shrugs. 'It's just how it is.'

And although he says it in a voice that makes it sound like it's okay, I don't believe him. I don't believe that if he really let himself think about it he'd be okay with it.

I keep staring at him. He brushes that blond tangle off his forehead.

'So, you've really been planning to be an astronaut since you were born?' he asks.

I nod. 'Blake said that when I was a baby, I loved to look up at the sky. And then, when I was old enough, he'd take me to the planetarium at the Smithsonian. He liked going because it inspired him for his songs and I liked the science stuff.'

We could sit there for hours, not talking, and when we came back into the bright, sunshine afterwards, it sometimes felt like we'd actually been to the stars and back.

The last time we went was the day before Blake flew out to London.

It was over 100F in DC. Totally sweltering. And the AC in the apartment wasn't working. And Blake and Jude had just had a massive row about the wedding and how Blake wasn't pulling his weight and didn't care about all the trouble she and Mom were going to.

To cool down, Dad had decamped from his study to the Georgetown Library and Mom took Jude out for yet another wedding dress fitting in a store in town. Jude was paranoid that she'd put on weight at the last minute and that the dress wouldn't do up. Of course, Jude couldn't put on weight if she tried. She's one of those naturally skinny people who could eat cheeseburgers for breakfast, lunch and dinner and still have clear skin and a wasp waist.

Anyway, once Mom and Jude went out, it was just me and Blake in the house. Which is how I like it. Minus the heat.

Leda, who was lying on the end of my bed, her tongue hanging out, her chest moving up and down really quickly, was feeling the heat too.

Blake put his guitar down on my bed. On Mom's orders, he'd been practising the song for Jude's wedding.

He caught my eye and smiled. 'Break it to me, sis – how was that, on a scale of one to ten?'

Blake asks me to rate his songs. Which is totally impossible. Because I want to give him a ten every time. Blake's brilliant. And he tries really hard too, which means that, most of the time, he sounds awesome.

But my big brother's smart enough to know that no one can be a ten every time. Not even him.

'It depends,' I said.

He raised one thick, dark eyebrow. '*Depends*?'

'Are we talking style or content?'

'Both.'

'Ten for style...and you don't want to know about content.'

Blake's face dropped. 'What do you mean?'

'The lyrics are cheesy – totally cheesy. And you don't do cheesy. Not ever. It doesn't sound like you, Blake.'

And it was true. Blake had spent longer on Jude's song than just about any other song he'd written – hours and hours scribbling away in his room. And although the tune was amazing, the lyrics made you want to stick your fingers in your throat and gag.

Blake pushed a pretend dagger into his heart. 'You do say the most hurtful things, sis.'

'The truth hurts, Blake. Why can't you write the kind of lyrics you usually write? Cool stuff.'

'This isn't a gig, Air. It's Jude's wedding. And people like cheese at weddings.' He jumped off my bed and walked over to the window. 'And you've got to give the people what they want – some of the time, anyway.'

He yanked open the window.

'You're letting hot air in,' I said. 'It'll make it worse. Scientifically proven.'

'I need to breathe,' he said, leaning out so far it made me nervous.

Though it shouldn't have – made me nervous, I mean. It's a well-known fact that Blake was a cat in a past life: no matter how high the drop, he lands on his feet.

He turned around, pulled up the bottom of his T-shirt and wiped his brow. Blake's got this long, smooth torso that looks toned even though he doesn't do any exercise. And because he's so tall, his T-shirts are all too short on him, which means he gets to show his perfect torso off to any girl – or guy – who's in noticing range.

People say that you can't tell whether your siblings are hot or not because biology's wired you to not fancy them. And I don't fancy Blake – *obviously* I don't fancy Blake. If I had a type, he wouldn't come close to being mine. But I can still see it, why all those girls go crazy for him. And guys. He's beautiful. In a kind of effortless way. Everything about Blake is effortless.

'Let's get out of here, find somewhere cool to hang out,' Blake said. 'As in cold cool.'

'Sure.' I climbed off the bed. 'Where?'

He came over and grabbed my hand. 'Let me take you to the stars.' He twirled me round the room until we were both so dizzy we flopped onto the floor.

The stars.

It being the middle of the day, this could only mean one thing: the planetarium. Our place.

We got to the Albert Einstein Planetarium, a few blocks from home, in time for the 1 p.m. *Journey to the Stars* show. Actually, we arrived about a minute late, but the guy at the ticket desk let us in anyway.

After we got our tickets, we ran to the auditorium doors, holding hands. A couple of girls standing in the hall outside the show looked me up and down. I was used to it. Girls mistaking me for Blake's girlfriend – mistaking me for *competition* – their thoughts so loud they may as well have been blaring them out through megaphones: *What's he doing with her? The girl with the pixie haircut and the cut-off denim shorts and sneakers? Surely he can do better than that?*

I gave the girls a smile, held Blake's hand tighter and we pushed through the doors.

We slumped into our special seats: five rows back, seven seats in. We'd been coming here since I was little, so we'd had the time to try out every viewing spot in the auditorium. These seats were the best for seeing the whole dome without having to strain our necks.

At the exact same moment, we let out a long breath. Compared to the house – compared to outside – the planetarium felt like sitting inside a refrigerator. Total bliss.

The lights went down and Whoopi Goldberg's voice came over the speakers, her words rich and full and fun and totally serious, all at the same time.

We'd seen this show so many times we could narrate along with Whoopi, but it didn't matter, we still loved it.

For a long time, we sat there, lost in the story of the universe, in the darkness of the auditorium, our heads tilted up to the blinking stars. And it felt good, to be here without having to think about or do anything else. Soon, I'd be starting my internship at the Smithsonian and Blake would be doing gigs around the UK and then we'd be all caught up in Jude's crazy wedding. This moment was ours, just ours.

'I've got a surprise planned,' he said, after a while.

'A surprise?'

'For Jude – well, for Jude's wedding. And for you. Both – kind of.'

'Mom doesn't like surprises. So I'd recommend keeping your surprise, whatever it is, well away from the wedding – that is if you consider your life worth living.'

'It'll be a good surprise – Mom will like it.'

I sigh. 'I hope so – for all our sakes.'

'You worry too much, sis,' he said.

'*You* worry me,' I said. 'Without you, my life would be totally stress-free.'

'But I'm worth it, right?'

Even though it was dark, I could see him wink, his long, dark eyelashes sweeping the top of his cheek.

I hit his arm. 'All I'm saying is that it had better be good – your surprise.'

'Oh, it'll be good.'

'Shush!' Someone hissed from behind us.

'Sorry,' I whispered back into the dark.

Because I was sorry – I didn't want to spoil it for him: The Whoopi-Journey to The Stars experience.

We didn't talk again until near the end of the show.

I could tell from how Blake's body slumped to the side that he'd dozed off for a bit. He's up so often in the night that he gets sleepy in the middle of the day. Takes naps like toddlers and old people.

'Looking forward to London?' I asked him.

107

'Yeah,' he says, his voice thick with sleep. 'I'd like to live there,' he mumbled.

I wondered whether he was fully awake, so I slipped my arm under his and gave it a squeeze.

'Really?' I asked.

'Yeah, really.'

'But – we'd be *here*,' I said.

By *we*, I meant me and Mom and Dad and Jude – and Leda.

'We'd be in America and you'd be in England. Like thousands of miles away,' I clarified.

Our family sticks together. It's who we are.

'England's not that far,' he said. 'And I'll come back. Stay in Grandpa's old flat in Nashville. You can come and stay.' He winks. 'I might even pop up to DC every now and then.'

Blake didn't hide his feelings about DC. How he found it soulless. The whole city carved up like a grid. Nothing but monuments. He'd written a song about it once.

He was awake now. Awake and actually having this as a serious thought.

A hollow feeling opened up under my ribs, thinking about Blake being so far away.

'You want to go into space, Air. At least I'll still be on land.'

'It's not the same.'

He sits up and rubs his eyes. 'No, it's worse.'

'Worse?'

'It's dangerous.'

'Not really.'

'Yes, really. I've seen Apollo 13.'

I rolled my eyes. 'I'll be fine. And the rest of the time, I'll be in *the US with our family*.'

I didn't want to guilt-trip him but I hated the thought of him not being here. That we wouldn't be able to run down a few blocks and hang out at the planetarium together, on a whim. But I knew that, sooner or later, this would happen – once he'd saved up enough money not to have to rely on Mom and Dad anymore, he'd move out. He'd talked of renting a place in Nashville once. And though I didn't like it, I could get my head around that – just.

But not London. Not an ocean away.

'I'll always be there, sis,' he said. 'You know that.'

'Not if you're somewhere across the Atlantic.'

He put his hand under my chin and tilted my head back so that I was looking at the stars again.

'It's not about distance, Air. You of all people should know that.'

I looked at the stars. Too many to count. Too many for us ever to fully understand. And I thought about the distance and time thing. How crazy it was to get your head round. How something could be there and not be there at the same time. And about how relative it all was.

I closed my eyes and leant my head against his shoulder and willed myself to believe him. Like I always did.

'Yeah, you'll always be here,' I said.

And even though it was dark and I couldn't see his face, I knew that he was smiling. And that he believed it too.

'My dad would totally love you,' Christopher says.

I'm jolted back into the present.

'What?' I ask.

'My dad – he'd love you.'

'Wow, so I'd get approval from both your mom and your dad?'

He nods.

'Mum would be into your whole feminist career thing and Dad, well, he'd like that you have a plan for what you want to do with your life. Something important. He's always saying that he wants me to do something big with my life.'

'You really don't have a plan?'

He shakes his head. And then he looks down into his coffee and starts stirring it with a plastic spoon even though there's nothing to stir. I shouldn't have said it like that.

'Have you spoken about it to your mom?' I ask.

He stops stirring but doesn't look up.

'About what you want to do with your life?' I go on.

He shakes his head. 'Mum and I don't have a relationship. She walked out when I was born.'

'But things change – maybe now—'

He shakes his head. 'She's busy with her new life. Dad told me she remarried – some guy called Mitch.'

'But you're her son.'

He shakes his head. 'She doesn't know me.'

I can't imagine living like that. Mom and Dad are totally different but they're also still totally in love. They kiss each other on the lips when they're saying goodbye or coming in from work and they leave each other slushy notes on the refrigerator door. Dad loves to say *We're the best team in the world*. And it's true. In their own crazy way, they are the best team. It must be horrible, having a dad living in one place and a mom in another. Living with one rather than the other.

All those splinters between people who are meant to be a family. For Mom and Dad and Jude and Blake – and me – family's everything.

'Your dad raised you on his own?' I ask.

'Yeah.'

'That's amazing.'

'Dad's like that.'

'Like what?'

He pauses.

Eventually, he says:

'He does the right thing.'

'Do you miss her – your mom?'

He shrugs. And the way he lifts and drops his shoulders, it's not like other people, who are just brushing something off or acting aloof. There are a thousand sentences in his shrug, sentences that, I guess, he's not willing to say out loud right now.

'It's hard to miss someone you don't really know,' he says.

I wonder whether that's true. Because I think you can miss the idea of something, even if you don't have it for real.

'That sounds hard – your parents being split up. Her leaving when you were a baby.'

'I'm used to it.'

It doesn't sound to me like something you'd ever get used to.

'Maybe you should call her,' I say. 'Your mom. Tell her you're coming.'

'I'll think about it,' he says. But the way he says it, I know he doesn't want to.

And I understand that it's hard. Like I can't tell my parents that I haven't got a clue where Blake is.

I glance at my watch – we've been here for over a half hour.

Then I notice the guy who bashed into me, standing at the counter, buying cigarettes. As he takes his change, he leans in and stares at the TV.

'Crazy – that stuff about the plane,' the driver says, handing the cashier a wad of dollar bills.

My eyes follow his to the screen. They're not showing the baseball game anymore. There's a picture of the plane, but it's different from the one back at the airport. There's a new piece of metal floating on the sea. Search and rescue boats circle the area. The aerial camera zooms in closer. My fingers go to my throat.

Oh God. It's the rudder of a plane, poking out of the top of the water. And it's got a picture of the Union Jack flag running up it.

Christopher's head snaps up towards the screen.

The guy behind the counter gets out a remote control and turns up the volume.

A newsreader's voice fills the Mobil store.

The wreckage spotted floating on the Atlantic has been identified as belonging to UKFlyer0217.

My stomach flips.

Passenger names have yet to be released.

The screen switches to a shot of the airport back in DC. My mind goes back to all those people waiting for the flight. How this news must be hitting them too.

A weight presses down on my heart.

The newsreader keeps talking:

A spokesperson for UKFlyer says that they're investigating mechanical failure but refusing to rule out pilot error at this stage.

A new picture flashes onto the screen. A pilot in a UKFlyer uniform. Dark hair. Tan skin. White teeth. A strong, confident gaze that says: *I've got this.*

Under it, there's a name: *Edward Ellis.*

Christopher gets up so fast his chair crashes behind him.

He doesn't bother to pick it up.

He just runs out of the door.

Chapter Twelve

22.01 EST
Mobil Station, I-81

'Where are you going?' I call after him.

Leda bounds ahead of me.

He runs past the car and out onto the highway.

'Christopher!' I yell after him.

Leda's barking: long, loud barks, no whining this time. So loud you'd never believe she was this tiny scrap of a dog.

'Christopher!' I yell again.

Eventually, I catch him up.

He's bent over, like he's been winded, his hands on his hips, breathing hard.

'Hey!' I touch his shoulder but he pulls away.

Up to now, Christopher's been the one holding it together and staying calm. Who kept *me* calm.

But after that picture on the TV, there's no more pretending, is there? The plane's crashed. More than that – it's split apart. Bits of it are floating on the Atlantic. And it's a UKFlyer plane. A Boeing. The one all those people were waiting for at Dulles. The one Christopher was waiting for.

Christopher slumps down on the side of the road.

'I can drive us back to DC,' I say.

He stares at the road.

'Christopher?' I say gently.

'It's bullshit,' Christopher says at last, shaking his head over and over. 'It's all bullshit.'

I sit down beside him.

'We can call the number,' I say. 'The one they gave us back at the airport. They'll be able to explain to us what's going on.'

He keeps shaking his head.

Sitting here, next to him, I feel the weight of what I've done. His dad's been involved in a plane crash and I've taken him off on this crazy road trip, jabbering on about Blake and where he might be and whether he's going to be late for the wedding. For Christopher, this is serious, way more serious than a wedding being messed up by my unpredictable, disorganised brother.

Back at the airport, Christopher might have got proper help. Counsellors or something. Someone other than me.

'They don't know what they're talking about,' he says.

'What do you mean?'

'When a plane lands on water, there are ways for the passengers to escape,' he says. 'Safety rafts. Life-jackets.'

He's upset because he thinks his dad might be *okay*?

'The plane was torn apart,' I say gently.

The thing is, we both saw the same image. Nothing good comes from a picture like that.

'It's better than a plane crashing into the side of a mountain – or on land,' he says. 'There's a higher survival rate for passengers when planes land on water.'

I wonder how he knows this stuff.

'So, you're saying that what we saw is a *good* thing?'

'I'm saying that we can't make assumptions.'

Leda tries to nudge his hand so she can nestle into his lap, but he ignores her.

'You think there might be some survivors, then?'

He doesn't answer for a really long time. And then he says:

'They're idiots.'

'Who – who are idiots?' I ask.

'Those reporters. The crew on board that airliner are professionals. They wouldn't have let anything happen to the plane. They've flown this route hundreds of times.' He keeps kicking at the tarmac. 'People are trying to find someone to blame, that's all.'

I try to remember what the news report said. All I could focus on was that image of the rudder with the Union Jack flag and how it confirmed what we'd been trying to ignore this whole time: that the metal they found floating on the ocean belonged to the UKFlyer flight we were waiting for back in DC.

I look around me. God this place is ugly. Gas fumes. The sound of the highway. No trees.

I touch his arm. 'Let's get back in the car.'

He doesn't seem to hear.

'You can't stay here,' I say.

'I'll be fine.'

'You won't be fine. We're in the middle of nowhere. And it's getting late. At least let me take you to Knoxville, then you can decide where you want to go. It's easy to get a bus from there. Or I can drive us back to DC.' I take a breath. 'Whatever you want to do, we'll work it out.'

I keep looking at him for some sign that he's taken it in but he doesn't move or say anything.

The truck that was filling up in the service station rumbles past us.

I look up at the stars and wonder where Blake is and what he'd be thinking about all this. What he'd be doing if he were here. God, he'd probably write a song about it. Yeah, that's totally what he'd do. While everyone's world was falling apart, he'd climb onto the hood of his Buick with his notebook and his guitar and he'd write a song. Something sad and true and totally beautiful. Blake believes that music can make things better, even impossibly hard things.

But how can anything make this better, Blake? I keep looking up at the stars. *How can anything good come out of a plane crash?*

I look back at Christopher, his head bowed low.

'I'll go and use the restroom,' I say. 'Give you some space. You take some time out here. Then we'll hit the road again.'

He doesn't move.

'Christopher? I'll be back in a minute. Just wait for me.'

I barely see the movement – but I think he nods. A small nick of the head to show that he heard me. And that he'll wait for me.

As I walk back through the Mobil store, the TV's on some other kind of news, like anything else in the world matters right now.

I try to focus on what Christopher said – that there might still be some hope that they're alive. That there'll be search and rescue teams all over the coast of Ireland. That should be on the news.

I use the restroom and then stand at the sink, staring in the mirror. I look at my short hair. Mom wanted me to get hair extensions for tomorrow: she said my pixie-cut wouldn't suit the look of the wedding. I told her that hair extensions didn't suit me and if she wanted *me* at the wedding – the real me rather than some hologram of a bridesmaid from a bridal catalogue version of me – then no one was touching my hair.

I already gave in to wearing a dress.

And having my nails done.

And scattering rose petals for Jude to walk on.

Enough's enough.

I lean forward and look at myself more closely.

I'm the odd one out.

Jude looks like Mom. Beautiful.

Blake looks like Dad. A hip version, obviously. Long-limbed with big blue eyes and thick dark hair.

And then me, a funny hotchpotch of all of them and none of them at the same time.

Like most kids, I'd gone through that phase of wondering whether I was adopted and that they'd been lying to me all this time – about being one of them. But the phase didn't last long. Because I *felt* it; that – in some totally unscientific, non-evidence based way – I belonged to them.

I think about what Christopher said, about not being able to relate to his dad or his mom and how that must be the loneliest feeling in the world: to feel like, even in your own family, you don't belong.

Blake's song comes back into my head, the one that made me swerve into the middle of the road, his cover of the Johnny Cash song he recorded at the Grand Ole Opry in Nashville:

Flesh and blood needs flesh and blood...

Yeah, we all feel it. Mom and Dad and Blake – and even me and Jude who can't be in the same room for more than a few minutes before arguing about something. We know that we're flesh and blood. That we belong. That we need each other.

Which is why, even when Blake is being his most infuriatingly self-centred self, he still shows up when it matters. On Mom's surprise fiftieth birthday party when, for once, it was down to us, the kids, and Dad, to do all the organising – and without letting her know, which was even harder. He wrote a song for that too. And yeah, it was the highlight of the party. It made Mom cry. In a good way.

I have to believe that he's still going to show up at the wedding. He has to. Because we're family. Flesh and blood. Letting each other down isn't an option.

I wash my hands, splash my face and dry it with some paper towels.

Then I look back into the mirror.

It's my turn to be there for Christopher.

Chapter Thirteen

22.23 EST
I-81

I run out of the Mobil store, ready to storm up to Christopher, pull him onto his feet and drag him back to the car.

But he's not where I left him.

I look up and down the highway, wondering whether he's decided to head off alone, but I can't see him.

Shit. I shouldn't have left him.

Then I hear a bark. Leda. I left him with Leda.

I spin round and try to work out where the barking's coming from.

Apart from the Mobil station and the Buick, the place is deserted.

More barking.

I look back at the Buick.

And then I see him, sitting in the front passenger seat, Leda on his lap, her paws up against the window.

I take in a long breath and release it slowly.

Thank God.

I go back to the car and settle in behind the steering wheel. I'm tired and shaken up by everything that I saw on the news and by the fact that Christopher suddenly went weird on me when he was meant to be the calm, sane one in all this. But I know I'm the one who has to keep their shit together now.

'Where to?' I ask him. 'Back to DC or onward?'

He stares out of the window and then, with a voice so quiet I can barely make it out, he says:

'Onward.'

I nod.

'Good,' I say.

And I pull out of the gas station and head back out onto the highway.

Chapter Fourteen

22.50 EST
I-81

As we drive, I switch the radio on and keep it low. I keep my phone on too, with CNN alerts set up. I get that Christopher doesn't like the way it's being reported but whatever's happened to the plane, we need to know what's going on. It was finding things out by accident, like back at the Mobil station, that made Christopher flip out.

Most of the stations are talking about the plane now.

They've found more pieces of metal floating on the sea belonging to it.

The search and rescue teams haven't found any survivors yet. But they haven't found any bodies either.

Every time they mention the reasons for the crash, like that pilot error might be involved, Christopher takes out his phone and looks stuff up, I guess about the plane.

The calm guy I saw sitting at Dulles, as though nothing could ever touch him, has vanished. Instead, Christopher keeps going through this stress cycle that's doing my head in. He scans his phone. Shakes his head. Cracks his knuckles. Jiggles his leg up and down. Then puts his phone away again for a bit, takes a scrap of paper from his backpack and starts folding. A few seconds later, he scrunches the model he's made up into a ball, drops it into the footwell, takes out his phone and starts scanning again.

I've been trying not to let it get to me but I can't help thinking about the plane and his dad and how he's going cope with it all.

He said the crew would have known what to do – and I try to believe that, for his sake. But everything they're saying on the news makes me feel sick to my stomach.

An investigation is underway, a spokesman said. *Search and rescue teams are working hard.* As if that's meant to make us feel better. A plane carrying over two hundred people has crashed into the Atlantic – what the hell else should they be doing except working hard?

Christopher keeps cracking his knuckles.

'Maybe you should call your mom,' I say.

I feel like, even if they're not close, he needs someone right now. And if he warns her that he's coming, at least he won't have to do all the explaining.

He stares out through the windscreen.

'I mean, if you're still going to see her.'

He still doesn't answer.

'I know it's hard,' I say.

He turns to face me.

'Have you spoken to *your* mum?' he asks.

I glance down at my phone, sitting on my lap. He must have noticed it lighting up over and over with messages.

I shake my head. 'No, I haven't spoken to her.'

'Well, maybe you should call her.'

I know what he's doing – pointing out that I can't get him to do something that I'm not willing to do myself. But it's different. His mom's not my mom. And our situations aren't the same. Blake wasn't on the plane.

123

'She won't let me talk,' I say. 'She'll go on and on about me being late and not doing the one thing I was supposed to do: get Blake to the wedding.'

'It's a lot,' he says. 'Being responsible for another person like that.'

'I don't mind.'

'You don't?'

'I love Blake. He's a pain in the butt but he's worth it. You need to know him.'

He nods slowly.

'Sorry, I shouldn't be talking about this stuff,' I say. 'It's stupid.'

His eyes catch mine.

'I'd rather talk about this stuff,' he says.

'Really?' I ask.

'Yeah, really.'

And then I get it. How it's easier not to think about the big stuff. How thinking about a wedding, even a wedding that's about to go horribly wrong, is better than thinking about a crash.

'Well, if I don't make it to the rehearsal dinner, I'm totally screwed. Mom's already going to be mad about the family breakfast but the rehearsal dinner's a whole different level of important: it's public. My sister's in-laws and their family will all be there.' I pause. 'I'm meant to wear a yellow dress.'

He cranes his neck round to the back seat where the two dresses in their plastic liners are now all bunched up.

'I wondered what the dresses were for.'

'Yellow for the rehearsal dinner, blue for the wedding. Mom made both of them.' I pause. 'Mom made everything for the wedding. And I don't even do dresses,' I go on. 'Not ever.'

'Even as a kid?'

'Especially as a kid. Mom tried to put me in dresses as a kid – Jude's hand-me-downs. But I was this really active kid and I couldn't crawl properly in them; I kept getting my feet caught in the hems and falling flat on my face. In the end, she packed the dresses away and brought out Blake's old stuff – shorts and T-shirts and jeans. Proper clothes.'

He smiles. 'I'd be crap in a dress too.'

I laugh and, for a moment, things feel kind of okay.

'But you're wearing those dresses to the wedding?' he asks.

'Yeah. I guess it matters to Mom and Jude.'

He nods and I know he understands: how it's both the most insignificant thing in the world but how it really matters as well; how in the world Mom and Jude are living in right now, nothing else matters more.

'Anyway, if I call Mom now she's going to ask me a million questions and then I'm going to have to tell her that I don't know where Blake is—'

Christopher's eyebrows knit together.

'You really don't have a clue?'

'No. I mean, he could be in Nashville or he could still be in London – I don't really know. Blake's unpredictable.'

I should shut up about Blake. And the wedding.

He keeps staring at me, so hard that I have to look away. And then, after a few beats, he says, 'How can you be so sure?' he asks. 'I mean, that your brother wasn't on the plane?'

My eyes burn.

'He's just not. Okay?'

125

I think about all the reasons I could give him.

That Blake shows up when it matters.

That he'd promised he'd be there.

That he was going to sing this special song for Jude and that he wouldn't let her down.

That the reason he was in England was because he was working on his dream of being signed by some big record label and living in London. And you don't step onto a plane that crashes into the ocean when you're working your dream.

And, most of all, because bad stuff doesn't happen to Blake. Which sounds crazy – I mean, why should one person be protected from the crap life flings at the rest of us, right? – but it's true. Bad stuff doesn't happen to Blake Shaw.

'I booked his flight to Nashville,' I say at last.

'So why were you waiting for him at Dulles?'

'I thought he'd got on the wrong plane. He sent me a message – when I was on my way to Nashville.'

'A message saying he was getting a flight to DC?'

'Yeah, but that doesn't mean anything. Blake's crap at organisation. He didn't even know what he was texting. He must have got it wrong.'

I'm beginning to regret talking to him about Blake and the wedding. It might have got his mind off the crash but now it's churning me up.

I stare out of the windscreen.

'I've got to get to the wedding,' I say.

He still doesn't say anything.

I take a hand off the steering wheel and rub one of my eyes. I've been staring at the road too long.

'Let's take a break,' I say.

Then I turn off at the next exit, take a right and park on the edge of a field.

It's ugly. Burnt grass. Flat tyres. Empty soda cans. Cigarette butts.

We sit in the car, looking out at the field, not saying anything. My eyes drift up and I feel grateful that, no matter how ugly the earth is, the sky stays untouched; the one thing we can't mess up. Or not yet, anyway.

'I've got an idea,' I say.

He raises his eyebrows. 'An idea?'

I nod. 'I'll call my mom if you call yours.'

He doesn't answer.

'You should give her some warning – that you're going to show up.'

He still doesn't answer.

'Christopher?'

'I don't know what to say to her.'

'Tell her you're coming for a visit.'

'It's not like that between us.'

'Well, tell her something came up with your dad – that he's had to go on another business trip—'

'A business trip?'

'Or whatever. Say that he's been delayed and that you're coming to stay for a few days.'

He stares ahead.

'And then, when you get there, you can talk properly.'

He raises his eyebrows. 'Talk properly?'

I guess that whether you're close to your family or not, talking about this stuff is near impossible.

'So, it's a deal?' I say.

He shakes his head and kind of smiles.

'What?' I ask.

'You're annoying.'

'I've been told.'

'*Really* annoying.'

'FI,' I say.

'What?'

'Fucking Infuriating. It's what Blake called me. Which was kind of hypocritical.'

'But kind of true.'

'Hey!'

He looks at me and then sweeps his hair off his forehead. He's a weird mix, Christopher. Totally introverted one second – like it hurts him even to be in the same car as me – and then he'll say something ballsy that makes me think that he's stronger than he lets on.

'Okay,' he says.

'Okay, you'll call her?'

'Okay I'll call her.'

'Good.'

I get out of the car and stretch my legs.

Leda jumps out beside me and does a big wee against one of the tyres. She must have been wanting to go for a while. I feel a wave of pity for her. I scoop her up in my arms and thread my fingers through her raggedy fur. She's so skinny and light you'd think she could float away into the night sky. She thought we were going to the airport to collect Blake. And then we left without him. And, instead, we've got this English guy I've known for like five seconds travelling with us and she can probably feel it too – how every muscle in my body is strained, how I feel sick at the thought of turning up at the wedding and having to face everyone alone.

I walk out to the middle of the field and breathe in the night air. In the distance, I can hear the highway, trucks and cars rattling past. Closer, the click-clicking of the Buick cooling down. And Leda foraging for something – probably one of those cigarette butts. And I can hear Christopher's voice too, quiet and slow and deliberate. He's kept up his side of the bargain.

So I dial Mom's cell.

She picks up after one ring.

'Ariadne!'

'Mom—'

She bursts into tears. It makes me want to cry too, hearing her like that. But I've held it together this long, I'm not going to lose it now.

'Why haven't you been answering?' Mom asks.

'I've been driving.'

'Driving where?'

'To Nashville.'

I hear her suck in her breath. 'What do you mean, *to* Nashville? You're *in* Nashville.'

'I'm not.'

I hear her sigh.

'You're not making any sense, dear.'

I pause.

'Ariadne?'

'I thought Blake got on a plane to DC. So, I turned round to pick him up from there. But it turns out I was wrong.'

'So, Blake *is* in Nashville?' Mom asks. 'And you're in DC?'

I can't cope with all these questions.

'Ariadne?' Mom says again.

I hear some frantic whispering through the phone. And then Jude's voice speaking to Mom, 'Is that Air? Where the hell are they?'

'Air's in DC,' Mom says to Jude. Her voice is far away, she's moved the phone from her ear.

'I'm not in DC,' I say, so loud I hope she hears.

'In DC!' Jude's voice is manic. 'What are Blake and Air doing in DC?'

Jude probably thinks that we've done this on purpose: that Blake and I have taken off somewhere and are leaving her out again. And that it's my fault. Because things are never Blake's fault. I want to tell her that I'm sorry – that we've let her down in the past. But that we would never mess up her wedding. That all of this is out of my control.

'I'm not in DC!' I yell down the phone again.

'You promised you'd be here.' Jude's voice is shaky now.

And I had. I'd promised that we'd be there: me and Blake.

'I know,' I say. 'I know.'

'So you'd better hurry up.'

Her big sister tone. Which under normal circumstances would totally trigger me. Like she thinks she can tell me what to do just because she's five years older.

There's a pause and some shuffling sounds.

'Air?' It's Dad.

Thank God.

'Your mother's a bit anxious,' he says.

Understatement of the century.

'What's going on, my love?'

It makes my eyes well up, the way he says *my love* and the way he asks me, like he's waiting me for me

130

to tell him about another Blake fuck-up that we're going to have to sort out. The way he doesn't have a clue what's really going on. And how bad it is this time.

'Just tell Mom I'll be there for the wedding,' I say.

'Well, that's the main thing,' Dad says.

'Yeah, that's the main thing.'

There's a pause.

'I love you, Dad.'

'I love you too, Ariadne.'

God, I don't know how I'd survive without Dad. He's the one sane person in our family. The one person who makes my blood pressure go down rather than up.

'Everything all right, Ariadne?' Dad asks.

Something comes loose under my ribs.

I don't know what to say. I've never lied to Dad. It's one of our family rules: *the truth, no exceptions.* Plus, Dad and I are close. Really close. He's easy to talk to. He doesn't judge me, even if the stuff I tell him is really screwed up.

'Not really,' I say.

I want to tell him. About everything. About the mix up with the planes and not knowing about where Blake is. And about Christopher, who I met at the airport, whose Dad was on the plane that was cancelled and then went missing, and then the images of the wreckage on the sea, and how I feel like I've got to help him because he doesn't have anyone else. And because I like him. Him being here, with me.

Because Dad would understand. It's Dad's thing. Understanding confusing stuff like this. Understanding *me*.

God, I wish we were sitting in his study in DC, just the two of us. I wish there was no wedding and no airplanes. Sometimes, I wish there was no Blake to worry about. Because it would be easier than this – having a bit of my heart walking around somewhere outside my own body, totally out of my control.

'Dad,' I start.

'Yes, my love?'

'Hand over the phone!' Mom's voice blares through.

There's a scuffle. I picture her actually wrestling the phone from Dad's hands and Dad not giving her any resistance because he's totally not into force, even if means he gets walked all over.

'Just get here safely,' Dad says, his voice so warm and kind I want to cry.

'I will,' I say.

And then, before Mom comes back on, I hang up. I bow my head and stare down at the burnt earth and the burnt grass of this God-ugly field.

When I get back to the car, Christopher's got into the back with Leda. They're both looking up at the sky.

I get in next to him and lean back too, following his gaze.

It's a clear night. We're far enough from any major town not to have too much light pollution.

'How did it go?' I ask him.

He shrugs. 'Okay, I suppose.'

'Okay?'

'She's expecting me.'

'How did she sound?'

'Surprised. That I got in touch.'

'Did you tell her about the plane?'

He shakes his head. 'I thought it was better to wait – until I saw her.'

'She thinks you're just coming for a visit?'

'I told her Dad was busy with work and that I had some time in the States before heading back to England.' He pauses. 'And that I'd like to see her.'

'That must have meant a lot to her – hearing that.'

'I don't know.'

He kicks at some stones on the ground.

'You okay?' I ask.

He shrugs and I get that I shouldn't push it.

After a while, he looks up at me, his eyes, shiny and dark under the night sky.

'How about you?' he asks. 'What did your mum say?'

'She's pissed – that I'm late and that I've messed everything up. Jude yelled at me down the phone: she thinks I'm doing this on purpose. Then Dad came on and it was good to talk to him but it also felt crap because I couldn't tell him the truth.'

'About Blake being missing?'

'Yeah.' I swallow hard. 'But at least I called, right?' I catch his eye. 'At least we called. It's all we can do for now, right?'

'I guess so,' he says.

I lean back and look up again.

Leda comes and sits on my lap. I rub the soft spot behind her ears and she leans into my hand.

We sit there for a really long time; I guess we're trying to process it all – what we've heard on the news and speaking to the people who are waiting for us and how we haven't got a clue what's going on and what we're going to do when we get there. And that, in a few hours, when we get to Knoxville, we'll be going our separate ways and probably won't ever see each other again.

And I know we've got to get back on the road. That he has to get his bus and I've got to make it in time for the wedding, but, right now, there's something else I want to do.

'Want a view that'll blow your mind?' I ask.

I don't wait for him to answer. I pull the telescope out of the footwell, along with the tripod, drag it out onto the burnt grass and set it up, bang in the middle of the field.

Christopher stares at me.

'You coming?' I ask him.

Leda jumps out and then Christopher follows.

I move back from the telescope.

'You want to take a look?' I ask him.

He nods and comes to stand beside me.

'We're getting close to September, so we should be able to get a good view of Altair – the brightest star in the Aquila constellation.'

'Right.'

He keeps standing there, awkwardly.

'You've never looked through a telescope?'

He shakes his head.

For a second – once my incredulity has subsided – I feel kind of jealous. That he's going to have his first taste of seeing the night sky up close.

When Blake saw how psyched I was by our trips to the planetarium, he bought me my first telescope, a kids' one that made everything look blurry. But it was still amazing.

'You need to crouch down.'

Christopher kneels in front of the telescope and puts his eye into the viewfinder; the telescope bashes against his glasses.

He takes his glasses off and rubs his eyes. Then he puts them back on and shakes his head.

'I'm blind as a bat.'

'Bats aren't blind.'

'What?'

'It's a myth,' I say. 'The bat blindness thing.'

'Oh.'

'You're short-sighted, right?'

'Totally.'

'So, keep them on, it'll be fine.'

He nods and puts his right eye back to the viewfinder, closing the left one.

'You can keep both eyes open,' I say. 'Otherwise your open eye will vibrate and everything will look fuzzy.'

'Oh – right.'

He opens his left eye.

'See anything?'

He shakes his head.

'Here, let me.' I push him gently to one side and look through the telescope. I focus the telescope until Aquila comes into focus. Then I step away.

'You should be able to see it now.'

He positions himself again and puts his eye to the telescope.

And then he sucks in his breath.

'Wow.'

He keeps staring.

I sit next to him, so close that I can hear his breath speeding up as he takes it all in. And my breath speeds up too, like I'm seeing it for the first time, with him.

'Wow,' he says again. 'It's like they're—'

'Falling?'

I remember that's what I thought too, the first time I looked through a telescope. That the whole universe was rushing towards me. Or like I was being dragged up into the sky.

Yeah, my breath's definitely speeding up. My heart too.

'No,' he says.

'No?'

He keeps looking. 'It's like I'm flying. It's like my feet have left the ground and – and the world's falling away.'

My body relaxes. I feel myself smile.

'The world's falling away. I like that.'

Like, when you look up at the sky, nothing else matters but this one moment. This one, good moment.

'Except you…' he says under his breath.

'Except me?'

Our eyes lock.

'You don't fall away. You're still here.' He gulps. 'In a good way, I mean.'

I can feel him blushing.

'Thanks,' I say.

Which is a pathetic answer. What I really want to tell him is that I feel the same: that everything's falling away apart from him and how that feels good. Except I guess I'm a coward. More of a coward than him.

So, instead, I lean in close and say, 'Can you see Altair, the brightest?'

'Yeah, I think so.' He pauses and I can feel him concentrating. 'Yeah, I can see it.' He reaches his hand out towards the sky.

Then he sits back down on the burnt grass. My body shifts back until it's aligned with his, until our legs and

136

arms are touching. And now we both look up at the sky, just with our naked eyes. It's really clear tonight. Even without the telescope, we can see loads of stars up there.

'Cool, hey?' I say.

He turns and looks at me, his pale eyes filled with light. 'Yeah, cool.'

We stare at the sky some more.

'They felt so close – the stars. All of them. But they're millions of light years away, right?'

'That's the big question.'

'The big question?' he asks.

'The one I want to try and answer: how far the stars are – from us.'

'We don't know that already?' he asks.

I shake my head. 'No, it's basically impossible. To know for sure. To know precisely.'

He looks back up at the sky. 'So, if the star's brighter…?'

'You'd think it was closer, right?'

'Yeah.'

'Well, it doesn't work like that. And if a star's dimmer, it doesn't mean that it's further away either. It turns out we could as easily be looking at a brighter star from further away or a dimmer star closer up. And if it weren't for supernovas, we'd never know.'

'Exploding stars?'

'Yeah. But not any supernovas. There's this special type, called 1a supernovas. They're the ones I've spent the summer researching. They're the ones that *everyone's* interested in. Well, everyone like me.'

'What makes them special?' he asks.

'Unlike other stars, they're a constant brightness, so we can work out the distance – and trust it. And this is the cool bit: we can work out whether they're moving away from us.'

'And are they?'

'Yeah.'

'And that's important because?'

'It basically gives us evidence for the Big Bang.'

He whistles through his teeth. 'Oh, only that, hey?'

'An astronomer worked out that these supernovas – type 1a – are moving away from us, which suggests the universe is expanding.'

'So, what you're saying is that we're going to go bang again?'

'That's what I want to find out. I mean, I want to be able to work out how far and how close each star is. But that just takes me to the next bit – which is even more important: finding out how fast the universe is expanding. The research suggests it's been expanding faster and faster over time. That it's pushing outward. There's like this energy or force that's pushing everything out – an energy created by space itself.'

I look at his face in case he's switched off. Loads of people switch off when I go on about space. Jude and Mom do. Blake's half-listened, part of him thinking about how he can use what I'm saying as material for a song. But he switches off whenever I get too technical. The only one who really listens – who gets it – is Dad.

Christopher doesn't look bored, not even close.

'After a while,' I go on, 'gravity will slow the expansion to a stop and then the universe will collapse in on itself – a Big Crunch to match the Big Bang.'

'So, the universe is going to fold with everyone and everything in it?'

'It's still a way off, but yeah.'

'And all this is because of some weird energy in space pushing everything away from itself and making everything expand?'

'Yeah, dark energy,' I say.

It feels good. To be talking about this stuff. Stuff that I know about. Stuff that, on any other normal day, would occupy most of my waking thoughts.

'Right, dark energy, I've heard of that.'

'It's an actual thing,' I say. 'And no one has a clue what it is. Not even the top astronomers.'

'And you think you can work it out?'

'I think that if I do some research, at college, NASA will take me seriously. And when I combine my research with an engineering MA at grad school, they'll take me *really* seriously. It'll make me stand out – the fact that I'm a researcher, an astronomer, and a technician. And if they're impressed enough, they might let me onto their programme.'

'To become an astronaut?'

'Right.'

'Sounds like hard work.'

I nod. 'And I have to work even harder.'

'Harder than who?'

'Guys. NASA took on its first female astronauts forty years ago. We're still outnumbered: only eighteen per cent of active astronauts are women. The odds are against me, so yeah, I have to work harder.'

'I get it,' he says.

And I think he does. More than most people, anyway.

'It's pretty amazing,' he says. 'Everything you're willing to do – to get to where you want to be.'

I shrug. 'I guess so. But then I find studying – working hard and learning – easier than the other stuff.'

'Other stuff?'

'The stuff that Jude does.'

'Getting married?'

'And being really sociable and having all these friends to keep up with and yeah, getting married and having kids. And it's easier than the stuff Blake does too.'

'Understanding the universe is easier than singing?'

'Singing is hard. Standing in front of all those people. Exposing yourself like that.' My throat goes tight. 'And making sure you don't let anyone down, especially when you're singing for a special occasion.'

'Singing for a special occasion? Like at a wedding?' Christopher asks.

'Like a wedding.'

He looks up. 'You've heard it – the song Blake was meant to sing?'

'A million times. I rehearsed with him before he left. I had to make sure it was perfect.'

'Perfect? That's tough,' Christopher says.

'If you meet Mom, you'll understand.'

And then I think about how he'll probably never meet Mom – or Dad. And how that makes me kind of sad.

'Mom's got high standards,' I explain. 'And the song was a big deal. He was going to sing it during the eclipse.'

'Wow.'

'Yeah, wow. And now that he might not make it, I'm trying to get my head around the fact that it's me who's going to have to do it. Or I at least have to prepare for it.'

'In case he doesn't make it?' His tone has changed. All the lightness has gone.

'Make it? Oh, he'll make it. He might not make it on time. He might not make it until the whole damn wedding is over. But he'll make it. Anyway, I know that me singing is a terrible idea—'

'No, no it's not.' His voice is still serious.

'You haven't heard me sing.'

'It doesn't matter. The fact that you'd do that – for your family – especially as you're not into singing—'

'Not *into* singing – I can barely hold a note.'

He pauses. Then he says:

'Showing up. That's what matters, right?'

I'd never thought about it like that. But I guess he's right. Showing up is what matters. And I can do that.

Again, it catches me off guard; how Christopher gets things on a deeper level than his clueless exterior suggests. The hard stuff.

I stand up and brush down my shorts. 'Well, if I'm going to show up, we'd better get going.'

He nods. But he stays sitting, looking at the sky. And I can tell he's still got the picture of those stars, up close, playing behind his eyelids.

Chapter Fifteen

23.15 CDT
Cherokee National Forest, TN

I glance at my phone and realise that it's adjusted to the time difference – we gained an hour when we crossed the Tennessee border. I remember how magical I found that as a kid, that the clock went back because we passed a sign saying *Tennessee Welcomes You*. This time, there's no magic, just relief that I've got one more hour to play with.

Christopher's asleep. After stopping for a break in the field, he relaxed a bit, quit all his phone scanning and knuckle cracking. Leda's asleep too, her head on his lap.

I don't know whether what we're doing is right – tearing across the country, me trying to make it to a wedding without a clue where Blake is; Christopher heading to a mom he barely knows. But for now, it doesn't feel like there are any other options.

In the last few hours, the landscape has changed. We're surrounded by tall, dark pines now, and beyond them, the sky is darker and blacker than I've ever seen it – like it's rehearsing for the eclipse tomorrow.

If I weren't trying to get to the wedding, I'd stop by the side of the road, take my telescope, run into the middle of one of these woods, find a clearing and stay there until dawn, looking up at the sky.

If Blake were with me, that's what we'd do.

There's always time, he says.

As though time itself were there to accommodate him.

The fact that Blake's late for everything never seems to bother him. Nor does it bother those waiting for him. Mainly, because when he does show up, he does it in this big, dramatic, Blake-like way which makes people forget that he's let them down and think, instead, that they're lucky he showed up at all.

Damn you, Blake, I whisper out at the night.

Leda stirs on Christopher's lap and looks up at me.

And then I see it, the sign for Blue Springs.

And Leda must have seen it too or heard the water or something, because she's standing on Christopher's lap, her head hanging out of the window.

Without even thinking, I press on the brakes.

The car slows.

Christopher straightens up and rubs his eyes behind his glasses.

'Where are we?'

And him saying that makes me decide.

I swerve off the road and into the clearing. The hidden entry point that Blake showed me when I was ten and he first took me to Nashville, the place he loved more than anywhere in the world.

And yeah, I have to keep going for the wedding.

And yeah, I know that seeing this place again, without Blake, is going to rattle me.

But I can't help looking at the picture of us taped to the dashboard, the one of ten-year-old me holding

Blake's hand before our jump. The first time he brought me here.

And I can't get his voice out of my head saying, *There's time, Air. There's always time.*

Even when he was talking, Blake made things sound like a song.

And it's more than that too. A tiny part of me thinks that he'll be here, waiting for me.

'You coming?' I call over my shoulder. I'm running. I can hear it, water crashing down rocks.

Christopher's still sitting in the car. He's blinking and yawning and stretching.

'We don't have long,' I yell, 'come on!'

'Come where? Where are we?' He cranes his neck out of the window and looks around.

'You'll see,' I say, like Blake said to me the first time he brought me and Jude here.

Leda bounds over the seats and out through her door. She runs around in circles like a crazy thing and then wees against one of the pines.

I hear Christopher unbuckling his seatbelt and stepping out of the car.

I breathe in deeply. It smells of earth and tree sap and pine needles.

'Come on!' I yell.

Leda dashes past me. She knows the way.

And then I hear him, his footsteps breaking into a run.

Chapter Sixteen

23.35 CDT

'We often stopped here on our way to Nashville,' I say. 'Blake knew I'd like it. You can see the sky from the water – it's the best sky in the world.'

'The best sky?'

'You'll see.'

And then he stops walking.

And so do I.

It's there.

The pool, surrounded by high rocks. The water gushing down from a high waterfall, as thick and dark as the sky.

As I look up, I see, us there, holding hands, like in the photograph – and it's like I'm looking at a hologram. How, any moment, the wind will shift and we'll vanish.

Because he's not here. Of course he's not here.

I swallow hard.

And then I realise that I'm standing where Jude must have stood, when she took the picture. I always forget that she was with us that day.

Although Jude's twenty-two and Blake twenty-one – barely a year between them – whereas I came along five years after Jude, the tag-along little sister, things didn't pan out between us like you'd expect. Since I can remember, it's been Blake and me on one side, doing the crazy stuff, and Jude on the other, telling us to be careful and taking the photos and trying to make everything look tidy and pretty and coordinated. And then acting pissed that she's the odd one out, even though she put herself there by not going along with us.

At least Jude's got Stephen now. And the wedding will be her chance to be in the spotlight for once. The only silver lining to me singing Blake's song instead of Blake singing Blake's song is that he won't detract attention away from her on her big day.

A thought flits through my mind: has Blake done this on purpose – ducking out of the wedding at the last minute? Could it be the big suprise he went on about at the planetarium? Because he didn't want to steal attention from Jude on her big day? Blake's as self-centred as they come but sometimes, just sometimes, he'll surprise you by how thoughtful he can be.

I guess it's a possibility. As much of a possibility as any of the other explanations for why Blake's not here yet. But then I know that he wouldn't miss it. He wouldn't miss the biggest day in Jude's life.

Christopher looks at the pool and the waterfall and the patch of sky in the clearing.

'It's beautiful.' His voice is full of hushed awe.

Leda sits beside him, thumping her tail. I can tell she's dying to go in.

'Yeah, it is,' I say.

'What's this place called?'

'Officially? Blue Springs. But Blake renamed it Leda Springs.' I pick Leda up and hold her close. 'We found her here, tied up to one of the trees. At first, we didn't know that she'd been abandoned – we thought her owner must have come here to swim or something. But there was no one else at the swimming hole that day. And by the time we were ready to leave again, she was still there, waiting. So, Blake took her.' I kiss the top of Leda's nose, wondering whether she remembers that day. Then I put her down. 'Plus, with her whole crazy jumping thing, we thought it worked: Leda Springs.'

I remember how I sat with her in the back the whole way. Jude in front with Blake, complaining at her whining, and at her damp dog smell, and at the fact that she could have fleas or any number of contagious diseases. Jude still doesn't pet Leda. Probably because Leda became the third part of mine and Blake's gang which made her feel, again, like she was left out.

Leda darts forward and puts her paws over the edge of the rock by the pool. She's definitely wants to go in. And I want to go in too.

I think about what I should do about clothes. If we didn't have our swimming costumes, Blake and I would strip down to our underwear.

But I'm not with Blake right now, I'm with Christopher.

And no one besides my family has ever seen me without my clothes on.

And then I think how stupid it is to even be thinking about all this stuff. It's a warm night, my clothes will dry.

So, fully dressed, I jump in.

Leda jumps in beside me.

Our bodies split the water into a thousand stars.

It's so cold, I go into a shock for a second, but then it feels good – like every one of my cells is coming back to life.

I shake the water out of my hair and look over at Christopher.

'You coming in?' I ask.

He looks over at me and I can tell he wants to, but that he doesn't know what to do.

'I'm fine,' he says, sitting down on a rock. 'I'll wait for you here.'

'Seriously, come in, it's not that cold.'

'I don't have swimming trunks.'

'Neither do I!' I laugh. It's good to laugh, despite everything that's going on. 'We'll dry off in the car. And you have some spare clothes in that enormous backpack of yours, right?'

He nods.

'So come on in.'

He still looks hesitant.

'You only live once!' I call out.

And then my stomach flips again. None of the usual words fit. It's like there's a whole vocabulary we're not allowed to use anymore.

But it's still true. And it's still what Blake would have said if he were here with us. And anyway, it works, because the next thing I know, Christopher is standing on the edge and from the way he's staring at the water, I know he's going to do it.

I splash him and he darts back.

'Hey!' he says.

'You have to do it in one go, or you'll chicken out.'

He looks at me like he's working out whether he can trust me. Then he takes off his glasses, places them on a rock – and jumps in.

When he comes back up, he gasps and thrashes at the water with his limbs and I'm worried that I shouldn't have asked him to come in, but then he laughs.

'You said it wasn't that cold,' he splutters.

'It's not – not when you get used to it. Blake and I have swum here when it was basically winter.'

He swims towards me and I notice goosebumps on his arms. His lips are a purpley-red. But he looks happy. Happier than I've seen him since he got into the Buick with me back in DC.

I float on my back, looking up at the sky.

'In just over twenty-four hours, it's going to be dark, like this, in the middle of the day,' I say. 'Isn't that amazing?'

'Yeah. It's amazing.' He tries to float beside me but then he bumps into me and goes back to treading water. 'Maybe the sun will decide not to come back,' he says. 'After the eclipse.'

That's the kind of thing Blake would have said: screwing around with science for the sake of poetry.

'Oh, it'll come back,' I say.

But what if it decides not to? I hear Blake saying.

I went to a lecture once, a visiting speaker at school, on how, centuries ago, people attributed a consciousness to the stars and the moon and the planets. On how we've evolved since then – now that we understand more about the universe.

Dad's into that stuff – says the Greeks knew more about the heavens than we give them credit for. That it's not just science, it's philosophy too. I say that those same Greek philosophers thought the world was flat.

Blake was on Dad's side. *One day we'll evolve past science*, he said once. *And then we'll understand that the things that really matter can't be proved.*

He liked to argue with me about that stuff. About the things that I knew were true because they'd been proved by science, and the things he believed were true because he felt them.

Neither of us ever won those arguments – we just got kind of worn out talking. A good worn out.

I wish I could argue with him now.

I wish I could tell him that if the universe really had a consciousness it would have made sure that he got on the plane to Nashville, the plane I'd booked. And it would have made sure that Christopher was in Oregon, with his dad.

Unless it's a screwed-up universe intent on hurting us. And I'm not willing to go there.

I swim back to the edge of the pool, climb onto the rock and hold out my hand. Christopher blinks and I realise he's not wearing his glasses, so I lean over closer. He grabs my fingers and I pull him out.

He puts his glasses back on and we sit next to each other, staring at the pool. He's shivering and his teeth start chattering. Thinking our clothes would dry off was probably a bit optimistic.

Leda scrambles up too and shakes out her fur.

I look up at the tall cliff face that stands above the waterhole and then stand up and hold my hand out to him again.

'Come on, I've got an idea for something that will warm you up.'

'We're going back to the car?'

I laugh. 'Not even close.'

I reach forward and ease off his glasses. 'Probably best to leave these down here.'

'I won't be able to see where I'm going,' he says. 'And what do you mean – down here?'

'You don't need to see where you're going; I'll show you the way.'

Before he has the chance to argue, I place his glasses down on a flat rock next to the pool, all the while keeping hold of his hand and then I guide him up a path between the rocks.

'You know why my brother brought me here – the first time?' I say.

He waits for me to go on.

'Because I was one of those scaredy-cat kids.'

'I can't imagine you being scared of anything,' Christopher says.

It makes me feel happy that he thinks that. I've worked my whole life on being brave. But it scares me too. Because if someone thinks you're not scared, you kind of have to live up to that.

'Oh, I was scared,' I say.

'What were you scared of?' Christopher asks.

I keep pulling him behind me.

'Everything.'

'Everything?'

'Yeah. I was scared of other people. And dogs.' I look over at Leda who hasn't budged from her rock. 'And of making new friends. And of big trucks. And loud noises. I was basically scared of every damned thing in the world.' I pause. 'I was even scared of those.' I look up at the sky.

He follows my gaze.

'The *stars*?'

I nod.

'How they're too far and too close all the same time. How we don't know anything about them – not really. And I was scared of the sky too, how big it was. And the dark. And the moon. And what might be out there.'

'You were scared of all the stuff you live for now?'

151

I turn to face him. *The stuff I live for* – no one's ever put it like that. Like they understand.

'Why are you staring?' he asks.

'You're pretty awesome, you know that, Christopher?'

He blinks and looks down at his feet.

'Come on, let's keep going,' I say, pulling his hand.

'So, Blake brought you here as a kid because you were scared of stuff?' Christopher asks.

'Yeah, he told me that if I could do this, I could do anything. And that the next time I was scared – of the dark or making friends or loud noises – I should think back to this moment. He said I should think about how I'd done the scarier thing and about how brave I was, and then I wouldn't need to be scared ever again, not about the small stuff.' I stop walking, drop Christopher's hand and look up at the top of the rock. 'Blake taught me to be brave.'

When I turn back to Christopher, he's staring up at the rock too. I wonder how much he sees – whether it's a blur to him or whether its sinking in, how high it is.

'What did he get you to do then?' Christopher asks.

I look back up at the tallest rock above the hole.

'Jump,' I say.

And then I take his hand again and drag him up the path.

Chapter Seventeen

23.50 CDT

Looking down makes every bit of my body spin – like my cells are shooting around my body so fast that they're going to burst through my skin.

It's good, to feel this alive.

And terrifying.

I look down at the rock where Leda's waiting for us; from up here she's a tiny speck. Occasionally, she lets out a yelp and it echoes around us. Jude stood in that same spot, that time we came here with her. She'd told Blake he was being stupid, taking me up here and she'd hated the fact that we'd ignored her and come up anyway. I wish that, just once, she'd joined us. That we could have jumped, the three of us.

I look at Christopher. He's standing really still. He's staring at the drop.

'Christopher?'

'I can't,' he stutters, beside me.

'Can't or won't?' I say.

'Both.'

'Why?'

'Seriously? *Why*? Because it's dangerous. I can't even see where we're meant to land.'

'It's not dangerous. There hasn't been an accident in like, for ever. And anyway, statistically, there are more chances of a meteor landing on your head than of you having an accident jumping from this rock.'

He frowns. 'That's not even a real statistic.'

'It should be.'

He doesn't look convinced.

'Fine, it isn't a statistic, but let's put it this way: it'll be quicker to jump than to walk back down. And safer.' I smile. 'It's dangerous to walk down rocky paths. There isn't a rail to hold onto. And you don't have your glasses.' I pause. 'Anything could happen.'

'Your brother's right.'

'What?'

'FI. Totally F-ing Infuriating.'

He smiles at me and then he looks down at the water. Slowly, I take his hand.

'We can jump together,' I say. 'That's what Blake and I did the first time.'

And I know that although it's going against every logical, sane, better-judgement-bone in his body, he squeezes my hand and says:

'Okay.'

With his hair lying flat and wet against his head, every angle of his face stands out, sharp and beautiful. I notice a constellation of freckles scattered across his nose and cheeks. Without his glasses, his face looks open and exposed.

'Can you really not see anything?' I ask. 'Without your glasses.'

'Not much.'

'Probably for the best,' I laugh.

'Hey!'

'I'm joking. It's going to be awesome.'
I squeeze his hand back.
And start counting:
'One.'
'Two,' he says.
'Three,' we say together.
And then, we jump.

Chapter Eighteen

23.58 CDT

It comes back to me. How jumping from this rock is like the longest and slowest two seconds of my life.

We bend our knees.

Push into our legs.

Our feet lose contact with the ground.

And then, there's a drop.

A *huge* drop into the darkness below.

For a moment, I'm suspended.

The night air brushes against my skin.

I hear an owl on a high branch. The grinding song of crickets in the long grass far below. The crashing of the waterfall.

And I wait. I wait to fall.

They say time's relative. That it stretches and contracts according to our perception. I guess that's true: it feels like I'm living a whole lifetime in these two seconds.

But there's something more relative than time.

Fear.

Because the things you *should* be scared of, sometimes, they don't even register.

I should be scared that my feet have lost contact with this crazily high rock face – and that I haven't got a clue where they're going to land.

I should be scared that I've talked Christopher into this when, much as I talked him into thinking it was safe, I don't have a clue. Not really. I only have Blake's words to go on and the time we jumped together. But anything could have gone wrong. We could have misjudged the angle. Jumped off from the wrong spot.

I should be scared because it's so dark that I can't see a thing – not the pool below or the sky above or even the guy I'm flying through the air with.

I should be scared that we're in the middle of nowhere. If we end up splattered on the rocks below it would take a good few hours before anyone finds us. Days, even.

Yeah, those things should scare the shit out of me.

But they don't. Not really.

Because however scary it is, it's nothing compared to what's going on out there in the world.

And I'm holding his hand.

A guy's hand that isn't Blake or my dad.

A guy I've just met.

A guy I basically don't know anything about besides the scraps he's given me about his mom and dad and the weird life he's had and how, somehow, he's not as cut up about his dad being on the plane as he should be.

But he's more than that too. He's the guy who's sat next to me for hundreds of miles already. Miles I would have had to get through on my own. A guy who's shy and strong and weird and basically a stranger but whose hand in mine feels like it could hold me through anything.

The further we fall, the tighter we hold on to each other.

And I don't want to let go.

I want time to stop still.

I want these two seconds to last for ever.

DAY 2
SUNDAY 20TH AUGUST, 2017

Chapter Nineteen

00.01 CDT

For a second, I feel every one of his fingers laced between mine – we're holding onto each other so tight that I'm not sure we'll ever be able to pull them apart again.

And then the water smacks our skin and we sink down under the surface.

The force of being pulled down into the swimming hole yanks our hands apart.

We come up coughing and spluttering and laughing and it's like in those few moments as we dropped through the sky, every bit of me was transformed – like all my cells renewed themselves in fast-forward and that I'm not the same person in this rock pool now as I was, standing up there on the ledge.

I cry out – from relief and exhaustion and out of a longing for everything to be okay. For me. For Christopher. For all those people who are waiting for news about the plane.

My cry echoes between the rocks around the pool.

Leda starts barking. I see her standing on the rock, wagging her tail, waiting for us to come out.

'You did it, Christopher,' I say, climbing out.

I get his glasses and hand them to him. He puts them back on and then stands there, like his body's still in shock. His legs are shaking. From the cold. From the jump. From what we just did together. But he looks more solid, somehow, more there.

Leda comes and sits on his feet and rubs her head against his shins, like she's trying to say well done too.

'It works, right?' I say. 'Now you don't need to be scared of anything ever again.'

He doesn't answer.

'It was amazing – at least give me that?' I prompt.

'Yeah,' he smiles. A big, open smile. 'It was amazing.'

We stand there, our bodies adjusting to being out of the water; to not being in freefall.

'Come on, let's get back on the road.'

He nods, but from how slowly he walks, his clothes dripping around him, I can tell he's still in a daze.

When we get back to the car I realise that the only bit of spare clothing I have with me are the two dresses scrunched up in the back seat. Mom and Dad took the rest of my stuff down for me a few days ago – Mom had pointed out that, with Blake's guitar and his suitcase, there wouldn't be much room in the Buick.

'You got any spare clothes?' I ask.

He looks at me bewildered.

I nod at his massive backpack. 'Just until my shorts and T-shirt dry? And you should probably get changed too.'

'Oh – right.' He opens his bag and starts pulling clothes out.

Everything's carefully folded. Not a wrinkle in sight.

'You iron your *T-shirts*?'

You iron anything, I'm thinking?

His cheeks go pink.

'They don't take up as much space when they're ironed,' he says. 'If I only have my backpack, I don't have to wait at baggage reclaim.'

He makes it sound like he spends his entire life travelling. I guess his dad must drag him around on his business trips.

'Sounds like you've given it a lot of thought,' I say.

'Dad taught me,' he goes on. 'How to pack only what I needed. And to use the space efficiently – not to leave any gaps.' His stares out of the windscreen at the dark pines. 'We'd compete, to see who could pack the lightest.'

I think about those paper models he makes, all those perfect folds. I wonder whether his whole life has been about that: folding everything up into small, neat little parcels. Not getting in anyone's way. It's kind of impressive. But sad too.

'Blake could have taken a few lessons from you,' I say. 'He travels with so much junk.'

I pick up one of his T-shirts and hold it up to my nose. 'God, I love the smell of laundry.'

'And it's not just the space-saving thing,' Christopher goes on, his mind obviously still on his dad. 'Before I went to boarding school, he taught me how to wash and iron. He has a thing about being well turned out, about his uniform being pristine.' He pauses and looks at me like he's expecting me to say something.

'Mom's like that – she's always smart when she goes to work,' I say. 'Jude's the same. Dad's got this whole scruffy professor thing going on and Blake wears ripped, faded stuff and as for me, I kind of just put on whatever's clean. Once I'm in space I'll be wearing a spacesuit anyway, so there's not much point investing in fashion. But I understand. Why some people think it's important.'

Christopher nods. 'Dad says that if you take care of your clothes, it makes people trust you.' He pauses again. 'It makes people feel safe.' His voice goes wobbly. And he catches my eye again.

'He sounds like a good guy,' I say.

'Yeah,' he says, biting his bottom lip.

I feel like there's more he wants to tell me. Like this is the first time he's ever opened up about his life and his dad and that now he's started he wants to carry on, because it feels good not to hold all that stuff inside. There are millions of things about him I don't know – and probably never will. But I'm guessing he's probably shared more with me in the last twelve hours than he has with anyone else his whole life. I wait for a beat to see if he'll go on but he doesn't say anything else.

I take a pair of Christopher's boxer shorts and place them on top of the T-shirt.

'Can I borrow these?'

'Sure… I guess…'

'Thanks.'

I scoot out of the car and go and get changed behind a clump of bushes.

When I come back I put my wet clothes on the back bench to dry. From the corner of my eye I see that the box with Blake's hat has slipped into the footwell and that his suit is all crumpled up. I reach back and straighten it out. It won't be perfect – not to Mom's standards – but at this point I don't care. Blake showing up on time, that's all that matters.

I turn back to Christopher. He's changed too – he's put on a pair of jeans and he's got a T-shirt over the top, which is basically the same as mine except mine is grey, his is white.

'Give me your wet clothes,' I say.

He hands them over and I place them next to mine on the back bench.

As I walk around the car, I can feel him looking at me and it does feel weird, wearing his clothes. But kind of nice too. I've always preferred boys' clothes. How neutral they are. And comfortable. I didn't want to wear clothes that made the boys at school look at me like I was one of the girly girls; like I couldn't join in with what they were doing. I wanted to be one of them. I've never minded being a girl but I do mind being told that I have to look a certain way. Anyway, thinking back, I guess it must have made Jude sad, that I wasn't a little sister she could play dolls and dress up with. I guess that's why it's important to her that I wear a dress for her wedding.

I pull up the roof of the convertible, get into the driver's seat and close the doors. Then I switch the heaters on. The car smells of dusty air and dog fur and pond water, which is kind of comforting.

I notice a tiny sketchbook on the front bench, smaller than the palm of my hand. Christopher pulled it out at the same time as the clothes. It's flipped open to a page filled with pictures of buildings. Weird, angular shapes. All glass and steel.

'What are these?' I ask, picking up the pad.

'Oh, nothing.'

'They don't look like nothing.'

'They're only sketches.'

'Sketches of what?'

'Pulkovo International Airport,' he says quickly. 'St. Petersburg.'

'You really have been everywhere.'

He hesitates and then nods. 'Sort of, yeah.'

I look back at his sketchpad. The drawings are really good. Like something you'd expect an architect to do.

'You like to draw airports, then?'

'I draw sketches before I make some of my more complicated models – to get the shape and the dimensions right.' He sounds kind of excited and embarrassed at the same time. 'Though sometimes I don't know what I'm going to make before I start. I kind of get this twitch in my fingers and after a few folds, I begin to get clues. Sometimes I don't work it out right until the end.' He's speaking so fast, he has to stop and take a breath. 'Sometimes I never work it out – the model just ends up being some weird abstract thing.'

'Blake used to say the same thing about his songs,' I say. 'That he could feel it in his body before he got the tune and the words down on paper. He said those were his best songs.'

My words sit between us.

The car heaters push out dusty air. We're starting to warm up again. Leda's sitting on her blanket in the back, her breath deep and heavy, exhausted after the swim.

'You make things really small,' I say. 'Why is that?'

'If they're small enough, they won't break. And it's easier to carry around.'

I remember that tiny bird he made back in Dulles. He's right – if it had been bigger and full of air, it would have needed some kind of box or protective casing.

'And people don't notice as much,' he says.

'Why don't you want people to notice?' I ask.

He shrugs.

'Is it because of your dad? Because you're hiding it from him?'

Slowly, he nods. 'I guess so. Maybe.'

'Well, I think they're beautiful. I think you should show them to the world.'

He doesn't say anything.

'Do you have a collection of all the models you've made? Back home?'

He shakes his head.

'What do you do with them?'

'I throw them out.'

'You *what*? That's insane.'

'They're not worth keeping.'

'The one you made for that woman, back at the airport – the small bird – that was worth keeping.'

'I give them away sometimes too. Mostly to kids because they don't mind—'

'Don't mind?'

'If they're not very good.' He pauses. 'I gave one to Dad once, for Christmas. I made this bird – a tiny warbler. I found out that they're the smallest birds who can cross the whole Atlantic without even stopping. I thought he'd like it. Like it was a symbol.'

'That's really cool.'

He shakes his head. 'I never saw it again.'

'The paper bird?'

'No. I think he must have binned it or lost it or something. I guess that's why I end up throwing most of them away.'

'Because your dad didn't value what you gave him?'

'Because they're not very good. Not good enough.'

I want to tell him that of course they're good enough – more than good enough. They're amazing. But I know how it is: wanting something you really care about to be perfect. And if it's not, you don't want it to be there, reminding you that you didn't get it right. And how crappy it is when people you care about shit over what you love.

'And they're still pieces of rubbish,' he adds. 'Like they were before I picked them up. That doesn't change because I made a few folds.'

'I don't believe that,' I say. 'I don't believe they're still rubbish.'

He shrugs.

I think about what Blake said about his singing once. How, if you believe in it hard enough, you can turn anything into something amazing – a poem, a piece of music, a painting. You can take the rubbish of life and make it beautiful. He said that was the point of art.

I wish Blake were here now. I wish he could explain it to Christopher. Help him see that the models he makes are beautiful.

'You ready to go?' I say.

He nods.

As I switch on the ignition, I can still feel him looking at me.

And I know he must think I'm crazy – getting him to jump off rocks into swimming holes in the middle of the night; wearing his clothes; tearing across the country to get to a wedding. And he's right.

But I think he gets it.

Why I'm doing all this.

Why he came with me.

And I think he feels the same as I do: that, right now, there's nowhere else in the world we should be but here, in Blake's old yellow Buick, shivering and dripping and wobbly-limbed from the jump we took, together.

Chapter Twenty

01.01 CDT
1-81

The car's warm. The road empty. We're both exhausted but kind of buzzing, too, from jumping off that rock at Leda Falls.

I keep glancing at my phone, sitting on my lap, expecting to see a message from Blake. It's been ages since the text he sent from Heathrow. He's pretty rubbish at staying in touch but even Blake would have sent me something to say that he'd landed – especially if I wasn't there to collect him. And if he still hasn't found his phone, he'd have blagged his way into borrowing some poor stranger's like he did the last couple of times. And I made him learn my number off by heart so that he could always reach me.

But there are no new messages on my phone.

My breath goes shallow. He should definitely have got in touch by now. His silence doesn't make any sense.

I close my eyes for a second.

For Christ's sake, Blake, I whisper to myself. *Why do you always make everything so fucking hard?*

I blink my eyes open, stare hard at the road and push away my thoughts. Then I grab my phone and shove it into the pocket of the door beside me.

Christopher and I are making good headway. We're getting to where we're meant to be. We have to keep going now. I grip the steering wheel harder. We have to believe it's going to be okay.

'You alright?' Christopher asks.

I nod. 'Fine.'

I can feel him looking at me and then he turns his head back to the windscreen.

'My dad would have liked that,' Christopher says.

'Liked what?'

'The swimming hole. The rock. Jumping.' He pauses. 'I think he would have been proud that I did it.'

I remember what he said to me about his dad back at the Mobil station – how he wanted Christopher to lead a big life.

'You forgive me, then?' I ask. 'For pushing you into it?'

He nods. 'Yeah, I forgive you.'

'I wish I could have worked out what I was going to do with my life, before—' his voice breaks. 'Before all this.'

My throat goes tight. The way he says it – before all this – it's like the first time he's acknowledging that something really bad might have happened to his dad. No excuses about the newspapers or the investigators or the UKFlyer officials. He's making it sound like it's all too late.

'You're going to work it out,' I say.

He doesn't answer.

I stare out of the windscreen and, for a second, I let myself think about what I would have wanted to say to Blake if the last time we were together was the last time I got to see him. If he really was on that plane. And then I push the thought away again.

I can't do this. I can't let myself think that anything bad has happened. Blake's probably in Nashville already. Knowing Blake, he's probably turned up at the hotel without me and I'll show up in the middle of the night, totally exhausted and end up walking down the aisle in a crinkled blue dress with massive bags under my eyes because I've spent the last two days chasing a brother who can't get his travel plans together.

I glance at Christopher. His shoulders are drooped. It must be hard, having a relationship like that with your dad – feeling like you're not good enough.

'I bet there's something you're amazing at,' I say. 'Something that comes naturally, that other people find hard but that you can do without even thinking.'

I think about how Blake can perform a song perfectly, even if he's only heard it once. And about how Jude can play these really old, classical pieces of music on the piano that people have heard a million times before – and make them come to life and sound new. And how she's amazing at making things match and look beautiful whether it's a homemade birthday card or her apartment or the clothes she wears – or this whole wedding that's about to take place.

He looks over at me.

'Can you do space stuff without even thinking?' he asks.

I scrunch up my nose. 'Space *stuff*?'

'Astronomy.'

'I have to work at it. I find Physics hard. Anyone who isn't a total genius finds Physics hard. And I know that if I want to be an astronaut, I'm going to have to learn to be a really good engineer, because understanding how to get to space – technically – is as important as understanding space itself. And engineering's tough. But yeah, when I look through my telescope, it makes sense to me – more than anything else does. So the hard stuff is worth it.'

'Well, I don't really have anything,' he says. 'Not yet, anyway.'

'You will.'

'Maybe.' His body slumps a bit and he stares out through the windscreen and I know he's thinking about his dad again.

I glance down at my phone. I don't know what Dad did to get Mom to stop calling me, but it's worked. The only notifications are news items. The eclipse. A replay of the Red Sox game. An update on the plane.

Christopher's gets out his phone and starts scanning through the pages.

'Any news about the plane?' I ask.

He keeps scanning for a bit, then he says:

'They're still trying to work out why it dropped so fast. It was meant to be on autopilot so it should have been flying at a steady altitude.'

'Are they giving any explanations?'

'They're investigating the conversation between air traffic control and the cockpit.'

'And?'

'There weren't any alerts.'

'What does that mean?'

'The crew didn't notice that there was a problem.'

I wait for him to go into defensive mode, like back at the Mobil station. To say that they're professionals and that they knew what they were doing and that the news reports are wrong. But instead, he says:

'God, all this is screwed up.'

'Yeah, it is.'

Christopher puts away his phone and, for a really long time, he stares out through the windscreen.

And then the thoughts crowd back in. The ones I've been pushing away, over and over. And for a second, I think about how Blake would have reacted if he'd been on the plane.

Would he have felt the drop?

And would that have made him feel scared?

Or would he have thought that it was simply a bit of turbulence, that in a few hours he'd land and then go to Jude's wedding? That, even if there were a few hiccups on the way, in the end, everything was going to be okay?

The last time we thought we'd lost Blake – *really* lost him in a way that actually worried us – was on a family holiday in Scotland. It was three years ago. We were celebrating Mom and Dad's twenty-fifth wedding anniversary.

Mom wanted to show us the exact spot on the shores of Loch Leven where Dad had proposed. She also wanted to show us the old white cottage where the Shaws, generations of her family were supposed to have lived. Dad, in this totally romantic, feminist move took on Mom's maiden name. That's why we're all called Shaw. It's one of the many reasons I love him so much. Guys from Dad's generation didn't do that stuff. Anyway, on that holiday, Mom and Dad took us to the grave of Robby Shaw, who was known for two things: his singing voice and his rebellious spirit. *He was an outlaw*, Mom said, like it was an accomplishment – which struck me as odd, considering she's a lawyer, until she said the next thing. Standing there in front of that mossy grave thousands of miles from DC, Mom turned to Blake and said: *That's where you get it from, my love.* As if this Gaelic ancestor who lived hundreds of years ago explained everything Blake had ever done wrong, including getting kicked out of high school for spending more days busking around DC than sitting behind a desk.

And that's when I got it. If an ancestor did it – and Mom loves all that ancestor, family – tree stuff – then Blake was forgiven. Because it wasn't his fault: it was written in his blood.

Mom finds excuses for Blake. I guess we all do.

Anyway, that summer, when I was fourteen, as the five of us stayed in a small B&B in Kinross, Blake performed one of his vanishing acts.

Mom gave us The Day Off. The Day Off is a family tradition. It's the only way we cope with the way Mom organises the hell out of every other minute of our holidays. The Day Off is always a surprise – Mom gets to choose. One morning, she'll announce it over breakfast and then go back to her room to sleep because having days without plans makes her anxious and sleeping gets her through them quicker.

The Day Off usually happens about halfway through any given holiday, when we're all in need of some alone time and some brain space and some time away from touring. It's everyone's favourite day, except for Mom, obviously.

So, on The Day Off in Scotland, we all went our separate ways.

I went off to explore the bits of the world that weren't covered by Mom's Fodor guidebook. The B&B

owner leant me an old bicycle she had hanging around in her garage. I grabbed a pair of binoculars Dad had given me for my birthday, packed a sandwich I'd made up from the breakfast buffet and headed off for a trip around the Loch.

As for Blake, he went off on foot, his guitar slung across his back – *to find inspiration,* he said. Inspiration and a local pub.

The bike I was riding ended up getting a flat tyre. Probably because I took it onto a dirt track to get closer to a wild bit of the lake. I had to walk back – which took ages and because the night sets in really early in Scotland, by the time I got back to the B&B, it was dark.

Before I even got through the front door of the B&B, I could feel that something was wrong.

When I saw Mom's face, I *knew* something was wrong.

Jude was standing behind her, biting her freshly painted nails. She caught my eye and I could tell that she was relieved that I was back. She'd clearly been absorbing Mom's stress for the last few hours.

'Where the hell have you been?' Mom asked.

'The bike got a flat tyre.'

'You couldn't have called?'

'I didn't think it would take as long as it did.'

She looked over my shoulder. 'So, you're not with your brother?'

'No.'

Then Mom tilted her head up to the ceiling and let out a long sigh. She was never really worried about me. Probably because I'd never given her much of a reason to be. She knew I'd show up. It was the fact that I'd come back without Blake that was rattling her.

'Blake's always late back, Mom,' I said.

Though, I remember thinking, even Blake can't have spent all day in the pub. And between the pub and the B&B and a whole expanse of lake, there wasn't much to do out here. And we were meant to have dinner together tonight to celebrate Mom and Dad's anniversary, so Mom had told him (like a million times) to be on time.

I slumped down into an armchair, my feet aching from the long walk home.

'Don't sit down, Air,' Mom snapped.

'Why not?'

'You need to help me look for him.'

Of course I did.

Mom held out her hand, waiting for me to take it so that she could pull me out of the chair again.

I pushed myself up to standing.

Mom put her hands on her hips.

'He was at the Bird and Stone. *All day.*'

'It's our day off, Mom, we're allowed to do what we want. And how do you know he was there *all* day?'

'I went and checked.'

I picture Mom storming into the old Scottish pub, yelling out for Blake. The locals would have loved that.

'And – what did you find out?' I asked.

'They said he drank too much.' She bit her nail in the exact same way that Jude did. 'Bad company, I bet,' she mumbled.

Mom didn't want to admit that Blake was perfectly capable of getting in trouble by himself. And drinking by himself. He loved that the drinking age in the UK was eighteen and took full advantage of that freedom by visiting every pub within walking distance of wherever we were staying. He said that pubs inspired him. That the people were interesting. And that, one day, he'd do a music tour of all his favourite pubs. Going to London this summer was a realisation of that dream – or the first part of it, anyway.

'He left three hours ago,' Mom went on. 'And the pub's only two miles away.' Her voice was shaking.

'Did you try calling him?' I asked.

Though I knew that was a stupid question. Reception here was rubbish. And Blake wasn't good at answering his phone. Especially when Mom called.

'Of course I tried calling him. It went straight to voicemail.'

'He's probably just gone for a walk,' I said.

'Or hooked up with some girl,' Jude said.

I shot Jude a *be quiet* look. If there was one thing that worried Mom more than Blake drinking too much or falling into bad company, it was Blake getting mixed up with a girl who would, in her words, *ruin his life*.

'It's dark, and it's been three hours and he's had too much to drink,' Mom said. 'And you know your brother…' Her voice trailed off. 'He gets distracted.'

Yeah, we all knew how Blake got distracted.

Then Mom went quiet.

'Where's Dad?' I asked.

'Upstairs,' Jude said. 'In the library.'

Of course.

'I'm going to call the police,' Mom said.

'It's not even that late, Mom.'

But she ignored me and got out her cell.

This is the weird paradox about Blake. He gets in trouble – *all* the time – which totally stresses Mom out. But he lands on his feet. Except, we're never allowed to just relax and wait for that to happen.

It's like this unwritten deal:

a) Blake messes up.
b) We go into action-stations to make sure he's okay.
c) Blake shows up fine and we're totally pissed at him but more relieved than pissed so we end up forgiving him.

And the thing is, we can never skip straight from a) to c). We *have* to go crazy finding him, because the one time we don't, he'll be in trouble and we'll have missed it.

So, we all did what we do when we're worried about Blake.

Mom called the cops.

Jude went into her supporting and there-thereing Mom mode (whilst mumbling her *I told-you-so-Blake's-always-doing-this* refrain reserved for these occasions).

Dad tried to help for a bit and then got swatted away by Mom for being annoying and ended up hiding upstairs in the library with a book.

As for me? My job was to come up with an actual plan to get Blake back. A logical one. So I did what I always did when Blake went missing: I retraced his steps by trying to work out where – if I were living in Blake's body with his particular personality and interests and blood chemistry – I'd be right now.

If I don't make it as an astronaut I'm seriously considering becoming a personal investigator.

But Blake was harder to trace on holiday. In DC, I knew most of the places where he hung out and which girlfriends or ex-girlfriends or any music friends he might have decided to crash with. In the middle of the Scottish countryside, there weren't that many options. And Mom was right: if he wasn't at the pub and if he wasn't on the road walking to or from the pub, where the hell was he?

I went up to the attic where the B&B owners had set up a small library, and found Dad reading a book on Scottish mythology, but his reading glasses were on his head rather than on his nose so he obviously wasn't actually reading.

He looked up at me and his eyes said it all: *Find Blake, Air.*

Every part of me wanted to bolt the door to the library and slump down in the armchair next to Dad and pull out a book and let my big brother sort out his own mess for once. He was eighteen, for goodness sake. Four whole years older than me. An adult. Why did I have to go out and find him?

But I knew it was my job.

I went over and kissed the top of Dad's head, because I knew that Mom would have given him a hard time, and then I walked back to the room I shared with Blake to do some thinking. Jude liked to have her space and Blake and I liked to share, so it all worked out. Kind of.

Anyway, it took me a few minutes to notice that some of the stuff in the room didn't quite add up to the current state of play.

Like that the black sweatshirt – the one Blake had gone to the pub wearing when he set off at lunchtime – was hanging on the back of a chair. As soon as I picked it up I could smell the beer and cigarettes.

Blake had gone to the pub and come back and then left again – without anyone seeing. Which wasn't hard. Mom would have been sleeping. Jude would have found an old piano so she could practise her scales: she was preparing for this really tough exam coming up in the fall at Julliard. Blake just played. Jude practised. Dad would have been reading in the attic and I was out exploring Loch Leven with my flat tyre.

The weird thing was that he'd taken off again, rather than stopping for one of his middle of the day catch-up-on-being-awake-all-night naps.

I looked around the room and noticed that his guitar was here too, tucked into the corner by his bed. Yeah, Blake had definitely been back. And gone again without his guitar. Which was strange. His guitar was basically like one of his limbs: wherever he went, it went too.

I kept looking. Nothing else seemed strange: an unmade bed, bits of music manuscript paper in a pile on the floor, clothes crumpled on top of his suitcase.

And then I noticed the heated towel rail in the en-suite bathroom. This morning, we'd taken it in turns to have a shower. And we'd both left our towels on the rail. And now his wasn't there.

I went into the bathroom and looked around in case he'd had another shower or something and left his towel on the floor but it was definitely gone. And it wasn't anywhere in our bedroom either.

Someone must have come to clean the room and taken the towel but forgot to replace it. But neither the bathroom nor our room looked like it had been cleaned. The trash can was still full and the sink was slick with soap grime.

I walked to the window, pulled it open, and looked out. For a moment, I let it all soak in – the warm night air, the water so still it reflected the moon perfectly.

And then I felt a jolt.

And I began to panic.

Blake liked to swim. Especially in random bodies of water. Ponds. Lakes. Rivers. Other people's swimming pools. The open sea, even in the middle of winter.

And swimming and alcohol don't mix.

I tore out of the room, down the stairs and through the front door.

'What is it?' Mom yelled after me.

But I kept running, images flashing in front of my eyes: Blake floating, drowned, face down in the lake. Blake caught in reeds, unable to scramble back to the shore. Blake knocked unconscious after tripping and hitting his head on one of the sharp rocks on the shore.

I pushed the images away. *Blake is going to be fine. Blake is always fine.*

It took me a while to find him.

He'd walked to a patch of beach from where he could wade into the lake.

But he'd never made it into the water itself.

He'd fallen asleep. Fully dressed. On the B&B towel.

When I found him, curled up like a kid, I nearly laughed I was so relieved.

And then I wanted to yell at him for being so stupid and so selfish and for stressing Mom out and for wrecking our parents' wedding anniversary.

Instead, I lay beside him and looked up at the sky with its millions of stars. And then I slipped my hand into his and closed my eyes and waited for my heart to stop hammering.

After a few seconds, he stirred.

I opened my eyes. The moon shone down so strong it felt like it was falling towards us.

'You're an idiot,' I whispered.

He groaned. Hungover. Stiff.

God he's infuriating, I remember thinking.

And then I remember feeling relieved. Because a part of me was scared, like Mom, that something bad had happened to him. That even Blake, my loved-by-the-gods big brother, might run out of his four-leaf clover luck one day.

I got up and yanked his arm until he was standing, wobbly, in front of me. He looked pale and his eyes were bloodshot and his hair fell into his eyes – but he still managed a smile.

'Yeah, a grade A idiot,' I said. Then I took his hand. 'Come on, Blake, time to go home.'

'Do you really think that they might be all right? The passengers on the plane?' I ask Christopher. 'Like you said back at the gas station?'

He goes still.

'Christopher?'

'I don't know.'

He's definitely shifted his thinking. Somewhere between the Mobil station and Leda Falls, the penny's begun to drop that the plane crash is real.

My shoulders slump. The thing is that, right now, I needed him to say that everything was going to be fine, to repeat that stuff about the crew being prepared to deal with this kind of thing.

'But you said—'

He takes off his glasses and rubs his eyes and shakes his head.

'What is it?' I ask.

He threads his fingers through his knotty hair and he grabs at it, like he's trying to pull the thoughts out of his head.

'I should have told you,' he mutters.

'Told me *what*?'

He doesn't answer.

I get a sick feeling in my stomach.

'Just say it. It's not like it can be any more shit than anything that's happening right now.'

He puts his glasses back on.

'It's about Dad.'

'Your dad?'

'His name's Edward Ellis.'

He says it like I should recognise the name. Like his dad's famous or something.

Christopher looks at me, his eyes wide through his thick glasses. His Adam's apple slides up and down his throat. He takes a breath and says, 'He's a UKFlyer pilot.'

His words hit me in the chest. My head swims. The road blurs in and out of focus. And I can't push the thoughts away anymore. About the fact that Blake should have been in touch by now. About how he might have been on that plane that crashed after all.

I hit the brakes.

The car skids and then I swerve onto the hard shoulder.

The car hums and clicks from the sudden stop.

'He's *what*?' my voice comes out shaky.

'He's a pilot.' His voice is jagged, like the words are struggling to come up out of his throat. 'He was the pilot – of the plane.'

As I watch his lips forming the words, it feels like he's speaking in a different language, one that I can just about get the gist of but without being totally sure whether how it translates in my brain is accurate.

'What do you mean?' I say slowly.

'I tried to tell you.'

'*You tried to tell me*? How? When?'

He gulps.

'I said I travelled a lot, with Dad. That I spent time in airports.'

'You thought I'd pick it up from that? You know how many people fly around the world for their jobs and *aren't* pilots?'

I grip the steering wheel and breathe in and out as steadily as I can. I need to keep it together.

'You said your brother wasn't on the plane,' he stutters. 'I didn't think it mattered who Dad was—'

'You thought it didn't matter?!' I yell.

My words get sucked into the dark night.

'I'm sorry,' he says. 'I'm really sorry.'

I look over at him and, for a second, I feel sorry for *him* – like I've felt sorry for him ever since I saw him sitting on the airport floor back in DC. But I push that feeling away. He doesn't get my pity, not after this.

I yank open the door and get out of the car.

I'm going to be sick.

'Air—' I hear him call after me.

The way he says my name, makes my breath catch in my throat. He says it like we're close. Like we've known each other for years rather than the truth: which is that we only met a few hours ago. That we basically don't know each other at all.

'Air!' he calls again.

But I don't turn around. Instead, I start running.

Chapter Twenty-One

01.17 CDT
1-81

When I've run so hard that my lungs feel like they're going to explode, I realise how stupid I'm being: running away from my own car. From *Blake's* car. In the middle of the night.

My brain yells at me:

What the hell are you doing, Air?

So, I turn around and run back.

I should never have taken Christopher with me. A total stranger. As if things weren't complicated enough already.

When I get back to the car, I rap my knuckles on the window next to him.

'Open up!'

He tries to roll down the window but it takes ages because the window's stiff and it sticks to the hood of the car. But I'm too pissed to care. He should be able to open a window for Christ's sake.

I keep banging at the glass, using my fist now.

He still doesn't manage to roll it down.

'Oh, for God's sake.' I yank open the door beside him.

He looks up at me, blinking and I can't tell whether he's relieved – or terrified – that I've come back.

You've got to tone down that fierce, Blake told me once, like he was composing the line of a song. *Or you'll end up lonesome.*

But lonesome is better than hanging out with someone you can't trust.

I close my eyes to still the arguing in my head.

And then I feel stupid – really stupid – standing there, in Christopher's T-shirt and boxers.

And I know Christopher feels stupid too, sitting in my car, not knowing what to do.

But I'm done with worrying about his feelings.

He lied to me. Period.

I look him right in the eye and say:

'*You* get out. It's my car.'

'I – I don't know where we are.'

It didn't seem to bother him earlier. When he ran away from the Mobil station. And then it clicks. The reason why he left like that, so suddenly. A hard lump, like a stone, sticks in my throat. They were criticising the pilot – on the TV screen, on the news – they were blaming Christopher's dad for what went wrong up there.

Don't feel sorry for him. Don't feel sorry for him. Don't feel sorry for him.

'You'll work it out.' My voice is shaking. 'Get out of my car.'

'I'm sorry,' he mumbles.

He's about to get up when Leda bounds over the bench of the Buick and settles in his lap.

Stupid dog. I try to lift her off him, but she makes her body go limp. *Stupid, stupid dog.*

And then, he just sits there, pinned down by a dog. And I just stand there, in his clothes. On the side of the road. Miles from anywhere either of us are meant to be.

'Let me explain—' he starts.

'Explain what? That your dad's responsible for all this and that you didn't think to tell me?'

His eyes go dark. 'Dad? *Responsible*?'

'That's how it works, Christopher: when you're the pilot, it's your job to keep everyone safe. So yeah, it's his fault.' I spit the words out.

There's a bitter aftertaste in my mouth. I know that what I'm saying isn't fair. That it's more complicated than that. That there are all kinds of reasons a plane can crash. But I want him to know how angry I am that he kept this from me.

He stares at me, his eyes wide and dark as the pool we swam in.

'No.' He shakes his head. 'Whatever happened up there, it won't have been his fault. You've got this wrong – I explained before. What they're saying doesn't make sense—'

'He was flying the plane, Christopher!'

'He's an amazing pilot.' His voice has gone shrill. 'He won't have let *anything* go wrong. And if something did happen—'

'Like what?' I snap back.

I wonder whether he's even thought it through. All the stuff that can happen up there.

'Even if he didn't cause it directly—'

'He didn't cause it!'

'*Even if* he didn't, he's not God, Christopher. What if it was a terrorist attack? Or what if there was a massive mechanical failure, mid-flight? Or an electrical storm?'

He goes pale.

'The pilot only has so much control,' I say. 'And he has plenty of chances to fuck things up.'

He puts his hand up, like he wants me to stop speaking. But I don't stop.

'The point is, he was in charge. And you didn't tell me.' I'm yelling now.

Leda starts barking at me. I know she's upset by my shouting. That she senses that I'm being unfair. But I can't stop.

'You didn't tell me,' I say again.

'Whatever happened, Dad would have sorted it.' His pale, grey eyes go watery. 'He doesn't even like his planes to be late.' He keeps staring right at me. 'Dad's smart. He's good at whatever he does. If he'd had the opportunity, he'd probably have been an astronaut or something – like you. Something really clever and technical.' He gulps. 'And he doesn't fuck things up. Ever.'

'I don't care if your dad's the best pilot this side of Mars. He's still the pilot. And the plane crashed.' I run out of breath.

Silence hangs between us for a beat.

'You said your brother wasn't on the plane.' He says it quietly this time.

I bite my bottom lip so hard I taste blood in my mouth.

'He's not on the plane,' I say.

'So why are you so angry with me?'

'Because it doesn't matter,' I blurt out. 'He *could* have been on the plane. And you lied to me.'

'I didn't lie to you.'

'You didn't tell me. That's the same thing as lying.'

He blinks, like he's taking it all in. Like he's never considered that his words could have implied anything else.

'You knew. And you chose not to tell me.'

'There wasn't time.'

'We've been driving for hours!'

'There wasn't the *right* time.' He looks at me, his brow folded. 'When was I meant to have told you? At the airport, when everything was going crazy and we didn't know what had happened to the plane? When you tore off saying you had to get to your sister's wedding? When we were busy getting your car back? While I was asleep? Or while you were making me jump off the highest rock face in the state of Tennessee?'

'It wasn't that high.'

He pauses.

'You should have told me,' I say.

'I know.'

Things go quiet between us. And I want to buy what he's saying – that somehow it never felt right to tell me. But I can't. Because I can see it in his eyes, how he's not quite able to look at me when he's talking – that he *chose* not to tell me.

So I stand there, waiting for him to get out. But he doesn't move.

I go around to the driver's side and sit down behind the steering wheel.

I stay there for a really long time, looking out at the dark, empty road. In any other situation, I'd have tried to listen, given this guy a chance. But this is different. I trusted Christopher. I told him about stuff. I took him to Leda Springs. And what did he do? He kept the most important bit of information he had to share from me.

'Did you lend me the money because you felt guilty?' I ask.

'The money?' He's looking right at me now.

'For the car. To pay the tow guy. You already knew it back then – you've known it the whole time. That your dad was the pilot and that bit of information was important and you've done all this stuff to cover it up.'

After what feels like ages, he says:

'I didn't lend you the money because I felt guilty.' He swallows. 'I did it because I wanted to.'

And I kind of believe him. But that doesn't make it any better.

'I can't see you right now,' I say.

I grip the steering wheel so tight my knuckles push up, white, under my skin.

He still doesn't move.

I turn around in my seat, reach for Christopher's backpack and throw it at his chest, just in time for Leda to jump out of the way.

'Just go!' I say, my jaw clenched.

In the second before he responds, I think back to how we stood on that rock, our fingers laced; how we flew through the darkness together. And I don't know how I can hold the feelings about that moment alongside how I feel about him now.

Slowly, he opens the door and stumbles out onto the side of the road.

I watch him stand there, tall, dark pines to one side, the long highway stretching out on the other. He looks around, not sure which way he should be heading.

Leda whines beside me and looks up at me, her ears flopped over.

'Shush,' I tell her.

I switch on the ignition, put the car into gear and go.

Chapter Twenty-Two

02.02 CDT
1-81

As I drive away, I watch him in my rear-view mirror. He stumbles out into the dark night and stands amongst the dark pines; I feel it, the dew from the grass verge soaking through his shoes and socks. The wind pushing against him making every step he takes an effort.

Leda's sitting with her paws up on the back seat, looking out through the rear window, whining, like she did when we were on our way to Dulles to collect Blake.

He brought this on himself, I tell myself. *Just let go.*

I force myself to look away from the mirror and focus on the road.

Sweat runs down my back but I'm still cold from the swim.

I feel sick. A hollow sick like my stomach's folding in on itself.

Why the hell didn't he tell me about his dad? I told him everything. *Everything.* About Blake and my family and the wedding.

A picture of him flickers in front of me. His tangled blond hair falling in his pale, grey eyes. His brows scrunched together. Listening. And I remember how much I liked that thought: to have someone sitting there, taking in my words, making me feel like I wasn't going crazy inside my own head.

Maybe I should have asked him more questions? Looked out for the signs? Had he tried to tell me, like he said?

I scan through the reasons why he didn't tell me about his Dad, trying to grab at some justification, but I keep circling back to that same thought: that he kept it from me, the most important bit of information about this whole situation that threw us together. The plane crash.

His father was the pilot? I still can't get my head around it.

I think about what he said. That he kept quiet because Blake wasn't on the plane. That he thought it wasn't relevant. But that doesn't make sense. Blake not being on the plane should have made it easier for him to tell me the truth. If Blake's life isn't at stake, then who cares if I know who the pilot is.

And of course, it's relevant. The national news thinks it's relevant. People who have nothing whatsoever to do with the flight see it as relevant to their lives. When something like this happens, everyone feels implicated.

So, it matters. Who the pilot was.

The guy in charge of the plane.

The picture they showed of him on the TV flashes in front of me. His pressed, navy uniform. His cufflinks shining. Not a crease. Not a hair out of place. His blue eyes strong and confident as if to say: *With me in charge, nothing can ever go wrong.*

The sick feeling in my stomach pushes up my throat.

But something did go wrong. Seriously wrong. And Edward Ellis, Christopher's dad, was flying that plane.

I try to push air down into my lungs but it's like there's not enough oxygen. Then I glance back into the rear-view mirror. It's dark and he's far behind me now, but I can still see him, a small figure with a backpack slumped on the verge of the highway.

How's Christopher's going to live with all this?

Losing his dad.

And worse.

Knowing that the crash might have been his dad's fault.

I keep trying to push the air down. My mouth is dry. The sick feeling in my stomach gets worse.

Through the windscreen I look out at the dark sky, at the millions of stars. More pictures flash in front of me.

I see Christopher sitting on the floor at the arrivals lounge, his back pressed to the wall, his head bent over that paper bird he was making.

I see him sitting beside me in on the curb, waiting for the tow-truck to bring the Buick back.

I see him reaching past me and grabbing the steering wheel to keep me from swerving into the oncoming track.

I see him leaning towards me, talking and drinking coffee – and then running out onto the road, furious that anyone could accuse the pilot of crashing the plane.

I see his face when he looked through the telescope for the first time.

I close my eyes and feel his hand in mine the moment before we jumped.

We only met a few hours ago but it's like we've lived a whole lifetime together.

I open my eyes and thump the steering wheel.

Damn it, Christopher, you should have told me.

I look up and down the highway ahead of me. At how empty it is. I think of all those hundreds of miles I'm going to have to do on my own before I get to Nashville. And then what? Even if I do make it to the wedding, what if Blake doesn't show up or get in touch? What if something really is wrong?

And what's Christopher meant to do? I'm the one who talked him into coming with me. And now I've dumped him the middle of nowhere. And I made him call his mom, pushed him to go there.

I feel dizzy.

God I'm an idiot. Why did I even suggest that he come with me? Why didn't I wave him goodbye at the airport and set off on my own? I'm good at doing stuff on my own. Besides my family I'm better on my own.

Just drive, I tell myself. *Just keep driving.*

I press down harder on the accelerator.

Chapter Twenty-Three

02.20 CDT
1-81

I keep driving, going faster and faster, ignoring the speed dial moving up on the dashboard.

This is how Blake liked to drive.

Take it from me, sis, one day, this Buick's going to take off and fly.

Another one of his comments that totally defied scientific logic but sounded cool and exciting.

Right now, I'd give anything for the Buick to take off into the air. To take me somewhere, far away from all this crap.

But the wheels keep clicking on the grooves on the road.

I look down and realise I'm still wearing Christopher's stupid clothes.

And a set of his clothes, the ones he swam in, are drying on my back seat.

What a mess.

My stomach groans. I haven't eaten since I left home this morning. And any energy I had left was burned up in the adrenaline rush from jumping off that stupid rock.

My legs are shaking. I'm worried my body's going to give up and that I'm going to swerve off the road. And this time, Christopher won't be there to save me.

Leda is huddled in the footwell of the back seat. She's gone really quiet. Which is even worse than her whining.

And that's when I realise that it's time to call it quits.

I've been trying to hold it all together. To make sure the wedding goes smoothly, no matter what's happening with Blake.

But I can't do this anymore.

Not after finding out that Christopher – the only person I've been able to share all this with – lied to me.

When I'm far enough to be sure Christopher can't catch up with me, I pull over again.

And I slump down against the steering wheel and this time, I don't hold them back: I let hot, thick tears roll down my cheeks.

Chapter Twenty-Four

03.01 CDT
1-81

When I look up again, the sky's so huge and dark that, for once, I find it more frightening than fascinating. I want it to be morning. For daylight to come.

I thought I could do this by myself. Get through to the wedding. Cover for Blake if he doesn't show up in time. Save the day. But it's no good.

Whenever there's a crisis – a real crisis – it's Mom who sorts things out. If there's one person I shouldn't have kept all this from, it was her. Christopher didn't tell me about his dad being the pilot and look how that turned out? No matter how much it stresses her out before the wedding, I have to tell Mom the truth about what's going on with Blake.

I get out my phone and call up the recent calls and press on Mom's name.

She picks up on the first ring.

I knew she wouldn't be sleeping, not with all her worries about me and Blake not showing up for the rehearsal dinner. And after Dad persuaded her to stop calling me, I bet she's been staring at her phone, waiting for me to call.

'Ariadne!' She lets out a long sigh. 'Thank goodness.'

Just tell her straight out. No hesitation. No chance for her to interrupt.

'Mom…'

'I promise I'm going to keep calm, Ariadne. I know you've got everything under control – your father was right, I shouldn't have been calling every two seconds.'

'Mom—'

'I was so upset – when you said you couldn't make it to our family breakfast.' There's a tremor in her voice. 'It was meant to be the last time – just the five of us, at Louis's—'

'Mom, will you let me talk?'

'Talk? Yes, yes of course.' She pauses for a millisecond. I open my mouth to speak but she leaps in again. 'Where are you? Why aren't you sleeping? You should be sleeping. I hope Blake's sleeping. You need to be rested for tomorrow. We have to go to the rooftop to make sure that everything's in place for the wedding. Do a run-through. And then there's the rehearsal dinner. And the pictures. I can't have you looking all tired for the pictures.'

Every time Mom speaks it's like she squeezes a bit more oxygen out of my lungs; like she's using up all the air I have to talk.

So much for telling her straight out.

I try a different tack. Maybe if I go at it more gently, she'll listen.

'I'll be there in time for the wedding,' I say. 'You don't need to worry about that.'

'Worry about that? Of course I'm not worried about that. You said you'd be there and I know you keep your word. That's why I put you in charge of getting that brother of yours to the wedding.'

A bit more oxygen gets squeezed out of my lungs.

'Yeah, I'll make it to the wedding, Mom. But there have been a few complications—'

'You should see the roof terrace, Ariadne. It's all set up. I even found the stool that your brother likes – I went to that music shop on the Broad, the one he loves, and I described how he likes to perch when he sings and plays his guitar and they found me just the thing.'

I recognise this behaviour. When Mom's stressed, she likes to talk. Dad usually gets the brunt of it but I guess he's asleep – and that he's been listening to her talk about this stuff for months. And Jude's probably getting her beauty sleep too. So that leaves me.

'And we've tested the microphone – like Blake does before a show.' Her words tumble over each other. 'And my roses – after all that worry, they survived the trip, I think they're going to stay fresh for the wedding.' She pauses. 'Oh, Ariadne, it's going to be perfect.'

I see her clutching her throat, closing her eyes, smiling – letting it sink in, all that hope and anticipation.

'Just perfect,' she says.

Sometimes I think Mom must be exhausted: chasing perfection in everything she does, how unrelenting it is. Because, no matter how hard she tries, there will always be things that are out of her control.

I open my mouth to tell her the truth: that I haven't got a clue where Blake is. But then his voice comes into my head again:

I'll be there, no matter what.

His eyes sparkle.

And then his words at the planetarium: *I've got a surprise planned.*

I see him smiling. A strand of dark hair falling into his eyes.

'Ariadne – you still there?' Mom asks.

I swallow hard. He promised he'd be there, no matter what. He'd planned a surprise. I have to believe him.

'It all sounds great, Mom,' I say. 'I can't wait to see it.'

I can feel her smile on the other end. Mom's super-confident – obviously, she's confident: she's an international human rights lawyer. But she still looks for praise.

'So, where are you, dear?' Mom asks.

'We'll make it, Mom, don't worry.'

She sighs. 'That brother of yours, getting the wrong flight – I just don't understand him.'

'Yeah…'

'Could you pass him over? I want to hear his voice.'

She thinks he's in the car with me?

Oh God.

'Mom, listen…' I start.

Leda lets out a whine.

'Is that your brother's dog?' Mom says.

Mom doesn't like Leda. Maybe because Leda doesn't follow her instructions. Sometimes, Leda does the exact opposite of following mom's instructions. And no one ignores Mom's instructions.

'I've got a kennel for her.'

'A kennel?'

'In case people are allergic.'

'The wedding's outside.'

'Some people don't *like* dogs, Ariadne.'

We've had this conversation before. I'm not Leda's greatest fan either but even I end up defending her to Mom.

'So she doesn't disturb people,' Mom goes on. 'It's a nice one. It'll be in a corner of the roof terrace.'

You think Blake's going to let you put Leda in a kennel in a corner of the roof terrace? I want to say. *Blake's going to want Leda sitting at his feet while he sings.*

Blake doesn't even believe in putting Leda on a lead. Even in parks where it's illegal not to.

But I don't say any of that stuff. There's no point upsetting Mom before the wedding. And by the time Blake shows up, she'll be so relieved, she won't even care about where Leda is.

'Can I speak to Blake?' Mom asks again.

'Um…'

But then my phone buzzes.

I pull the phone away from my ear in time to see that there's a news alert.

Latest on the UKFlyer0217…

'Hang on a second, Mom.'

I click onto the alert. The screen opens.

Autopilot disconnected. Flight lost altitude fast before the crash.

'Ariadne, are you still there?'

Investigators are listening to the recordings from the cockpit to determine the cause of the error.

'Ariadne!'

No passenger names have yet been released to the public.

I think about Christopher and a lump forms in my throat.

He shouldn't have lied. He *really* shouldn't have lied. Not to me. But he needs to know what's going on with the plane. And he shouldn't be alone.

'Ariadne?' Mom's voice is desperate now.

'Sorry – I've got to go, Mom.'

'I need to talk to Blake – we need to go through some details—'

'I'll see you tomorrow, Mom.' I pause. 'Try to get some sleep.'

'Ariadne!'

'Bye, Mom.'

And then I hang up.

Chapter Twenty-Five

04.50 CDT
1-81

He's not hard to find. Apart from the occasional car, the highway is deserted. And he hadn't got very far.

Before I get to him, a pick-up drives past and Christopher sticks out his thumb but the truck doesn't stop. I'd be surprised if the driver even saw him.

I remember the thought I had the first time I saw him in the airport: *The kind of guy you walk right past.* And how, ironically, that was what made me stop and notice him. Because I liked it: how he wasn't trying to be the centre of attention, like most of the people do.

I dip the headlights and press on the brakes until the car's crawling beside him.

'You're going the wrong way,' I say.

Leda barks beside me, her paws up on the window ledge, her tail wagging.

'And if you're going to make a habit of hitchhiking, you're going to have to learn to be a bit more assertive.'

He keeps walking, not looking at me.

I stop the car and whisper in Leda's ear:

'Go get him.'

Leda jumps out of the window and runs up to Christopher.

He tries to ignore her but she jumps up at him so hard she nearly knocks him over. Eventually, Christopher stops walking, puts down his backpack and rubs her behind the ears.

I march up to him.

'You're an idiot,' I say.

'I know,' he replies.

'You do?'

'Yeah. I should have told you.'

'So why didn't you?'

He pauses for a second. 'I guess I've never been in a situation like this before.'

Our eyes catch.

'I mean,' he goes on. 'I've never had to explain something like this – not to someone—'

'Someone?'

He looks down at his feet.

'Like you,' he says.

'I'm not sure what you're saying…'

'Someone who matters.'

'Matters?'

He looks up. 'To me.'

Our eyes catch again for a second and this time I'm the one who can't look. I bow my head.

'Oh.'

'But I realised,' he says, 'when I was walking, that that's the reason I should have told you. It's because you matter – to me – that I should have told you the truth.'

He shakes his head and clenches and unclenches his fists like he's trying to get all the tension out of his body.

I take his hand and unfurl his fist.

'I'm sorry too,' I say. 'I'm sorry I kicked you out of the car.'

He looks at the back of his hand cradled in my palm like somehow his hand doesn't belong to him.

'It's okay,' he says.

'No, it's not okay. Not with everything that's going on – with the plane. With your dad.'

He doesn't answer.

I get out my cell, swipe open the page from the CNN news and place the phone in his hands.

'Have you seen this?'

He shakes his head.

And then he starts reading.

His face freezes. Then he takes a breath. His eyes go massive behind his glasses.

'The autopilot doesn't just get disconnected,' he says. 'This doesn't make any sense.'

I don't know what to say.

'And if it had got disconnected, Dad would have noticed. He's always checking things, even when he doesn't have to. I've seen him work.' He pauses. 'Dad doesn't get that stuff wrong.'

'Everyone gets things wrong sometimes,' I say gently.

He shakes his head violently. 'You don't know Dad. You don't know how he works.'

I think about Mom. About how, until two years ago, I'd never seen her lose a case. And how it took her months to get over it when she did. How every time something related to the case was mentioned in the news or someone we knew brought it up by mistake, she'd kind of go into herself.

Yeah, everyone messes up sometimes. Even those you think never will.

'Why don't you get back in the car,' I say gently. 'We'll drive to Knoxville as planned. Keep an eye on the news. You can call the number UKFlyer gave us, see if they have any more information.' I pause. 'Whatever happens, you shouldn't be on your own right now.'

He stares at me. Like properly stares.

'What is it?' I ask.

'You.'

'What about me?'

He keeps staring.

'*What about me*?' I ask again.

'You're so sure of everything.'

I laugh. 'Right now, I'm not sure of anything.'

'But you make it feel like it's going to be okay.'

I pause and look right at him.

'It *is* going to be okay.'

'You see?' he says. And then he shakes his head. 'I've never met anyone like you.'

'Thank you. I think. Now stop staring, it's embarrassing.'

But he doesn't stop staring. And the thing is, I don't really want him to. I want him to keep standing there, looking at me like he believes in me. Because right now, all I can think about is that I've screwed everything up. That Mom still doesn't know what's going on. That I'm scared to death that Blake won't show up on time, even for the wedding, regardless of his promises. And worse, that something has happened to him.

I step forward. Christopher's so close I can feel his warm breath on my skin. I stare right into his eyes.

'Just don't keep the truth from me ever again,' I say. 'Promise?'

Then I step back.

My whole body spins. More, even than when I was standing on the top of that rock. I can still feel his breath on my skin – I can feel how it felt when he was close.

'I promise,' he says.

'Good.'

Then I turn around and go back to the car.

He doesn't move.

'Are you coming?' I throw over my shoulder.

'Yes,' he mumbles.

And then I hear him pick up his backpack and stumble after me.

Chapter Twenty-Six

07.05 CDT
1-81

We drive for while, not saying much. Christopher slumps beside me, drifting to sleep. I look at the clock on the dashboard. If I push myself and keep driving, through Knoxville, to Nashville I'll make it in time for the rehearsal dinner. But what then? I'll have to stand there, on my own, in that yellow dress, being stared at by my family and Stephen's family and have to explain why Blake isn't with me. And worse, I'll have to explain that I still don't know where he is or whether he's even going to make it to the wedding. At least, if I don't show up, if they think Blake and I are still on our way, they can go on with the party and all the preparations and get through the night, thinking that by morning, we'll show up and that even if we've missed some of the stuff leading up to the wedding, we'll be there for the important part. The vows. The I dos. Blake's song.

And if, in the meantime, Blake gets to the rehearsal dinner and I'm not there – big deal? They can go ahead without me. They'll get over it.

I see a turn-off ahead and remember how this, too, was a detour Blake liked to take. How he spent more of his life taking detours than actually getting anywhere.

I take it as a sign and flip on the indicator.

'You like hiking?' I ask Christopher.

Leda barks, like she's answering for him. She has a tiny body and tiny legs but it's like she's got rocket fuel running through her veins. She can hike for hours, up the steepest hills, and not get tired.

'Christopher?'

But he's already asleep.

'I'll take that as a yes,' I whisper, taking the exit. 'We'll get some sleep and then I'll show you the coolest view in the states of Virginia, Tennessee and North Carolina combined.'

Christopher shifts slightly in his sleep. His head drops towards me.

He's in no rush to get to Atlanta, I think. His mom will still be there, whatever happens. And I'm not ready to say goodbye to him yet. Maybe that, in the end, is why I take the detour.

Chapter Twenty-Seven

13.00 CDT
Deer Ridge Trail,
Cherokee National Forest, NC

'Where the hell are we?'

Someone's nudging me. I try to swallow, but my throat's dry. My eyeballs gummy with tiredness. I can feel the afternoon sun pounding down on us.

'Air – what's going on?'

I rub my eyes and force them open.

Christopher's eyes dart around. One minute they're on me, the next they're taking in the dirt track and the map on the side of the road marking out the trail that will take us to the summit of Deer Ridge mountain.

I glance at the clock on the dashboard. 12 pm. We must have slept for hours.

If we'd followed Plan A, Christopher would be on a Greyhound heading to Atlanta by now and I'd be on my way to Nashville, in time for the rehearsal dinner.

But while Christopher was sleeping, when I decided to take that turning, I ditched Plan A.

'I thought we could do with a break,' I say.

'A break?' He looks down the winding mountain track behind us. 'There weren't any rest stops off the highway?'

'I wasn't looking for a rest stop.' I get out of the car and stretch my stiff legs. Leda jumps out too and runs around me in circles. Then she starts sniffing at the earth and wagging her tail. She remembers this place.

'You coming?' I ask Christopher.

'Coming where?'

'You'll see.'

'You're doing this again?'

'No jumping off high ledges this time, I promise.'

'Oh, thanks, I'm reassured.'

I tilt my head to one side and smile. 'Come on.'

Finally, Christopher gets out too. He's got a big crease mark from sleeping pressed up against his seatbelt.

'So where are we?' he asks.

'Deer Ridge.'

'And we're here because?'

'I want to show you something.'

He tries to smooth down his hair from where it's got all smushed in his sleep, only it makes it worse – though it makes him look kind of cute, a bit like Leda actually, a dishevelled kind of cute.

'I don't understand, Air. I thought you had to get to Nashville in time for the rehearsal dinner.'

'I decided not to go.'

His eyebrows shoot up. 'You decided not to go to the wedding?'

'No, I'm still going to the wedding. But if I show up tonight, without Blake, everyone's going to flip out. I want to give him some more time to get there. Otherwise the whole wedding will be ruined. Mom will send out a search party—'

'Perhaps a search party would be a good idea. For Blake.'

'What's that supposed to mean?'

It's the first time he's challenged me about how I'm going about finding Blake.

'It's been a long time, Air – for someone not to be in touch. Someone who's meant to be here already.'

Leda comes and sits at my feet and looks up at me.

I blink away Christopher's words and shake my head.

'Blake's going to show up. And in the meantime, I've got to let my family believe that we're coming.' I swallow hard. 'No search party.'

Christopher nods and then kneels down and rubs the soft spot on the top of Leda's head, a bit that's a lighter brown, like it's been bleached by the sun. Leda rests into him. She totally loves him.

'You're not sad you'll miss the dinner?'

'Sad? God no. I mean, of course, I should be there for Jude. But no, I hate those things. Dresses and sitting at a table for hours and being polite to relatives.' I pause. 'The only way I survive those things is if Blake's there.'

'You're fine about going into space but you're scared you won't survive a family dinner on your own?'

'Fear's subjective.'

'I guess so.'

'Anyway, it looks like Blake's not going to show for the dinner. Otherwise he would be there already. And I'm not showing up without him.'

'And if, for some reason, he does show up – and you're not there?'

I give Christopher a big smile. 'Win-win.'

'*Win-win*?'

'Everyone will be thrilled Blake's there. No one will mind that I'm not. Not really. I'll avoid the dinner. And

I'll still make it to the wedding, that's the main thing, right?'

'I think they'll mind that you're not there.'

'Maybe. But they'll get over it.' I step closer to him and touch his arm. He flinches a little and the top of his cheeks go pink. 'And you're in no rush to get to your mom, are you?'

He shakes his head. 'No rush at all.'

'So, I thought we could buy ourselves a few more hours.' I swallow. 'Before we say goodbye.'

He looks up at me.

'I'd like that.'

'So, you forgive me?' I ask.

'Forgive me?'

'For driving you off course when you were sleeping?'

'Do I have any choice?'

'Not really.'

'Well, then, I guess I forgive you.'

Christopher look up at the tall pines, at the fierce blue sky, at the mountain track I drove up this morning and then at the opening of the trail which leads up to Deer Ridge.

I look down at his flip-flops. 'You've got some sneakers, right?'

He nods. 'Why?'

'We're going for a walk.'

'A walk?'

'I want to show you something.'

I grab a bag of kibble from the boot of the car along with a water bottle and fill Leda's two bowls. She bounds past me and starts wolfing down the food. Then I grab a couple of cereal bars from the glove box and throw one at Christopher.

'We'll get a proper meal when we head back down the mountain. These should keep us going until then.' I reach further into the glovebox and pull out two foil wrapped rectangles and throw one to him. 'Oh, and for dessert.'

He pushes his glasses closer to his eyes and turns over the wrapper. 'Strawberry ice cream?'

I nod. 'From the Air and Space Museum. It's delicious.'

He scrunches up his nose.

'Don't knock it 'til you've tried it,' I say.

'Can't be worse than airplane food.'

He puts the cereal bar and the astronaut ice cream in the pocket of his shorts. Then he grabs his backpack and pulls out a pair of sneakers. As he's lacing them up, I say:

'Oh, and another thing.'

He stops lacing and looks up at me. 'Do I want to hear this?'

'You're going to do some talking. Walking means talking. Or it does in my family.' I look at the map at the side of the road. The squiggly green line mapping out the trail to the top of Deer Ridge.

'It was Dad's thing,' I say. 'He said it went back to ancient times. That when people had things weighing on their minds, they'd go out into nature and walk it out of their systems. When we were kids and he'd sense we were upset about something, he'd say: "Get on your hiking boots." And he'd take us off. Sometimes for a hike around DC. Sometimes we'd take the car and go into the woods, further out. But it worked. Even if we had to walk in silence for a few hours, sooner or later we'd open up to him and by the time we got back, things would better.'

216

It's the reason we first came to this place, as a family. We were driving to visit Grandpa in Nashville and Jude, Blake and I were arguing in the back seat. Dad swerved off the highway and drove us up here and made us hike to the top of Deer Ridge until we'd stopped bickering and started talking to each other properly. When we got back in the car, we were nice to each other the rest of the way to Nashville. Or maybe we were too tired from the hike to argue. Whatever, it worked.

'You're taking me on a hike up a mountain so that I'll talk?' Christopher asks.

'Kind of. The mountain's cool anyway. But yeah, you could do with talking. You don't do enough of it. Which is why you didn't tell me about your dad. And if I'm going to have you in my car and drive you all this way –' I swallow, my mouth still dry from sleep. 'If we're going to be friends – well, then you're going to have to start telling me stuff. That's how it works.'

Christopher ties a knot in his laces and then stands up.

Leda finishes her bowl of kibble, slurps some water and darts towards the trail. I put away her bowls, then I grab my telescope and swing it over my shoulder.

'Ready?' I say.

'You know that I've talked more to you since we left DC than I have to basically any other human being in my whole life, right?' Christopher says.

I think about how I've probably talked to him more than anyone else outside my family. And how that's a big deal too.

'I'm honoured,' I say.

He gives me a sideways smile. 'You should be.'

'And now you've warmed up, you can do some more talking.'

He shakes his head.

'Your brother's right, you know.'

My head snaps up.

'Excuse me?'

'You are FI – totally, unquestionably Fucking Infuriating.'

I smile. 'So that means you're coming?'

'Do I have a choice?'

'Nope.'

He smiles back, then reaches into the car, lifts his backpack onto his shoulder and steps towards me. I grab his hand and pull him towards the mouth of the trail.

Chapter Twenty-Eight

15.10 CDT
Deer Ridge Trail,
Cherokee National Forest, NC

For a long time, we don't actually do that much talking. It's good to be out of the car, listening to woodpeckers high up in the trees; to our breathing, deep and steady at the effort of the climb. Sometimes we stop and stare, catching a glimpse of a view through the branches, our hearts speeding up at the thought of what it will be like when we get to the top.

Leda keeps darting ahead of us and we have to call her back. She's running off all that excess energy from being cooped up in the car for all those miles. And she's excited to get to the top too. And there's something else I've noticed too. Whenever we stop in a place where Blake would stop too – stop with her, when they did this route together – it's like she's looking for him.

I brush away the thought. I don't want Blake in my head right now.

I stop and check my phone for the time. We've been walking for hours. It feels good to have left the world behind for a bit.

Before I put my phone away again I notice the reception bars.

'Thank God,' I say.

Christopher turns around. 'What is it?'

'Off grid.'

'Sorry?'

'No one can get in touch with us now, not until we get back to the car.' No messages from Mom. No panicking from Jude. No aching silence from Blake. And, though I wouldn't say it to Christopher, no news from the plane either. For now, we can put it all down.

I put my phone away.

'Come on, let's keep going, we're nearly halfway.'

'*Nearly* halfway? How long is this walk?'

'It's a hike, Christopher. Hikes take time.'

'Okay, fine. But if we're going to expend all this energy, I think we should stop for some of that delicious ice cream you mentioned,' Christopher says.

I swipe at his arm. 'Hey, I told you not to knock it.'

'I'm not. I could do with an ice cream break.'

It comes back to me. That ironic tone that British people have so that you're never quite sure if they're kidding or not.

'Okay,' I say. 'Let's have an ice cream break.'

He nods and smiles and we find a log to sit on and ceremoniously unwrap our foil parcels. Christopher takes a bite. He makes his jaw work really hard, like a toffee's got stuck between his molars. Then he swallows hard.

'Wow,' he says.

I roll my eyes.

'Seriously – wow. Strawberry polystyrene: who knew that that was what was missing from my life this whole time?'

'Hey!' I punch his arm again.

He holds his hands up. 'I'm joking, I'm joking. It does taste pretty good. In a weird kind of way.' He takes another bite.

We sit there, munching. Leda sniffs around at our feet for a while and then dashes into a bush after some critter or other.

Christopher pulls a bottle of water out of his backpack and we take it in turns to sip, like I do when I'm hiking with Dad.

Yeah, Dad would like Christopher. He'd make him laugh. And he'd like how calm he is. How he doesn't make a drama out of everything just for the sake of it.

'You must have seen some pretty amazing places,' I say. 'Travelling around with your dad for all those years, before you went to boarding school.'

'I guess so.'

'You didn't like it?'

'It was amazing – and I'm grateful, of course. I mean, what ten-year-old kid has been to the Taj Mahal and the Great Wall of China, Niagara Falls and the Galapagos Islands, and all the standard tourist places too – Venice, Paris, Berlin, Iceland…?'

'You've really been to all those places?'

'Those are just the highlights.'

'Wow, that's incredible.'

'I guess so.' He pauses. 'But I'd have swapped it all in a second…' His voice breaks off.

'For what?'

'It's going to sound stupid.'

'Try me.'

'To get to do some of the boring stuff.'

'The boring stuff?'

'Spending time at home. Waking up late on a Saturday morning and watching TV in my pyjamas. Ordering pizza with Dad. Just hanging out.'

'Well, you can come and do that with my family anytime. We have the local pizza delivery guy on speed dial.'

He looks up at me and his eyes go sad and I feel bad for making a joke when he was trying to tell me something.

'It's the everyday stuff that matters. More than the Taj Mahal, right?' I smile. 'Even though the Taj Mahal does sound pretty cool.'

He nods. 'It is.'

I hear voices behind us and then footsteps. A young couple walks past us. When they see us, they smile and nod their heads as a hello. I notice the woman's eyes lingering on me – I look down and realise that I'm still wearing Christopher's T-shirt and boxers. My face flushes red.

'Beautiful day,' the woman says.

'Yes,' Christopher answers.

I think about how, for the rest of the world, this is just another beautiful day. All those billions of people on earth haven't got a clue what's going on in my life – or Christopher's. How we're going through all this stress and worry, how a plane has dropped out of the sky, how Blake's disappeared off the face of the planet, and how that's turned our lives upside down, but for most people – like this couple – they'll never know. It doesn't touch them.

I get that feeling I sometimes get when I'm looking up through my telescope or when I'm sitting in the planetarium: a kind of sinking feeling as I realise how small we are. How, in the grand scheme of things, our lives are just a speck of dust in this huge universe.

'See you at the top,' the young man says and then they keep walking, holding hands, leaning their heads towards each other and picking up their conversation.

Leda runs after them and bounces around them in circles so they can't walk any further.

I put two fingers in my mouth and whistle.

'Leda! Back here!' I yell.

I go after her and grab her collar.

'Sorry.'

The man and the woman laugh and make a fuss of her.

'We don't mind,' the woman says.

'She likes to adopt people,' I say.

'Well, she's very charming.' The woman gives her another pat and stands up.

I wonder how things would have turned out for Leda if Blake, Jude and I hadn't found her that day at Leda Springs. Would anyone have picked her up? And how would her life have been different?

I pull her back towards Christopher and we both sit down beside him. She slumps her body over him and he gives her long strokes from under her chin right across her body to the base of her tail.

After a while, I say to him:

'You know what you said, back then, about not having talked to anyone as much as you have to me?'

He takes another sip of water, closes the lid, puts the bottle away.

'Yeah.'

'Is that really true?'

'Really true.'

'What about your dad? You spent all that time together growing up, travelling around the world. You guys must have shared so much.'

He leans back and looks up into the high branches of the pines.

'We were never really alone. Just the two of us, I mean. Like I said, we didn't do the everyday stuff. And when we were alone together, he didn't like to talk much.'

I wait for him to go on.

'Travelling around – airports and planes and visiting places that he thought would educate me; there were always people around. And noise. And activity. When he was at work, he was in official mode, welcoming passengers, joking with the air stewards, giving updates from the cockpit. When we were visiting places, he'd talk loads about the history of what we were seeing, kind of like a lecture, I suppose. And then he'd get tired and go quiet. Really quiet. When we were driving on our own or hanging out in a hotel room, he sometimes didn't say anything for hours.'

My family never stops talking about their feelings and probing into each other's business. Dad's the quietest one but even he likes to know what's going on with us.

'I guess it's kind of ironic,' he says. 'If you count up the hours, Dad and I have probably spent more time together than just about any father and son. But when I see other kids with their parents – even at boarding school, now – they seem to have a closer relationship than we do. It's like time doesn't really matter. Not if you're not really tuned into each other.'

Christopher coughs and then takes another sip of water, like his throat's sore from all the talking.

'That sounds lonely,' I say. 'Being with one person all that time and not feeling close to them.'

His eyes go far away. 'Yeah, I guess it is.'

'And you didn't try to talk to him?'

'Maybe, when I was younger, but I guess I soon worked out that he preferred not to chat about personal stuff, or boring, everyday stuff. So, I stopped asking questions. Let him do his thing. It was easier.'

He looks down into his hands.

'I think he liked it that way,' he says.

'What do you mean?'

'Not being alone with me. Not talking to me.'

I feel a lump in my throat.

'I'm sure he cared about you, Christopher. He was crap at showing it, that's all.'

'Maybe.'

'He was probably so wrapped up in showing you all this cool stuff that he forgot to check in. And maybe he felt guilty – about things not working out with your mom—'

'Or maybe we just aren't suited.'

'Suited?'

'Just because he's my dad, it doesn't mean we're made to get along.'

I'd never thought of that. Sure, kids and parents and siblings sometimes don't get on. But they're still family. They're biologically wired to be together. That should count for something, shouldn't it?

Leda comes back out from a bush, her fur knotted with leaves and twigs and pine needles. She bounds up to Christopher, puts her paws up on his knees and licks at his hands.

I think about getting up and walking on but words push up my throat.

225

'He just needs to see you, Christopher,' I say. 'I mean, really see you.'

He looks at me and blinks.

'Like I see you,' I say. 'Or the bits you've let me see anyway. Because I reckon that if he did then he'd want to spend every second being with you and talking to you and getting to know you.'

Once my words are out, I can hear them echoing between us and I'm scared that I've said too much and totally put him off. And worse: that he's not going to want to tell me any more stuff.

'I'm sorry—' I start.

He looks up at me and shakes his head.

'Don't be,' he says. 'Don't be sorry for anything.'

For a while, we sit there, staring at the pine needles and the track ahead of us. Then I put my hand on his.

'Shall we keep going?' I ask.

He nods.

We get up, brush down our shorts and pick up the trail, Leda jumping up and down between us.

Chapter Twenty-Nine

17.54 CDT

It's good to make progress, to feel the mountain disappearing under our feet. The trees start thinning the higher up we go and there's a change in the air too, how it makes my head go lighter.

Leda keeps darting ahead of us or disappearing under bushes, chasing critters.

'So, you were really fine with it, not going to school growing up?' I ask.

'We're still talking about me?'

'We're not nearly done.'

'FI,' he whispers.

'I'm just getting to know you. It's what people do.'

'Right.'

'So, tell me, I'm interested. It must have been weird, having your dad as your school. Not going to classes with kids your age and stuff.'

'It was all I knew,' he says. 'And Dad said I was lucky. That by travelling, I was seeing the world for real, not just in books. He said that I was going to "The School of Life".' He puts on a grand voice. 'I guess I believed him.'

I realise that's what I haven't been able to put my finger on – that weird contradiction in Christopher, how part of him seems totally wise about the big world stuff, how calm he is, how he seems to let things float off him, stuff that rubs the rest of us up the wrong way, but how he's totally clueless at the same time. Because, I guess he's never had the chance to be a kid. To make friends. To have a crush on a girl and ask her out and then break up. All that mindless shit that takes up every waking minute of most of a kid's life growing up.

And for a second, I kind of envy him.

'That's allowed – travelling around rather than going to class?' I ask.

'Dad had to prove that I was following a curriculum, covering the basics – but as long as that was in place, it was fine.'

'And did it work? Your Dad's philosophy? Do you understand life?'

'What? You can't feel the deep wisdom radiating off me?'

'Yeah, I can, actually.' I pause. 'It's just—'

'It's not enough, right? That's what you're thinking.'

'No—'

'I mean, what's the point in learning to meditate with Tibetan monks if you can't even talk to a girl.'

'You are talking to a girl.'

'Under duress.'

'Really?'

'No. Not anymore.'

'Not *anymore*?'

'It's hard for me – at first. To make small talk. To walk up to someone and start a conversation.'

His shoulders slump and his pace slows, like his thoughts are weighing him down.

'Was it hard starting school, after all that time?'

He nods but doesn't look up.

'A boys' boarding school, you said?'

He nods again.

'I've heard those can be rough. Dad went to one here in the States. He's still scarred by the experience.'

'It's not that bad. They leave me alone, mostly. I'm lucky I joined in the sixth form; everyone's grown up a bit by then. We get our own rooms. And if you do your work the teachers leave you alone too.'

'So, you haven't made any friends then?'

'I'm not sure.'

'What do you mean, you're not sure?'

'I sit next to people in class. And at meal times. I do projects with other guys. Sometimes we talk in the TV room. If that's having friends, then I guess so, yeah.'

That's not having friends. Not even close.

I step towards him and take his hand lightly. He stares down at my fingers.

'We're friends,' I say.

'We are?'

'Of course.'

'We haven't known each other for long.'

'It's like you said, Christopher – knowing someone isn't about time.'

He looks up at me. His eyes are such a pale grey and so wide it hurts to look at them.

'I said that?' he asks.

'Yeah, you did.'

I stop walking, put my hands on my hips and bend over. The air's getting even thinner and we've been walking fast. Every time I look up, my head spins.

'You okay?' Christopher asks.

'Yeah – just catching my breath.'

229

I close my eyes and listen. To my breathing. To Christopher's. And beyond that, to the long, thin silence between the mountain ranges.

Then my eyes dart open.

'Where's Leda?'

I spin round.

Christopher looks round too. 'She was here a moment ago—'

'When?' I snap at him. 'When did you last see her?'

'I – I don't know. She kept darting off. But then she'd come back. I don't know – a few minutes?'

'Shit.'

'Dogs know how to come back, right? She'll smell her way back to us.'

I shake my head. Tears dart into my eyes. The dizziness gets worse.

'She gets confused – she's not good at finding her way back to places.'

Christopher looks down the path where we came and then back up to where it keeps climbing up the mountain.

'Shit, shit, shit.' I kick at a stone.

Leda's tough and she can keep going for hours, but the thinness of the air up here will be getting to her. She'll get disoriented, especially if she can't find us.

'I bet she's at the top already,' Christopher says.

I keep shaking my head. 'She could be anywhere.'

'Yeah. But she knows the path, right? You said you brought her here before – with Blake and your dad. Don't dogs remember the trails they've walked, like for ever?'

'You've seen Leda – she's a total nutcase. Who knows what she remembers and doesn't remember.'

'She's a dog, Air. She's hard wired to remember.' His voice is low and steady and it calms me down for a second. 'We'll keep walking. And we'll find her.'

'But how do you know – what if she's run back down or thrown herself off one of the ledges or got stuck in a bush?'

He steps forward and this time he's the one who takes my hand.

'We've got to make a decision and I reckon that the best decision, right now, is to keep walking. If she's not up there, we'll turn back.'

I take a slow breath in and out to calm myself.

'Okay?' He searches my face.

I take another breath. 'Okay.'

Chapter Thirty

20.07 CDT
Deer Ridge Summit

It takes us twice as long to get to the top than it should have done – every time we saw a trail leading off the main path or heard a rustle in the bush we detoured to check whether Leda was there.

I've shouted and whistled so hard and so long that my mouth feels like it's on fire.

'Leda!' I yell, as we come out into a clearing.

And then we both stop.

It's there. The summit. The long, smooth plane at the top of Deer Ridge.

I hear Christopher take in a sharp breath.

'Wow.'

The sun sets early here – it's already beginning to sink behind the mountain range, a huge orange ball.

And then I snap back into the present. I scan the ridge. But she's still not there.

My stomach turns inside out. Maybe we missed her on the way up. Maybe some crazy mountain animal got hold of her. Or maybe she tried to make her way back down to the car.

A bit further along, I see the couple who walked past us. They're sitting on a slab of stone looking out at the sunset.

'I'll go and ask them if they've seen her,' Christopher says gently.

I don't answer. I know it's stupid to be pissed at him but he's the one who said to come up here. And I trusted him. And she isn't here. And I know it's not his fault but I can't help feeling angry at the time we've lost.

When I don't answer, Christopher walks off.

I turn away from him and look back out at the mountains – layers of blue tissue paper thinning out towards the sky, the sun almost gone now. If we're going to make it back to the car before dark we need to start heading down now.

Which is what Jude said to Blake the last time the three of us came up here.

'We need to get back – it's dangerous, being out here after nightfall. We won't see the path.'

'We're here to see the stars, Jude – dark's kind of the point.'

'You didn't tell me that when we set off,' Jude said.

Blake and I had found that when it came to Jude, seeking forgiveness was usually better than asking permission. She worries about things. If we told her the details of our plans, she'd put a stop to them before we even got started.

'It'll be worth it,' Blake said to Jude, his smile wide and charming. 'You only live once, sis.'

Jude hung around for another half hour and then got cross and stomped off back down the mountain by herself. And took a wrong turning. And got like a million bug bites because it was bug season. And Blake and I got down the mountain before her and when she joined us, she was furious. Because if she'd waited for us, she'd have been fine. And because, once again, she felt left out.

I feel a pang of guilt now. At how she must have felt all those times when Blake and I went off together. And how even when she was with us she was always out on a limb by herself.

And the thing was that, most of the time, Jude was right about things. Blake's decisions were crazy and irresponsible and ended up inconveniencing people and costing Mom and Dad loads of money they didn't have when they had to bail him out. If it was Blake getting married, Jude would have turned up on time. She'd have turned up earlier than anyone. Made sure everything was organised. Done a load of work so that his day was perfect. And even if she didn't like Leda, she would never have let her get lost.

Maybe all that fun, charming, who-gives-a-shit kind of attitude isn't so cool. Maybe it's more people like Jude that we need, not Blake. Dependable people. People who make plans and stick to them and show up and keep each other safe.

I close my eyes and swallow hard. God, everything's such a mess.

'Hey, Air!' Christopher calls over to me.

I open my eyes and look over to him.

The couple's standing up now, putting their backpacks back on.

Christopher's kneeling by the rock.

He waves me over.

We have to find Leda. We don't have time to look at the view. To stop.

'Air! Come over here!' he yells.

'We've got to get back down the mountain,' I call out as I run towards him.

But he doesn't budge.

When I get to him, he smiles.

'What?' I say.

He nudges his head to his side and looks down.

I don't see anything at first. But then I catch sight of her tail caught up in a tangle of yellow leaves, the exact same colour as her fur.

I crumple onto my knees and throw my arms around her.

Her body's limp but she's breathing hard.

'When she got up here, she ran around like a crazy thing for about a minute and then flopped down and fell asleep. Dead to the world,' the young guy says.

I keep hugging her, burying my face in her rough fur, kissing her. A warm tear drops from my cheek onto her belly.

'You silly, silly dog,' I say.

'Well, she sure is a strong one – for a little dog,' the woman says.

'Yeah, she is,' I say, gulping back more tears.

I lift her into my arms. She stirs slightly but stays asleep.

'She'll be too tired to walk back down,' I say.

Christopher crouches beside me. 'I'll carry her. She's light.'

I look up at him, my eyes swimming, and say. 'You knew she'd be here?'

He shakes his head. 'A lucky guess.'

'We've got a headlamp – should get us through the last bit of the trail if it gets dark,' the man says. 'If you're happy to walk back with us.'

I look at the couple properly for the first time. They're totally equipped for the hike. Proper hiking boots. Hiking backpacks. Water bottles slotted into the side. Hats. The kind of clothes that protect you from the sun and dry off quick if you're caught in the rain and stop you from sweating too much all at once. If Jude and Stephen were ever to hike, this is how they'd do it.

'Thanks,' I say, 'that would be great.'

Christopher looks up. 'Would you mind if we took a few minutes – to take all this in?' He looks around the mountain range. 'If it's no trouble?'

The man and the woman smile at him. 'Sure – you've walked all the way up, you should get to enjoy the view.'

'Thanks,' Christopher says.

Still keeping hold of Leda's sleeping body, he puts his backpack down. Then he looks at me and holds out his hand.

I shift my telescope onto my other shoulder and take his hand and we walk towards the highest point on the ridge, to the point where it feels as though you're closer to the sky than to the earth.

For a long time, we sit on the ridge, Leda sleeping between us. Occasionally she twitches and lets out a small whine but she stays asleep.

We stare out at the sunset.

Christopher goes really quiet beside me.

'It's pretty awesome up here, isn't it?' I say.

He doesn't answer, he just keeps staring out at the sky.

'Blake wrote a song up here once – about how it was like we could touch heaven.' I pause. 'Which is kind of cool…if you believe in heaven, that is.'

He's still quiet, too quiet.

A moment ago, he was really excited about finding Leda and about coming over here to look at the view. I don't understand what happened.

The sun is setting fast now, a ball of fire dropping behind the mountain range. It'll be dark soon.

I look over at the couple. They've got their backpacks on.

'We should probably get going,' I say. 'They're waiting for us.'

But Christopher still doesn't answer. It's like he's in some kind of trance.

'Christopher?'

And that's when I see it. A light aircraft, more like a glider than an airplane, so thin it could be made of paper. It's sweeping between the mountains, its wings tilted to one side. And then it disappears. Christopher doesn't take his eyes off it. Or the space where it disappeared.

'Oh, Christopher…'

He takes off his glasses and bows his head between his knees. His shoulders start shaking. And then his whole body.

A few minutes ago, he was fine. He was so happy to have found Leda. Seeing that plane, being up here, so close to the sky, must have flipped some sort of switch.

He's shaking uncontrollably now.

Leda's head shoots up. She nudges Christopher.

He doesn't acknowledge her. His shoulders slump down further. And then he starts crying. Loud, deep sobs that seem to come from somewhere deep inside him.

'Hey, hey, it's going to be okay.' I put my arm around his shoulders.

He shakes me off so hard I nearly fall backwards.

'Christopher?'

'It's not going to be okay,' he says.

'They're still investigating—'

He shakes his head.

'He's not coming back.'

'You can't say that.'

Tears drop down his cheeks. 'He's not coming back and I never even got the chance to show him...' He lets out a gulp.

'Show him?'

'That I could be someone. That I could make him proud of me.'

'He *was* proud of you.'

He shakes his head. 'You don't know my dad. I was a disappointment, Air. His only son and I was a disappointment.'

'I don't know your dad, but I know you. You've sat beside me for two days straight and that's long enough to know that you're the kind of guy any dad would be proud of – should be proud of. And I get that he gave you a hard time but that's on him, Christopher, not on you. We think parents know what's best for us, but most of the time they're making it up as they go along – like we are. And they make mistakes. Big mistakes.' I pause. 'Even your dad.'

My words are just bouncing off him. He's not ready to hear them, not yet.

I look over at the couple. They're still standing there, waiting for us.

'Look, why don't we get off the mountain. Get some food. Then we can talk properly.'

He shakes his head.

'I can't.'

'You can't what?' I ask.

'I can't move. I don't want to move.'

'Christopher?'

He looks up at me, his eyes red.

'Just go. Leave me up here. I'll work things out.'

'Work things out? Seriously, Christopher? You're miles from anywhere. No. I'm not going to leave you at the top of a mountain after dark.'

His shoulders start shaking again. 'I can't do this anymore.'

I get then that he's serious. That unless I physically drag him down the mountain, he's not going to budge.

'Well, I'm not leaving you here,' I say.

He doesn't respond.

I get up and run over to the couple. Leda stays with Christopher, her small body pressed up against his like she's trying to pin him down; like she's scared he's going to drop off the edge of the mountain.

'Is everything okay?' the woman asks.

'Not really.' I look over at Christopher. 'We're going to have to stay up here for a little longer.'

The man and woman exchange a glance.

'You can go – you should go,' I say. 'We'll work it out. I've walked this trail before.'

The man puts down his backpack. 'No. We can wait.'

'Really – you don't have to do that, we'll be fine,' I say.

The woman touches my arm. 'We're in no hurry. We'll stay here and enjoy the night sky.'

I want to throw my arms around them and thank them – for not leaving me up here alone. For being here when everything's falling apart.

'Thank you,' I say.

'Sure,' the woman says.

Then I walk back to Christopher and sit down beside him. Leda's head is resting in his lap but her tail's twitching: she knows that something's wrong.

'You can take as long as you like,' I say. 'But I'm not leaving without you. None of us are. We're going to wait here until you're ready.'

He doesn't answer but I see his shoulders relax a bit and he puts his glasses back on.

And then we wait.

And we watch the sky.

Until the sun's disappeared.

Until the sky goes from red to grey to dark blue to black. Until the stars come out. Until the night noises start to echo around us. Owls. Deer. The wind in the pines. Until it starts to get cold. Goosebumps flare along my arms. The wind picks up.

After a while, I lean my head against his shoulder and, this time, he doesn't push me away.

When the sky's totally dark and the stars are bright, I take out my telescope and hand it to him.

'Here,' I say.

Because I don't know what else to do. To make him feel better. I just know that it's what I'd do if I felt like my life was falling apart: I'd look up at the night sky, at the stars.

He hesitates and then he takes the telescope and presses it to his eye. I let him watch for a few minutes. Then, I say:

'Sometimes, it takes time to get to the people we're really meant to be with.'

He puts down the telescope and turns to face me, his brow scrunched up. His eyes are still puffy from crying but I can feel that he's calmed down.

'You've spent all these years with your dad. And you talk about how you feel like you didn't really belong. And now, with everything that's going on, you've been forced to find your mom again—'

His eyes go wide. '*You* forced me to find my mum again.'

'I guess I kind of did. But what I mean is – whether it was me or what's going on with the plane or whatever, maybe it's meant to be?'

I can't believe I'm even using this language. I don't believe in *meant to be*. Blake's the one who's into that superstitious stuff. How life's full of signs. How the universe has a purpose for us.

'Finding your mom could be a good thing. A really good thing. Maybe you're more like her – maybe she'll get you. I love both my parents but I'm way more like Dad. Mom's amazing – totally amazing. She's a kickass attorney for the White House and she's always there for us and she has like a million different skills and talents. But when I'm with Dad, it's like my whole body relaxes. He makes me feel like I belong.'

'Mom left,' he says.

'But now she wants to see you, right?'

'Only because I called.'

'Maybe that's true. Or maybe there's a whole load of reasons why you guys haven't been together. I know it's not my place to say this stuff. But I want you to know that it's not on you – the fact that you've never had anyone get you, or see you for who you are. You just haven't met the person who will make you feel like you belong. And it could be your mom.'

He looks at me, his eyes swimming.

'Dad didn't want me to see her.'

'What?'

'I asked him once: why we didn't visit. I knew other kids who had parents who weren't together and they split their time between their mum and dad, even if their parents hated each other.' He swallows hard. 'He said she didn't deserve to be in my life.'

'Wow, he really said that?'

'He said that when she left me with him, she made her choice. That she doesn't get to change her mind. Dad's black and white about stuff like that. He has such high standards for himself and he holds other people to them too. He believes in people doing the right thing, no matter how hard it is.'

'Sometimes life's more complicated than that though, right? Sometimes people mess up.'

'Dad doesn't have time for people to mess up.'

'You think she tried to get in touch with him? That she wanted to reach out to you? I mean, it's been seventeen years, right? That's a long time. People change. She's still your mom. She'd still be thinking about you.'

'I don't know. Maybe. Whenever I asked Dad questions about Mum, he clammed up. So, I stopped talking about her. And I guess I thought he knew best – and—' his voice chokes up. 'Oh God.'

'And?'

'And I didn't want to hurt him. He's the one who's always been there for me.'

I want to remind Christopher about what he said about his dad: that although he was always around, he never spent proper time with Christopher; that he didn't make him feel like he belonged, or that he was valued. And that Christopher has a right to find someone who gives him those things. Everyone does.

'I think you should see her, Christopher.'

'I don't know.' He looks down again. 'I don't know.'

'Look, I get that you think that you'd be betraying your dad. And that it feels totally crappy, especially right now, with everything that's going on. But I stand by what I said. That there are people out there who we're meant to be with – sometimes the people we least expect. It could be your mom. That's all I'm saying.' I pause. 'Or it could be someone else – someone who's not even related to you.'

'Someone else?'

'You're amazing, Christopher. And whatever your dad said, you're leading a big life already – because of who you are. I see that.'

Very slowly, he takes my hand and brings it up to his mouth. He kisses the space above my knuckles and, for a second, he closes his eyes.

We stay for a while longer, staring out at the dark sky and then, very slowly, he puts down my hand and stands up.

'I'm ready now,' he says.

I look back at the couple and give them a wave. It blows my mind, how total strangers can make things feel better when your life's been turned upside down. How, a moment ago, Christopher was a stranger too and how, right now, there's no one I feel closer to.

Leda gets to her feet. She stretches out her limbs and then does a little jump.

We both laugh, watching her, the tension of the last few minutes flooding out of our bodies.

'I guess she won't need to be carried,' I say.

Christopher leans over and strokes her back. 'I guess not.'

Then I pick up the telescope, Christopher goes over to get his backpack and we set off down the mountain again: two kids who only met a few hours ago, with a crazy dog bounding in front of us and a couple of strangers who've basically just saved our skin.

The whole way down, all these thoughts and feelings crash around in my body and I can't make sense of how they're meant to fit together. I think about Blake and where the hell he is and whether I'm even going to make it to the wedding. I think about what Christopher's going through and how, if his dad really is dead, if his mom's the only one left, his life is never going to be the same again. And though I know I shouldn't even be thinking about it with all this crap going on, my mind can't help going back to how, a moment ago, he held my hand and pressed it to his lips.

My heart flutters like a butterfly is trapped under my ribcage. And in this moment, I'd give anything for this feeling to go on for ever.

Chapter Thirty-One

21.16 CDT
Burger King Rest Stop, I-81, TN

We're so hungry that we wolf down our burgers and fries without talking. We're kind of talked out after our walk up the mountain. We fed bits of burger to Leda because I couldn't be bothered to go back to the car to get the fancy food Blake makes me give her. Now she's lying on Christopher's lap, fast asleep, her teddy bear head resting on her paws. Christopher has totally got this service dog thing nailed: none of the staff even questioned us when we brought Leda in.

When he finished eating, Christopher ripped off one side of the brown paper bag our food came in and started folding down the edges. Every now and then he stops folding and gives Leda a rub behind the ears.

'You two suit each other,' I say.

Christopher looks up and brushes his straggly hair out of his eyes.

'What?'

'You and Leda. You go well together.'

He gives me a sideways smile. 'What – small and scrappy and kind of irritating?'

'Small and scrappy – and not to be underestimated,' I say.

He laughs. 'I'll take that.'

'You should get a dog. When you go back to England.'

My words hang between us and from the way his brow scrunches up I wish I could take them back. Everything is so messed up right now that it's wrong to imagine anything concrete. Maybe he'll never even go back to England.

'Boarding schools don't allow pets,' he says. 'Not for the students anyway.'

'You could try the service dog act. You've got it nailed, you know?'

He smiles for the first time since he had his breakdown, up on Deer Ridge.

'The English are a bit more cynical about that kind of thing,' he says.

'Hey, are you saying that we Yanks are dumb?'

'No. Just more generous in what you're willing to believe.'

'Well, one day, whatever, you should have a dog. You're a dog person.'

He reaches down and gives Leda a kiss between the ears. 'The problem is, she's set the bar high. It'll be hard to find a dog that lives up to Leda.'

As Christopher's hair falls over his face into Leda's fur I realise that the colour is so similar – a kind of sandy, golden blond with bits of caramel and bits of brown woven in – that it's hard to tell where Christopher's hair ends and where Leda's fur starts.

Leda nestles deeper into his lap, pressing her head into his stomach and Christopher goes back to folding his brown paper bag.

I watch them for a moment and then, when Christopher goes back to folding his brown paper, I look around us.

I look at this ugly diner with its strip lighting and its plastic chairs and its smell of fryer grease.

I look out of the scratched windows, past our booth and out onto the highway, trucks and cars rushing past, all on their way to some life or another.

And then I think about the rehearsal dinner. Those long tables with white tablecloths. Mom's heirloom roses nodding their heads in tall vases. Yellow silk bows tied around the chairs. Everyone there except me and Blake. And although it should feel wrong, me sitting in this dingy fast food joint with a guy I've only known for a few hours when I should be there with the people I love – it doesn't. Right now, sitting here, watching Christopher folding that paper bag, Leda on his lap, the restaurant nearly empty except for us, it feels like there's nowhere else in the world I should be.

He stops folding and looks up. He pushes his glasses closer to his eyes, like he needs to see me more clearly. His eyes still look a bit red. Whenever my mind goes back to those hours up on the mountain and how scared I was that Christopher would never agree to come back down with me. Panic rises up my throat. I don't know what I would have done if he hadn't come back with me.

'Will you teach me?' I ask Christopher.

'Teach you?'

'To make something – out of paper?'

He frowns. 'Seriously?'

'Seriously.'

'Why?'

'Because I want to know. The things you make are amazing.'

And I want to take a bit of you with me, I think. But I don't say it out loud because I know it will sound cheesy and will probably freak him out. And me. It's not the kind of thing I say. Not to boys who aren't my brother.

'The life of an astronaut can be pretty boring,' I say. 'It will be good to have an activity to pass the time.'

'The life of an astronaut – *boring*?'

'I once heard someone say that the most exciting jobs are ninety per cent boring and ten per cent exhilarating. That you need all the boring to get to the exciting.'

'I suppose I get that.'

'So, will you show me?'

'Sure.'

He shifts Leda off his lap and puts her on the floor. She moans a little but then goes back to sleep. Then he comes around and sits beside me in the booth. His thighs brush my bare legs.

'What are you doing?' I ask.

'It'll be easier to show you if I'm sitting next to you – that way you don't have to watch me folding upside down.'

'Oh, right, of course.'

'So, first things first. You need to choose your material.' His voice is strong and confident – like he's enjoying being in charge for once.

'My material?'

'I only ever work with found paper. Airline tickets. Receipts. Napkins – though I wouldn't advise those, they're a bit floppy. Flyers. Posters. That kind of thing. Something that speaks to you.'

'I don't have any paper with me.'

'Then you need to find something.'

'Here?' I ask, looking around.

'Yep, here. It's part of the challenge.'

I look around the restaurant and then I see a noticeboard by the restroom. There's a poster that catches my eye. It has an acoustic guitar on the front.

'Okay,' I say and walk over to the noticeboard.

The poster is out of date so I don't feel bad taking it. It's advertising a concert – this old guy who's known for having this really amazing technique when he plays the guitar: he uses it as several instruments. The side as a drum. The chords to makes sounds like a cello or a harp. Blake's talked about him loads. Says he'd love to get some lessons from him one day.

I bring the poster back to the table.

'Perfect,' Christopher says.

Then he pulls out a piece of printed paper from his backpack. I notice that it has all the booking details for the flight he was meant to take to Oregon with his dad.

'So, what are we going to make?' he asks.

'I have to choose that too?'

'Yep. You're in charge of the material and the subject.'

I look past him again at the highway and above it, at the sky. There's a haze of orange from the light pollution but above it, I can see a smattering of stars. But no moon. Not the night before an eclipse.

'Can we make the moon?' I ask.

'Wow, you don't make it easy, do you?'

'The moon's hard?'

'The moon doesn't have any edges. We're going to have to fold our papers into a globe. That's pretty advanced.'

'Oh.'

'But you chose your subject – so we'll go with it.' He looks at me and winks. 'Plus, you don't strike me as the kind of girl who likes the easy option. So, the moon it is.'

I bite my lip, feeling weirdly nervous. 'Okay.'

'Right, follow me,' Christopher says. 'One step at a time.'

At first, it's not too difficult. He folds his paper down the middle and I copy him. Then he folds another side in and I copy that. My poster paper is a bit stiffer than his, which makes it harder, but I try to get the folds smooth and accurate. As our papers get smaller – as his folds get more intricate – I start losing my hold on the model I'm making. Folds keep bouncing back up and my corners aren't nearly as sharp as his. And that's when I see it. How making things really small and strong is way more challenging than making big models. It's more intricate. It's more beautiful. And it's damn hard.

I can feel my cheeks flushing as I concentrate, but the harder I try the more it falls apart.

'I'm crap at this.' I push my model away to the middle of the table.

'Hey, we've only just got started.'

'No, we haven't. We've been folding for ages. And I can't do it. Not like you.'

I look over at his model – all those sharp corners, the paper forming a beautiful white globe. And then I look at mine, this misshapen blob with bits sticking out of it. Even the colour of the paper looks wrong because one side of the paper was black so my moon's this weird monochrome.

'Hey – you nearly got it,' he says.

He leans past me and picks up my paper moon. I can feel his breath on my neck as he gently pulls and pushes at the folds in my model with his delicate fingers. It makes me feel a bit like when I watch Jude playing the piano or Blake finding the chords on his guitar: it's beautiful and effortless and totally out of my reach.

'There,' he says, handing it to me.

It does look better – at least it's vaguely spherical. But it's not a patch on his.

The backs of my eyes sting.

'It's pretty pathetic, right? I want to study engineering – I want to fly to the moon – and I can't even make a paper model.'

'It's your first try, Air. And it's not really a big deal. It's just paper.'

'It's not just paper.' I poke at my model. 'It was meant to be the moon. A beautiful moon.'

He puts his hand over mine to stop me from poking at my model.

'You're the first person who's ever asked me to teach them how to fold paper – you know that, Air?'

I look up at him. 'I am?'

'Yep.'

'Your dad never asked?'

'*My Dad*?' He laughs. 'No. Never.' He places my moon in the palm of his hand and holds it up, inspecting it like it's some kind of special jewel rather than a scrunched up old poster.

'Can I have this?' he asks.

'Seriously?'

'As a memento.'

'A memento of what?'

'My first student.'

'Oh, so I'm your student now?'

He blushes. 'My friend.'

I nod. 'A misshapen paper moon from your friend. Okay.'

He takes the small moon and puts it on the table next to his perfect white moon. Then he takes both of them and places them in a small pocket in the front of his backpack.

I let out a long yawn. Suddenly, every part of my body feels tired. My limbs and eyes are heavy.

'You look really tired,' he says.

I nod. 'Long day.'

'Long *days*,' he says.

He's right. We've been on the road together for nearly two days now.

I nod and yawn again. I try to stretch to snap out of the tiredness but it doesn't work. I slump back down in my seat.

'You should get some rest,' he says, turning back to me. 'Some proper sleep. You've got a long drive tomorrow to Nashville and you haven't stopped.'

'I slept a bit in the car this afternoon.'

'Not long enough. And car sleeping isn't proper sleeping. We drove past a motel on the way here. Why don't we get a room?'

'Why don't we get a room?'

His whole faces flushes pink. He pushes up his glasses.

'That's not what I meant – I was thinking that it would be good to have a place to crash. Somewhere with a proper bed.' He gulps and his eyes water. 'Don't worry, I'll sleep on the couch or the floor or whatever. I can even sleep in the car if you like. I think you should get some proper rest. Especially before the wedding.'

Staying in a roadside motel with an English guy I hardly know. It's probably the last scenario I had in mind when I pictured the eve of my sister's wedding.

'Okay,' I say.

'Good.'

I look up at him. 'And thanks.'

'For what?'

'For looking out for me.'

He blinks at nods and then smiles. 'Come on, let's go.'

He stands up, hitches his backpack on, gives Leda a little nudge, scoops her up into his arms and then holds out his hands.

'Ready?'

I nod and take his hand.

DAY 3
MONDAY 21ST AUGUST, 2017

Chapter Thirty-Two

03.00 CDT
Roadway Inn Motel, I-81, TN

I lift Leda's small body from where it's resting against my arm and swing my legs out of bed. She nestles in closer to Christopher. Yes, we ended up sharing a bed – with a wall of pillows and Leda between us. It was the only room left in this crummy motel. There wasn't a couch and although Christopher valiantly offered to sleep on the floor, I didn't want to be responsible for him contracting any diseases from his contact with a carpet which, I'm pretty certain, hasn't been cleaned properly since the last solar eclipse.

The walls are yellow with cigarette stains. I can hear people talking in the room to the left of us and the TV blaring to the right of us, and everything smells. The sheets. The carpet. The walls. But we needed to sleep. So, after we'd eaten our fries and burgers from the Burger King down the road, we crashed here.

And I did sleep, for a few hours. Like the dead. But then I had a dream about Mom banging on the door and finding me in here with this guy she's never met rather than showing up at the rehearsal dinner and totally flipping out. Which I guess she'd have a right to do.

Everything about the last two days has been totally screwed up.

Before going to sleep last night, I left a voicemail for Dad, apologizing that Blake and I hadn't made it to the rehearsal dinner. I knew Dad's cell would go straight to voicemail; he hates talking on the phone. I also know that he checks his messages and that he'd pass it on to Mom. And that, somehow, a voicemail would go down better than a text – and would definitely go down better than me trying to explain to Mom, who probably hadn't got over the fact that we'd missed the breakfast at Louis's. Plus, I was banking on Dad picking up on the fact that I needed his help. He knows I come to him when I feel I can't go straight to Mom. And he doesn't mind being the punching bag instead of me. Taking her flipping out and shouting and stomping around so that she gets it out of her system and she's calmed down a bit before talking to me. He doesn't mind because he totally loves Mom and he gets that the only reason she reacts like that is because she cares so much.

As I sit on the edge of the bed, I whisper, 'I'm sorry, Dad,' hoping that wherever he is and whatever he's doing right now – sleeping hopefully – he knows how much I love him and that I'm grateful for all the crap I know he'll have taken from Mom.

The curtains of the motel room don't close. It's still dark out there. I look over at Christopher, sleeping. Leda's rearranged her body since I got out of bed and is now totally nestled into him. Yeah, Mom would totally flip if she found me sleeping in a bed with Christopher but she doesn't know how I couldn't have got through all this without him. How, with Blake missing and her, Dad and Jude in Nashville, he's been family.

I grab my telescope and head to the door. I need to get some air.

As I press down the handle, Leda lifts her head and looks up at me, her eyes dark pools in the half-light of the room.

I pat my thigh lightly, hoping she might join me. I could do with company. But she nestles back into Christopher's body.

'Wow, so that's where your loyalties lie, hey buddy?' I whisper.

She lifts her head again for a second and then snuggles in even closer to Christopher.

The thing is, I don't mind that Leda loves Christopher. That she's got someone now too. And that she understands, in that way that dogs do, that he's a good guy.

My throat goes tight. In a few hours, we're both going to have to say goodbye to him. And I'm not sure I'm ready for that.

I sit on the concrete steps outside the door to our motel room and look up at the strange, moonless night. There are a few stars but the sky's getting lighter already. I get out my telescope and point it at the sky, at any old where, at a patch of dark blue far enough away to make me feel calm again.

And then my phone buzzes.

I turn it over. It's Jude.

Up until now, Jude hasn't interfered. I guess Mom's told her that she's got it in hand. That, whatever happens, Blake and I will be at the wedding.

I'm not sure I can handle her right now.

I read her words.

Why are you doing this?

She really thinks we're doing this on purpose?

I check the time. It's 3 a.m. If she's up at this time, the morning before her wedding, it's not a good sign. Jude needs her sleep she's all over the place.

I close my eyes for a second to prepare myself for what's coming next and then dial her number.

She picks up on the first ring.

I expect her to yell. She's a yeller, like Mom. Needs to get her whole body involved in communicating her anger. But there's no yelling. There's no sound at all.

'Jude?'

Still nothing.

'Jude – are you there?'

'You're not coming, are you?'

'Not coming? Of course I'm coming. I'm a couple of hours away. I'll be there.'

'Don't lie, Air.'

'Why would I lie about this?'

'I know you never wanted to come to the wedding. How you and Blake joked about it behind my back. How you thought it was a waste of time and money'

'What? No. Of course it's not a waste of time. It's your wedding, Jude, we wouldn't miss it, not for anything. This isn't like—'

'All the other times you two have blown me off?'

I think back to how often Blake and I have let Jude down. How we've gone off and done things on our own – mainly because she wasn't interested in coming with us or because we knew she wouldn't approve. And I guess I knew that she felt it, and that it must have hurt her, being left out like that. And I think about all the complaining I've done over the past few months, about having to wear a dress and be this cheesy out-of-a-catalogue bridesmaid and how I haven't done anything to hide my views on marriage being totally old-fashioned and unnecessary and, in fact, damaging to the advancement of women in the twenty-first century. Worse: damaging to Jude and what she could be.

'We'll be there, Jude.'

'Did you plan all this?' Jude asks, like she didn't hear what I said.

'Plan what?'

'Messing up the wedding. Missing the family breakfast. Not showing at the rehearsal dinner.'

'No – of course not. Why would we want to do that?'

'Because you wanted to make some kind of statement.' Her voice is hard and cold.

'A statement? No. Jude, you're getting this all wrong. Blake's messed up his flights. He messes up, you know that. He can't help it. And I've been trying to sort it out. Because we both want to be there.' I pause. 'We love you Jude – and we get what a big deal this day is.'

'You don't want me to get married.'

'We want you to be happy, you know that.'

'But you still don't want me to get married.'

I pause for a second. What am I meant to say?

'We like Stephen,' I say. 'He's a great guy.'

'But you still don't want me to get married.'

It feels wrong having this conversation now, at 3 a.m., a few hours before her wedding.

'You need to get some sleep, Jude.'

'You think I'm throwing my life away,' she says over me. 'You think I'm making a mistake.'

We've never spoken this openly about her getting married before. Blake and I have made our views clear but more in the abstract – in passing comments. Indirectly, when we've tried to persuade her to keep up with her piano. In family debates about the place of marriage in the twenty-first century. Jude held her own against us, argued as hard as we did. But we've never sat down and actually thrashed it out; as siblings, on a personal level: why Blake and I don't think Jude should be getting married and planning to have babies at twenty-two.

'You're so talented, Jude. You could do anything. You went to Julliard for Christ's sake. Do you know how few people manage that? I guess we – I guess I – can't get my head around it, why you'd give all that up.'

For a long time, Jude doesn't answer. For so long that I think she might have hung up on me.

'Jude?'

'I'm still here.' She pauses. 'You don't understand me, Air. Neither you nor Blake ever have.'

'That's not true—'

'It is. Competing. Trying to be the best. Performing in front of all those people. It wears me out. It's never made me happy.'

'But you love to play the piano – and you're so good at it, Jude.'

'I love to play, Air. *Just* play. I don't want all the other stuff that comes with it.'

'But you've worked so hard.'

'Yeah. Because I thought it was what people wanted.'

'What people wanted?'

'Mom and Dad. You. Blake.'

'I don't understand.'

'Everyone in this family has to be so goddamn special.'

'*You're* special.'

'Not like you. Not like Blake. I don't want to go and find lost planets in outer space. I don't want to be an international celebrity, like Blake. I don't want to be a famous lawyer and negotiate international peace deals like Mom. Or even be this ground-breaking academic like Dad. I want to have a normal life, Air. I want to be a wife and a mom. I want to stop having to compare myself to you guys or be judged because I'm not doing something to change the world.' Her words tumble over each other. I can hear her voice thickening and by the end she's sniffing and gulping.

'Oh Jude—'

'So, it's not going to work.' Her voice is trembling. 'You and Blake trying to sabotage my wedding. I'm still going ahead with it. I'm not changing my mind. Because it's what I want, Air. It's the one thing that makes me happy and you can't take that away.'

My body is shaking. I'm struggling to take it in. All these things Jude's been feeling about us. And how she's right. We haven't understood. And we have judged her. And all that stuff I've been saying to Christopher about how being him is enough – how leading a big life isn't about doing big, showy things, that he doesn't need to live up to this big ideal his father has for him – was totally hypocritical. Because I've been doing the same to Jude.

263

When Jude first told us she was engaged, Blake and I gave Mom a really hard time for going along with it when she was the one who was always pushing us to fulfil our potential and to make the most of our talents. She'd just said, *I think Jude's made the right decision.* So, she understood Jude. That's why she's gone all out for this wedding. That's why she didn't give her a hard time when she didn't take up any of those amazing offers after Julliard. She got her more than we ever did.

'I'm sorry, Jude. I know that I've got loads to make up to you. But you have to believe me, Blake and I were planning to be in Nashville on Saturday – well ahead of all the wedding stuff. We love you. We were going to be there for you. We'd never let you down.'

She goes quiet again. Then she says, 'So why aren't you here?'

I look up at the inky sky, trying to find the words to explain, words that won't make my only sister, who's getting married in a few hours, feel even worse.

'We're on our way. We'll be with you soon – ready to watch our amazing big sis walk down the aisle.'

I hear the door to the motel room open behind me. Christopher comes to sit beside me and then he realises I'm on the phone and holds up his hands and mouths: 'Sorry.'

'It's okay,' I mouth back and pat the space beside me.

I could do with his company right now.

He sits down. Leda follows him out and sits beside him, his warm body between us.

'It's my fault,' Jude says after a while.

'What?'

264

'That day, in the apartment – after the suit fitting. I told Blake not to bother coming to the wedding.'

Blake and Jude have had so many arguments that they all kind of blend into one. But it comes back to me now, a couple of days before Blake left for London, before my internship. How Jude dragged Blake out for his suit fitting. And how it all ended in a horrible argument.

I was with Dad in his study – he was preparing a lecture on Persephone, his other favourite Greek goddess, for the fall, and I was reading up on black holes so I'd be up to speed with the other interns at the Air and Space Museum. When we heard the front door slam shut and raised voices in the hallway, Dad and I looked up at each other: we knew this wasn't going to be good.

Jude had dragged Blake out to have him fitted for the morning suit and the top hat she wanted him to wear for the wedding. Proper, old-fashioned hat and tails. The works. He'd avoided her for weeks and this was the last day they could measure him up before he left for London.

'You didn't even let her measure you properly – if it doesn't fit right, you're going to look ridiculous.' Jude's voice out in the hall.

'I'm going to look ridiculous anyway,' Blake threw back.

'It's a traditional wedding suit – it's smart. It's what guys wear – Dad's wearing it and Stephen, and Stephen's dad, and his brother, and his best man—'

'So why do you need me to wear one as well? Looks like all the other guys have got it covered.'

'Seriously, Blake? You're my brother. Everyone's going to wonder why you're the one guy in my family who's wearing ripped jeans to my wedding.'

'Everyone knows I wear jeans. They'll hardly be surprised, Jude.'

'God you're arrogant. For once in your goddamn life could you get your head around the fact that not everything is about you, Blake?' Jude's eyes were welling up.

Dad and I exchanged another look. This definitely wasn't going well.

Jude and Blake had been arguing about the suit thing for weeks. They'd been arguing about loads of things that Blake had been asked to do to fit in with the wedding. But I'd talked to him. Told him that this was important. That it mattered to Jude – really mattered.

'You're my brother, Blake – people are going to be expecting you to wear what the other guys are wearing.'

'Oh, you should have told me – people are *expecting* me to look like an idiot. Why then, that makes everything fine.'

I hear Jude throwing her handbag and keys into the bottom of the hallway closet.

'You're going to ruin my wedding.' Her voice was tearful.

I put my notes down and got up off the chair. Dad came out from behind his desk.

'So why don't I just not show up – wouldn't that be easier?'

'Well, maybe it would,' she threw back. 'If it's all such a hassle, don't bother coming.'

When I came out into the hallway, Jude stood there, facing Blake, hands on her hips, her torso tilted forward, chin jutting out. Blake was propped up against an old chest, his body slouched, his hair swept over his face, inspecting a plectrum. He was acting like all this was nothing but I could tell, from how red his ears were and from the rash at the base of his throat, that he was barely holding it together.

The thing about Jude and Blake is that they totally love each other. It's just they've always been in competition. Treading on each other's toes. Jude hadn't even started walking when Blake showed up, probably singing and strumming a guitar as he appeared from the birth canal. Suddenly she wasn't the baby anymore. And part of her didn't mind. There are pictures of her looking over his crib and giving him cuddles and helping Mom give him baths. Even then, she was maternal. But he totally eclipsed her. Because he was this funny, gorgeous, charming baby that everyone stopped to stare at. I don't think anyone even noticed when she took her first step – they were too busy focusing on Blake.

And ever since they've been tiny, they've had this pattern of interacting that has become so familiar to me, Mom and Dad that we've accepted that it's part of our family dynamic.

For a few weeks, Blake and Jude are fine.

Then they start getting on each other's nerves. They sigh and roll their eyes and whisper comments under their breath. But they press down their irritation.

And then there's a trigger. Like Blake having to wear a morning suit. And all that built-up tension explodes and they have a massive row.

Mom, Dad and I are actually quite grateful when they have the row – it clears the air, like a good thunderstorm. And afterwards, they're back to normal for a while, kind of liking each other and getting on.

Anyway, this explosion had been building up for some time. People say that family dramas are heightened when there's a wedding and that was definitely the case with Blake and Jude.

Jude started sobbing.

Blake pretended not to notice but I knew it would be getting to him.

So, Dad and I swung into action.

Dad walked over to Jude and put his arm around her and steered her into the kitchen. When the door closed behind them, I walked over to Blake.

'You couldn't go with it, Blake, just this once?'

He shrugs. 'I don't get what the big deal is.'

'Yes, you do.'

'You should have seen it Air, really—'

'I have to wear a dress too, remember. Believe me, I know. But it's going to make Jude happy. And Mom too.'

He didn't say anything. Because he knew I was right. And because, despite it all, he loves Jude. They fight like cat and dog but they'd defend each other to the death too. Mom told me how, when Blake got into a scrape on his first day at preschool, Jude single-handedly tackled the biggest guy in the class who was giving Blake a hard time. Climbed onto his back and started pummelling him.

'So you'll say sorry?'

'I'll wear the damned suit, Air.'

'And the hat?'

'Seriously?'

'You can't wear the suit without the hat.'

'Okay, *and the hat*.'

'And you'll say a proper sorry – like you mean it? You know all this wedding stuff is stressing her out.'

'Okay, I'll say sorry.'

'So let's go and practise the song – before you leave for London.'

He leant back and rolled his eyes. 'God – she's going to want me to sing and play looking like a fucking penguin.'

'Blake!'

'Sorry, but it's true.'

'You'll look dashingly handsome whatever you're wearing – I'm sure that Blake Shaw can work out how to rock a morning suit.'

He looked up at me through his hair and grinned.

'I reckon I could, you know.'

'There you go. Now come and practise the song.'

He gave me a salute and we went off into his bedroom.

I didn't give it much thought at the time because I'm so used to Blake and Jude knocking heads and because there's been so much stress surrounding the wedding. But I realise now that Blake never got to say sorry to Jude: about the argument they'd had or about having been a total pain in the ass about the suit. And she never got to say sorry about having told him not to come to the wedding. And she never got to see how, after she left the apartment, he spent ages rehearsing her song because he knew that, whatever happened, no matter how much they were getting on each other's nerves, he would never miss his big sister's wedding. He'd agreed to the suit and we'd practised the song and there was no question that he was going to show.

'I know how all this looks, Jude. How late we are. How we missed the family breakfast. And the rehearsal dinner. It looks really bad. And you're totally entitled to be pissed at us. But I need you to trust me. We know that today means more to you than anything in the world. And although Blake was a total ass about the suit, he gets that too. He loves you. He totally adores you, Jude. He wants your wedding to be amazing. We all do. It's going to be okay.' I pause. 'I'll make it okay.'

She goes really quiet.

'Jude?'

Then I hear a sniff.

'Jude – what's going on?'

Another sniff.

'Jude, talk to me,' I say gently.

'What if all this is a sign?' she says, her voice small.

'A sign?'

She sniffs again. I imagine her sitting alone in her hotel room, tangled in sheets, tears dropping down her face and I get an ache in the pit of my stomach. I should be there.

'Maybe you're right. Maybe the wedding's a mistake.'

'You've spent the last half hour explaining to me why getting married is what you want – that it's who you are. We're the ones who've been getting it wrong. Who haven't given you the credit for making your own decisions – the *right* decisions, for your life. And we're going to make it up to you, I promise—'

'But nothing's right, Air.'

'Look, Jude, you've just got the pre-wedding jitters. And me and Blake messing you around like this – it hasn't helped. But you're going to be amazing. An amazing, beautiful bride and amazing wife and the best mom ever. And I'm banking on you doing this stuff because it's not like I'm going to give Mom and Dad any grandchildren. And I want to be the cool auntie,' I take a breath. 'And I can't wait for the wedding.' And for the first time, I mean it. I really mean it. I want to be there for her, more than anything.

Christopher shifts beside me. I guess he wasn't expecting this stuff to come out of my mouth. *I* wasn't expecting this stuff to come out of my mouth.

'Jude?'

'Just promise me you'll be there.'

I swallow hard. Because I know that she's talking about me *and* Blake.

'I promise. Now get some sleep. We can't have the beautiful bride walking around with bags under her eyes.'

I hear her let out a small laugh and then she sniffs again.

'I love you, Jude.'

'I love you too,' she says.

And then she hangs up.

I put my cell down beside me and let out a huge sigh. That might have been the first real conversation I've ever had with my sister. It feels crap: that it's taken this long. That I've been totally blind to her feelings.

'That was intense,' Christopher says.

I nod.

My eyes well up. I tried to hold it together while I was talking to Jude but I can't anymore. I let hot tears drop down my cheeks.

'I'm so angry at Blake,' I blurt out. 'Couldn't he have got things right, just this once?' I clench my fists at my side, digging my nails into my palms until it hurts. 'He's so selfish.'

Christopher reaches out his arm. I can feel him hesitating for a second but then he puts it around my shoulders. I lean my head against his chest and we sit there, on the sidewalk outside the motel, watching the sky. It's still dark enough to see a few stars. Sitting here with him steadies my breath and, slowly, I uncurl my fists.

'There's no moon,' he says.

'It's waiting in the wings,' I say.

'Waiting in the wings?' he asks.

'It's still there,' I say. 'Of course it's still there. But the night before an eclipse, the moon is close to the sun – it stands between the sun and the earth. Preparing for the eclipse, I guess. It doesn't move much on its orbit, not like it does on a normal night. So, we don't see it.'

'Weird.'

'Logical, really,' I say.

He laughs. 'For you, I guess.'

We watch the sky lighten and the stars fade.

'You going to be okay?' he asks after a while.

'I don't know,' I say.

I straighten my spine.

'But I'm going to have to be, aren't I?'

I look at him and he holds my gaze.

'Wherever Blake is, I'm going to make sure that he doesn't ruin Jude's wedding. For once, I'm going to be there for Jude. She needs me today, more than anyone.'

He takes my hand and looks right into my eyes.

'You're amazing, you know that, don't you, Ariadne?'

'Ariadne?'

'The sentence called for your full name.'

I smile.

'*Totally* amazing.'

I shake my head. 'I've let Jude down. And not just by failing to get Blake there or showing up on time myself. I haven't respected who she wants to be.'

'You're amazing because you've got the balls to admit that you might have got this wrong. And because you're putting her first now. Families can go a whole lifetime before doing that. Sometimes they never do.'

I think about his dad. Whether he'll ever get the chance to understand Christopher for who he is – to really see him. And I feel a heavy weight on my chest.

'Thanks,' I say. 'Thanks for being here.'

He gives me a sideways smile. 'Thanks for not leaving me by the side of the road.'

As I think about how, in a few hours, he won't be there anymore, how he'll be on a bus heading to Atlanta and I'll be heading to Nashville, I feel a hollow thud behind my ribs.

Looking at him, I realise how tired he looks. Shadows under his eyes. Even paler, if that's possible, than the guy I saw back in the airport in DC. He hasn't eaten properly in two days, or slept properly. And he's been listening to all my problems without ever complaining about his, which are way, way bigger. I wonder whether it's not just Blake who's selfish; whether it's me too. Whether we've both spent too long thinking the world revolves around us.

'Is there any news?' I ask. 'About the plane?'

He adjusts his glasses and then shakes his head. 'Just more speculation. They're trying to work out what happened in the cockpit moments before the plane crashed.'

So, they're still blaming his dad.

'How are you holding up?' I ask.

'I'm fine,' he says, too quickly.

'No, you're not,' I say. 'You can't be. And you don't need to pretend to be, not with me.'

He looks at me like he's weighing up whether he wants to even go there.

'You're allowed to be scared,' I say gently.

He shakes his head. 'You want to hear something totally screwed up?'

'I'm good at screwed up.'

'Of course the stuff that's going on with the plane and my dad is totally doing my head in. But it's like, when I was sitting up there on the mountain, I realised how powerless I was. That it was all totally out of my control. And now, the thing I'm really scared of,' he shakes his head. 'It's kind of stupid.'

'Tell me.'

He swallows hard. 'I'm scared of seeing my mom.'

He looks away from me and out to the road that runs past the diner.

'What if she doesn't want to see me,' he says.

'She wants to see you, Christopher.'

'How do you know?'

274

'Because she's your mom. And because whether she knows it or not, she's been missing out, big time. And if she didn't want to see you, she would have told you not to come when you called her.'

'She didn't exactly have a choice,' he says. 'I caught her off guard.'

'She's going to love you, Christopher. You have to trust me on this one. You have to trust yourself.'

He doesn't answer. And I know that my words probably sound hollow. I mean, what do I know, right? I've never met his mom. I hardly know him. But from the last two days we've spent together, I've seen enough of Christopher to know that unless there's something really wrong with her, his mom *is* going to love him – she has to. Because he's one of the most awesome human beings I've ever met and even if his dad didn't see him like he wanted to be seen, I know he loved him too. He must have done.

'You're still going though, aren't you? To Atlanta?'

He nods. 'I don't know where else to go.'

I get that sense again, of how lonely he is. How few people he has in his life looking out for him.

I look out towards the diner.

'You hungry for breakfast?' I ask.

'I could do with some coffee.'

'Then I've got just the place.' I hold his gaze again. 'A goodbye breakfast.'

He raises his eyebrows. 'A goodbye breakfast?'

'Yep.'

I stand up and hold out my hand.

'It's not somewhere crazy, is it?' he asks.

'No, it's not somewhere crazy,' I say and pull him up.

He stumbles into me and our bodies crash into each other awkwardly and, before I know it, we're hugging.

'Thanks for being here too,' he whispers into my hair.

And, for a moment, I allow my body to rest into his and I let the rest of the world fall away.

Chapter Thirty-Three

04.33 CDT
Pancake Stack Diner, Knoxville, TN

I lean into the car. 'It opens in an hour,' I say. 'And your bus leaves in an hour and a half. So, I vote we wait.'

I'm standing there, in the bluey-black light of dawn, still wearing Christopher's T-shirt and boxers.

He nods.

I get back into the car beside him. I notice goosebumps on his bare arms. I lean over and switch on the heater.

We're sitting in the car park of this diner Blake took me to whenever we drove to Nashville. At this point in the drive, we'd get hungry and need something to keep us going for the last 180 miles.

I can see him now, throwing his arm around Suzy, smiling.

This girl makes the best pancakes in Tennessee, he'd say.

And she'd blush and smile.

Suzy was Blake's girlfriend. On and off for years, actually. The only girlfriend I've ever liked. There was a time when he came down to Nashville nearly every weekend. Before Grandpa passed away he'd stay with him in his apartment on Music Row. Sometimes he

277

took Suzy with him. And even when he was busy, he'd take the time to drop into The Pancake Stack.

My heart skips a beat. Perhaps Blake's been in touch with her – told her where he is. That would be typical of Blake: sharing his plans with an ex-girlfriend rather than his actual family.

The Greyhound bus stop is on the other side of town. If Christopher gets the 6.30 a.m. bus, he'll be with his mom just after lunchtime.

And by lunchtime, I'll be standing at Jude's wedding, making up some excuse for Blake not being there. Or maybe he'll be there already. Or maybe he'll storm in at the last minute, make one of his grand entrances, and save me from having to sing that damned song of his. Whatever happens, when all of this is over, I'm going to give him hell for having put me through this. Up until now I've always had his back. And when it's come to Jude being pissed at something he's done, I've been right there, at his side, defending him. But not this time. I think about how she was on the phone, how she thought we'd done this on purpose to upset her and then how scared she sounded, that she thought she was making a mistake. What Blake's done has made her doubt the one thing she believes in. No, today, Blake doesn't get to let Jude down.

I yawn and rub my eyes.

'You should get some sleep,' Christopher says.

I shake my head. 'I'm fine.'

'Look, you're going to need some energy,' he says. 'To get through your wedding. At best, you only got a few hours back at the motel. Even Leda's asleep.'

I look down at Leda settled between us on the front seats. She must still be exhausted after her hike up to Deer Ridge. She lets out a snuffle and twitches her paws, like she's chasing after something in her dream.

I yawn again. 'You're *making* me tired, I was fine before you said anything about sleeping.'

'You've got a long drive. I don't want to be responsible…' his voice trails off.

'Responsible?'

'For anything happening to you.'

It's crazy. How two people who hardly know each other can get so tangled up in each other's lives that they come to care about each other in a way that goes way deeper than you'd ever expect. When he says those words – about being worried about something happening to me – I believe him. And I want to believe him: I want him to care.

'I'll wake you as soon as the diner opens,' Christopher, 'Then we'll get breakfast.'

And then we'll say goodbye. For good. And the thought of that makes me feel empty. I've got used to having him beside me. More than used to it: I've grown to like it.

'Okay,' I say, leaning my head against the side of the car. The car door feels hard under my head. I shift uncomfortably.

'Why don't you lean on my shoulder?' he says.

I look at him for a second. His cheeks are bright pink, his eyes watery with embarrassment. But he's holding my gaze.

'If…if you want to, I mean,' he stutters.

I hesitate for a second but tiredness washes over me so hard that I give in to it. I shuffle up on the seat and lean against him. My head falls onto his shoulder but I don't have the strength to move it.

'You smell of pines,' I mumble, my voice far away and sleepy. *Pines and sky and the cool water.*

He squirms his arm out from between us and puts it round my shoulders.

I wonder what Blake would think. Me and a guy – a guy who's not him – sitting together in his car.

And then it comes back to me, how this really bad thing has happened.

And I can't get my head to undo those knots: the knots of how my body feels, leaning into Christopher like this – when I've never even been on a date before, not a proper one, and the knot about what's happened to Christopher and his dad. What's *really* happened. And when we're going to know for sure, and what we're going to do when we find out.

I don't know how to make all those feelings fit in my body at the same time.

I notice Christopher get his phone out to check the news but then he switches it off again, like he doesn't want to see, not now.

My body slumps more heavily against him.

Yeah, he smells of cool, dark water. And mountains. He smells of all the places we've been together and all those amazing faraway places he's been to that I'll probably never see. I can feel his breath against the top of my head and it feels kind of familiar. More familiar than it should for someone I've only known for a just over a day. More familiar than someone I should still be totally mad at for having lied to me.

I look over at the diner. I can see through one of the back windows into the kitchen. Suzy is getting things ready: pouring filter coffee into thermos flasks, pulling muffins out of the oven, beating eggs into the pancake batter.

There's something soothing about watching her going through her routines, preparing for another ordinary day.

The windows steam up as the kitchen gets hotter and soon, she disappears.

My eyes flicker.

As my eyelids begin to fall, I feel Christopher lean forward – he holds my head lightly so as not to disturb me. I watch him grab a scrap of paper from his backpack, and then he starts folding.

And then my eyelids get heavier. And the car's really warm. From the fan heater. From our breaths – mine, Christopher's and Leda's too.

I want to stay awake. I want to watch him, folding that paper between his long fingers.

But my body begins to go slack.

And then I can't keep my eyes open any longer.

My eyelids close.

My body slouches into the seat.

And then I'm somewhere else.

'Wake up, Air.' He's shaking my shoulders.

I can smell him in the room. Cigarette smoke. Leather jacket. Hair gel. Cold air from having climbed in through one of my two windows, the one that faces out onto the street.

I'm thirteen; he's seventeen.

I rub my eyes.

'Come on – let's go.' He tugs at my pyjamas.

I rub my eyes some more.

'I've got an assignment due tomorrow,' I say.

Physics. A presentation on the moons of Jupiter. I've been preparing for weeks and I'm determined to get the best grade in the class.

'You'll be fine,' he says.

I straighten up and look at him, sitting there on the end of my bed. Light from the window falls across his face. It's a full moon.

'Go where?'

'To chat. On the roof.'

This is what he does. Goes and does a gig somewhere in Georgetown, comes back totally wired and unable to sleep and gets me up – because he doesn't want to be alone. Blake's never been good at being alone.

'And we should check out the moon,' he says. 'Say hi.' Then he smiles at me. 'It's missing you.'

He does that too: makes it sound like the sky is as interested in me as I am in it.

'Fine – for a few minutes,' I say.

I never say no to Blake. No one ever says no to Blake. Because we know that whatever he's asking, it'll be worth it. Spending time with Blake is worth it, period. And we know that he'd do anything for us too. If I asked him to stand outside the window of my Physics class tomorrow holding up cue cards for my presentation, he'd so be there.

I swing my legs out of bed and a moment later we're climbing out of my other window, the one that leads onto the roof rather than to the street.

He starts rolling a cigarette.

'It'll kill you,' I say, nodding at the cigarette. 'Scientifically proven.'

'Ah, the beautiful die young.' He flashes me a smile.

I remember getting a sinking feeling in my stomach whenever he joked about stuff like that. He didn't understand – how, if ever something did happen to him, none of us would survive it.

A gust of cold air brushes over my skin. I shiver.

'Here,' he says, taking off his leather jacket and draping it over my shoulders.

I snuggle into it, breathing in the smell of his aftershave and his skin.

'So, how did it go?' I ask.

'I think I messed up the last song.'

He was doing a Johnny Cash cover in a bar. Greatest hits. Blake gave them his own spin.

'Which one?'

'"Flesh and Blood."'

'But that's your best song.'

He'd sung it to me a million times.

'Yeah, that's why I messed it up.'

I got it. It was the same with me at school. It was the same with this project tomorrow. Sometimes choosing your favourite thing to talk about in a project is a total risk – because if you mess it up, you're left with this horrible empty feeling inside, like you've let it down, the thing that you love so much.

'I bet it was amazing,' I say.

'Didn't feel like it,' he lies back.

We lie there in silence. Then he says:

'Stars look good tonight.'

I shake my head. 'Too much light pollution.'

'Damn it,' he laughs. 'I forgot to ask the city to switch off all the lights.'

I laugh too. I know that Blake would do that for me if he could – switch off every single light in DC so that I could get a better view of the stars.

'You think I'll be up there one day?' I ask.

'You bet, little sis'.' He takes my hand. 'As far as the stars – that's where you're bound.'

'As far as the stars,' I whisper back.

I think about the millions of times we've been out here together, lying side by side on the roof of the house, looking at the stars. How it's what got me interested in space to begin with.

I hear some sounds coming from my room, below us.

'I'm going to go out again,' he says, getting up.

'But it's nearly morning.'

'Exactly. Too late for sleep.'

He starts humming the tune to 'Flesh and Blood'. He's hard on himself; I bet he totally rocked it.

'If you're not back for breakfast, Mom will kill you.'

He keeps humming. And then he answers, singing, 'I'm always back for breakfast.'

From down in my room, I hear the desk creaking, the one we have to climb onto to get to the skylight which leads onto the roof.

I take off the leather jacket and hand it back to him.

'Thanks, Airbug.' He puts it on and walks to the edge of the roof.

'Where are you going?'

'Shortcut.'

Someone's behind me on the roof, I can feel it.

'It's not a shortcut,' I call after him. 'The street's on the other side.'

He's singing again. He's not listening.

This isn't the window he uses to get out of the house. This is the roof window, where we talk. He should be going back into my bedroom and using the other window, the one with the drainpipe that leads onto the street.

'Blake!'

'I'll get there quicker!' he says.

284

'But—'

'See you little sis,' he says.

And then he jumps.

'Air?'

I spin round.

'What are you doing out here?' It's Jude. She looks hurt. Like she does whenever Blake and I hang out without her.

'I was just talking to Blake.' I look back over to the edge of the roof.

I notice that my whole body is shaking.

'Blake?' I hear Jude say, though she sounds really far away. 'Blake's not here.'

I rub my eyes again and stare hard at the spot where, a second ago, he was standing.

But she's right. He's gone.

Chapter Thirty-Four

07.45 CDT

Someone's shaking my shoulders, so hard I can feel their fingers digging into my collarbone.

'Air?'

'Blake! Come back!' I yell.

Lights shine behind my eyelids. I feel tears on my cheeks and realise that I'm crying.

'Blake!' I'm screaming now.

'Air! Air! Wake up!'

My eyelids fly open.

He's staring right at me, his grey eyes lit up by the morning sun that's pouring through the windscreen. Sometimes, his eyes and his skin and his hair are so pale, it's like he's not there at all: like he's a ghost.

'It's okay, Air. It's okay,' Christopher says. 'You were just having a bad dream.'

Sweat runs down my back. I stare at him, confused by who he is and why he's here and why, at the same time, he feels so familiar. I notice that he's holding my hand, squeezing it tight like he's worried I'm going to take off.

'It's okay,' he says again.

I blink at him. And I nod. But it doesn't feel okay. Not even close. And from his eyes and from the fold in his brow, I know that he knows it too.

'I have to get to Nashville,' I say, my words jagged. 'I have to be there for Mom and Dad and Jude.'

I wipe my eyes on the back of my hands.

'I know,' he says.

'He's always leaving,' I blurt out and then wish I hadn't said that, not out loud. Not even in my head. I don't get to say bad stuff about Blake, not with him missing. But I feel a ball of anger in my stomach.

'Leaving?' Christopher asks me gently.

'He's always taking off. Even when we were younger and he wasn't allowed to go out without telling Mom and Dad, he'd climb out through my window in the middle of the night and ask me to cover for him, and then, just when I thought I'd have to tell Mom that he was missing, he'd sneak back in.'

'Where did he go?'

'I never knew. Which made it worse. At least if I could have pictured where he was, I'd have known how close he was – or how far away.' I catch my breath. 'I'd have known he was okay.'

'And was he okay?'

'Yeah, Blake's always okay. When he came back, I'd find out that he'd gone to sing and play his guitar in some bar in Georgetown. Or that he'd just taken a walk. Or got onto the subway and skipped from one train onto the next, not going anywhere.'

'A free spirit.'

'More like annoyingly unpredictable.'

'And he likes to go out at night?'

I nod. 'He says that night time is when he's most inspired to write songs – that that's why he never sleeps.' I see Blake, standing in the frame of my window – my bedroom was the only one that faced out onto the street – giving me that massive smile of his, the smile that got him out of anything. Tears sting my eyes. 'And of course I cover for him. Just like I'm covering for him now. I cover for him because I know he'll come back. Because, every time, he promises me he'll be fine. And I believe him.' Tears are rolling down my cheeks so hard I don't even bother to wipe them away. 'No matter how much I begged him to take me along, he always left me behind.'

Christopher digs around in his backpack, pulls out packet of tissues and hands one to me.

'Thanks,' I say and blow my nose hard. And then I look at him, my eyes blurry. 'I'm sorry, I keep going on about myself. And I know you had a hard time too – with your dad and how he was never really there for you.'

Christopher gives me a sad, sideways smile. 'I guess he and Blake have more in common than either of them would ever realise. Dad's always kind of leaving too.'

I sniff and look up at him, waiting for him to go on. He started opening up to me on the mountain – I want him to feel like he can tell me anything.

He nods.

'When I was younger, I hated him going to work,' he says. 'I know it sounds stupid, because I was with him so much of the time, but I'd have done anything for him to have a different job. Something boring and ordinary. A nine to five in an office somewhere.' He closes his eyes and shakes his head. 'When he was in the air – he was in his own world. I might as well have been on the ground – in a totally different country from him – for all the difference it made having me on board. He never came out to check on me. His air stewards would look out for me, give me special treats like the desserts from business class, but when we were in the air, Dad acted like I was just another passenger.' Christopher clenches his hands together on his lap, his head bowed.

'And when you got older?'

'He hasn't really changed. I sometimes think that he's embarrassed about me.'

'Embarrassed? How could he be embarrassed?'

'I'm not like him.' He looks down into his hands. 'I don't want the same things as him. He says I should be grateful – for all the opportunities he's given me.' He pauses. 'I shouldn't be saying bad stuff about him—' His voice breaks. 'Not with all this going on.'

I shake my head. 'You're wrong.'

He looks up at me, searching my face.

'You *should* be saying this stuff about him.'

He waits for me to go on.

'Because it's what you feel. And because talking about the bad stuff means that there's still hope.' I gulp. 'And there *is* still hope.'

'I don't follow.'

My throat goes tight but I push out the words. 'It's this unwritten rule, isn't it? That when something bad happens to someone, you're only allowed to say the good stuff about them. No one dares to say the stuff that made you mad, that drove you crazy, that they wish had been different. So, wherever the hell he is, I have to talk about Blake like he's going to be okay.'

'Air—'

'Because they are,' I say quickly. 'Whenever they are, they're both okay.'

He goes really quiet.

'Tell me something else about your dad,' I say gently. 'Something he does that drives you crazy.'

He hesitates for a second and then he says:

'He burns toast.' His cheeks flush pink.

'Toast?'

He nods. 'Yeah. You'd think someone who could fly a plane could operate a toaster, right? But basically, every time he makes me toast, we end up having to scratch the burnt bits off in the sink because he'll have forgotten to pick up more bread so those two burnt slices are the only ones we have left to eat. He's crap about food. Crap about cooking. We mostly have takeaways. Sometimes he even brings home leftover food from first class. But it's the toast that pisses me off most. It's like, this is the one normal thing we have together, sitting down and eating breakfast, having toast with butter and jam – and he spoils it, every time. And then the flat smells of charcoal for ages. And then he goes to work and I go back to school and all I can think about is the burnt toast.' He pauses. 'So most of the time, I make the toast. The cooking, generally. Whenever he has time off work or I'm home from school and he's not dragging me off to the other side of the world to see something, I make us stuff.'

'You cook? Like properly?'

'Kind of.'

'That's cool.'

'Only easy stuff. Spag bol, chicken curry, that sort of thing.'

'Still cool.'

'Dad likes my baked bean lasagne.'

I wrinkle my nose. 'Baked bean *lasagne*?'

'It's delicious,' he says. 'To start with, it was an experiment. We ran out of tomato sauce. The only thing I could find were a few tins of baked beans at the back of a kitchen so I layered the beans up between the sheets of pasta and the layers of beef and the cheese. Dad really liked it, so that's how I made it after that.'

I smile. 'What a delicacy.'

'You bet it is.' He laughs and his eyes well up at the same time and I can tell he's got that same crazy tug of war going on his head that I do: of feeling guilty and sad and relieved at the same time.

I lean back and sigh.

'Blake zones out.'

'Zones out?'

'We'll be out having a hot chocolate in a coffee shop or walking down the street or hanging out in my room at home, and one minute we'll be having a conversation and the next minute his mind will be in a different place – usually when I'm saying something that really matters to me, like a fact I might have learnt in astronomy.' I snap my fingers. 'It's like from one second to the next, he's gone.'

I close my eyes and think about the last time he did that, when I drove him to the airport to get his flight to London. For the millionth time, I was giving him instructions about the wedding. He didn't take in a single thing. Which is how we got into this whole mess. If he'd listened to me this time – or any of the times before – he'd have got his own ticket to Nashville without asking me to book it for him at the last minute.

And he wouldn't have had to check his phone to look at the flight details, and he would have got on the right plane, the plane *I* booked for him.

I open my eyes and look over at the diner. Blake composed a song there once, while we were sharing a stack of blueberry pancakes.

'He gets inspired, that's what he says – to excuse the zoning out thing. Says that he notices how someone looks, or he overhears what someone says, or he gets drawn in by the light in the sky, and then he thinks of a lyric or a tune and a moment later he's forgotten I'm even there. And I get that he's an artist and everything, but still, it's not cool. And I've told him that.

I yelled at him once, right in the middle of a Starbucks. I stood up and said: *Stop being so rude, Blake*, and I stormed off. But he didn't even hear it, not really. Or he didn't care. Because what matters is that he's found another song.' I pause. 'And he knows that I'll come running back to him. And so then he'll do it all over again. He'll be in the middle of eating a bowl of cereal or doing some washing or something and he'll go off in his head somewhere and leave the soggy cereal and the pile of dirty clothes and then forget to come back to them. A bomb could explode right in front of Blake and he wouldn't notice, not if he's lost in composing a song.'

I don't think I've ever spoken to anyone this much about Blake before. I don't think I've even said all this stuff to myself before.

Christopher looks at me, his brow folded, his eyes soft, like he wants to take it away: the feeling I get every time I think about Blake and how he does all this stuff that upsets me and how I'm scared that one day he'll take off and never come back and I'll never get to feel upset again – like he'll never get to smell his dad's burnt toast again.

My eyes are swimming. 'I wish he'd think about someone other than himself for once.'

Christopher shifts his head and looks through the side window. Streaks of pink and orange and purple slash the morning sky.

'Sometimes,' Christopher says, 'I feel like flying matters more to Dad than I do. That even if we had all the money in the world so he could retire and be around more, like normal parents are, he still wouldn't do it. Because being up there, above the clouds, makes him happy. Happier than anything I could give him.'

I've sometimes wondered that about Blake: whether if he had to choose between us – his family – and his music, which way he'd go. And I never let myself reach a conclusion. I guess because I was scared of the answer.

I want to reach out and touch Christopher in some way, to make him feel even a tiny bit better and to let him know that I get it, how the people you love more than anything in the world are also the people who hurt you the most.

'When Dad gets frustrated with me, he uses his captain's voice. It annoys the hell out of me.' Christopher's on a roll now. I can tell that, in some weird way, it's doing him good, to talk like this. He clears his throat. 'We will soon be beginning our decent into London…the local time is 13.25 p.m. *You only have one year left at school, Christopher. Not even a year. You need to make some decisions…*Cabin crew, prepare for landing please…*You have to have a*

plan, Christopher. You can't just let life happen to you.'
He pauses. 'It's like he thinks that if he says it clearly enough, I'll pay attention and give him the response he wants.'

'Just after Blake has been totally annoying or gone off without telling me and I've decided that I'm not going to be that little sister trailing after him anymore, how I've got my own life, Blake will do something totally awesome and suck me right back in again.' My voice is thick. 'Like he'll wake me up in the middle of the night and ask me if I'm hungry and he'll put my coat on and take me to this bar where he knows the owner because he does gigs there and asks them to make a kids' cocktail for me and I'll feel like the luckiest sister in the world.'

'Yeah. I've always thought that about Dad – about being his kid. Even when he's really annoying, I know that I've lucked out. He's one of life's good guys, you know? The kind of guy who'd save babies from burning buildings and get cats down from trees and help old ladies cross the road. He does all that disaster zone rescue stuff too. He makes people feel safe; they think that when he's around nothing bad can happen. And I've always been totally proud of that, that he's better than all the other dads put together.' His voice chokes up but he keeps talking. 'When I was little, I thought that he must be a superhero or something, like he was fuelling the plane through his own special powers.' He pauses. 'I know it was stupid…'

Something goes still between us. I think back to how I found out about his dad being the pilot of the plane. How angry I was about him not telling me. It's all gone now, the anger. Whatever happened up there, it's not his dad's fault. Maybe it was nobody's fault. Maybe it's one of those things that should never have happened but did anyway, and, somehow, Christopher and all those other people waiting for their friends and relatives to show up are going to have find a way of living with it.

'No, it's not stupid,' I say. 'I thought the same kind of thing about Blake. Not that he was a superhero but that somehow he wasn't quite real.' A thick nausea settles in the back of my throat. 'I was worried that someday he'd take off and never come back – because he got sick of living at home or whatever – but I never thought anything bad could ever happen to him.'

Then I turn around to look at Christopher. His eyes are closed.

'Your dad could still be okay, couldn't he?'

He keeps his eyes closed.

'The plane landed on water,' I add. 'You said that was better…'

He doesn't say anything.

'And you said it yourself – your dad's a pro. He would have done everything to keep the passengers safe.'

Christopher's head drops.

'Say something, Christopher.'

But he doesn't answer.

And that's when I glance at the clock on the dashboard.

'Shit! It's gone seven – your bus.'

Slowly, he opens his eyes.

'There's another one,' he says.

'What?'

'I looked it up on my phone. There's another bus at 10.30 a.m.'

'God, I'm sorry. I shouldn't have fallen asleep.'

'You were exhausted. We both were. I decided to let you sleep.' He gulps. 'And...'

'And?'

He blushes. 'I wasn't ready to go yet.'

I'm not ready for you to go yet, either, I think. But I know it wouldn't be fair to say that. He needs to get to his mom. He has to focus on what's going on with his dad. I've dragged him far enough into my mess.

I lean back in my seat. The night's over; it's morning. In a few hours, the wedding will start.

At least we won an hour, crossing the state line. It'll take me another three hours to get to Nashville, but I should make it in time for the wedding.

I look back at the diner and see Suzy, arranging chairs and tables on the porch. She notices the car and waves. My heart sinks. She recognises the Buick. She thinks Blake's here.

'You know her?' Christopher asks.

'Blake used to bring me here for pancakes.' I pause. 'They dated – Suzy and Blake. On and off for years.'

'On and off?'

'Blake lives in DC, Suzy lives here, in Knoxville. He'd hook up with her every time he swept through on his way to Nashville and they never broke up, not officially – not even when Blake dated other girls.'

'That must have been hard for her.'

That makes me like Christopher. He may not have had many normal relationships growing up but he gets how people feel.

'You'd think so,' I say. 'But in the context of my brother, it was a compliment – she was his most long-

296

standing girlfriend. The constant, while all the others came and went.'

Christopher scratches his head. 'So they're still going out?'

'No. She finally ended it last summer – she met someone else. Someone she can settle down with. But I think she still likes him.'

'*Love*-likes him?'

I bet Christopher doesn't have these conversations very often. *I* don't have these conversations very often – not outside Blake's world.

'Yeah, I reckon she loves him. But Blake's hard to love – even for his family.'

I realise what a paradox that is. How everyone falls in love with my brother because he's so interesting and talented – because he draws you in. But how really loving him, in a relationship kind of way, is nearly impossible. Because you're always waiting for the next time he'll let you down.

Christopher nods and I can tell that he gets it. That it's how he feels about his dad too.

'It's a shame. She's nice,' I say.

I look back at the diner. Even though Suzy's with someone else now, I know that she'll be excited to see me – that she'll look over my shoulder for Blake, like the rest of the world does.

Unless he's there.

Unless he came here because he knew that, somehow, I'd come by and find him.

Because that's the kind of thing Blake does. Showing up, out of the blue, to surprise you.

My stomach flips on itself and this time, there's no tug of war inside me, I just feel sick at it all. At the fact that I'm here with the wrong person. That Christopher should be in Oregon, with his dad. That no matter how many stories we share about how annoying Blake or his dad are – or how amazing they are, it doesn't change the fact that everything's totally screwed up.

Chapter Thirty-Five

08.12 CDT

The bathroom's off to the left, before the main door to the diner. I tell Christopher to meet me inside.

In the bathroom, I take off Christopher's boxers and T-shirt and pull on the bridesmaid's dress. It's too tight and too frilly and too bright, and it's got scrunched from flying around on the back seat. But I don't have a choice: next to the rehearsal dinner dress, it's the only dry, clean bit of clothing I have left. And if I get into it now I won't have to stop again – I can park the Buick and run straight to the wedding.

Then I look down at my sneakers. *Shit.* I forgot the dress shoes back in DC – the ones that were meant to match the dress. Blue satin. A small heel. Gross. But, as far as Jude and Mom are concerned, absolutely essential to complete the look.

If Mom doesn't kill me for being late or for singing Blake's song – she'll kill me for the sneakers.

Shit. Shit. Shit.

I force myself to calm down. Shoes are the least of my problems. I'll crouch a bit, make sure the hem goes over my feet, and Mom won't notice.

When I come out of the bathroom, I walk into the diner and stand by the door, scanning the booths.

299

I know which one Blake would have gone for – by the window, overlooking the main road that leads into Knoxville. The best place for looking out onto the world and getting inspiration – and being noticed by the world too. Whatever he says, Blake likes the attention.

But he's not here.

Like he wasn't at Leda Springs.

It's all right. I press the words into my brain. *If he's not here, maybe he's already made it to Nashville.*

Christopher's chosen a booth at the far end of the diner, also by a window. He's folding one of the paper napkins again, like back at the Mobil station. And even though the napkin's too floppy and the folds don't hold, I recognise it: he's making a model of Leda.

Then he sighs and shakes his head, screws the napkin up into a ball and puts it on the plate in front of him.

I wish Christopher hadn't done that; I wish I could have kept the paper model of Leda. Because soon, he'll be on that bus to Atlanta. He'll be gone too. And the model was good. Leda's ears pricked up just right, her head cocked to one side, her tail trapped between her paws. A beautiful, scruffy, tiny Leda.

I wish he'd see how good he was.

Apart from an old couple sitting at the counter, drinking their filter coffees, we're the only ones here. The local radio's on: the presenter's talking about the countdown to the eclipse.

I wonder about the conversations they must be having in newsrooms up and down the country: what matters more? That a plane has dropped out of the sky on its way to the US or that, in a few hours, the world's going to go dark? And who decides, I wonder?

I notice Christopher looking down at his phone. As it blinks to life, my stomach clenches.

It will have been on all the news channels. Mom and Dad and Jude and everyone else at the hotel must have seen it when they were having breakfast and getting ready. And it would have made them feel sick for a moment, like everyone feels sick when they hear about a plane crash, even if it's totally unrelated to them. But then they'd have gone back to whatever it was they were doing.

I walk up to the table.

'Any more news?' I ask.

'The coastguard is widening its search for survivors and they've been speaking to a fisherman who said he saw the plane at the moment it lost altitude.'

'God, that must have been scary – watching a plane dropping out of the sky.'

The words hang between us.

'Investigators are still looking for the black box,' he says without looking up. 'They say they won't know anything for sure until they find it, and that takes time, especially when a plane has crashed into the sea.'

I think about all the other plane crashes I've heard about in my life. How rarely anyone survives, especially when it's a big crash, like this one. And even if, by some miracle, one or two passengers make it, the pilot never does. There's a reason people who are scared of flying reserve seats at the back of the plane.

I brush away the thought. We can't make any assumptions, not until we know for sure.

'Thanks for these,' I say, holding out Christopher's T-shirt and boxers.

At last, he looks up. His eyes go huge and his mouth drops open.

'Wow.'

'Wow, what?'

'You look—'

'Ridiculous?' I ask.

'I was going to say—'

'Over the top? Like a blue meringue? Or a schlumpf?'

'No. Beautiful. I was going to say, beautiful.'

My cheeks burn. 'Really?'

'Really.' He smiles. 'Especially for someone who doesn't do dresses.'

For a second I look at the dress differently. I was so against having to do the whole girly-dress-up thing that I never considered that Mom and Jude had done a good job; chosen something nice – chosen something that made *me* look nice.

'Thanks,' I say.

It's what Blake would have done: made me feel good about something that I didn't want to do.

I realise I'm still holding Christopher's clothes.

'Here,' I say.

I stare down at them and think about how good it felt to wear his boxers and T-shirt compared to how it feels wearing this dress. It might look nice but it's too tight and frilly and it's impossible to walk in properly.

I'd give anything to go and get changed again.

'Why don't you keep them,' he says. And then he goes bright red, like I did a second ago. 'I mean, just in case.'

'In case what?'

He shrugs. 'I don't know. In case you decide to go for another swim?' He smiles. 'Seriously, keep them. You can give them back to me another time.'

And then he goes quiet. And I don't say anything either. Because we both know that it's unlikely that there'll be another time.

But I don't care. I hold the clothes to my chest and say: 'Thanks, I will.'

Then I sit down in front of him.

'You ready to order?' Suzy's standing next to us.

My heart lurches.

I look up.

'Air! I thought it was you!' she says. And then she throws her arms around my neck and squeezes me really tight, like the first time Blake introduced me to her. Like loads of women who've fancied Blake over the years have done. As if hugging the baby sister was a way for them to get closer to him. Except with Suzy, I know it's not fake. She likes me.

'And you!' She bends down and stretches her hand under the table to give Leda a rub.

It's one of the reasons Blake liked to stop here – Suzy let him bring Leda in.

'Blake's not here,' I say quickly, pre-empting her question. 'He's travelling.'

She sighs and smiles. 'Of course. Never could pin that brother of yours down for more than two seconds.'

I look at her smile and at her wispy blonde hair and at her pretty blue eyes and, I wish, again, that she'd been able to win Blake's heart. That he'd fallen head over heels in love with her and proposed to her; that they'd have got married and lived with her above this diner or in Grandpa's flat in Nashville. That he'd been so in love with her that they'd have had a kid together and that he'd have loved the kid so much that he'd have decided to stop going on tour. Because Blake totally loves kids. He's pretty indifferent to Jude getting married but he's totally psyched about the possibility of being an uncle. And, of course, he'll be perfect. The crazy-fun, totally loveable uncle who feeds the kid too much candy and gets away with it. Anyway, if Blake had fallen for Suzy and they'd got together and had a kid, they'd both be at the wedding right now, Suzy would have got him there. I'd have handed over my *sort out Blake's shit* mantle to her and the only person I'd have to worry about getting to the wedding was me.

'Blueberry pancakes?' she asks. 'Extra maple syrup?'

I snap back into the present.

'Pancakes?' she asks again.

Even though I've hardly eaten a thing, I'm not hungry. Not anymore.

I look over at Christopher, hoping he'll order so that I don't have to talk.

'Could we have a couple of coffees first?' he says.

I breathe out. He gets it.

'Sure,' she says. 'Cute accent by the way.'

She winks at me, because she's totally thinking that I've hooked up with Christopher. And she goes off to get the coffee.

I glance out of the window beside us. The morning light streams in, catching the edges of his tangled hair.

I look down the road in the direction of the bus stop and my stomach clenches. At the thought of having to get back into the car alone. At the thought that, once the wedding's over, once the world has gone dark and the sun's come up again, and Blake's not back – I don't know what I'm going to do.

'Two coffees.' Suzy places a couple of mugs in front of us and fills them from her pot of filter coffee.

'Thanks,' Christopher says.

'Sure you don't want anything to eat?' Suzy asks.

'We don't have much time,' I say. 'Christopher's getting the bus to Atlanta.'

She smiles at him. 'Well, you can come back and try our pancakes another time.'

Christopher smiles back but his face looks strained. 'That would be nice.'

I get a lump in my throat. The likelihood of Christopher ever coming this way again is basically zero. The likelihood of us ever seeing each other again once he gets on that bus is basically zero.

When Suzy's gone we drink our coffees and listen to the radio from behind the counter. A newsreader on a local station is talking about the eclipse. They're worried about the weather – that clouds might obscure the totality.

'You'll probably see it from the bus,' I say.

'Yeah.' And then he laughs but it's a sad laugh. 'Dad would have been disappointed. We were meant to see the eclipse from a boat on the ocean in Oregon – and now I'm going to see it through a bus window.'

'It's still the same eclipse,' I say.

He looks at me and his eyes brighten and he sits a bit straighter. 'Yeah, I guess you're right.' Then he looks back through the window.

I look out at the sky too and as I think about standing up at the wedding, in front of everyone, singing Blake's song, my stomach tightens. I don't know how I'm even meant to stand up and breathe, let alone sing.

I tilt back my head trying to get the tears to drain back into my eyes. Then I look at him.

'They're lucky to have you,' he says.

I look at him. 'What?'

'Your family,' he says. 'You're lucky to have each other. To be so close.'

And that's what does it. I totally break down. Because family is what this whole wedding is about. Us coming together to celebrate Jude. To welcome Stephen into the family, officially. Without Blake, that won't work. Blake's the one who *makes* us a family. The glue and the sparkle and the thing that makes us feel like we're the most special family in the whole damn world. If he doesn't show up in time, it's going to ruin the whole wedding.

'Oh God, I can't do this. I can't show up at the wedding on my own. I can't sing Blake's song for him.' I start sobbing. My nose streams and tears pour out of my eyes and I can feel my face going red and blotchy.

He gets out of his side of the booth and then he's sitting beside me.

'And they'll blame me. For ruining everything,' I say, hiccupping between each word. 'They love Blake. More than anyone. If anyone had to be there, it was him.'

Christopher pulls some paper napkins from the dispenser and puts them on the table in front of me. I grab one of them and dab my face.

And then I feel bad. Because Blake not showing up to the wedding is like nothing compared to Christopher's dad being on that plane. But it somehow feels like this is a turning point for us. Like maybe, if Blake doesn't keep this promise, if he doesn't show up, then he may as well not come back at all. Because it will prove that, in the end, no matter how much we love him, Blake puts himself first.

'Even though he was the most unreliable person on the planet, in the end, he was always there – when it mattered, I mean.' The front of my dress has gone soggy from crying. I dab at the fabric with my snotty tissue. And then I break down again. 'All this is my fault.'

I put my head down on the table and let my body slump into itself. Right now, I can't imagine ever getting up again.

After a few seconds, there's a hand on my shoulder blades. He's hardly pressing down at all but it feels like, through that hand, he's holding the whole of me together.

'None of this is your fault, Air.'

He rubs my back in gentle circles like I'm a kid and it feels good, to let go of everything that's going on, just for a second.

'And you're going to do to it. You're going to do whatever it takes for your family. Because they mean more to you than anyone. And you're going to do it for Jude, because it's her wedding. And Blake, no matter where he is and no matter how badly he's messed up, you're going to do it for him too. And most of all, you're going to do it for you – because it's who you are.'

I look up at him.

'It's who I am?'

He nods. 'Like I said before. It's showing up that matters. And, from the sounds of it, you show up.'

I wipe my eyes and sniff.

'But it isn't fair, that Blake – that *everyone* – expects that of me, every fucking time.'

'No, it's not fair.'

I keep shaking my head.

'I can't do this,' I say.

He puts his hand over mine.

I look back up at him.

'You want to get into a rocket and fly off into space, right?'

I nod.

'So being brave is part of your DNA.' He pauses. 'You can do this,' he says again, pronouncing each word really slowly like he's trying to press them into my brain.

For a few moments, I don't answer. Then I say:

'I'm the odd one out.'

'Sorry?'

'I'm the only one in my family who can't do music.'

'Oh.'

'Mom played the cello growing up and Dad played the French horn and they both sang in this acapella group when they were at Oxford. They wanted us to be musical too. When we were little they let us pick our own instruments. Blake chose the guitar. He wanted to be like grandad. Jude picked the piano. And, because I'm competitive and the youngest – and stupid – I chose the violin.'

'Stupid?'

'Because it's the hardest, right? With the piano or the guitar, you can make up a small tune and everyone sings along and it sounds nice. The violin sounds totally crap until you're good. *Really* good. Which was this big joke because it turned out that whereas Blake and Jude are totally gifted musicians, I spent years screeching away while my family clamped their hands over their ears.'

'Do you still play?'

'God no. I gave up as soon as I could.' I pause. 'It's the only thing I've ever given up. I'm not a quitter.'

Mom still plays her cello sometimes, to wind down after a long day at the White House and Dad's part of this really dorky orchestra in DC where he gets to play his French horn once a week and even though Jude's given up pursuing a career as a concert pianist, she's still amazing at it. Sometimes, when she thinks we're all out of the apartment in DC, I've come back to find her playing on the Grand that Dad bought her when she got into Julliard. I know she still loves it. And then there's me. Hardly able to hold a note.

At Christmas, they all get out their instruments out. My job? To turn the pages for Jude at the piano.

The music thing made me realise – along with a whole load of other things that have happened over the years – that how you relate to your family is like this really complicated Venn diagram.

There are some things we all share. Like that we're all obsessives: me about outer space, Mom about her legal stuff, Dad about his Greek, Blake about his music, Jude about her teaching and wearing colours that match and the whole getting married stuff.

And there are some things we share with only one other person. Like Mom and Jude's thing about making everything look pretty, which Blake, Dad and me totally don't care about. Well, Blake likes to make himself look pretty, but that's kind of different.

And there are some things others share that I don't get to be part of – like Blake and Jude and Mom and Dad being good at music.

And there are some things that are totally our own, that make us feel kind of detached and lonely but strong too, because it's our thing. Like how, whenever Blake walks by, the whole world notices, because he's got that magnetic, look-at-me thing going on.

None of the rest of us have that. Not even Jude, who's really pretty. That's Blake's thing. That and the fact that things work out for him, no matter how badly he messes up.

I blink some tears out of my eyes and sniff.

Christopher looks at me, his head tilted to one side, his eyes wide and unblinking behind his glasses, and then he gets up and goes to talk to Suzy. I don't know what about. Maybe he got hungry, though it seems a bit abrupt.

I stop crying and, slowly, I straighten up.

When he comes back, he holds out his hand.

'There's access to the roof,' he says.

'What?'

'Suzy said we could use it.'

'Use it for what?'

'You'll see.'

'I'll *see*? What does that mean?'

He's still holding his hand out. He's totally not being himself – the Christopher who barely had the courage to look at me back at the airport is now directing me to the roof of a diner?

'You spoke to Suzy?' I ask.

He nods. 'When you were in the bathroom.'

'Oh.'

So, this isn't an afterthought: he's planned it.

'It'll help,' he says. 'I promise.'

310

'Help what?'

He keeps holding out his hand.

I hesitate for a second but then I take his hand and he pulls me up onto my feet.

'Okay,' I say. 'Okay.'

Chapter Thirty-Six

08.30 CDT

Christopher asks Suzy to watch my telescope and his backpack and then he guides me through the kitchens. Leda bounds behind us.

He walks fast, his head held high, like he's been here before.

It smells of pancake batter and bacon and freshly baked muffins. There's a tray of eclipse-themed donuts on the counter. The diner is on the main route out of Nashville, so I guess Suzy's expecting quite a crowd today. I have to hold Leda's collar to stop her from jumping up and grabbing something. I'm pretty sure her being here goes against every food hygiene rule but Suzy hasn't said anything. Maybe she gets that today isn't a normal day. That sometimes, we get to break the rules. And if she loved Blake, breaking the rules would have been part of the deal.

For some reason, Christopher picks up an eggplant from one of the vegetable bins.

Yeah, he's acting totally weird.

He holds open the back door, which leads straight out to the fire escape.

Our feet clatter on the steel steps. I have to hitch up my dress to avoid stepping on the hem. Leda darts past us so she's the first to get to the top.

When we get to the roof, we stand there for a bit, staring. Leda goes to the edge and looks down and barks at the Buick. I wonder whether she keeps expecting Blake to show up. Whether maybe, in that mysterious way dogs seem to know stuff, she's got a clearer idea of where he is than I have.

I scan the skyline. I've never seen Knoxville from above. And it's not that it's pretty: a big road runs through it and it's kind of industrial, but when it's hitched up to the sky – the big, endless sky – it looks beautiful.

I think about the pictures of the earth taken from outer space. How all you see are those blue and green swirls, the ocean, the earth and the white clouds sweeping round the earth's atmosphere – how looking at things from the sky edits out all the garbage of life.

I can tell that Christopher likes it too, behind here, above everything, like somehow, for a few seconds, we've stepped out of all the crap that's going on in our lives.

I wonder whether Blake's ever been up here. Maybe with Suzy.

The sun's rising, a big ball of fire under the horizon. And the sky's a pale, brilliant blue.

A few hours, I think. *A few hours and the world will go dark.*

But still, I don't know why he brought me up here. For the view? Because I told him about my dream, the one where I was sitting on the roof of my house in DC with Blake? Though that would be a bit weird; I don't need to be reminded of that. The eclipse isn't for a while and it's daylight now, so it's not like we can do any stargazing. Plus, my telescope's with Suzy.

313

I wait for him to explain but he simply keeps staring at the sky, like he did on the summit of Deer Ridge. I realise he must be thinking about how if something has happened to his dad, he won't ever be able to look at the sky again without thinking about what he's lost.

He still hasn't explained why he brought me up here though so, eventually, I ask him. We don't have much time before his bus and if I have a chance of getting to the wedding on time, I have to get back on the road.

'So, what are we doing up here?'

He looks back at me.

'Dress rehearsal.'

'Excuse me?'

He hands me the eggplant.

Yeah, he's totally lost it. I guess it was going to happen. Those calm, quiet, keep it all inside types end up flipping sooner or later.

'You need to practise,' he says.

'Practise what?'

'Blake's song.'

Oh God.

'The song you're going to sing at the wedding?'

Yeah, I'm going to sing it. But I've been trying not to think about it. Because, barring my solo performances in the shower, I don't do singing. And I don't do audiences, not when they're looking at me.

I pull at the collar of my dress. Already, the day's getting hot.

'You know the words, right?'

I nod and gulp and hope to God that he isn't going to make me do this.

He sweeps his hands across the roof.

314

'The wedding's taking place on the rooftop of a hotel in Nashville – that's what you said.'

I nod.

'Well...' He keeps sweeping his hands in the air. 'Imagine you're there.'

Except I'm not there. I'm standing here, with Christopher, on the roof of a diner – a horrible roof, patched and grey and tinny. Holding an eggplant.

I feel like a total idiot: standing up here in my blue-meringue dress.

And then I look down at the parking lot and notice Blake's car. His yellow Buick that, when I was a kid, seemed like the biggest, brightest, most exciting thing in the world – like an extension of Blake himself. And then he taught me to drive. And gave me a set of keys. Because he trusted me with the things he loved.

I look back at Christopher.

'Okay,' I say.

He nods. 'Good. Now stand up straighter.'

'What?'

'You're slouching.'

'You're telling *me* off for slouching?'

'Yeah. If you slouch, the sound won't come out. If you want to project your voice, you need to open up your lungs.'

He puts his hand on his stomach and says: 'Breathe in.'

I'm beginning to wonder whether Suzy slipped something in his coffee.

'What do you know about singing?'

The tops of his cheeks go pink. 'Dad made me take singing lessons.'

'I thought you were home-schooled?'

'Yeah. One of his flight attendants used to be a singing teacher.' He pauses. 'And when I went to boarding school, Dad made me join the choir.'

I look at Christopher and think about all the things about him I don't know. Things I'll never know.

'So, you can sing – I mean, *really* sing?'

'Sort of. Now stand straight, hold your head up, and breathe.'

Weirdly (I make a point of not taking instructions from guys my age), I straighten my spine. And it does feel better.

Then I take a few breaths.

And then I break down. Again. Tears and snot start coming out and I can't stop them. I grab one of the ruffled layers from the skirt of the dress, pull it up and wipe my face.

From the edge of the roof, Leda looks back round at me and lets out a whine, like she's joining in, and that makes me want to cry even more.

'I can't, I just can't,' I stutter.

'You can.'

I shake my head. 'I'm totally going to ruin it. They're expecting to hear Blake. That low, crooning voice of his. No one will want to listen to me.'

I think about what Mom said about the special stool she found for Blake. I picture him placing his hand on it, slipping onto it, leaning towards the audience, getting off again – every move perfectly choreographed.

Christopher steps towards me.

'You're not going mess up it. But even if you do, it doesn't matter.'

'It doesn't *matter*?'

'No, it doesn't matter. This isn't about you, Air. It's not even about the song.' He looks me right in the eye. 'It's about your family. You're doing this for them.' He pauses. 'And for Blake.'

'For Blake?'

'Because he wanted to be there.'

'If he wants to be there, he'll be there.'

'Maybe,' he says.

And the way he says it makes my breath catch.

'Anyway, the song's bigger than you,' he goes on. 'Or your ability to sing it. Right?'

I don't answer.

'Right?' he says again, his voice so loud and sure that, without even thinking about it, I nod.

'Right,' I say.

He steps back again and pats his thigh. 'Come on, Leda – this is your cue. Go sit with Air.'

Leda runs over and sits at Christopher's feet.

'Not me, silly – Air.' He laughs and drags her over to me.

'What are you doing?' I ask.

'Leda will be with you while you're singing, right? And it'll help, having her there. It means you won't be alone.'

I shake my head. 'She won't be.'

'Won't be what?'

'With me. Mom's built Leda a kennel, so she doesn't upset people.'

'A kennel? Wow.' He scratches his head. 'Look at the sky, then.'

'What?'

'Look at the sky – that'll still be there, right?'

I nod.

'And it'll make you feel better.'

I nod again. And then I look up at the bright blue sky, at the pale sun, at the thin clouds shifting overhead.

And then I take a long breath.

And I start singing.

'Louder!' Christopher says, walking away from me.

I take another breath and push the words out.

'*From the first time we met to the last breath we take…*'

I stop singing and curse Blake in my head. And I think back to the argument we had about the song when I told him it was too cheesy. The thing is, however crummy the words, Blake would make them sound good, because he's Blake. Because he could make the phone directory sound like a Johnny Cash classic. All I've got are a bunch of crummy words and a crap voice.

'Keep going!' Christopher says.

'I can't do this.'

'You've *got* to do this.'

'He'll probably show up.'

Christopher hesitates. Then he says. 'You want to be prepared though, right?'

I don't know what I want anymore. All this is so messed up.

'And anyway, I want to hear it,' he says.

I look up at him. He gives me a small smile. Kind of crooked. Kind of cute.

'As I won't be at the wedding, I won't get to hear the song. I want my own personal performance.'

Ever since we had our fight and Christopher got back in the car, he's been acting more confident.

Talking more. Talking louder. Talking like he believes he's got something to say that's important. I'm not sure whether I like the old or the new Christopher better.

'Your own personal performance, really?'

He smiles.

'Really.'

I roll my eyes but then, for some reason, I go with it. I take a breath and open my mouth:

'*From the first beat of my heart to your last embrace…*'

Christopher folds his arms across his chest. He nods as I sing and his hair falls in his eyes. As I push through each verse, a smile spreads across his face.

When I stop singing, I feel the words vibrating in the air around me.

And, for a second, I understand – the feeling Blake has when he sings, how it's like the whole world has whooshed through your body.

Then I hear clapping coming from somewhere below us. I look down and see Suzy standing on the porch of the diner. She must have heard me singing and come out. I wonder what she thinks I'm doing, standing up here, singing, with this guy she's never seen before.

I hold out the eggplant, my fingers shaking.

Christopher takes it.

'You're going to be fine,' he says.

I look at him. 'I wish you could be there.'

He nods. 'So do I.'

'*Flesh and blood needs flesh and blood*,' Blake's voice comes into my head again. '*You're the one that I need.*'

I realise that, right now, Christopher's the most solid thing in my life.

But I know he has to go to see his mom. And that I have to face Mom and Dad and Jude and Stephen and all the other guests at the wedding.

'Are you going to be okay?' I ask. 'With your mom and everything?'

He shrugs. 'I guess I'll see.'

I wonder whether it's easier for me: having the wedding, the song to focus on, the day to get through.

'Thanks,' I say. 'For bringing me up here.'

'I'm forgiven, then?' he asks. That small, wonky smile again.

'Yeah, you're forgiven.'

We walk back down the fire escape, through the kitchen and into the diner, Leda weaving between our legs.

Suzy's putting those sun-filter glasses on all the tables for her customers to use when the solar eclipse starts.

I sit down in the booth and my body crumples into itself. I feel like I've run a marathon.

'Got any more coffee, Suzy?' I call over.

'Sure,' Suzy says and goes off to the kitchen.

I expect Christopher to come and sit in front of me in the booth but instead he kneels down, takes Leda's face between his hands and kisses the spot between her ears. He stays there for what feels like ages and when he stands up again, he picks up his backpack and hitches it up onto his shoulders.

'Where are you going?' I ask.

'I think I'll walk to the bus.'

'But – I can take you—'

He shakes his head. 'It's not far. You pointed the stop out to me on the way into town. It'll be good to stretch my legs for a bit before the long bus trip.'

I hadn't prepared myself to say goodbye to him, not yet.

'But—'

All this feels too fast.

'I hate goodbyes,' he says quickly.

Then he leans over his shoulder and pulls something out of one of the side pockets of his backpack and places it in front of me on the table.

'For you,' he says.

It's a star. A tiny paper star attached to a piece of string. The star looks like it has a thousand folded angles. It's beautiful. Maybe as beautiful as an actual star.

His words come back to me:

I make them small so they don't break.

And he's right. Although the star is made of paper, the folds are so tight, so precise, that it looks strong.

'When did you make this?' I ask.

He looks at me through his glasses, his eyes huge.

'While you were sleeping.'

I think back to those hours before the diner when we were both in the car. How good it felt to fall asleep and let my mind and body go to a different place, knowing that he was there, beside me.

'You could wear it,' he goes on. 'Like a necklace or something. And when you get scared again, about what you have to do, it can remind you to keep going.'

I pick up the paper star on the piece of string and put it over my head and then tuck the star under my dress. The sharp edges push into my skin, but it feels good, to have a piece of Christopher so close.

Then I stand up and put my arms around his neck and hold him really tight for a second. His body goes stiff like he doesn't know what to do and then he puts his arms around me too, very lightly.

'Thanks,' I say. 'Thanks for everything.'

We hold onto each other for another second and then he pulls away, hitches his backpack onto his shoulders. He leans under the table and gives Leda a final stroke.

'Good luck, buddy,' he says.

'What does that mean?' I ask.

'Oh, you know. The wedding. The kennel.'

'Right, the kennel.'

Leda lets out a small yelp, and I know that she wants him to stay.

I don't know what I'd imagined our goodbye would be like, but it wasn't like this: walking away from each other, as though we'd only met for a few seconds. As though saying goodbye was nothing.

As I watch him walk away I whisper in my head: *Please turn around one more time, please...*

But he doesn't. He just keeps walking.

Chapter Thirty-Seven

09.15 CDT

Through the window, next to the booth, I watch Christopher walk down the road, his massive backpack full of ironed clothes and tiny paper models bouncing up and down on his shoulders.

I never thought I could miss someone I've known for less than two days but I do. I miss him already. And I'm not sure how I'm going to get back in the car by myself.

Leda's got her paws up on the windowsill and is whining. It makes me realise how she hasn't whined in a really long time. Not like this. Christopher made her feel better about Blake not being here. He made me feel better too.

Suzy comes up to the booth, puts a hand on my shoulder and follows my gaze out through the window.

'He was cute,' she says. 'In his way.'

In his way. I smile. Yeah, he was cute in his way.

I keep watching as Christopher's body gets smaller and smaller. Until he's gone altogether.

'Air?'

I look up at her.

'You think Blake would approve?' Suzy asks.

'What?'

'He's protective – and you're his little sis'.'

Although I'm the one who spends all my time looking out for Blake, Suzy's right, he would never let anything happen to me. Especially when it came to guys. He warned me about the total losers he came across who treated girls like crap. Not that he needed to worry. Between studying, being his PA, keeping peace between Mom and Jude, and doing all the other family stuff that my parents were into, there wasn't really time for getting into trouble. And I'd never met a guy I liked. Not before yesterday. And Christopher's not exactly the bad boy type Blake had in mind when he warned me off guys. And anyway, he's gone now.

'I mean,' Suzy goes on, 'you hooking up with that guy and showing up at the crack of dawn – wearing his clothes.' She pauses for dramatic effect. 'You thought I didn't notice when you came in?'

Yeah. Of course she noticed. Crap liar. Crap actor.

'It wasn't like that,' I say.

She smiles. 'Like what?'

She thinks I spent the night with him. That he's my boyfriend. Or worse: a one-night stand.

'I was just giving him a lift,' I say.

She puts her hands on her hips and laughs. 'Oh, *just a lift* – in your brother's car, in the middle of the night, miles away from your home?'

'Yeah, just a lift.'

'And the clothes?'

I look at Christopher's clothes folded up on the table and think about how good it felt to put them on after the swim. And how I wish I was wearing them now rather than this frilly bridesmaid's dress.

324

'And what was with the singing? Planning to join Blake in the music business?'

'The music business? No. Never. I can't sing.'

'Sounded pretty good up there.'

'Thanks. But no.'

She smiles. 'Still planning to take a rocket to the stars?'

'Yep.'

'What's going on, then? Why are you here?'

'It's a long story.'

'Right.' She winks. 'It always is.'

And then I realise that I've got to tell her about Blake. Perhaps she knows something – that would be Blake all over: swinging by the diner, telling Suzy about some crazy plan he has which will provide a totally logical explanation for why he hasn't shown up yet. Maybe he told her about whatever surprise it is he had in store for the wedding. Maybe she's even helped him. She's like that: the kind of best friend sidekick in films that gets taken for granted by the hero.

'Could you talk for a bit?' I ask.

She looks around the diner. There's only one other customer.

'Sure, honey.' She sits down.

I know what she's thinking: that I've decided to give her the gossip about whatever it is that happened last night.

'It's about Blake.'

She smiles and opens her mouth and I know that she's going make some kind of a joke about my brother, something that's going to make it even harder for me to say anything.

'He's missing.'

She rolls her eyes. 'What's new? If only that brother of yours could stay in one place long enough, one of us girls might have a chance—'

'No – this is different. He was meant to get a plane into Nashville from London. I booked the flight for him. Told him to make sure he checked the details. And he got things mixed up and the last I heard was that he was getting a plane to Dulles and he's not answering his phone—'

'Sure sounds like Blake.'

For a second, it feels good talking to Suzy. Someone who knows how crazy and impulsive and infuriating Blake is.

But then she scrunches up her brow. 'You said the plane to Dulles?'

'Yeah, I drove all the way back to DC to pick him up but it turned out he wasn't on that plane either.'

'Oh, Air.' She swallows hard. Her hand flutters to her throat. 'You don't mean *the* plane to Dulles. The one from London that's been all over the news?'

Very slowly, I nod. 'Yeah, that one.'

Suzy looks past me at the TV screen behind the counter. I follow her gaze. The picture of guy in a UKFlyer uniform fills the screen. Curly, dark hair trapped under his cap. Every button sparkling.

Edward Ellis. My throat goes tight.

There's a strapline under his picture:

Pilot suspected of failing to recognise a technical error in the cockpit.

'Oh God,' I say.

And I want to tell her about how Christopher's dad was the pilot but then I think about how cut up he was about what everyone was saying – that the crash might have been his dad's fault – so I don't say anything.

'It's horrible,' Suzy says. 'All those people...'

'Yeah.'

I pray that Christopher hasn't seen the update. Not yet. He needs to get to his mom, first. He needs someone with him.

I look back at Suzy.

'Did Blake tell you anything?'

'Tell me anything?'

'Any special plans he had – linked to the wedding – or the eclipse. Or Nashville. Something that might explain why he hasn't shown up yet?'

'Doesn't Blake always have special plans?'

'The wedding?'

'Yeah – Jude's getting married later today.'

Her face drops. He hasn't been in touch then. Not for ages. She doesn't even know about Jude.

She sits back like she's been punched.

'He was meant to be in Nashville already,' I say gently. 'And he said he had a surprise planned, for the wedding.'

She looks back at me, her eyes far away like she's trying to process it all.

'We've missed the rehearsal dinner and he hasn't been in touch since he was in London.'

'He said he'd be there?' she asks.

I swallow hard. 'He promised. No matter what, he said.'

Suzy's eyes go clear again. 'Then he'll be there.'

I look up. 'You think so?'

'Yeah. Probably at the last minute. Knowing Blake, probably at the last *second*. But if he's said he'll come, he'll come.' She pauses. 'Family's everything to him, you know that.' She looks right at me. '*You're* everything to him. He wouldn't let you down, Air. Not unless—'

My heart lurches.

'Unless what?'

'Unless it's out of his control.'

Her words hang between us.

'And what if it *is* out of his control?' I say, my words breaking.

She stares at me for a moment and then closes her eyes, takes a breath, opens them again and, trying to smile, says, 'You'll give him hell and he'll forever be in your debt.'

We both go quiet again.

Then I let out a laugh that sounds kind of forced but I go with it anyway, 'Yeah, you bet I'll give him hell.'

She smiles and puts her hands over mine. 'Want me to come with you? To Nashville?'

My eyes well up. She'd close the diner – on a busy day like today – for me? For Blake?

I shake my head. 'This is a big day for you – for the diner.'

'There'll be another eclipse.'

'Not for another seven years, not like this one, a total eclipse, in North America.'

She shrugs. 'Seven years? I'll still be here.'

And she will. Because Suzy's the exact opposite of Blake. If he can never stay in one place for more than a few seconds, she's the kind of person who puts her roots down deep and doesn't budge. Her grandma opened this diner sixty years ago. The whole putting her roots down is probably what made Blake fall in love with her: opposites attract and all that. And what made him keep leaving her too.

'You really think it's going to be okay?' I ask.

'You bet it is,' she says.

And I want to believe her, I really do. But all I can think about is that one word she said after she went on about how Blake would never let me down.

Unless it's out of his control.

Chapter Thirty-Eight

10.01 CDT
1-40

I give Suzy a big hug and then I pick Leda up, along with the boxer shorts and the T-shirt Christopher left behind, and I go back to the car.

It's starting to get hot already, so I put the top down.

I lift Leda into the back and place her on her blanket. The seat beside her looks empty without Christopher's backpack.

And then I look at Blake's morning suit, still scrunched up on the back bench and the box with his hat with its big dent in the side.

I swallow hard.

I can do this. I press the words into my brain. *I can do this.*

Then I lift the paper star over my head and place it on the dashboard, close the door and start the ignition.

For a moment, I sit there, the car rattling, staring up at the hot, white sky. It's nearly lunchtime. I've got three hours to get to Nashville, in time for the wedding. And then everything will go dark.

As I turn the car, I notice that Suzy's come out onto the porch. She holds up her hand and waves.

When this whole wedding stuff's over – when I've made Blake feel totally guilty for putting me through all this – we're going to come back here and eat pancakes and everything will feel normal again. And I'll tell him to stop taking Suzy for granted. I'll make him see how awesome she is.

I wave back.

And then I pull out of the parking lot.

Chapter Thirty-Nine

10.04 CDT
1-40

I drive down the road that takes me out of Knoxville.

By the time I get to the highway, the sun is so strong and so low that I can barely see where I'm driving.

Cars and trucks rush past. Too fast. Too loud.

A dull pounding sets in at the back of my skull.

Something feels weird. Wrong-weird.

There's too much space around me.

And my body feels hollow. Right down to my bones.

And the thing is, it's never been a problem before.

Having space.

Sitting, waiting, walking – *being* – alone.

My family's so intense that I love the time I get to myself.

Being alone has always been fine.

Except now it's not.

It's really not.

And I don't know what to do.

Through the windscreen, I stare at the heatwaves rising off the asphalt. At the cracks in the road. The faded lines.

And I think about all those hours we sat next to each other in the car. How we swam together. How I got used to the sound of him folding paper beside me. How I grew to like it.

And I think about all those things he said about his dad. How he was the only one he had but how they weren't even close. And how he's on his way to a mom who might not even want to see him. No one should have to face all of that alone.

I stop and look over my shoulder. I can still see it. The diner. It's neon sign blinking by the side of the road. The roof where I sang. How, for a few minutes, he made me feel like I could go to the wedding and sing instead of Blake.

I want to call him and tell him how I don't know what to do now, with all this space around me. And then I realise that we didn't even swap numbers. Not once did we stop and think about how we might get in touch again.

Then I think about how he has to focus on his own stuff. Even if I did have his number, it wouldn't be fair to call him. He has to get to his mom. This isn't about me.

And I think about how we were never really meant to meet.

And how, whichever way you look at it, this whole thing was going to have to end sometime.

Maybe it's for the best that we didn't swap numbers. That we're making a clean break. That, whatever we shared these past two days, stops here.

I reach over to the passenger seat and pull at the glovebox to get out some sunglasses. Blake has more sunglasses than anyone I know. He stashes them away in different places so that he always has a pair to hand. It's part of his look.

As I shut the glovebox again, my hand brushes against my telescope case.

Only a few hours ago, Christopher and I sat in a field, looking at the stars. I remember how his face lit up when he got that first look at the night sky through the telescope.

It's like they're so close I can touch them, he said. *Like the rest of the world is falling away.*

And so, I knew he felt it – how amazing they were, those balls of fire lighting up the universe, so beautiful and so close and so far away.

And then I think back to what he said about how his dad wanted him to see the eclipse from a fishing boat out on the sea in Oregon and how, instead, he was going to be seeing it through the window of a bus.

I look back at the telescope. At the empty seat beside me. And then at the tiny paper star on the dashboard, the sun lighting it up like a lantern.

Just let him go, just let him go. I force the words into my brain.

But my brain's not listening. And neither's my heart.

Damn it.

I glance back at the clock.

It won't take long, I tell myself.

I take the exit, turn the car, and head back into Knoxville.

Chapter Forty

10.15 CDT
Knoxville Bus Station, TN

The bus is already there. Christopher's queuing to get on.

I park the car next to a sign that says 'No stopping at any time' because it's the closest space to the station, praying that there are no traffic attendants around.

'You stay here,' I say to Leda. 'And don't let anyone tow us.'

She lets out a small yelp – she sounds happier, like she knows that Christopher's close.

Then I grab the telescope and run into the station.

The bus is already there.

And Christopher's the next in line to get on.

'Christopher!' I yell out.

My heart's pounding.

There are so many bus engines running and it's so echoey in here that my voice doesn't carry.

I push past the other people in the queue and catch Christopher's arm.

He turns around. Behind his glasses, his pale grey eyes widen with confusion.

'Air?'

I push the telescope into his arms. 'I want you to have it.'

'I – I don't understand.'

'To see the eclipse.'

'But—'

'You can use it through the bus window. It will help you see it better.'

'But, how will I give it back to you?'

'You can have it.' I pause. 'I mean, for good.'

His eyes go even wider.

'It's got a special lens,' I say quickly to cover his embarrassment. 'So you can look right at the sun without burning your eyes. Look through it, like I showed you.'

'Are you sure?'

I nod. I'm sure. I'm going to spend my life looking at the stars. At the moon. And something tells me that when I get to the wedding, I won't be getting out my telescope to look up at the sky.

'Take it as payment – for the parking fine and the gas and the coffee…And maybe, one day, you can tell me about it. I mean, what you saw, and what it felt like.'

'Are you coming or not?' The bus driver calls down to us from his seat.

'Yes, he's coming,' I call over.

Because even though every bit of me wants to reach out and grab Christopher and persuade him to turn around and come back to the Buick, I know he's got to get to his mom; that we both have to work out the next bit on our own.

'You could make it – afterwards,' I say.

'*Make* it?'

'A model. Of the eclipse. Out of paper.' I look at him.

'If he's coming, he needs to get on the bus,' the driver says.

I step away.

Christopher's still looking at me.

And then I jump back up the steps and throw my arms around him and press my cheek to his and whisper into his ear:

'They're not a waste of time – your paper models. They're beautiful, *really* beautiful. And I think you should spend your life making them. That would be a really big thing.'

When I pull away from him, he stares at me, his eyes wider than ever.

I step down off the bus.

'You're an artist, Christopher!' I call over to him.

And he keeps looking at me. Then he puts the telescope on his back and gives me a nod, like he's saying *yes*.

Yes to the telescope and to looking at the eclipse and to telling me about it one day and to making a model.

Yes to everything we've been through in the last two days.

Yes to how we held each other, just now, and how, in that moment, things felt like they might be okay.

And then he turns, steps into the bus, and is gone.

Chapter Forty-One

12.51 CDT
6th Avenue N., Nashville, TN

I don't have time to go through the proper, hotel parking procedures, so I abandon the Buick on 6th Avenue.

I take the paper star on the piece of string, pull it over my head, tuck it into my dress and close my eyes for a second.

You can do this. His words come back to me. *Being brave…it's part of your DNA.*

I grab Blake's suit from the back, along with the dented hat box. Then I pick up one of the bits of scrunched up paper from the footwell on the side where Christopher was sitting, pull it open and flatten it out. It's a printed email from his dad, dated from a week ago – an itinerary of all the places he wanted Christopher to visit when he was in DC. After the long list of places he signed off: *See you soon. Dad.* My heart jolts.

For a moment I feel like I can't breathe. Like I can't put one foot in front of the other, let alone turn up at Jude's wedding and face my family and then sing that damned song.

Hold it together, Air. Hold it together.

I grab a pen from the glovebox and scrawl across it:
Please don't tow me – my sister's getting married.

Parking attendants aren't known for their compassion but I can't think of what else to do. If I do get towed, Blake's paying for it.

I stick the note on the windscreen under one of the wipers and look over at the hotel.

Music drifts down from the roof terrace. Mom had a ton of jazz pianists come to the house to audition for the wedding. In the end, she went with someone Blake recommended.

And then I think about how Mom will react if I sing the special wedding song rather than Blake and a sick feeling pushes up my throat.

You'd better be here already, Blake, I say through gritted teeth.

Getting to the wedding, that's what I've got to focus on right now.

I take out my phone. I stopped looking at my phone when I left Knoxville – I had to concentrate on driving without the stress of taking in more news – or of having to read Mom's messages. She must have taken our phone call last night as a green light to start sending me texts again. I guess she's got a right to be stressed: the wedding's started and I'm not there yet. Not that she's called for the last hour. Which means that either a) she's too busy – which would make sense or b) that Blake's here and the crisis is over.

I send Mom a quick message as I grab Leda from the back seat:

I'm coming.

The bottom of my dress catches on the Buick door. I hear a loud, clean tear.

'Damn it!'

I look down at the jagged hem.

At least, now, the hem covers my sneakers.

Before I walk through the big glass doors of the hotel, I look up once more at the roof of the hotel and this time I send up a prayer rather than a curse: *Please, please be here, Blake. I can't do this alone.*

The small, sharp points of the star dig into my skin at the base of my throat.

I hold Leda tighter, and walk through the doors.

Chapter Forty-Two

12.59 CDT
The Blue Ridge Hotel, Nashville, TN

It's beautiful. *Obviously*, it's beautiful. Mom wouldn't have settled for anything less than perfect. But it's more than that. Up here, on the roof of the hotel, in the heart of Nashville, under the big sky, it's as though all the ugliness I've been seeing on the news – the broken wreckage of the plane, the stories about what happened in the cockpit – is part of some other world. A world that, for now, doesn't touch this one.

There are chairs arranged in rows, draped in sky blue silk. At the back of each chair, the silk has been gathered and tied into big bows. I bet Mom tied each one of those herself, probably at some crazy hour last night.

I scan the roof terrace, my heart hammering – maybe he made it, just before me.

I look over at the cluster of jazz musicians Blake recommended, thinking that that's where he'd be, jamming with them. But he's not there either.

Even without looking, I can feel it – that he's not here.

When Blake's around, the energy's different. He draws everyone in towards him. There's a centre for people to focus on.

No, he's not here.

The chairs face an arbour of soft, pale pink roses under which Jude and Stephen are going to get married. The two-hundred-year-old roses from Mom's rose garden in DC, the ones she had flown down on ice, along with the white roses for last night's reception.

Even the roses made it, Blake! I want to scream. *Where the hell are you?*

On every chair, there's a pair of glasses for looking at the eclipse. Mom had them made especially: the frames in whites and blues to match the colour scheme of the wedding.

The same roses that are draped over the arbour are everywhere else too. In low vases on the round tables where people will be having their meals. In flowerbeds that Mom had brought in to run along the perimeter of the roof terrace. And soft, single heads nodding in lapels of the men's jackets.

In the corner of the roof terrace, there's a microphone and the stool Mom bought for Blake.

My heart contracts.

As I try to imagine myself standing there, I start to feel dizzy, like the air up here is too thin.

Maybe he'll show up just in time. Like Suzy said. He'll come running in at the last second and snatch the microphone from my hands and before I've had the chance to sing even one flat note, he'll launch into the song.

And by the time he's finished singing, everyone will have forgotten that he was even late.

And everyone will forgive him.

'Ariadne!' Mom's voice booms across the roof terrace.

She runs towards me.

'Where on earth have you been?'

Her face is flushed, her arms flail around her, expressing the frustration and incredulity she's feeling at how late I am. But behind the stress, she's beautiful. She's wearing the same shade of blue as my bridesmaid's dress and as the silk draping the chairs. The colour of Jude's eyes – and of Blake's eyes too. Her trim jacket pinches in at her waist, under it a fitted skirt. She made it herself. She's made every bit of this wedding herself. She didn't trust anyone else to get it right.

'They're here! We can start!' Mom calls over to Reverend Drew, who's milling around with some of the guests.

Rev Drew married Mom and Dad and baptised every one of us, and even though he's retired and ancient, he agreed to come to Nashville to marry Jude and Stephen.

He gives her a nod and goes over to talk to Stephen, who's standing with his best man, Josh, the friend he's had since he was in middle school. Stephen waves at me, his face flooded with relief at the fact that I've shown up.

I'm sorry, I want to tell him.

Sorry for adding to everyone's stress.

Sorry for not getting Blake here on time.

Sorry, in advance, for making a total hash of the song.

Mom turns back to me.

'Will you put that dog down, Ariadne.'

'What?'

'Your dress.'

Oh God, she's seen the hem.

Mom nods at Leda. 'She's shedding on your dress.'

'Oh. Right.' I put Leda down and bend my knees a bit, hoping that the hem will keep covering my sneakers and kind of fold over itself and disguise the tear.

Leda rubs her head against Mom's ankles like a cat.

Mom shakes her off and looks at her watch.

I notice the kennel in the corner of the roof terrace. It has a bow on it too. And my heart sinks.

She looks over my shoulder.

'Where's Blake?'

I feel sick.

She looks back at the suit and the hat box I'm carrying.

'And why isn't he dressed already?'

I take Mom's hand and get her to focus on me for a second.

'Mom,'

Her eyes flit around, searching for him.

'Mom,' I say again.

At last, she looks at me.

I put the suit and hat box down on one of the chairs.

'He's not going to make it, Mom.'

Mom's face folds.

'I don't understand what you're saying, Ariadne.'

'I said Blake's not coming. There was a mix up.' I choke on my words. 'With the plane.'

All the colour drains out of her face. 'A mix up?'

I nod and try to sound casual. 'You know Blake.'

Mom pulls her hands out of mine, grabs her throat and kind of chokes.

'But he was in the car with you. You picked him up.'

'I didn't— He wasn't—'

'You're not making any sense, Ariadne.'

'It's fine, Mom, it's all fine.' I force the words out. Because, for a few more hours, it has to be fine. 'Blake's not here but it's going to be okay.'

'*It's okay?*' Mom throws her hands up in the air. 'This is your sister's wedding, Ariadne. Couldn't he have made sure he got it right just this once? Was it *that* complicated? All he had to do was to show up and sing a song.' She pauses. 'And all you had to do was to make sure that happened.'

I let out a cry. 'I tried Mom, I really tried!'

'You didn't try hard enough!' She puts her hand to her throat, as though she's struggling to breathe. 'You're the one who doesn't let me down, Ariadne. And you know how important this day is for all of us. What on earth happened?'

I let her get it out of her system. And I let her take it out on me. She needs this right now.

'I don't know, Mom. I'm sorry.'

Mom sweeps her palms down the front of her dress, flattening wrinkles that aren't there. It's what she does to calm herself down when she's wound up: she tries to put order back into the world around her. Smoothing wrinkles. Tidying. Clipping dead heads off her roses.

'So, where is he?' she says, her voice strained.

'I don't know.'

'What do you mean, you don't know?'

'He's on his way.'

'*On his way?*'

'He'll show up – sometime.'

'Sometime?'

It's stressing me out, how Mom's repeating everything I'm saying. But it's not really the right time to tell her she's being annoying.

I look around again. 'All this is beautiful, Mom.'

Seeing all this, what she and Jude have created, how special it is, how much it all means to everyone, has convinced me of this more than ever: I have to keep it together. My family needs this one good thing, this one moment in our lives when things feel perfect.

Mom looks kind of paralysed, like she's been trying really hard to make it all work but, with this last bit of information, about Blake not coming, she doesn't know what to do anymore.

I squeeze her arm. 'Let's get started, Mom, like you said.' I look over at Stephen and Josh and Rev Drew and all the guests. 'It's going to be amazing.'

'But what about the song?' She's welling up now.

'I've got a plan, Mom.'

'You've got a *plan* – what plan?'

'Trust me, please.'

She looks at me for a moment. And then nods.

I don't know why she should believe me or what she thinks I can possibly do to work out a song that Blake's meant to sing when he isn't here, but something makes her nod and then she kisses my forehead, straightens her spine and goes back into Mom mode.

'I'm so glad you're here, Ariadne.'

I nod. 'Me too.'

Then something catches the periphery of my vision.

It's a baby grand piano, in a corner of the roof terrace, not far from the mic Mom set up for Blake.

'You had a piano brought in?' I ask.

Mom shakes her head. 'No, it just showed up.'

'What do you mean, it just showed up?'

'A couple of Blake's friends from downtown had it delivered. I asked them what it was about – I *told* them it wouldn't fit – there were no plans for a piano. I had to take a table out. But they insisted.'

Blake's surprise, I think. But it doesn't make sense. He doesn't even play the piano. Maybe he hired someone to accompany him. But that's not his style.

'They dropped something else off too,' Mom says, looking over at the stool where Blake was meant to sing the song. I notice a big white envelope. There's one sitting on the piano too.

'Did you recognise the friends – the ones who brought the stuff up?'

'No. I guess I might have met them sometime but you know what Blake's like.'

Yeah, I know what Blake's like: it's impossible to keep track of all the people Blake calls friends. He has friends everywhere. Hundreds of them. Real. Virtual. And everything in between. It could have been anyone.

'They said Blake was meant to have the things delivered himself – the piano and those envelopes, two days ago, but that he never showed up.'

So Blake thought he'd be here two days ago? That means he knew he was meant to fly into Nashville.

I tug at the collar of my dress.

'Ariadne?' Mom asks. 'You look pale.'

I breathe in and out slowly.

'I'm fine, Mom. Just tired. What's in the envelopes?'

'I don't know.'

'You haven't looked?'

Her eyes well up. 'I thought your brother wouldn't like it. I didn't want to interfere.'

Mom's annoying in a million and one different ways but she's always been really good at respecting our privacy.

'Well, I'm going to have a look,' I blurt out. Because stuff Blake's privacy and stuff his Big Surprise. He doesn't get the right to secrecy, not anymore.

Before Mom can stop me, I go over and pick up the envelope on the stool next to the mic. It has *Blake Shaw* scrawled across the front. In the corner of the envelope, there's a stamp from the music store Blake loves in downtown Nashville. The one over by the piano has the same stamp but this one has Jude's name on it.

My mind races.

I look back down at the envelopes. Then I rip open the one with Blake's name and pull out a small booklet. It's a manuscript. A proper, printed, copyrighted manuscript. Music. And words. For someone to sing. A guitar to accompany. My eyes are burning. I blink and look closer.

As Far as the Stars.

That's the title, typed across the front.

My eyes well up. I swallow hard to stop myself from crying and keep reading.

Under the title, there's a dedication:

For Jude. Written by Blake, inspired by Air.

This is his song. His gift to Jude. And it's meant to be from both of us – our wedding gift to her. And he's had the manuscript professionally bound. He was going to give it to her, probably after he'd sung the song.

I feel like my insides are being wrenched out of my body. Like I'm coming apart from the inside out.

Why aren't you here, Blake?

I look back at the song.

The tune is the same – I know enough about music to recognise that much – but the lyrics are totally different. The words aren't the cheesy words we'd rehearsed together. They are the kind of words I recognise from Blake's other songs: beautiful and surprising and completely his own. Not a cliché in sight.

As I scan the lyrics, I realise that Blake *had* listened when I talked to him about the stars. Really listened. He understood all the stuff that I was so excited about and he'd turned it into this amazing metaphor for Jude and her love for Stephen and what they meant to each other.

I gave him the science and he turned it into a song for Jude.

And that cheesy song we sang – that was Blake taking me for a ride. Because he wanted this to be a surprise. For all of us. And it's awesome. Totally awesome. But I haven't practiced this song.

I look back at the sky.

Whatever you're playing at, cut it out, Blake. We're going to get this wedding started and you're going to come and sing this song. You're going to show up, damn it, like you said you would.

I put down the manuscript and tuck Jude's envelope under my arm. Whatever's inside, I feel like she should have it.

'You opened the envelope?' Mom asks.

'One of them.'

'And?'

'It's the latest version.'

'Of the song?'

'Yep.'

'At least he's been organized about that,' Mom says.

'Yeah, at least that.' I look around. 'Where are Dad and Jude?'

'In the suite – just below us. They've been waiting for you. The other bridesmaids are there too.'

'Okay, I'll go and find her.'

Mom nods, biting her lip.

'It's amazing, Mom. All of it.'

She nods again.

I take her hand. 'You're amazing.'

She stares at me and for the first time in my life I see the Mom who lives behind the confident, plan and organize and make everything perfect and win every case Mom. The real Mom. The Mom who's scared, like the rest of us.

I lean forward and kiss her cheek.

'Go, go speak to Rev Drew,' I say. 'We should get this wedding started.'

'Okay.'

She sucks in her breath and nods. I can tell that she's willing herself to be strong.

As she walks over to Rev Drew, I stay standing there for a beat, trying to find the courage to move on to the next thing I have to do: face Jude.

You want to get into a rocket and fly off into space? Christopher's words come back to me. *Being brave is part of your DNA. You can do this.*

I can do this, I say to myself, over and over. *I can do this.*

Though I know something Christopher doesn't: that getting into a rocket and flying off into space is a piece of cake compared to facing your own family.

I knock on the door.

It flies open. Jude's face is in mine: big and angry and stunningly beautiful.

'Where's Blake?' she says, looking past me.

'He's not here.'

'Not *here*?'

'Not yet.'

'I'm going to kill him!' she says. 'I'm going to kill *you*.'

I'm glad that Jude's back to her usual self – that she's pulled herself together since our phone call: if she has the energy to be mad at me, it means she's back on track. It means she can get through today.

'I'm sorry,' I say.

'You don't come to my rehearsal dinner and then you show up late to the wedding and now Blake's not even here?'

'I'm sorry.'

'It was your only job, Air. To get Blake to my wedding.'

'I know.'

Then she pauses and looks me up and down. Her gaze stops on the tear at the hem. 'What happened to the dress?'

'I'm sorry,' I say again. Because I don't know what else to say.

And I am – really sorry. About being late. About the dress. About all the other thousand and one ways I've failed my sister.

'You said *not yet*,' Jude says. 'You said Blake isn't here *yet*. What does that mean?'

She never misses a thing.

'He might still show up,' I say.

'*Might*?'

'He promised he'd be here. He wouldn't let you down, Jude. Not intentionally.'

And then it hits me. People don't make promises – not the kind Blake made, not the *no-matter-what* type of promises – unless they think there's a chance they might not be able to keep them.

I wish Blake never made the stupid promise. I wish he'd just made the kind of throwaway comment he usually does: *Sure, I'll be there...* Something casual. But he promised.

'Here, this is for you.' I hand Jude the envelope with her name on it.

'What's this?'

I guess she hasn't been upstairs since Blake's friends popped by.

'It's from Blake. One of his friends dropped it off.'

'He's left me a letter?' she says.

'I don't know what it is, Jude. I just thought you should have it.'

Jude takes the envelope and goes to sit in one of the satin-lined chairs by a dressing table.

'Hey – there you are!' Dad comes bounding up to me and gives me a bear hug. 'Thank God you're here, Ariadne,' he whispers.

'Yeah, I'm here.' I hug him back.

It feels good, to have one person who's not laying into me.

'I've missed you, Dad,' I whisper, close to his ear.

He hugs me a little tighter. 'Missed you too.'

And we both know it's a weird thing to say — we saw each other a week ago in DC. But when stuff like this happens, a week can feel like a lifetime. And Dad and I have always relied on each other to get through the hard stuff.

Dad's a go-with-the-flow, make-the-best-of-it-whatever-happens kind of a guy, which makes me happy and drives Mom and Jude crazy because they're big-time planners. But his laid-backness only goes so far: when things go wrong and Mom or Jude flip out and Dad can't fix it, he worries. And nine times out of ten, he comes to me for advice. We're good allies, me and Dad.

Except I haven't been here to help him. And he's probably been through hell in the past forty-eight hours. And yet he's calm. Really calm, like he's worked out that this time, he can't go and lock himself in his study and hide behind his books on Greek mythology.

Out of the corner of my eye I see Jude opening the envelope. She pulls out a booklet that looks identical to the one in the envelope with Blake's name on it, the one I opened and left on his stool by the mic. Her mouth drops open and then she shakes her head. I want to go over to her but then Dad, letting me out of his bear hug, says, 'I take it that now you're here, we can get started? If we don't get started soon there's no telling what your mother's going to do. She's being remarkably calm, but—'

'She's about to flip?'

'I wouldn't have put it in those words, but yes, Ariadne, she's close to the edge.'

Dad doesn't even mention Blake. I guess he's decided to go with him not being here.

I think of Mom talking to Rev Drew upstairs. And then this cello music that Jude picked out for her and Dad, and me and the other bridesmaids to walk down the aisle to, starts playing.

I look over at Jude. She's got an Audrey Hepburn kind of dress: a high, boat-necked collar, sleeveless, long gloves.

I don't like dresses – not on me, not on other people. But Jude's wedding dress is different: it's like it's an extension of her; like it's part of her skin.

She looks terrified. And beautiful. My beautiful, terrified big sister.

I go up to her and take both of her hands and kiss each palm.

'It's going to be perfect, Jude. Just perfect.'

Her six best friends, all bridesmaids, start gathering around her. She asked me to be Maid of Honour, which is a joke considering that any one of her friends looks ten million times more the part than I do. But I guess that being her sister counts for something. So, I hold my head up high and tell myself, again, that I can do this.

Jude goes over to a friend who did her make-up and hands her the white envelope and whispers something to her.

Then, she comes back to us.

'Ready?' Dad asks her.

She gives him a nod.

And then we climb the stairs. The six girls with their perfectly styled hair and their perfect make-up and their non-ripped-dresses follow me. Behind us, Dad, his arm tucked under Jude's.

Chapter Forty-Three

13.10 CDT

I'm struggling to concentrate. Because I'm tired. Because my body's shaking with relief that I actually made it on time. And because I'm scared of what I've got to do next. And I'm holding onto the hope that, by some miracle, Blake might show up so that I don't have to sing his song.

But I still take it all in. How everyone gasps as Jude walks down the aisle.

How Stephen stares at her like she's some kind of alien (a totally stunning alien, obviously) that's randomly landed in his life and he doesn't understand how he got so lucky.

How Mom starts crying when Dad reads 'A Red, Red Rose' by Robert Burns, the same poem that Mom's dad read on their wedding day.

How beautiful it is up here, looking up at the sky and down at Nashville below us.

Every few seconds I turn around to look at the door but Blake hasn't shown up yet.

Leda whines from the kennel in the corner.

And then, it starts to get dark.

And everyone gasps, like they did when Jude walked past them in her dress.

Dad stops reading, just before the final stanza, and stares at the sky.

'Michael!' Mom hisses.

Dad snaps back into the present and finishes:

And fare thee weel, my only Luve! And fare thee weel, a while!

The poem's framed in our kitchen back home. Blake made up a song to go with it once, an off the cuff improvisation after dinner one Sunday, but it made Mom well up all the same. Mom's tough, but Blake's songs get to her every time.

My phone, that I've been trying to carry without anyone noticing (it turns out bridesmaid's dresses don't have pockets), vibrates.

And I will come again, my Luve, Tho' it were ten thousand mile!

I go to silence it but then a notification flashes up on the screen.

There's a missed call – a number I don't recognise.

And then an email alert.

UKFlyer Customer Survey: Take a minute to tell us about your experience and we'll enter you in our airmiles prize draw.

My heart stops. A customer survey?

In a moment, I'm going to have to get up and sing. Which means I should switch off my phone.But I can't look away from that message from UKFlyer.

Before I have time to think, I open the screen.

The words swim in front of my eyes.

Flight UKFlyer0217, Heathrow to Dulles International Airport...

I grab my throat.

The email was sent to my account because I booked the flight.

And I booked it to Dulles.

To Dulles!

I can't breathe.

How the hell could I get that wrong?

I was *meant* to book the flight to Nashville. I told Mom and Blake – I told *myself* – that I'd booked it to Nashville.

My body feels like it's going to pull apart.

I scan through the last forty-eight hours.

I remember being jolted awake by Blake's message pinging into my phone. You know that crazy mix of totally exhausted and totally wired? When every noise makes you jump? That was me that night. I'd been working for days on writing up the findings of the research I'd been doing on my internship at the Air and Space Museum. I wanted the paper to be good. Really good. I thought that if I impressed my advisor on the internship programme, she'd write me a glowing recommendation when I applied to MIT. Maybe even put in a good word for me – she was an MIT alum.

So even though it was three in the morning, I woke right up when Blake left that voicemail.

It took me a moment to work out what he was actually saying: that he hadn't booked a flight back to the US. That, if we didn't do something – like *now* – he'd miss Jude's wedding.

I remember texting back a whole load of messages, not caring if whoever had lent him the phone read them first:

Seriously, Blake!?
You couldn't have got your shit together?
Just this once?

But, of course I'd helped him.

Because that's what I do.

I remember getting out of bed, dog-tired, my limbs lead weights, my head stuffed with wool.

I remember opening my laptop and going onto the UKFlyer website to book a last-minute flight. I'd booked flights from this site so many times that it had stored my preferences.

I remember sending Blake another text about how expensive the flight was and that Mom wouldn't let him hear the end of it.

He didn't answer. He was probably asleep, or off getting inspiration somewhere. Blake wasn't worried; he knew I'd take care of it.

So, I booked the flight.

I remember sending Blake a final text to tell him that he totally owed me. And then I forwarded the flight confirmation without even bothering to check the details. Because I didn't need to check. I was organised. I got this stuff right. Always.

BE ON TIME! Was the last thing I wrote. All caps. Me shouting at him that I'd got him as far as I could; the rest was on him.

And after that, I closed my laptop and went back to bed.

And the next thing I knew, I was driving to Nashville. And then he texted to say he was on the way to DC.

Breathe…Breathe…Breathe…

I look out across the rooftop. My body's somewhere else, drifting far above all these people.

I feel like I shouldn't be here.

I screw shut my eyes.

So I was tired? Big deal. I'd done things before when I was tired and hadn't messed up.

I don't mess up. Ever. Not when it matters. God, I don't even mess up when it *doesn't* matter. I totally rock the details. It's my fucking USP!

I press the palms of my hands against my eyeballs until I see darkness and stars and flashes of red.

And I picture what must have happened next: when Blake got to the airport and actually looked at his email, and realised the flight was to Dulles.

He must have done a double take.

Didn't she say Nashville? he must have thought.

But only for a second.

The mix-up wouldn't have bothered Blake.

He'd have shrugged. Gone with it.

Because he trusted me.

Because he knew that his little sister would have got it right.

And because going to DC made sense. I'd pick him up after my internship. We'd drive together to Nashville.

Yeah. It made sense.

But it was wrong.

It wasn't the plan.

You were meant to go to Nashville, Blake.

My heart speeds up.

I put Blake on that plane. The one that crashed.

I drop my phone.

My eyes fly open.

The first person I see is Dad. His head is bowed. He's stopped reading.

Dad catches my eye, comes over, sits back down and puts his hand on my shoulder.

And that's when I look over to the mic and to the stool. It's time for the song. And Blake's not coming. Not ever.

Chapter Forty-Four

13.26 CDT
The Eclipse

I don't think anyone notices me get up; they're too busy looking at the sky through the glasses Mom put on everyone's chairs.

No one except Leda, who runs out of the kennel and follows me over to the mic.

As I perch on the edge of the stool, every bone in my body shaking, she lies down at my feet, her warm body resting against my ankles.

Every second, the world gets a little darker. And one by one, the stars come out.

And I'm grateful for it – for the darkness. So that no one can see me. And for the stars, because they make me feel a bit less alone.

I look across the roof terrace and I think I see someone standing in the doorway. Maybe a guest who's late.

All this time, I believed he'd show up. But he couldn't have, could he? Not even if he wanted to.

I'll be there, no matter what. I promise.

My heart contracts.

I swallow hard, trying to chase the dryness out of my mouth. Trying to get some oxygen into my body.

You can do this, you can do this, you can do this…

And doing this matters now, more than it ever did. Because it's all I've got left to do before I tell my family that Blake's never coming back. And that it's my fault.

Then I take the manuscript out of the envelope. The new song, the one that Blake wrote. His surprise for the wedding. For Jude. For me.

The words blur in front of me:

As far as the stars are from the earth… As far as the moon is from the ocean…

Singing the cheesy song I'd rehearsed with Blake was one thing; singing *this*, the words inspired by the thing that I loved most in the world – the way Blake had made his gift from both of us – I don't know if I can handle that.

I don't know if I can handle anything anymore. Not after what I've just found out: that I'm to blame for getting Blake on the wrong plane.

My legs are shaking so hard now I think that, any second, I'm going to crumple.

Then I notice the shadow in the doorway again, shifting.

It's so dark that besides a few faces lit up by the candles Mom put on the tables, it's hard to see.

Maybe he didn't get onto the plane to Dulles, I tell myself. *Maybe he worked out that I'd got it wrong. Which means he could still make it.* I clench my fists at my sides. *Maybe he borrowed some money from a friend – he's done that before – and booked a new flight to Nashville. Which means he could still make it. And if he does, I want him to see that I can do this.*

I scan the wedding guests and my face falls on Jude. Her head's resting on Stephen's shoulder: they're both

362

looking up at the dark sky. Any moment now, she'll look back down and see me at the mic.

Oh God.

I think about what Blake said about confidence – that it was the most important part of his performances. That confidence gives off this magnetic energy that pulls everyone in. That sometimes, people don't even take in what they're hearing; they simply buy into it because they see how in control you are of what you're doing.

I don't know if that's true. Blake's an awesome musician – *that's* what makes him good. But right now, faking confidence is the only thing I've got.

I tap the mic, like I've seen Blake do. It gives out an electronic whine, which makes a few people turn their heads but they quickly look back at the sky. They think it's the sound system playing up.

Jude looks over to me. I avoid her gaze. I can't cope with her, *What the hell are you doing up there?* look. Or her disappointment that I'm not Blake.

But then, from the corner of my eye, I see her get up. She kisses Stephen's cheek, then she hitches up the train of her dress, floats between the tables and makes her way to the baby grand piano.

She takes the envelope from the piano bench – her friend must have placed it there at some point during the ceremony. She pulls out the booklet and places it in front of her. Then, like I've watched her do a million times before, she straightens her spine and takes a deep breath. She looks over at me and mouths, 'Ready?'

My heart stops. She's going to play? At her own wedding? Was this Blake's plan all along? That they'd play the song together, like they used to play when they were really little? My heart contracts. He really got it for once: that this wedding was meant to be about Jude, not him. Even when he was performing, she would be in the spotlight. He must have had a piano partition drawn up for her.

God, I love you, Blake, I think. *And God, I hate you for not being here.*

My whole body shaking, I nod and mouth back, 'Ready.'

Then I close my eyes.

Leda's body slumps against mine, heavy and warm on my feet.

I hear the piano starting. Jude's fingers light as water over the keys, like she's played this song a thousand times before.

And then I open my mouth and start singing.

Chapter Forty-Five

13.27 CDT

By the time the sun comes back out from behind the moon, I worry that everyone's staring at me.

I fix my eyes on the arbour of Mom's heirloom roses so I don't have to look at the guests – or Mom and Jude's faces either.

I've got through the first few lines of the song but my voice is wavering and now that everyone can see me, I don't know whether I can do this anymore.

My voice sounds shrill. I don't think I'm even in key. I know that I'm ruining it – that if I stopped singing and let Jude play, it would be better.

My pulse beats in my wrist and behind my ears and at my throat.

*You can't do this...you can't do this...*my brain yells at me.

The words on the manuscript paper swim in front of my eyes.

Then I notice someone shifting in the doorway again.

I blink.

My heart contracts.

For a second, I think that maybe, through some crazy twist of fate, he's here after all. That even though I messed up, the universe had his back, and he made it.

Leda stands up beside me.

And then he steps forward.

I blink again.

My eyes wander back to the doorway. He's still there, the guest who came late. And now, with the sun back up, I see the tangled hair. I see the telescope held up to his eye. My telescope. And then, as though he can feel me watching, he lowers it and cradles it in his arms and looks right at me.

I scan the wedding guests around him. I was wrong. People aren't looking at me. They're looking at Jude. Most of them have never heard her play; she's private about her piano. Besides her friends at Julliard and her family, people could know Jude really well and never have a clue that she was an amazing musician. But now they know. That she's brilliant. Totally brilliant. So brilliant that she can take up a partition on her wedding day that she'd never played before and turn it into magic. So brilliant that it doesn't matter how bad my singing is – or whether I'm singing at all. Blake planned for this. Not the part about me singing but the part about everyone seeing Jude for who she was: a beautiful bride but also the amazing piano player.

My eyes flicker back to the guy standing in the doorway.

He brushes his tangled hair out of his eyes. Pale grey eyes. A sideways smile.

For a second, I actually convince myself into thinking it's Blake; that all the facts I know about what's happened to him have somehow vanished, that he made it: that I wished him into being here.

But it's not him. Not even close. It's Christopher.

Christopher, who should be on his way to Atlanta.

And in this moment, I feel angry at him for being here; for standing in the spot where Blake should be, just like he did at Dulles airport.

Leda rushes through the guests towards him.

And that's when I break down.

I close my mouth – halfway through a line, I just stop singing.

And now there's no sound, only my breathing in the mic.

I drop the mic. It crashes to the floor. A dense thud.

Leda turns and runs back to me. She sits at my feet, looking up at me, waiting.

Jude stops playing.

A gasp ripples through the guests. Not the gasp like the one when Jude walked down the aisle or when the eclipse started. They're gasping because they know that something's wrong.

And then I run.

I run between the tables, keeping my eyes low. My dress catches and rips on the back of a chair but still, I keep running.

Lead weaves between my feet. Silent. So close.

I run across the dance floor.

I run to the door.

I run so fast I nearly crash into Christopher.

He steps back.

I stare at him for a second. He's just standing there. Looking at me. His brow furrowed.

'Hi…' He mumbles.

Leda jumps up at him.

I shake my head.

It wasn't meant to be him.

Christopher holds out a hand.

'Air—'

But I push past him, run through the door that leads to the rooftop terrace and head down the back stairs of the hotel.

Chapter Forty-Six

After the Eclipse

I collapse onto the stairs and sink into myself.

My head pounds.

I've messed everything up. *Everything*.

Leda sits down beside me and settles her muzzle on the ripped hem of my dress. Her body's shaking.

I know she wants me to hold her. Because she feels it. Of course she does. Maybe she's felt it this whole time – that Blake's not coming back.

But I can't pick her up.

I don't have the strength.

And more than that.

I don't get to make her feel better. I did this to her. I did this to all of us.

My thoughts crash into each other.

Why didn't I look up the flight details back at the airport? Did I know all this time that I was the one who was responsible for all this?

Nothing makes sense. Nothing's going to make sense ever again.

I don't know what to do or where to go. How can I face them – Jude and Mom and Dad, my family, the people who trusted me to take care of Blake?

I think about getting back into the car and driving. Driving for ever. Maybe the wedding will keep going without me. Maybe, once the guests have gone home and Jude and Stephen have headed off on their honeymoon, Mom and Dad will go back to DC and pick up their work and everyone will forget about me.

And then I'll disappear.

And no one will ever have to see me again: the girl who ruined their lives.

I shut my eyes.

Please make me disappear, I say to myself. *Please make me disappear.*

And then I hear footsteps echoing down the stairs above me.

Leda gets to her feet and skitters up the steps.

He comes and stands on the step beside me.

I want to get up and run but I can't move.

Christopher's standing too close. He brushes his hair out of his eyes and takes a few steps away.

'Why aren't you on the bus to Atlanta?' I ask.

The words come out hard and small and mean. But I don't care. Why the hell did he have to come here and stand in the doorway like some kind of ghost?

His face is flushed. A trail of sweat runs down the side of his brow.

'I – I – I'm sorry,' he says.

'You're *sorry*?'

My fists are clenched and my jaw juts out. I try to relax my body but I can't. Every part of me is shaking.

'When I heard— When they released the names of the passengers—'

My head spins. 'They released the names?'

370

'Not to the public. Just to the families.' He pauses.

He knows that Blake was on the flight to Dulles.

'Did the airline call you?' Christopher asks.

I think about the missed call on my phone – the number I didn't recognise.

'I thought you'd want—' he goes on.

'Want *what*?'

He doesn't answer. He knows that there's nothing he can say right now to calm me down.

'If you hadn't shown up like that, I could have kept singing,' I clench my teeth. 'You ruined everything.'

'I'm sorry,' he stutters.

'It wasn't meant to be you!' I say, choking on my words. 'Not in DC. Not in the car. Not at Leda Springs. Not at Deer Ridge. Not at the diner. And not here.' I swallow hard. 'You're not the one who's meant to be here.'

My words ricochet off the walls of the stairwell.

Our eyes catch for a second and then he bows his head.

We sit in silence for a beat.

And I know it's not fair. I know it's *really* not fair. Blaming him like this.

And I want to tell him that the song doesn't matter.

And that it wasn't his fault that I stopped singing.

That it's my fault – all of it. That I put Blake on the wrong plane.

But I can't find the words to tell him that right now.

I hear footsteps again. My eyes drift upwards; I see the shimmer of a white dress coming down the stairs.

Christopher notices too. I hear his breath speed up.

'I'm sorry,' he says again.

And then rushes down the stairs to the next floor and through the doors that lead to the elevator.

Leda follows him and I'm about to call out when I hear more footsteps. A moment later, Jude's standing on the step beside me, looking down. I can smell her perfume – crushed pink roses, to match the theme for the wedding.

Why did everything have to be so damned perfect?

Everything except me. And what I did.

I can't face her.

I can't face all the stuff that she's going throw at me.

I can hear her words already: *All you had to do was to get Blake here...You messed up the song...You ruined the most important day of my life...You ruined everything, Air.*

And she doesn't even know the worst of it.

I look down at my feet. At my sneakers. I couldn't even get the shoes right.

There's nothing more I can say or do.

Jude sits down next to me.

I want to get up and run but I can't move.

And then Jude puts her hands on my shoulders and I think she's going to shake me in that way people shake those they're really mad at. Like words aren't enough.

But she doesn't shake me.

And she doesn't yell.

Instead, she pulls me in close and whispers into my ear:

'Thank you.'

'*Thank you?*'

She nods. 'It must have been really hard – getting up and singing Blake's song like that.'

I sigh and choke at the same time and squeeze her back, really hard.

She's thanking me? After everything I've done?

'You were amazing, Jude – how you played.'

'I don't know about amazing.'

'You were. Totally amazing.'

She smiles at me. She looks tired but there's a light in her eyes and I can tell she's happy. That she knows she's done the right thing: getting married to Stephen. And it's not a compromise, not if it's what makes her happy, not if it's who she is. And playing in front of all her friends, on her wedding day, that made her happy too. If Blake had suggested it she would never have agreed; I guess that's why he kept it secret. But it was perfect.

'It felt good,' she says. 'To play. It felt good to perform with you.' She lets out a light laugh. 'Who would ever have thought, hey? You and me, up there. When we were kids, you never wanted to join in when we played – Mom, Dad, me and Blake.'

'I didn't join in because I knew I'd spoil it.'

'Well, you didn't spoil it.'

Jude pulls away, takes both my hands and kisses my palms one at a time. Then she looks down at my feet.

'But don't think I didn't notice.'

'What?'

'The sneakers.' She rolls her eyes. 'The *dirty* sneakers.'

'I'm sorry.' My voice breaks. 'I'm so sorry.'

I try to steel myself to tell her. But the words won't come.

'I'm going to kill Blake for bailing on my wedding.'

A hot, raw feeling pushes up my throat.

'Jude…'

'I mean, it's my wedding, damn it!' she says. 'He could have at least *tried* to be here.'

'He tried…'

'I guess we can Photoshop him into the pictures,' she says sarcastically.

'Jude, listen.'

Jude looks at me like she's got her head around the fact that Blake's late and that I ruined her song and that, somehow, it's not the end of the world because she got to wear the dress and got to marry Stephen and the roses were beautiful – and, if she's honest, she kind of thought Blake would mess up. We all did. Because ever since we were old enough to remember, Blake messing up has been part of our lives. And that, sure it's disappointing, but it's our normal. And like she said, she'll give him a hard time for it. But in the grand scheme of things, it's okay. Everything's going to be okay.

The way Jude looks at me, grateful and sad and relieved and pissed off at Blake but happy too – because she's married and her wedding was beautiful – makes something inside me break.

I'm going to have to tell her. I'm going to have to tell all of them.

I choke and then I let out a sob.

'He's not coming back.'

I feel her pull away.

'Blake's not coming back. Not ever.' I swallow hard. 'And it's my fault.'

Once I've told Jude – all of it: that Blake was on the plane to Dulles, the one that crashed, that there are no known survivors, and that he was on the wrong plane because of me, she just sits there. Then she tilts her head up, runs the pads of her thumbs under her eyes to brush away the smudged mascara, and says:

'Let's go back up to the roof.'

'What?'

'People will be waiting for us.'

'But—'

'We need to do this, Air. For Mom and Dad. For everyone.'

They say that at times of shock and tragedy, everyone resorts to their true selves. That either they totally fall apart or they do something amazing, something that no one expects. Out of all of us, I never thought my big sister would turn out to be the strong one, but in this moment, as she stands up and brushes down the creases in her long, white dress and holds out her hand to help me get back on my feet, I realise that it could be that she's the strongest one of all.

So, we go back up to the wedding.

And we wait.

We wait for the photos to be taken.

We wait for her and Stephen to cut the cake.

We wait for Dad to give his speech, which is kind of embarrassing and not really funny, even though he tries really hard for it to be, but he's so obviously proud of Jude and so emotional about his little girl growing up, that everyone gets swept along and claps really loudly at the end.

We wait for her and Stephen to have their first dance.

We wait for her to change into her going away outfit, also made by Mom.

We wait for her to kiss all the guests goodbye.

And for all that time, somehow, I manage to keep it together.

Jude was right. We needed to do this. We had to finish the wedding, right up to the end, because afterwards, when everyone finds out about Blake, it will be all we had to cling to. And we'll never be able to go back.

All through this, I wonder where Christopher is. And I realise that I shouldn't have yelled at him. None of this is his fault.

The small paper star presses into the base of my throat.

I'm sorry, Christopher, I whisper. *I'm sorry.*

'Let us know as soon as you've landed,' Mom says, hugging Jude tight.

She hasn't said anything yet, about Blake not being here and about me messing up the song. I guess she's holding out too, until the wedding's over.

I have to say something now.

Jude holds Mom extra tight. 'Thank you, Mom,' she says.

All of us know that this whole wedding, everything from the napkin rings to the rose petals on the tables, is down to her.

Mom closes her eyes and rests her head on Jude's shoulder. 'Of course,' she says.

And then Jude takes Mom's hand and Dad's too and looks over at me.

'Air and I have to talk to you guys.'

Jude looks at me and our eyes lock.

I thought I was going to have to do this alone. But Jude's here with me now. She's taken it on.

'Why don't we go down to the lobby?' Jude says.

'But, that's not how we planned things,' Mom's voice is strained and tired. 'You and Stephen were meant to say goodbye up here. You're meant to throw your bouquet—'

Jude takes Mom's hand gently. 'Mom, please go with it, just this once.'

'It would be nice to see you off from downstairs,' Dad says. 'Let's do that.'

I shoot him a grateful look.

'Okay,' Mom says, still a bit wary.

We all get in the elevator. Mom doesn't stop talking about the wedding, how perfect and beautiful everything was despite me being late and wearing sneakers and having a tear in my dress and breaking down in the middle of the song. Despite Blake not showing up at all.

And that's when I lose it. Cooped up in that elevator with my family, with the people who trusted me. As soon as the doors open, I run out through the lobby onto the street.

'Air!' Dad calls after me.

Tears are running down my cheeks now. I can't face them. I can't.

'Air!'

When I get outside, I look up at the dark sky, at the billions of stars, and my legs buckle. I slump down onto the steps of the hotel and sink my head into my knees.

Dad sits down next to me. He puts his arm around my shoulders.

'It's all been a bit much, hasn't it, my love?' he says.

And that makes me break down more.

He thinks that I'm upset because I'm tired. Because the wedding's all been too much. Because Blake messed up his plans. And that just makes me feel worse. He hasn't got a clue how bad it is.

My shoulders are shaking. And then every part of me starts convulsing, like I don't have the strength anymore to live in my own body.

'Oh, Air...' Dad says.

I shake my head. 'You don't understand, Dad.'

'So, tell me.'

'I can't... I can't... Not this time.'

I tilt my head up to the sky and let hot tears rush down my cheeks.

'He said he'd always be here,' I choke out the words. 'He promised.'

'Air?'

'He said I'd feel it – that even if he was gone – I could look up at the stars and see him. Know he was with me. But he's not here, Dad. I just feel empty.'

He rubs my back gently. 'You're going to have to start at the beginning, Air.' He draws me in and kisses my cheek. 'Start from first principles.'

It's something he always says when I'm upset and he's trying to comfort me – *Start from first principles.* And usually, it steadies me, trying to talk things through like they're a logical equation.

But not this time. There's nothing logical about what's happened.

My brother's died. And it's my fault.

My throat tightens. I feel like I've forgotten to breathe.

Dad takes my hand: 'Breathe in slowly, Air...take your time.'

He breathes in and out, trying to get me to follow him. I try but my breath comes in and out of my body in jagged gasps.

'I can't do this, Dad...' I blurt out. 'Not without him.' I look down again.

Dad takes my face between his hands and makes me look at it him.

'Whatever it is, Air, you can tell me. You can *always* tell me, you know that.'

I bite my lip and nod and try hard to get myself back into a place where I can talk but I'm still shaking and I'm still crying and I don't know how I'm ever going to get through this. How am I meant to live when he's not here? And when I know what I've done.

I guess Dad senses that it's too hard for me to talk. That somehow, this is different from the other times when I've come to him upset. He places his hand behind my head and draws it into his chest and we sit there for a while, my whole body leaning into his, his hand stroking my hair. And he doesn't ask me anymore – about what's wrong or what I'm so upset about or why I'm falling apart on him like this. He just waits with me, in the silence, and lets me cry. After a while, our eyes drift up to the sky and I wonder whether he feels it too, even without knowing why; that nothing's ever going to be the same again.

I don't know how long we sit there. Maybe for a few seconds or a few minutes. Maybe longer. But as I lean into him, feeling held for the first time in days, it starts to fill up again, the emptiness that I've been feeling ever since I found out that Blake was on the plane that crashed. And I know that the emptiness is never going to go away, not completely. That it's going to be inside me for ever. In all of us. Because nothing will ever be able to fill it – to make up for the huge hole that Blake has left in our lives. No matter how much we love each other, no matter how much time passes. But I know, too, that I'm not alone.

When Dad and I get back to the lobby, Jude, Mom and Stephen are sitting on a bunch of armchairs in the corner.

I exchange a look with Jude; I guess she found a way to keep Mom waiting inside while Dad went after me.

'What's all this about?' Mom says, standing up.

Jude opens her mouth to speak.

And then I interrupt her. Because it's on me. I have to tell them.

'Something's happened, Mom,' I say.

'Shall I give you guys some space?' Stephen asks, standing up.

Stephen knows how intense our family can be. Because we're so close. Because we're all kind of crazy. Because of Blake. But he never minds. It's part of what persuaded me that he'd be good for Jude. Good for all of us.

'No, stay,' Dad says. 'You're family now.'

It surprises me – how Dad takes control like that. Usually it would be Mom who stepped in to make the decision. It surprises me like his calmness did earlier. But when he looks straight at me and gives me a small nod I know that he's going to be strong for me, no matter how bad things are.

I hear the lift ping and look up. It's Christopher. He walks out, Leda following him. When she sees me, Leda dashes over and comes to lie at my feet. He brought her back to me.

Christopher catches my eye for a second.

He walks over and takes the telescope off his shoulder and places it at my feet beside Leda.

I can feel my whole family staring at him.

'Thanks,' he says.

And then he walks off down the lobby and out through the hotel doors.

'Who was that?' Mom asks. 'And why did he have your telescope?'

She's flustered. She hates not knowing what's going on.

'Christopher,' I say.

'Who's Christopher? And why was he at the wedding? And how do you know him?'

Christopher wasn't part of Mom's plans for the wedding. He wasn't part of my plan, either.

I press my hand over hers.

'It's not important, Mom. Not now.'

Then I look up at Jude and Dad and Stephen.

And I think about Blake. How he should have been the one who messed up, not me. That that's why I didn't even bother to check the flight details. Because I never get stuff like that wrong. *Infallible-Air* he'd called me once. And I'd laughed. But I went with it. Because he was right. If Jude was the beautiful one and Blake was the charming, loveable one – then I was the reliable one. A sure thing.

Only no one's infallible, right?

'He was on the wrong plane,' I say.

Mom looks up.

'You said that already.'

'No, Mom. This is different.'

Jude chokes. Her shoulders slump and she starts shaking. She's been holding it all together for too long.

'Jude?' Mom says, startled. 'What's the matter?'

Stephen puts his arm around Jude.

Jude's sobbing now. Big, loud gulps that don't go at all with the Jude who's wearing a beautiful dress with perfect hair and make-up.

'So, where is he?' Mom asks.

I look over at Dad. He looks at me too and we hold each other's gaze. And usually his gaze is steady. He's going to help me. He's going to make sure they're okay – Mom and Jude and Stephen and all the guests up there, and all those people who are going to fall apart when they realise that Blake's not coming back. I don't have to do this alone. And right then all I want to do is go to Dad and bury myself in his arms, like when we were outside – and stay there, until all this goes away.

But I have to face it. I owe it to them. To Blake.

I straighten my spine.

'It was my fault,' I say.

Mom's head snaps up.

'*Your* fault?'

'I was the one who booked him onto the wrong plane.'

I want to make excuses:

Blake was meant to have booked his own plane.

I booked the same flight I always do: Heathrow to DC. I was so used to booking that flight path that I didn't even think.

I was tired after working so hard on the research paper.

And stressed about the wedding.

And so I made a mistake. The biggest mistake of my life.

But I don't say anything else. Because none of those reasons are good enough. It was my fault. Period.

Everything goes silent. Jude's fingers slip into mine.

'He's not coming back, Mom,' I say.

The words feel like stones in my throat.

Mom's face folds in on itself.

Behind her, I see a TV screen. The news is on. An aerial shot off the coast of Ireland. And then they're interviewing a guy standing on the shore next to a fishing boat. The guy's pointing at the sky and shaking his head. A rolling banner with a phone number for friends and relatives of the victims comes up on the screen. And a tag line: *No known survivors.*

'Blake got a plane into DC,' I explain, as calmly as I can. 'He was meant to fly into Nashville – as you know, that was the plan.' The words stick in my throat but I force myself to keep going. 'I was going to drive down and pick him up and bring him to the hotel. But I booked a flight to DC instead. And the plane never made it.' I pause. 'So it's on me.'

Everything goes very still.

Stephen takes Jude's other hand.

Dad puts his arm around Mom.

And I sit there, Leda still at my feet, staring at the TV screen.

Silence.

I'd tried to prepare myself for this moment.

For all the questions I couldn't answer.

For making sense of the Blake-shaped hole that my family was going to have to face.

For Mom being Mom and jumping in and trying to solve the problem before I'd even finished explaining.

And then for it really sinking in. That if weren't for me, Blake would be with us. He'd be alive.

But I wasn't ready for this. For silence. More than silence. A stillness, like everyone and everything around me has stopped breathing.

And that's when I get it. Really get it. That I've known all along that Blake wasn't coming back. But that I couldn't let myself believe it. Because of this. Because of what it would do to them.

Jude's stopped crying. Her eyes are rimmed red. She's leaning into Stephen, staring into space. I guess she's used up all that strength she had getting through the wedding, and now it's sinking in, what I said to her as we sat on the stairs under the roof terrace.

Dad's holding Mom's hand, stroking it over and over with his thumb.

All the colour's drained from Mom's face. She keeps shaking her head slowly from side to side.

Even Leda's quiet, her head between her paws, her ears flopped over her eyes.

Then the silence breaks.

'What do we do?' Mom's voice comes out small and wobbly.

My heart sinks. Not once in the seventeen years of my life have I heard Mom ask this question. A meteor as big as the Empire State Building could crash into our back yard and she'd know what to do. She'd take charge.

'This is what we're going to do,' Dad says.

Every one of us shifts a bit and looks at Dad like we've never seen him before.

He clears his throat. 'It's the middle of the night, so we're going to go back to our rooms and get some sleep and then, tomorrow, we'll work out what we're going to do next.' He looks around at us, catching each of our eyes. 'We'll face it, together.' He pauses. 'Like we always do.' Dad speaks in this strong, confident voice like, for once in our family's life, he's going to get to make a decision. And like he knows it's the right one.

Mom shakes her head. 'I want to go to DC now.'

'And do what?' Dad asks. 'By the time we get there, everyone will be asleep. There's nothing more we can do tonight.'

Mom looks from Jude to Stephen. 'But they were meant to leave for their honeymoon – we haven't booked a room for them. And the hotel's full. The wedding guests. The people who came to see the eclipse—'

'We'll find them a room, my love,' Dad says, gently.

Then he takes Mom's hand and kisses it. I notice that her skin is red and chapped from all the flower arranging she's been doing for the wedding.

'You're exhausted,' Dad says. 'We all are. Let's go and get some rest. Tomorrow's going to be a long day.'

Mom looks up at him, her lips trembling, and nods. Then she leans into his chest. He kisses the top of her head and closes his eyes. I can feel his relief that Mom's agreed to stay here rather than tearing off to the airport in the middle of the night.

Jude starts sobbing. Stephen holds her.

Dad opens his eyes and looks over at me and I can tell that he's grateful I'm here with him, to hold the family together.

I think about how, already now, before any of us have had the time to process any of this properly, the concentric circles of our family have shifted.

And then I think about Christopher. About how he came all this way. How he sat with me for hundreds of miles while I kidded myself into believing that if I got to the wedding in time, Blake would be here and everything would be okay. And how he went with it. More than that, how he helped me. Because he understood, somehow, that that was what I needed to do.

I realise how I'm not ready to go back to the hotel room Mom booked for me and to lie in bed unable to sleep, replaying all the details of what's happened.

And I don't want to be alone.

Jude has Stephen, and Mom has Dad. Blake was the one I turned to when things fell apart. Not because he could do anything to sort it out but because just being with him made things feel better.

More than anything, I think they need space from me: the person who got things so badly wrong.

I stand up slowly.

'They can use my room,' I say. 'Jude and Stephen.'

Mom stares at me, like she can't process any more information right now.

'Air,' Dad asks. 'What's going on?'

'There's something I've got to do,' I say. 'Somewhere I've got to go.'

All four of them look at me, stunned.

Leda gets onto her feet and starts thumping her tail against the hotel lobby.

'Where?' Mom asks, her voice wobbly. 'Where on earth do you have to go?'

'To Atlanta.'

I know it's crazy. But right now, it's the only thing that makes sense to me. It's the only way I can get through this.

Mom lets out a sob. 'Atlanta – what are you talking about?'

'I'm going with a friend. I met him at DC. At the airport. He had someone on the plane too.'

I'm starting to walk away already.

'Air!' Mom calls after me.

'I don't understand what's going on,' Jude says.

I come back and take her hands and kiss each palm in turn, like she did mine when we were talking in the stairwell.

'His name's Christopher. The guy you saw just now – the one who had my telescope. He's going to Atlanta to find his mom and I need to go with him.' I pause. 'He lost his dad – in the crash.'

Jude's eyes fill with tears.

My throat feels thick with guilt at leaving them, but I have to go.

'He's been here for me – through everything.' I swallow hard. 'And he doesn't have anyone.'

I wipe a tear from Jude's cheek.

My eye catches Stephen's and although he doesn't say a word, I can see from how he's looking at me that he's going to look after her for me. And everything that's going on right now, I'm grateful again that he's here – that the wedding happened, that he's in our family. That there's this one good thing for us to hold onto.

'I'll come back. As soon as I've done this, I'll drive to DC and then we'll be together, I promise. I have to do this,' I say.

I kiss Mom's forehead, trying not to look at her eyes. If I don't go quickly, I'll lose my nerve.

Then I turn to Dad and give him a hug, like the one he gave me before the wedding.

'You got this, Dad?' I whisper in his ear.

His head nods against my cheek. 'I've got this.'

He holds me for a really long time and I know that, once I've got back from Atlanta, when I'm back in DC, it's Dad who's going to be there for me. He's the one who's going to help me from going crazy thinking about what I've done.

'Thanks,' I whisper back.

He gives me one last squeeze and then I pull away.

I know that going like this might be wrong. That perhaps I'm running away from things again, like I ran away from the truth that Blake was on that plane. From having to watch Mom and Dad come to terms with what's happened. From having to live inside me – the person who's to blame for all this. But I know that even though going might be wrong, it's right too. And that no matter how crazy it sounds, being with Christopher is the only thing that makes sense right now. And that he deserves to have someone with him.

I pick Leda up, hold her tight against my chest and feel her head rest into my shoulder. Then I turn and run out through the hotel doors.

Chapter Forty-Seven

6th Avenue, Nashville, TN

He's walking past the Buick when Leda catches up with him. She jumps up at him.

'Hey, buddy.' Christopher takes her into his arms. Leda licks his face.

I can tell that he's avoiding having to look at me. He probably thinks I'm going to lay into him again.

'I'm sorry I yelled at you,' I say.

He still doesn't look at me.

'It was kind of you to come,' I go on.

His spine straightens a little.

'It's just …' I can't find any words to say it. That Blake's gone. That nothing's going to be right ever again. That although Christopher coming all this way is like the nicest thing anyone's ever done for me, it doesn't make any of it go away.

'It's okay,' he says, 'I understand.'

'I've told them,' I blurt out. 'I've told my family.'

He nods.

'Everything, I mean.'

Christopher takes his backpack off his shoulders, places it on the sidewalk, kneels down and rubs the soft hairs under Leda's chin.

'I told them that I was the one who booked the flight,' I say.

He stops stroking Leda but he doesn't look up.

'Did you hear what I said? It was my fault.'

He doesn't move.

'I booked Blake onto the wrong flight. I put him on the flight to DC. The one that crashed. It was all my fault.'

He still doesn't say anything.

I slump down on the curb.

'It was all my fault.'

He sits beside me.

'It wasn't your fault,' he says.

'How can it not be my fault? I put Blake on that plane.'

'It doesn't work like that.'

I look up at him, waiting for him to explain. '*It doesn't work like that?*'

'You didn't know the plane was going to crash.'

'I know this is true. Logically. Objectively. But the point still stands: if Blake had flown into Nashville – if I'd booked him onto the right plane – he'd still be here.'

'It's still not your fault that the plane crashed.'

I look out across Nashville. My brother's city.

'They're still in shock, I think, my parents, about Blake.'

Christopher nods.

I think about those first hours in the car together. How we were kind of numb too. How I nearly crashed the car when Blake's voice came over the speakers. Did I already know it then? That he was on the plane? That he was already gone?

Christopher looks up at the windscreen of the Buick and smiles. I see the scrunched-up piece of paper that was once one of Christopher's models. And then my words.

'You thought a note would do the trick?' he says.

'Well, the car's still here, isn't it?' I say.

'Or maybe the parking attendants took the day off because of the eclipse.'

'Maybe,' I say.

Christopher looks down and nods at the bag on my shoulder. 'Thank you for the loan of the telescope. The eclipse was cool, hey?'

'I was so busy messing up the song I didn't see it.'

'You didn't mess up the song.'

'I did.'

'You showed up.'

'And then I left.'

'You still showed up. And you tried.'

'Yeah, I tried.'

He looks up at the sky. 'And we'll get another chance.'

'Another chance?'

'To see an eclipse.'

My mind fast forwards to a time, years ahead, when I get to see the world go dark in the middle of the day. I wonder where I'll be and who I'll be with and whether it'll even matter to me, what's happening up there, in the universe.

'How did you get to Nashville?' I ask.

'I hitched a ride.'

'*You did*?'

'Yep. I upped my game.'

'Someone actually stopped?'

'Yeah, someone *actually* stopped. A red pick-up in fact.' He smiles. 'Between the Buick and the pick-up, I've had the all-American experience, right?'

'Right.'

I think back to the first time I saw Christopher at Dulles. *The kind of guy people walk right past*, that's what I'd thought. Invisible. And I have the same thought that I had when I watched him coming out of the water after we jumped at Leda Falls: that he's become more solid, somehow – more *here*. Or maybe it's me. Maybe it's because I know him now – because I know that he's not invisible – that he's real, one of the most real things in my life.

'Why?' I ask.

He shrugs. 'I guess he felt sorry for me. Or maybe he liked my accent. I was shouting pretty loud.'

'I mean, why did you come *here*?'

'I wanted to hear you sing.'

'You've heard me sing.'

'I didn't want you to be alone.' Then he shakes his head. 'No, that's not true. I mean, it's true – I didn't want you to have to face all this by yourself. But I knew that you could do it.' He pauses. 'I came for me.'

'For you?'

He nods. 'I missed you.'

My throat's gone dry. 'You did?'

He nods again.

I think again about how there are a thousand sentences in those nods and those shrugs of his.

'And now?' I ask.

'I need to go and speak to Mum.'

He gets up and pulls his backpack onto his shoulders.

I stand up too, step past him and open the door of the Buick. Leda jumps in and settles on the dress that I was meant to wear for the rehearsal dinner. I put the telescope beside her.

I think about Blake's suit and his hat box, how it lay there, on the back seat, for all those hundreds of miles.

They've probably been dumped in some back room upstairs in the hotel.

Even with all the news about the plane, I kept believing that he'd find a way of getting to the wedding. That he'd walk in at the last minute, and take over the song. But it was Christopher who showed up.

I go around to the front, open the door to the driver's seat and sit down behind the steering wheel.

I look up at him. 'Need a lift somewhere?'

He stares at me, his eyes wide and pale behind his glasses.

'Sorry?'

'It'll be faster than taking the bus.'

'What will be faster?'

I roll my eyes. 'If I drive you.'

'But your parents – your family?'

'I told them I had to do this.'

'You did?'

I nod.

'And they're okay with that?'

'I don't think anyone's okay with anything right now. But yeah, Dad's going to work things out tomorrow.'

He keeps standing there, staring and blinking. I guess he's weighing up whether he can handle it – another road trip with me and the possibility of me blaming him for everything again.

'You getting in, then?' I ask.

Leda lets out a yelp from the back seat.

I turn the key in the ignition.

And then Christopher takes off his backpack, places it on the back seat next to Leda and gets in beside me.

DAY 4
TUESDAY 22ND AUGUST, 2017

Chapter Forty-Eight

I-24, TN

After getting out of Nashville, I turn off the I-24 and park the Buick on the side of the road.

I get changed out of my bridesmaid's dress and into my T-shirt and shorts, the clothes I swam in, now dry and stiff as cardboard. Then we both sleep. I stretch out on the front bench; Christopher goes in the back and curls up with Leda.

We know that we can't keep going if we don't at least try to rest.

When we wake up, it's nearly dawn. A kind of half-light. A few stars, the bright ones, still shining.

Before getting back onto the highway, we stop by a small grocery store, pick up some sandwiches and then set off for Atlanta.

Our body clocks are all over the place, so driving at some crazy hour in the morning won't make a difference.

And the half-light, the stillness of the early morning, makes it easier, somehow.

Easier not to talk.

Easier not to have to think too hard about everything that's happened. And whether I should have stayed with Mom and Dad and Jude. And whether Dad's strong enough to hold them together through all this. And what's going to happen when I get back to DC and Blake's not there and I have to find a way of living with the fact that it's because of me.

Besides stopping to sleep, we only take one break at a rest-stop outside Chattanooga.

And that's when Christopher tells me about the news that came in during the wedding. And the news that's come in since then, while I was driving and he scanned his phone for more information.

About what really happened to the UKFlyer0217 that left Heathrow for DC on Friday 18th of August 2017. The flight his dad was on. And Blake.

After we've eaten our burgers and fries from the McDonald's at the rest stop, Christopher gets out his phone and starts reading, 'Edward Ellis failed to realise that the autopilot had been switched off.'

'I don't understand...'

He keeps reading.

'The UKFlyer pilot received inconsistent readings which suggested that the plane's speed sensors had become blocked.'

'So it was a mechanical failure,' I leap in. 'It was out of your dad's control.'

Christopher's eyes are still fixed on the screen. He keeps reading.

'When Edward Ellis, a UKFlyer pilot with over fifteen years and hundreds of hours of flight experience, realised he was losing altitude, he raised the angle of the plane's climb. The plane stalled three times and finally fell into the ocean...' His fingers, holding the phone, are shaking. 'The crash killed all on board.'

The words hang between us.

Very slowly, he puts down his phone.

'It was Dad's choice to tilt the plane upwards as a response to the plane losing altitude.'

He pulls one of the napkins out of the dispenser and I think he's going to start folding it but, instead, he smooths it out on the table.

He bows his head. His knotty hair falls into the space between his eyes and his glasses.

'It was Dad's fault.'

'You said the autopilot disengaged...?'

'He should have realised that it had been switched off. It's his job to notice that kind of thing.'

'People can't get things right every second of every day of their lives, Christopher.' I swallow hard. 'People make mistakes.'

He looks up at me. 'Is that what you're going to tell your crew when you go up into space for the first time? That people make mistakes?'

I think about what Christopher said about how his dad always got things right; how people trusted him because he made them feel safe.

And I think about me. About how my place in my family has been defined by being the reliable one. The one who sorts out other people's messes – Blake's messes in particular. The one who, like Christopher's dad, was never meant to get things wrong.

But I got this wrong too. We both did.

I look back at him. I can't lie to him, not anymore.

'No, it's not what I'd say. I'd make my crew feel safe. I'd make them believe that we were going to make it. Because that's what they'd need to hear.'

'You'd say it even if it wasn't true?'

'I would believe that it was true. And that's why I'd say it.'

'But you couldn't *guarantee* their safety.'

'No one can guarantee anyone's safety.'

It's the first time I admit this to myself. Maybe it's the first time I believe it. That no matter how good we are – how experienced, how reliable – we make mistakes.

Christopher's eyes go far away.

'There are jobs where you don't get to make mistakes,' he says. 'Dad knew that. *You* know that.'

'Your dad tried to do the right thing – by lifting the angle of the plane. It could have worked.'

'But it didn't work. And, it turned out, it wasn't the right decision. It made the plane stall.' He swallows hard. 'Which caused the crash.'

Christopher keeps smoothing the napkin down against the table.

'If I ever get to talk to a crew before going into space,' I say, 'I wouldn't talk to them about human error. Not at that moment. I'd inspire them. I'd tell them they could do it. That we were going to make history. That what they were doing was amazing. But they'd know it; that something could go wrong. That bad things happen – big things, life and death things – and that some things are out of our control.' I take a breath. 'And sometimes it's our fault and we have to live with that knowledge no matter how hard it is.'

'Dad said that there was no such thing as human error – only human negligence,' Christopher says.

'Well, he was wrong.'

Christopher looks up at me.

I keep going. 'Getting things wrong is part of the deal – the cost. We all know that.'

'The cost?'

'Of doing stuff like this. Flying, taking off in rockets, doing things that I guess we were never really meant to do.'

'Overreaching,' he says.

'Yeah, overreaching.'

He nods and begins to lift up the sides of the napkin. A fold on each corner.

'And even when we're not overreaching,' I add. 'We make mistakes then too. Important mistakes.'

Even when we're just booking a plane ticket.

My body slumps into itself.

All I had to do was to get him to Nashville.

Christopher keeps folding. The bits of tissue paper split and fan out. He's making a flower.

I look through the window at the new day. Neither of us thought that we'd be sitting here today, together, the day after the eclipse. Neither of us knew we'd ever see each other again.

My gaze drifts to the sky and I try to picture Blake, sitting in the plane, shortly before the crash. Maybe he was asleep or watching a movie – or maybe he was composing a new song because he'd been inspired by the sky through the small oval window beside him. Did he feel it? The plane dropping? Did he know that something bad was happening – more than a little turbulence? That in a few minutes, his beautiful, blessed life would be over?

He once said that he'd like to look death right in the eye. To have the experience of it so that he could write about it. Because between love and death there wasn't much else. That that was all anyone ever really wrote about and sang about, he said. I didn't take it seriously at the time. Blake's always coming up with that weird, philosophical stuff. But I think about it now. Whether, as the plane was falling, he was inspired, whether the lines of a song started to come to him. Or whether he was scared, like everyone else.

And then I think of Mom and Dad and Jude and Stephen, back at the hotel, trying to get their heads round the fact that Blake's never coming back. And that I'm the one who put him on the wrong plane.

I don't know if I can ever go back to them. Whether I can bear looking into their eyes knowing that it's because of me that Blake's not coming back.

Looking back at the paper model Christopher's been making, I realise that it's one of mum's heirloom roses, from the wedding. He must have seen them when he came to the rooftop. I wonder whether one day he'll get to meet her. Whether she'll show him the roses she grows in our garden back in DC.

'I could take one of those into space with me,' I say.

He looks up at me.

'One of your paper models,' I explain. 'Put it in a time capsule or something. As a souvenir from earth.'

He smiles. 'I'd like that.'

Chapter Forty-Nine

Atlanta, GA

In the stretch between Chattanooga and Atlanta, we don't really talk. I guess there's not much more to say, now that we know what happened. Or know as much as we ever will.

We're tired. Too tired to go through all the emotions again.

Christopher sleeps for a bit but his sleep's so light that as soon as Leda barks or I go over a bump in the road, his eyes dart open.

He's nervous about seeing his mom; I can feel it coming off his body in waves.

Leda shuffles onto his lap; she senses it too.

By dawn, we're pulling into Sandy Springs.

We wait outside the house. It's too early to ring the bell.

There's a white moon in the sky. It makes me think of the paper moons we made back in that Burger King outside Knoxville. How hard I found it to make some folds in a piece of paper.

And I remember the strange, moonless sky the night before the eclipse. How that time we spent together, before we knew what was really happening, was kind of unreal.

You've come back, I say to myself.

The sun sits under the horizon, lighting up the world from below.

At around 7 a.m., a guy, about my dad's age, comes out through the front door, wearing a green dressing gown. He's followed by a golden lab who crouches on the lawn to relieve himself.

Leda jumps up and down on the bench behind us and starts barking with excitement.

Which makes the man look up.

'Who's the guy?' I ask.

'Mitch. My stepdad, I guess.'

'You guess?'

'I've never met him.'

Mitch puts his hand over his brow to block out the sun, trying to work out where the barking's coming from. The front door opens again, and a woman walks out.

She slips her arm around Mitch's waist and leans her head against his shoulder.

And then she sees us.

I guess it's not every day that a Yellow 1973 Buick convertible parks in front of your house.

And it's not every day that the son she hasn't talked to in years shows up with no more warning than an oblique phone call the day before.

'Mom! Dad!'

A little girl skips out of the house. I'd say she was about five or six. The same tangled blonde hair as Christopher, only longer. The same grey eyes. They both look like their mom.

'You didn't say you had a sister.'

And then I realise, from how he's staring at her, that he didn't know.

His leg starts jiggling up and down.

You'd think that what I've done was harder: standing up in front of all those guests at my sister's wedding – in front of my family – and singing the song that my brother was meant to sing. And then telling the people I love most in the world, right there, at the wedding, that Blake was in a plane crash. That he wasn't coming back. And that it was my fault. You'd think that was harder than just driving to your mom's house. But you'd be wrong.

It's the quiet that makes this so hard.

And the fact that it's just another ordinary Tuesday morning.

And that they're going about their normal lives: letting the dog out, giving each other a morning hug, looking out onto the street.

If it hadn't been for us, they'd have gone back inside and had breakfast and showered and got ready for work and taken the little girl to kindergarten. Like any other day.

And Christopher's going to have to break it, the quiet, happy, everydayness of all this. And somehow, their lives will never be the same again either.

I grab his hand.

'You can do this,' I whisper. 'I'm not going anywhere. I'll wait for you in the car.'

He keeps staring out at Mitch and his mom and the little girl.

Leda starts barking again.

'And take Leda with you.'

He looks at me, confused.

'She adores you.'

'But—'

'You should have her. For good.'

I haven't planned this. Hadn't even had the thought until it popped into my head a second ago, but I know that it's the right thing. Leda should be with Christopher.

'You'll take better care of her than I will. And it'll be one person in your camp.'

'In my camp?'

'So you don't have to face your family alone.'

The yellow lab bounds across the lawn towards our car.

'And it looks like she might have a friend.'

Christopher leans over and kisses me lightly on the cheek. I feel it in my whole body, the way his lips brush against my skin.

'Thank you,' Christopher says.

The little girl follows the golden lab, the hem of her night-dress brushing the sprinkler-wet grass.

'Come back!' she yells after him.

Her mom and dad follow her.

Christopher gets out of the car, pulling Leda behind him and walks towards his mom.

'Who's that?' The little girl points at Christopher and then looks back at her parents.

Christopher's mom stares at him for a second, and then steps forward. 'This is your brother, Christopher.'

The girl tilts her head to one side. 'The one from the photo?'

Christopher looks at his mom. My body floods with relief: so she'd told the little girl about him. That must count for something.

'Yes, the one from the photo.'

They're too wrapped up in each other to see me. Which is a relief. I don't have the energy to face anyone right now.

I scoot down in my seat and watch them all walk back into the house, Leda and the golden lab tumbling over each other like they've known each other for a lifetime. Maybe Leda's been waiting to find her true home too. Maybe she was only with Blake – and with me – for the ride.

Tiredness sweeps over me. A thick, heavy tiredness like I could sleep for a million years.

Before he goes through the front door, Christopher turns one last time to look at me.

'You can do it,' I whisper to him.

And then he gives me a small nod and turns to go inside.

I must have fallen asleep because the next thing I know, the sun's beating down on me and there's the little girl – Christopher's sister – staring at me through the car window. She's on tiptoes. And she's grinning.

When she notices that I've spotted her, she takes a step back.

Behind her, Leda and the golden lab are tumbling over each other on the lawn.

'Don't tell Mom I woke you,' the girl says quickly.

I rub my eyes. 'Okay...'

'She told me to let you sleep. We came out to check on you a few times but Mom said you seemed really tired and Christopher said you'd been driving for days and so we thought it was better to leave you.' The girl takes a strand of her long, tangled hair and chews the end.

'But...' she starts.

'But?'

'I wanted to see what you looked like with your eyes open.'

'Oh…'

'You look pretty.'

'Thanks.'

'I think I might cut my hair short too…It must be nice not to get tangles all the time.'

'Yeah, it is. But your hair's nice –' I think about how it reminds me of Christopher's hair. How it made me realise, straight away, that she must be his sister.

I glance at the clock on the dashboard. It's gone noon. I must have been asleep for hours.

'Do you want to come inside?' the girl asks.

'Um…'

'We're going to have lunch. Mom's not going in to work today and she's given me a home day because I told her it wasn't fair that she got to stay home with my brother while I had to go to school.'

The word brother startles me. I guess it must have startled Christopher too. It's amazing how small children adopt complete strangers into their lives. Or maybe Christopher's mom had prepared her in some way. Maybe they've been waiting for him. I hope so.

My brother…

And then it comes flooding back to me. How I had a brother too. And how now, he's gone. I press my eyes shut.

'What's wrong?' the girl asks.

I push the heels of my hands into my eyes, take a breath and then turn back to face her. 'I'm just really tired,' I say.

'Mom told me to play outside while she was talking to Christopher.' She lets out a small sigh. 'They've been talking for *ages*.'

That's a good sign, I think.

'So, will you come in?'

'Nina!' Christopher's mom is standing at the front door. She's got dressed: she's wearing jeans and a sweatshirt and sneakers. She looks younger than Mom but more worn out somehow.

She comes up to the car.

'Sorry,' she says to me. 'We told her to leave you alone.'

'It's fine,' I say.

'Air's going to come inside and have lunch with us,' Nina announces.

She knows my name. I wonder how much Christopher has told her about me: how he's explained the fact that he showed up with a girl in a yellow Buick rather than on a Greyhound bus.

'Well...' I start.

'If you'd like to come in, you'd be most welcome,' Christopher's mom says. 'You could probably do with some food. And you can take a shower or a bath and maybe rest a bit...'

I notice Christopher coming out through the front door. I try to read his body language: to work out how he's feeling – whether he's surviving all this; meeting the mom who walked out on him when he was a baby. But he just looks kind of blank, like he hasn't processed it yet. I guess it's a lot to take in. At least he doesn't look upset. And if things had gone really badly, he'd have come back to the car and woken me up and said he wanted to leave. He's still here. That's a start.

I'm torn between getting on the road and heading to Nashville to be with Mom, Dad and Jude, and staying here. I'm exhausted. And I could do with a wash. And some food. And I want to make sure Christopher is okay before I leave him.

'It's your decision, of course, but the offer's there if you'd like it,' Christopher's mom says.

'I'd like to come in,' I say.

Nina jumps up and down with excitement and as I step out of the car Leda runs towards me and licks my hand like she approves of my decision.

'Wonderful,' Christopher's mom says. 'I'm Amy by the way. And I'm so pleased that I got to meet you.'

'Me too,' I say.

When I walk towards Christopher, still standing at the front door, I suddenly worry that this is a bad idea – me gatecrashing his big family reunion. Maybe he wants to be with them alone. But when I get to him, his face relaxes and he smiles and, as we walk into the house, he catches the back of my hand and whispers, 'Thanks.'

The afternoon slips away from us. We have some sandwiches sitting in the garden and then I soak in the bath for ages, letting the hot water numb my body. It's good to let go for a bit. Christopher's mom lends me some of her clothes – she says I can keep them when I go: a pair of leggings and an old sweater. They're soft and they smell of laundry detergent and make me feel comfortable for the first time in days. And then Mitch comes back from work and grills some burgers and hot dogs in the back yard and before I know it, it's getting dark.

'I should probably get back on the road,' I say.

'Are you sure that's wise?' Amy says. 'It's a long drive back to Nashville.'

So she knows about Nashville. And there's something about the way that she's been acting all afternoon that makes me think Christopher must have told her about Blake too. I keep catching her looking at me, her brow crinkled up, as if she's checking that I'm okay.

'You'd be welcome to stay the night; we have a guest room made up. You could leave first thing in the morning.'

Although I know I should be heading back to my own family right now, I like it here. It's helping. And I haven't had the chance to talk to Christopher yet – not alone. I want to know whether he's okay. Really okay.

'She's right,' Christopher says. 'You'll be fresher in the morning.'

I'm relieved that he wants me to stay.

'If you're sure it's no trouble,' I say to Amy.

She smiles at me. 'No trouble at all.'

She seems so easy, I think. So ordinary. Good ordinary. And kind too. She doesn't look like the type of person who'd abandon her baby. I don't know what I'd expected when Christopher told me about her, but it wasn't this.

When we go upstairs to bed, Christopher shows me his room: his *actual* room. Amy's been keeping it for him, hoping that he might come and stay one day. It makes me feel both really happy for him – that she wants him this much – and sad too, that all these years, he could have come here and had her as a mom.

When we say goodnight, I want to ask him to come into my room to talk; I want to hear what happened in those hours when I was asleep in the car and he was chatting to his mom. But once he's walked me to the guest room, all he says is, 'See you in the morning, Air.' And then he turns to go.

'Christopher...?'

He turns back round. 'Do you have everything you need?'

'Yes...'

No, I want to say. *No. I want you to stay...I want you to talk to me...*

I thought I'd taught him something on that long road trip – and on our trek up that mountain. But I guess he's not ready.

I take a step towards him.

'Is everything okay?' I ask, hoping I might get him to open up. 'We haven't had much of a chance to talk.'

He shrugs and says:

'We'll see...' And then he leans in and kisses my cheek. 'Goodnight, Air.'

And before I can say anything, he turns around again and heads down the hallway to his room.

I get into some PJs that Amy put out for me on the bed and then call Dad to give him an update on where I am. I tell him that I'm staying the night with Christopher's family. I can feel that he's worried about where I am and who I'm with but he doesn't challenge me. I guess he trusts me that I'm not going to do anything stupid. Not with everything else that's going on.

He tells me that Mom's been on the phone to DC non-stop. That she's pulled a few favours and got some more information about the plane. Though, from the sound of it, more information was really no information. They're saying that it's unlikely they'll find any bodies. That we have to prepare ourselves for that.

I thought it would upset me – hearing that they couldn't find Blake. But, after we finish the call, as I lie in bed, looking out through the open window, I think about how, if Blake could have chosen a way to go, this might have been it: to disappear between air and water and earth. He would have found it poetic. He would have wanted to write a song about it, if he'd had the chance.

My eyes well up. *I miss you, Blake*, I whisper into the dark room.

I try to sleep; my limbs are aching with tiredness but my mind won't stop whirring. Every time I close my eyes I see the dashboard of the Buick, the clock, the speed dial, and then I'm standing on the rooftop of the hotel, at the wedding, singing and then I'm in Dad's arms, my body shaking…

I find an old bathrobe on the hook behind the guestroom door, wrap it around me and walk downstairs, out through the back door and into the garden.

It's a clear night. And there are stars, of course. But they feel so far away that it hurts to look at them.

I sit on a bench swing, tuck my legs up and hug my knees.

It's nice to be outside, the cool night brushing my skin.

'You still awake?'

I look up. Christopher stands in front of me in his boxers and T-shirt, his bare feet in the dew-wet grass.

'Couldn't sleep,' I say.

'Me neither.'

He sits down beside me.

'It's weird, isn't it?' he says. 'Us being here.'

'Yeah,' I say. 'Though it's probably the sanest stop on our road trip so far.'

He laughs. 'Yeah, I guess it is.'

'An ordinary house and an ordinary family…' I say, thinking back to what Christopher told me about how he wished that he could just do normal things with his dad rather than shooting off around the world.

He nods.

'Do you like it here?' I ask.

'I think so.'

'If you don't want to talk, you don't have to,' I say.

He raises his eyebrows and smiles. 'Really? I get a choice about not talking? That's new.'

I punch him playfully in the arm. 'Hey.'

He leans in to me and gives me a small nudge. 'It's okay,' he says. 'I don't mind talking. I just didn't want to burden you.'

'*Burden* me?'

'You've got your own stuff to deal with. You can't be worrying about me.'

I look at him and wait for his eyes to find mine.

'I *want* to worry about you,' I say.

Even though it's dark I can see the tops of his cheeks flush pink. I want to touch them, to feel whether his skin is as warm and soft as it looks, but I'm scared that would totally freak him out.

He leans back and looks at the sky. I follow his gaze and notice a red tail light in the sky. We must be under a flight path.

I wonder how many times Amy must have looked up and thought about him. And his dad.

Christopher goes really quiet. I don't think we'll ever be able to get used to planes flying overhead.

I take a breath.

'So you guys talked,' I say. 'This morning, while I was sleeping in the car.'

He nods.

I hear a clattering of paws on the patio. Leda runs across the lawn, jumps up onto the swing and sits between us.

'Like old times, hey?' I say, rubbing her behind the ears.

He smiles. 'Yeah. Like old times.'

The golden lab lumbers over too and sits at our feet.

'Did you talk about what happened – when you were a baby?' I ask.

'She said she was sorry.'

I wait for him to go on.

'She was young when she got pregnant. She said she was scared that she wouldn't be able to cope – that she wouldn't be a good enough mum. She said she understood books and science but not babies.' He pauses and looks up at the house. There's a light on in what must be Mitch and Amy's bedroom. I wonder whether they're talking about today too – about Amy seeing Christopher after all this time. 'She admitted that she never really wanted kids. That kids didn't feature in her plans.'

'But she got pregnant…?'

'Yeah, she did.' He goes quiet for such a long time that I think he's decided he doesn't want to talk about this after all. He pulls Leda onto his lap and buries his hands in her raggedy fur.

And then, he starts talking again.

'She'd decided not to go through with the pregnancy.'

'Wow…she actually told you that?'

He nods.

'That must have been kind of crappy to hear.'

'Not really. I guess I was glad she was honest. Saying it like it is. Dad would never give me a straight answer. And it wasn't personal – it's not like she knew me.'

'What happened then? She obviously did go through with the pregnancy.'

'When Dad found out she was pregnant, he said he wanted her to have me. He didn't believe in abortion. And he said he wanted to be a dad.'

I think about all the things he's said about his dad – how they never really spent any proper time together, how Christopher didn't feel seen for who he really was. The funny thing is that I get the sense that things would have been different with Amy. And yet she was the one who was scared that she wouldn't be a good mom. I guess it goes to show that we can't always tell, in advance, whether we're cut out for something. Especially not when it comes to being parents.

'But it was still her choice, though, right?' I say. 'It was her body.'

I'd had this drilled into me by Mom more times than I can remember. She's worked on human rights abuses in countries where really young girls get pregnant and then don't have the option to end their pregnancies because men make the decisions for them. It's one of the things she feels really strongly about: that a woman gets to decide.

'She said that she thought he would be a good dad, that he'd do right be me – and that if he really wanted me, then maybe it was the right thing, to go through with the pregnancy.'

'So, she had you for your dad?'

'I guess so.'

'That must have been hard.'

'Yeah.'

'And then, when she had you, she didn't change her mind? She went through with giving you away?'

'She said that giving me up was the hardest decision she'd ever had to make. Dad came to the hospital with a ring and asked her to marry him. He thought he could persuade her to stay and give it a chance. He told her that they could make it work. But she got scared. On the day she was due to be checked out of the hospital, she left early. Dad was in another room giving me a bottle. By the time he came back to see her, she'd gone.'

'Just like that?'

'Just like that.'

'But she's had this room waiting for you all this time – something must have changed?'

'She said that she tried to get in touch a few times. That she talked to Dad about wanting to see me. But he was still angry with her for walking out on us all those years ago. He told her that she'd given up her right to be my mom.' He pauses. 'Dad's always had this really strong sense of justice – of right and wrong. He felt that she'd made the wrong decision and that she had to live with that.'

'And your mom accepted that?'

'She said that she felt she had to respect his wishes. That he'd brought me up, done all the hard work. She didn't want to push him.'

'But she always hoped, right? To see you again?'

'She thought I might come looking for her one day, when I was older, when I got to decide.'

'Are you angry with your dad, for what he did?'

He shakes his head. 'Dad was trying to do the right thing. He didn't want me to get hurt. I guess he didn't know that Mum had changed.'

'That she'd had Nina, that she was a mom?'

'No, I don't think he knew about Nina. I suppose he couldn't wipe it from his head: the picture of her running out of the hospital. Of how he she just left us. Or the fact that she'd wanted to end the pregnancy.'

'You're being amazingly calm about all this.'

'It's still sinking in.'

'Yeah, I know what you mean.'

I look back up at the house. The light in Mitch and Amy's bedroom has gone out now. Nina must be asleep too. Maybe she's dreaming of the new brother she has. How easily people can come into our lives, I think. And how easily they can leave too.

'So, are you going to stay here for a while?' I ask.

'I suppose so. I haven't thought ahead, really. School starts again in a few weeks, back in England – Mum and I talked about that. But she said that, for now, we should just take things one day at a time. Get to know each other.'

I lean my head against his shoulder and look up at the sky. I notice a comet dashing by. And the stars, they feel a bit closer again.

'I like her,' I say. 'Your mom. I mean – not taking into account the whole giving you up thing.'

'Yeah, I think I like her too.'

'I guess that's a start, hey?'

He nods. 'It's a start. And how about you? How are things?'

I look down at Leda, sleeping beside us. 'I can't believe Blake's not coming back.'

'I know.'

'I keep expecting him to jump out and surprise me, like he has a million times before. I can see him giving me that apologetic smile of his, knowing that he's messed up but that I'm going to forgive him anyway.'

Christopher takes my hand and threads his fingers through mine.

'I keep expecting Dad to send me a text, confirming that he's landed, asking me to meet him at arrivals.'

'I guess we'll feel like that.'

'Yeah, I guess we will.'

We let the pictures in our heads sit between us: images of the people we love showing up, like they were meant to, two days ago.

'So, you'll drive back to Nashville tomorrow?' he says after a while.

'I thought I might drive straight back to DC. Meet Mom, Dad and Jude there rather than in Nashville. I kind of want to do the trip on my own. I'll take it slow. It will give me time to sort things out in my head. I want to be in Blake's car, on the road, to have a few hundred miles not having to do anything but drive.'

'You sure you'll be okay?'

'I'm going to fly to the moon someday, remember? I think I can manage a few highways.'

He smiles. 'I remember.'

'And I won't have you distracting me, this time.'

'I was a distraction, was I?'

'What do you think?'

Our eyes lock for a moment and then we both smile.

Then we sit there, swinging gently back and forth, Leda falling asleep between us and I wish that this moment could go on for ever – that we never had to face tomorrow.

But after a while, he stretches out his legs and says: 'I'd better get some sleep – and you should too. You've got a long drive tomorrow.'

'I think I'll stay out here for a bit longer,' I say. 'I'll come in soon.'

He stands up. 'Okay.' He leans in and his lips brush my cheek, right up, close to my mouth. 'Goodnight, then.'

'Goodnight,' I say.

As he walks away, I call after him:

'I think you're doing the right thing, you know.'

He turns around.

'Giving your mom a chance,' I say.

He gives me a smile. 'Thanks.'

And then he keeps walking until he disappears into the house.

When he's gone, I lean back in the swing and close my eyes. Behind my eyelids, I see the stars, pulling in closer and closer. I feel Leda's breath, heavy and warm beside me. And, far overhead, I hear another plane making its journey through the dark, night sky.

One Year Later

Chapter Fifty

August 2018
London

'Cabin crew, please take your seats for landing.' The captain's voice comes over the speakers.

I wonder what Edward Ellis would have sounded like. And how many times Christopher heard him say those words. And whether, when Christopher was small, he said the words too, pretending he was the pilot. Maybe there was a time when he wanted to be like his dad.

In those hours we spent together in the Buick, on the way to Knoxville and then on to Atlanta to meet his mom, Christopher and I talked for hours. But there's still so much I don't know.

I look out of the window. Mom booked a night flight but I haven't been able to sleep. Too much sky to look at through the window. Too much to think about.

Blake was in a window seat too. 27A. Looking out at the sky and sea. Except, for him, it was light.

Jude pulls off her sleep mask and yawns. 'Are we here yet?'

'Nearly,' Stephen says. He's sitting on the other side of her.

I'm by the window. Mom and Dad are across the aisle.

This trip to London is going to be the honeymoon Jude and Stephen never had. They're going to spend a few days with me, Mom and Dad in London, doing touristy things, and then Jude's going to take Stephen to Scotland, back to Loch Leven, show him where our ancestors came from. We'll fly back together in two weeks, in time for me to start at MIT.

It's the first time I've been on a plane since what happened to Blake. Even before that, I'd only flown once or twice, mostly short, internal flights. I've never been this far from home.

I lean over and look through the window, down at the Atlantic. Blake wrote a song about it once, how vast it was; how, on our planet, there was more sea than land. How the real mysteries we still had to uncover were not in outer space but down there, in that dark, silent world.

Maybe, if I don't end up in space, that's where I'll go. Maybe it's possible to do both, to tie it all together: what goes on above and below us.

We've all been pretty quiet through the flight. Because of the night thing. But also because we've been thinking about Blake. How he did this trip in reverse. How he never made it.

The investigators said that they didn't think the passengers realised what was happening until the last minute. The cabin voice recording only registered cries in the final seconds before impact.

It took a few months for all the facts about the crash to come out.

There was no rational explanation for why the autopilot disengaged. And the wisdom of Edward Ellis's last-minute decision to change the angle of the plane is still up for debate: some think that it was bound to make the plane stall; others say that it was the only option he had left to try and save the passengers. I guess that even mistakes aren't clear cut.

Like there's no rational explanation for why I booked Blake onto the wrong flight. I was tired. I was used to him coming into Dulles rather than Nashville. But that's not enough to explain it. In the end, I just got it wrong. And I'm going to have to live with that, just like Christopher's going to have to live with the fact that his dad might have made a mistake too. That sometimes we mess up.

It's been a tough year, watching the investigation unfold. Wishing, over and over, that we could turn back time and somehow stop that plane from ever taking off.

But we're okay now.

Well, that's not true: we'll never be okay, not really. But we're trying to make it work.

Some days, we pretend that the reason Blake's not around is because he's on tour somewhere or that he's gone off on one of his random drives because he got tired of staying in the same place.

Some days, we talk about him in the present tense, like he's still here. We know we're doing it. And we know it's not accurate, grammatically – that it's not the truth – but we do it anyway, because it feels good to acknowledge that he's still part of us.

Mom will pick up some Ben & Jerry's Mint Chocolate Chunk from the grocery store – even though none of us like mint chocolate much – because it was Blake's favourite. And then we eat it together, sitting in the living room, watching the video of the wedding. We even laugh when it comes to the bit where I try to sing Blake's song. Because no matter how you look at it, it was pretty embarrassing and pretty bad.

Jude will drop by with Stephen for dinner and complain that Blake's jackets are taking up all the space on the coatrack. He had as many jackets as he did sunglasses.

Some days, we feel so sad that none of us can even look at each other. On those days, Mom lets the house get messy and doesn't get out of her PJs and Dad eats too many donuts, even though he's been working really hard on lowering his cholesterol, and Jude sits on the living-room floor, sobbing her eyes out as she looks through the wedding album Mom made, because every picture screams out that Blake wasn't there.

And me? I sit in Blake's room, listening to his songs, and it feels like my heart's going to break into a thousand little pieces and never go back together again.

And some days, we're just plain angry. Mainly because each of us carry all this *what-if* guilt around.

What if I'd gone to bed early that night instead of bellyaching about the research paper?

What if I'd only seen Blake's message the next morning, when I'd have been clear-headed enough to book him onto the right flight?

What if I'd refused to book his flight, told him to deal with his own mess? He might have been late for the wedding. He might not even have made it at all. But he'd still be here.

And what if Mom had insisted that Blake come home earlier and that we all drive down to Nashville together?

What if Mom and Dad had put their foot down and said that, this summer, he wasn't going to London, that he had to stay in DC and focus on the wedding?

And what if Blake himself had been with it enough to realise that he shouldn't be flying to DC? That I'd got it wrong? That he shouldn't get onto the plane?

Even Jude feels guilty. Once, she said she wished she'd never got married at all. If it hadn't been for her wedding, Blake would still be alive.

Those angry, guilty days are the worst.

But they're rare now. Mostly, we try to get on with things. Mom goes to the White House to do her legal stuff; Dad grades his papers and prepares his lectures; I do my prep reading for MIT; Jude orders a million baby clothes and nursery items so that everything's ready in time. She's due in five months. A Christmas baby.

My stomach turns in on itself. The plane's started its descent into London.

I close my eyes and reach for the paper star pendant hanging from the piece of string around my neck. I've worn it every day. You'd think that it would have got damaged over time. That paper wouldn't last. But it's so small and strong, the folds so intricate, that it's stayed in one piece.

A moment later, the wheels hit the tarmac, the plane shakes and judders and there's a loud drag as the pilot slams on the brakes.

As we come into land, I switch my phone back on and a message pings up from Christopher's mom, Amy:

Hope the trip went well. So good of you to come. Can't wait to see Christopher's face when you show up. X

We'd planned it together, me and Amy, the trip here – the surprise for Christopher. It's weird how, when crazy things happen – when bad things happen, like the plane crash – lives collide in ways you don't expect. You end up having relationships with people you never knew even existed. And I don't just mean Christopher.

After that afternoon and night I spent at her house in Atlanta, Amy and I stayed in touch. As part of her work as a marine biologist, she runs workshops around the country for kids, for girls, especially, to inspire them to go into science. She passes through Boston, NYC and DC a few times a year. Whenever she came to DC she took me out for lunch and we talked about how my school work was going and my application to MIT – she acted like she was really interested, and like she believed in me, and that meant a lot: that someone outside my family was rooting for me. She asked me how things were at home without Blake and it was easier to talk to her about it than to Mom or Dad or Jude, I guess because I didn't need to worry about her being upset. And then we talked about Christopher.

Christopher stayed to finish boarding school in England. His mom thought it would be less disruptive than transferring him to a school in the US. She's been out to see him regularly. Sometimes with Nina and Mitch, like last Christmas when she thought they should all be together. Christopher hasn't been back to the US yet. He told me he wants to give travelling a rest for now. That he's not ready to get back on a plane. Which is another reason I decided to fly over for this.

Mostly, though, Amy went out to see Christopher on her own. She said she wanted time, just the two of them, so they could get to know each other. She's been helping him with his studies too. He was able to switch one of his A-Level choices to include Art. And she's the one who persuaded him to enter the competition to exhibit in a gallery in London. I think she's helping him to understand that what he does is amazing – that it's a big thing. A big and important thing. And that he's brilliant at it.

Christopher and I FaceTime sometimes and write emails but he still feels far away. When I talk to Amy about him, he feels closer. That's why I like to see her. And to call her. And I guess I like her too. I love Mom and we're close in our way, but sometimes it's easier to talk to someone else's mom. Especially a mom who doesn't have all the answers. Who knows she's got stuff wrong. Big stuff.

I've told her some of the details of the long car trip from DC to Nashville and then on to Atlanta. I shared some of the things Christopher told me about his dad, things I didn't think he'd mind me saying. And maybe I'm seeing what I want to see but when I sit in front of Amy, thinking about the time she's taking to talk to me, some random girl her son met a year ago, when I think about how often she goes out to see him in England and how, when she does, they just hang out together, like he wanted to do with his dad, my heart gets a bit lighter. Like maybe, despite the fact that she walked out on him as a baby, despite the fact that it will take her a lifetime to make up for that, maybe, for once, he feels like there's someone he belongs to.

I look down at my phone and type:

Landed safely. Can't wait either.

And then the plane jolts to a stop.
And we're here. In London.

Chapter Fifty-One

Shoreditch, London

There's a picture of him on the billboard outside the small gallery in Shoreditch. It feels strange to see his face like that, on a poster. I remember how shy he was when I first met him in Dulles – and then how crazy he acted on the roof of the diner in Knoxville, persuading me to rehearse Blake's song. How it was like, with every mile we drove, he became more alive.

And here he is, staring into the camera, his grey eyes wide and confident.

I notice that he's wearing new glasses – black, artsy frames that make him look kind of hip – a bit less Christopher Robin than this time last year.

Next to him, there's a write-up about the art competition he won earlier this year and the prize: a chance to exhibit his work in a London gallery.

At the bottom of the write-up, there's a dedication: a photograph of his dad, in his pilot's uniform and under it, his name: *Edward Ellis, 1975–2017*.

I considered telling Christopher that I was coming but then I thought that, after how he showed up at Jude's wedding without any warning, bang in the middle of my song, he deserved a taste of his own medicine. Plus, Amy liked the thought of it being a surprise.

'Ready?' Dad asks me.

I nod and we walk into the gallery.

It's dark. Only a few lights flicker above us. It makes me think of the planetarium back in DC where Blake and I spent so many hours: a thick, hushed, dark silence, full of other people we'd never know.

From the other side of the room, I can hear his voice. He's doing a Q&A.

'Why do you work with paper?' someone asks.

'Because it's beautiful,' he answers. 'And simple. And because it's everywhere. Paper is part of our everyday lives.' He smiles. That's more confident too, his smile. 'And because I loved to make paper planes when I was a kid.'

His words send a shudder through me. It's the answer he gave me when I first asked him why he made those models.

'And you made every single one yourself?' someone else asks.

I stand up on tiptoes to look over the audience. He's wearing a suit. A tie. It's the first time I see a bit of his dad in him.

His mom is standing in the front row. She notices me and gives me a small wave and a smile. Mitch, Christopher's stepdad is there too, and between them, in a green dress, stands Nina, the little girl with the long, tangled hair I saw running across the grass that morning in Atlanta. Her head is tilted up to the roof of the gallery: she can't take her eyes off all those folded pieces of paper.

'Yeah, I make them all,' he says. 'It's therapeutic – all that folding.'

His audience laughs.

He told me that in one of our Skype chats. How, when he folded paper, especially for installations that required lots of repetitions, his mind stopped whirring and allowed him to get lost in what he was doing. For those hours, his fingers and his mind busy with paper, he didn't have to think about what had happened – about how his dad had tried to save everyone's life and how close he'd got but how, in the end, even he couldn't do it. And now he'll never see him again.

I leave Mom, Dad, Jude and Stephen in the main bit of the gallery and go up the back stairs to the balcony.

I want to see the installation from above.

'They're made from airplane tickets – is that right?' a young woman asks.

Christopher nods. 'I used to collect them, when I hung out with my dad at the airport. Once people had got to wherever they were meant to be, they discarded them. In the front pockets of aeroplane seats. On the ground. In bins. I've always made models out of found bits of paper. Receipts. Flyers. Menus. Old posters. Sheets of newspaper. After the crash, when I went home, I found all of these – I had thousands of them, stacked up in boxes in my bedroom. So, I thought I'd use them for this.'

The room goes still. They've probably done their research. They know that, a year ago, Christopher Ellis lost his dad – the pilot of the plane – that crashed into the Atlantic. There was lots of news coverage in the weeks following the discovery of the black box.

'Why stars?' someone asks.

My heart jolts.

Christopher looks up at the ceiling from which his installation hangs. His hair's shorter, smarter somehow; it's still curly but the tangles have gone.

Christopher's head shifts to the cascade of stars that hang from the ceiling. Hundreds and hundreds of them, every one of them a plane ticket, folded by him.

Each star has a small light inside. That's where the flickering came from.

He keeps scanning the ceiling. And then he notices me. His eyes go wide.

I look back at him and smile.

You didn't think I'd miss your official opening, did you? I try to say with my eyes.

Christopher looks back to the guy asking the question.

'A friend once taught me about the stars,' he says. 'How they're always with us. Even when we can't see them – even when they're hundreds of light years away. I guess that inspired me.'

Someone starts clapping. And then others join in. Soon, the whole room is applauding him.

He gives them a small nod and steps away from the lectern.

I wait on the balcony while he shakes people's hands and answers more questions that people didn't get to ask in the official Q&A.

Mom, Dad, Jude and Stephen walk up to him and give him a hug. It's like they know Christopher, when really, besides that brief glimpse they got of him in the lobby of the hotel back in Nashville a year ago, this is the first time they've met him properly. I guess they've heard so much about him that he feels familiar.

Then Christopher disappears from the crowd for a bit and I think he's gone to the bathroom or that he's slipped outside to get some air because it's all too much. It would be killing him, all this attention.

I sit down, my back pressed to the wall, and look up the hundreds of paper stars.

'You showed up – again.' His voice comes in from behind me.

I turn to see him in the doorway. He's got taller this past year. And he's standing straighter. And he doesn't have that ridiculous backpack weighing him down.

'Wouldn't have missed it,' I say.

He comes and sits down beside me.

'And you're wearing a dress,' he says, touching the hem of the yellow cotton dress Jude helped me pick out for tonight.

'It's a special occasion,' I say.

He looks up at me. 'It is?'

'Yeah.'

For a while, we both sit there, our backs pressed to the wall, our legs stretched out, just touching, looking up at the dark ceiling and those hundreds of flickering paper stars.

'So, you finally got it,' I say.

'Got it?'

'That they're art.'

'I'm still not sure about that.'

I laugh. 'You won a major art competition and your work's in a gallery and you've got people asking you questions about your installation – and you got an art scholarship to Central St. Martin's – and you *still* don't think you're an artist?'

He shrugs.

'You're an artist, Christopher. A totally kickass artist.'

His eyes go back to the ceiling, to all those stars.

'I'm a bit of a fraud, you know,' he says.

'A fraud?'

'I stole someone else's work.'

'What?'

He points to a corner of the room. 'Once upon a time, this American girl made a paper moon…'

And that's when I see it. My odd-shaped, black and white, paper moon, hanging from the ceiling, side by side with the one he made at the diner.

'You hung them up!'

'They complete the piece, don't you think.'

I laugh. 'Well, I'm honoured.'

He smiles and then sits back. The sound of clinking glasses, the murmur of voices, jazz music, playing low, swirls below us. Then he says, 'I keep wondering what Dad would have thought.'

'Your dad would have been totally proud. This is a *big* thing, Christopher. A really big thing.'

'Maybe.'

'Your mom's so proud too.'

'You spoke to her?'

I nod. 'I called her to check the details – for today.'

'So, the two of you conspired?'

I smile. 'Yep.'

I think he kind of likes that we're in touch, him and his mom.

'Mum's good at showing up,' Christopher says. 'Like you.'

Christopher hasn't said all that much about his mom and I know it must be hard, getting used to having her as his main parent when she walked out on him and his dad all those years ago. But I know that it's a good thing too, that they've fond each other again.

'Are you staying for a bit?' he asks.

I nod. 'Until school starts.'

He was the first person I called when I got into MIT. If he was still here, it would have been Blake. But it felt good to share it with Christopher.

Although it's dark up here, I see his eyes light up.

I open the palm of my hand. The star's sitting there, the one he made for me a year ago. The star that gave me courage to sing Blake's song at Jude's wedding; the star that's helped me get through this past year.

'You've still got it.'

'Of course.' I hold it up and look at it in relation to all the other stars hanging from the ceiling and I wonder whether one day, we'll work it out: how far the stars really are from us.

'I'm going to take it with me,' I say.

'Take it with you?'

'This – your art.' I hold out the paper star. 'On my first trip into space.' I smile.

He takes the star from me and places it on the ground.

Then he holds my hand.

'You still believe that thing about astronauts and personal relationships?' he asks.

Blood rushes to the surface of my skin.

'The statistics don't lie,' I say.

'Let's not be a statistic then,' he says.

'I'm not sure we get to decide.'

'Yeah, we get to decide,' he says.

And then he leans in and, very lightly, he presses his lips to mine.

Everything goes still.

All I can feel is his breath and his touch.

Through his lips, he whispers, '*This* is big enough for me.'

And then I kiss him back.

And the kiss feels like it lasts a lifetime. And like a second. Like time in space.

When we stop kissing, we sit back and look at the stars Christopher made for the exhibition.

And although we don't say it out loud, I know that we're thinking about Blake and Christopher's dad. How they were booked onto that flight from Heathrow to DC, like all those passengers from the discarded tickets were booked onto flights too. And that those passengers made it. And that Blake and Christopher's dad didn't. And that no one will ever understand why.

I feel Christopher's hand slip into mine.

I lean into him and rest my head on his shoulder.

And we look up at the hundreds of paper stars that once belonged to people who flew through the sky.

And, for a while, the world falls away.

Acknowledgements

This has been my hardest novel to write to date. Conveying the unbearable grief of two teenagers who lose those they love most, whilst simultaneously exploring how they find each other and fall in love, was a balancing act that threatened to defeat me many times over. But then I'm told that the stories we wrangle with are often those that end up touching readers most: I hope that is true.

Thank you to my unwaveringly faithful agent, Bryony Woods, for reading oh so many drafts of this novel and for never giving up on me or on this story. Thank you to Charlotte Mursell, my new editor at HarperCollins, for taking over the project and putting so much love and creativity into getting my story out to readers.

Thank you Darik Velez, for teaching me about dark energy, Type 1a supernovas and how tricky it is to work out the distance between us and the stars.

Thank you to my dear friends who have cheered from the side lines and who encourage me, every day, to keep going in my life as a writer: Helen Dahlke, Aryn Marsh, Hannah MacBride, Jane Cooper, Karla Kittler, Margaret Evans Porter, Marjorie Burke, Steve Del Deo and Michael Herrmann.

Thank you to the people who help me hold up the scaffolding of my life and so allow me to write. The wonderful staff at Live Juice and the Gibson's True Brew Café who keep me fed and watered as I scribble.

The incredible teachers at Woodside St. Paul's who love and care for my little girls every day: Melyssa, Justina, Kelly, Maddie, Penny, Abby, Kathy, Carol and the rest of the amazing team. I couldn't do it without you.

Thank you, finally, to my dear, dear family. Mama, who reads and re-reads each of my novels and who believed I'd be a writer from the moment she named me. My wonderful, spirited little girls, Tennessee Skye and Somerset Wilder, who run me ragged and often make it feel like it's impossible to write a single sentence, but who also provide the fuel that I need to keep creating – love, inspiration and endless, endless entertainment! My darling husband and soul mate, Hugh, who talks with me late into the night about my plot and my characters and who helped me rethink this novel a hundred times. Thank you for walking with me on this journey, my love, and for showing me the way back when I get lost.

ONE PLACE. MANY STORIES

Bold, innovative and
empowering publishing.

FOLLOW US ON:

@HQStories